Acclaim for David Jones's
Behind the Locked Door

"From a dying brother's letter of despair and hope, David Jones creates a harrowing mix of humanity and inhumanity; love and terror; medical madness, and mirages of miracles. The searing journey the author imagines for his brother compels readers to confront profound questions of how life is best lived and death best met."

>—Jeffrey Amestoy, Former Chief Justice, Vermont Supreme Court; author of *Slavish Shore: The Odyssey of Richard Henry Dana Jr.*

"David Jones is one of the great thinkers and writers. He pours his intellect and life experience into *Behind the Locked Door*. Run, don't walk, to devour it, and be ready to be consumed."

>—Gary Evans, former World Bank economist and financial advisor to the Republic of Poland

"It requires skill to twist a thought to express a sensation, a tender emotion. David has that skill—to create a mood, a reality for the reader. It is another form of truth made out of illusions."

>—James Maxwell, painter, sculptor, graphic designer; author of *My Ghosts*

"David Jones has delighted us for years with his blog www.thinkinthemorning.com. Now, in his engaging first fiction, he takes readers to Mexico as a young man searches for the gift of healing."

>—Katy M. Tahja, author of *An Eclectic History of Mendocino County 1852–2002*

"I'm delighted to be able to fully immerse myself in the richness of David's imagination, truth telling, and writing talent. Hurray—and more, please!"

> —Susan B. Wood, artist and "teller" of the secrets of an amazing, aging, single, woman artist

"David Jones has chosen a difficult subject: The story of a desperate 'everyman' grasping at any straw in hopes of surviving incurable cancer. Set in Mexico, the novel is liberally sprinkled with indigenous mysticism and surreal interludes that enhance the story and help make *Behind the Locked Door* a wonderful read."

> —Gil Gevins, author of *1967: The Autumn of Post-Coital Despair*

"In this genre-bending ode to his beloved older brother, David Jones has imagined an inner and outer life for a dying man. Imagine a gritty tale of intrigue, international crime and corruption, and the cruelest, most savage details of high-tech medical reality merged with the shimmering world of shamans, visions, totems, and magical realism. The reader ponders the age-old question: Do we dream that we are awake, or are we awake when we are dreaming—and is there a difference?"

> —Eleanor Cooney, author of *Death in Slow Motion* and *Midnight in Samarra*

Pieces of Time

Short Stories

David Herstle Jones

Think in the Morning
Mendocino, California

*These are stories about what might have happened but didn't.
That makes them fiction.*

For Cathy

everything
That ever was still is, somewhere
—Tracy K. Smith

Contents

The Fifties

Ménage à Trois

Devon huddled in the back seat of the Cadillac, wrapped tightly in a soft brown blanket patterned with small red squares. The air was cold and the glass fogged slightly with each breath. He could hear his father and Louie up front, their voices muffled and distant, but from where he sat, he couldn't see them. Beside him sat Louie's wife, Dolly, a small woman with bobbed red hair, lips painted the same shade, and a face powdered so pale it reminded Devon of a street clown he'd once seen on a trip to San Francisco. Dolly's perfume was heavy and sweet, the kind that clung to the back of your throat.

On the trip they had parked in a loading zone. His father turned and said, "If the cops show up, tell 'em I'm making a delivery." Then he disappeared into the dark entrance of the building.

A man in a black-and-white harlequin outfit tapped on the window, his face ghostly white under the streetlight. He did a little jig right there on the sidewalk. Devon stifled a laugh under the blanket when he thought about it.

When he glanced at Dolly again, he noticed smudges of lipstick on her teeth. In the dim light inside the car, with her painted face and stiff smile, she looked less like a clown and more like a witch.

Louie wanted Henry to pull over. The snow fell harder now; fat flakes swirled in the headlights like ash.

Henry kept on, determined to get back home and confident, as usual.

Devon sat in the back. He thought about last winter—how they'd gotten stuck in a drift off Highway 20. They'd been lucky. A trucker came by to help. Without him, they might have frozen out there.

Devon saw his father only during school breaks. His parents were divorced.

"The snow's picking up, Henry," Louie said, a note of concern in his voice.

"Relax," Henry said with a grin. "I've got it under control. The snow and I have an understanding. It's like an open marriage. Complicated, but it works."

Henry caught Dolly's eye in the rearview mirror and shot a wink at her.

Devon saw it. He didn't like that look on his father's face.

Dusk sank into a sullen black as snowflakes hurled themselves against the car window, then vanished in rivulets. Devon shivered and drew the blanket tighter around his shoulders.

"Are you cold, sweetheart?" asked the witch. Her red lips curled into a smile that showed sharp teeth, glossy and wet.

Devon's mother had told him to be polite, no matter what. Dolly was good to Devon in her own way, but she didn't understand him. Not really. Not the way he wanted to be understood. He knew she meant well, but she treated him like a baby.

"No," he said softly.

Beside Dolly, though he never quite believed that was her real name, rested a book. Something about Brothers. Devon had just started to read books on his own. He traced the strange word with his eyes. *Dos-toe-ev-sky*. It sounded like a toe floating in the sky. He didn't ask. Dolly was a bookworm. It was the one thing Devon liked about her.

He turned his face into the scratchy wool seat, the fabric rough against his skin. With one hand, he flicked the chrome ashtray open and shut, open and shut, and listened to the crisp little clicks like a code only he could understand.

"Don't mess with the ashtray, sweetheart," Dolly said. "It's irritating. You might hit the window switch by accident and let that cold air in."

Does she think I'm an idiot? Devon scowled. He knew perfectly well what was what—ashtray, window, door handle. He knew about cars. This wasn't his first trip.

"The snow won't stick," Henry said from the front seat. "I'll get us home. Just watch."

Louie didn't look convinced. He shot a sharp glance into the rearview mirror, his jaw clenched tight.

Devon didn't say anything. He pulled the soft blanket over his head and tucked it under his chin until the world disappeared. Snow tapped against the car in soft, wet thumps—*pluh, pluh, pluh.* The wipers kept their rhythm, slow and tired—*shuh-shuh, shuh-shuh, shuh-shuh.* He imagined a kitten curled up outside his blanket purring softly just for him. It made the sadness smaller.

"I think we better pull over, Henry," Louie said. "It's worse. Ballard's is just past that bend up the hill. We should stop there for the night."

Henry shook his head. "I want to make it all the way home, pal. It's Friday night."

From beneath the blanket, Devon peeked out and caught Louie's reflection in the rearview mirror. His mouth was tight with frustration.

"Relax, Louie," Henry said. "The snow's really not that bad. I'll get us through this, like always." He knew Louie had a point. The road was slick, the sky dark, but he didn't want to break the Friday-night routine. It was his turn with Dolly, and everything would be easier at home.

Dolly lit a cigarette. The smell curled around Devon like smoke from a campfire.

The windshield wipers beat back the snow in tired swipes. In the corners where they couldn't reach, slush piled up in grimy crescents. One clump broke loose and stuck briefly on Devon's window, then slid off and vanished into the dark shoulder of the highway.

"Don't smoke, Dolly," Henry said. "You know it makes Devon sick. We'll stop at Ballard's. I'll call ahead about the storm. You can smoke then."

"He's not going to get sick," Dolly snapped. She turned toward Devon. "You're fine, aren't you, Devon?"

Before he could answer, Dolly took a long drag and exhaled a dense white cloud that rolled across the ceiling of the car like fog.

Devon pulled the blanket back over his head. His world plunged into darkness. The smoke crept in anyway. It smelled like wet leaves smoldering in a ditch.

By the time they reached Ballard's, his eyes stung.

Henry eased the Cadillac beneath the overhang at the hotel entrance. Louie and Dolly climbed out first. Louie leaned in close and said something under his breath. Dolly jerked back, startled, then dropped her cigarette and stormed toward the door, her powdered face flushed pink.

"Jesus, it's cold!" she shouted. "I'll get us drinks. You make your call, Henry."

She slammed straight into a bellboy as he hustled outside.

"I'll park the car, sir," the boy said after he caught his balance. He held out his hand, palm up, waiting for the keys.

"Don't worry about it, kid," Henry said. "We'll only be a few minutes. I just need to make a call."

Henry was always the last to admit defeat when the weather turned. No matter how heavy the snow or how dark the road, his optimism clung like frost to glass, but now, evening had fallen hard, and the snow piled up fast.

The young bellboy stepped forward, hand outstretched. "Sir, please. You can't keep going. The road's closed up ahead. The Highway Patrol just radioed in."

Henry hesitated, jaw tight. Then, with a sigh, more irritated than defeated, he handed over the keys. Without a word to Devon, he brushed past, already lost in his own thoughts.

Devon stood outside, alone. He watched as the Cadillac eased toward the far side of the lot. Only when it was parked and the engine cut did he head inside.

Ballard's Lodge looked just the same as he remembered: pine-log rafters above, thick granite walls mottled like salt and pepper. Hardwood floors stretched beneath mismatched oriental rugs. The one in the reception area was a dull green, the color of split-pea soup, with orange and brown flowers. The colors reminded Devon of his nausea. He didn't feel sick now that he was out of the car.

When he was here last with his dad there was a little white dog around. He wondered if it was still here.

"Feeling better, Devon?" his dad asked as he looked down at him.

Devon nodded. "Yeah. I got sick from that cigarette but I'm better now."

Henry sighed. "I know. I'm sorry about that." He paused, then brightened. "Hey, you got any change?"

Devon dug into his pocket and came up with a dime.

"Here, let me have that," Henry said.

"What for?" Devon asked, holding it tight.

"I'll trade you this," Henry said. He pulled a pocketknife from his coat and placed it in Devon's hand.

Devon's eyes widened. "But Dad, that knife's worth way more than a dime."

Henry smiled. "It's a special knife. They say the less you pay for it, the longer your friendship lasts."

Devon got a pensive look. "Then give me back my dime, I'll trade you a penny instead."

"Ha-ha!" Henry laughed and clapped a hand on his son's shoulder. "You're a clever one, pal. Come on, let's go find Louie and Dolly."

As he settled onto a stool at the bar, Henry said, "I guess we can spend the night here and follow the plow out in the morning."

"Fine by me," Louie replied, a satisfied glint in his eye. He liked being right, but knew better than to gloat around Henry.

Louie was French Canadian. His motto was "everything in moderation," and he lived his life accordingly. He met Henry at Wells Fargo Bank on Montgomery Street in San Francisco when the bank approved Henry's loan to construct a hotel in the Sierras at the halfway point between Sacramento and Reno. Working as a loan officer at a bank was not Louie's dream job. He was drawn to Henry and to the idea of the hotel. The two of them formed a partnership and a lasting friendship, though there was never any doubt who was in control. Louie was Henry's alter ego. He offered sage advice and reined Henry in when danger threatened as it did sometimes with Henry's headstrong nature.

"Hey, Tommy," Henry called. "Set us up with another round and have your girl up front get us a couple rooms."

Tommy Logan, who owned Ballard's, gave a nod. Henry, Louie, and Dolly co-owned the Rainbow Lodge across the valley.

"I'll give you two doubles and a twin for the kid," Tommy said. "Kitchen closes at eight, so don't wait too long if you're hungry."

Henry turned to Dolly with that smile that made Devon uncomfortable. It was nearly seven. Devon stood by the jukebox and pretended to study the song titles.

"Come over here and say hi to Tommy," Henry called.

Devon made his way to the bar. Tommy leaned across the counter, his bald head gleamed under the lights, and his mustache was thick above a toothy grin.

"Hello, Mr. Logan," Devon said.

"Stand up straight, Devon. Shoulders back," Dolly chimed in. "Slouching causes curvature of the spine."

There she goes again, thought Devon. *The witch.* She meant well but he didn't like her. He straightened up, just a little, and kept his eyes forward. *Polite,* he reminded himself. *I'm supposed to be polite.*

"Would you like a cherry coke, Devon?" asked Tommy.

"Yes, sir. Thank you," Devon replied.

Tommy dropped a splash of grenadine into a tall glass packed with ice, added a spoonful of chocolate syrup, filled it to the brim with Coca-Cola, and crowned it with a bright-red cherry.

"Here you go, kid," he said, as he slid the glass across the bar, "and take these two quarters for the jukebox." He handed them over with a smile. The hair on Tommy's fingers was thick and black, the same wiry black hair curled out from the collar of his shirt. Devon wondered how a man so hairy could be completely bald on top.

"Thank you, Mr. Logan," said Devon.

Henry leaned over. "Devon, we're gonna have a couple of drinks, then head to dinner. That okay with you?"

"Sure, Dad."

Devon walked over to the jukebox. He slid one of the quarters into the slot and pressed D8, *D* for Devon, and *8* for his age. The other two songs he picked at random. He watched the machine come to life, its internal arm swung back and forth with smooth mechanical grace until it plucked a record and dropped the needle.

He wandered over to a window booth, the one farthest from the bar, and sat down alone. Outside, the world was swallowed by snow and darkness. He pressed his forehead to the cold glass and stared into the night

The jukebox clicked and came to life with *C'est Si Bon* in Eartha Kitt's sultry voice. At the bar, Henry leaned in to talk with Tommy, while Louie and Dolly spoke quietly on their own. None of them seemed to notice the music.

Devon sat alone and turned the pocketknife over in his hands. It had two blades, one slightly smaller than the other, each with a little notch for his thumbnail. He opened and closed them a few times. The metal snapped back with a satisfying click. Then, using the smaller blade, he carefully scraped the dirt from beneath one fingernail.

When he finished his cherry Coke, he returned the empty glass to the counter, and slipped the second quarter into his pocket. He'd save that one for later.

"Can I go sit by the fire in the lobby, Dad?"

"Sure, pal. Stay close. I'll come get you when it's time for dinner," Henry said.

"How was that Coke, Devon?" asked Tommy from behind the bar.

"It was great, Mr. Logan. Hey, what happened to that little white dog?"

"White dog?"

"Yeah, the one that was here last Easter."

Tommy shrugged. "Hmm. Maybe a mountain lion got him."

Devon's eyes drooped.

"I think one of the guests took him home, didn't they?" Dolly chimed in casually.

Devon knew what she was up to.

"Oh, right," said Tommy, who caught on.

"I remember now. A lady guest fell in love with the little guy. Couldn't leave without him. Took him all the way back to San Francisco, I hear." He winked at Dolly.

Devon turned and headed toward the lobby. *What a bunch of liars,* he thought. *They think I'm a dumb kid, but I'm not.*

Devon knew it was a mountain lion that killed the dog. That's how it was in the mountains. He tried to picture how it happened: the quick blur of fur, the claws, the teeth. Did the little dog fight back, or did he die quickly without a sound?

Devon felt for the pocketknife in his coat pocket. His fingers found the cool metal and held it tight. His father had killed a mountain lion once; had the head stuffed and mounted. Devon looked into its glass eyes a hundred times, wondering how it would feel if the real eyes had locked with his. He tried to imagine what it would be like to be hunted.

An older couple stepped out of the bar and began their slow ascent up the spiral staircase.

"Good night, Mr. and Mrs. Wilkins," said the girl at the front desk. "The attendant left extra blankets in your room. Sleep well."

The girl at the desk was pretty. Devon liked the way she smiled when she spoke.

The woman walked partway upstairs and stopped. As she turned slightly, her gray dress caught the light. A black shawl rested neatly on her shoulders. She reminded Devon of his mother.

"We will, dear, thank you," she said with a kind smile, then continued up the stairway.

Devon's chest tightened. He missed his mother. He wished his parents would get back together. Once he'd asked his dad if that might happen. His father had only said, "It's complicated, son."

When he asked his mother, she said, "Maybe," but it didn't happen. He didn't ask again.

The girl at the desk noticed him sit by the fire.

"Does your dad know you're here, young man?" she asked. Her voice was soft, curious. She really was very pretty.

"Yes," Devon said. "He asked me to get something from the car." He didn't mean to lie but he wanted to go outside. It was too hot by the fire.

She raised her eyebrows but didn't press further. "It's cold out there. Don't stay long."

Devon didn't reply. He pushed through the front door into the quiet darkness. The cold didn't bother him.

Past the awning, his shoes left prints in the snow. The walkway along the side of the restaurant was covered in a thin white layer. He wandered along, and listened to the snow crunch beneath his feet.

Through the tall windows of the dining room, Devon saw the flicker of candlelight on the tables. A waiter stood beside a couple seated near the window. They didn't notice him as he watched from the dark. He walked slowly in the snow, separated from the warmth inside.

He reached a storage shed at the end of the walkway and tried the door. It was locked. A small overhang above the entrance kept the ground there dry. He sat down beneath it, leaned back against the door, and closed his eyes. Sleep came quickly.

⌛ ⌛ ⌛

"It must be dinnertime," Dolly said. "I'm starving." She stood up and Louie followed.

At the bar, Tommy and Henry were deep in conversation.

"Sure, they're illegal," Tommy said, and lowered his voice. "Those guys made it clear, Henry. If I didn't take the machines, they'd come back and torch the place."

"Goddammit, Tommy," Henry snapped. "We can't let that slide. I've got contacts in Sacramento. I'll make some calls."

Dolly drifted over, and leaned in close to Henry.

"Where's Devon?"

"Somewhere in the lobby," Henry said.

"It's Friday night," she murmured.

Henry smiled. "It sure is. Still on?"

Her cheeks flushed. Louie turned away and walked off. Tommy just grinned.

"All right, enough of that," Dolly said, recovering. "Go find Devon. Louie and I will grab a table in the dining room."

When Henry stepped into the lobby, Devon was nowhere to be seen.

"Hey," he said to the girl at the front desk. "You seen my boy?"

She didn't look up right away. She was busy filing her nails. After a moment, she glanced at him.

"Your boy? Hmm... yeah, he came through here. Said he was going out to the car for something. I don't think I saw him come back."

Henry's face tightened. "Jesus, he's just a kid. It's freezing out there. Why didn't you keep an eye on him?"

She gave a half-hearted shrug. "I thought he came back in... I was busy in the dining room."

Henry turned and bolted for the door.

"Devon! Devon!"

No answer.

He circled the parked cars, scanned the dark lot, then moved toward the dining room windows. Inside Louie and Dolly sat calmly at a table, flipping through menus. Outside, along the walkway, a set of small footprints marked the snow, which now fell faster and heavier.

Henry followed the trail until it ended at the storage shed. There, curled up against the locked door, was Devon, fast asleep. His hands were tucked inside his sleeves, coat collar pulled up around his face like a makeshift cocoon.

"Devon! Devon, wake up! Are you okay?"

Devon stirred, and blinked up at his father, still tangled in half-sleep.

"Huh? What...?"

"I said, are you all right?" Henry crouched beside him and helped him sit up.

Devon rubbed his eyes. "Yeah, Dad. I just... I don't like that woman."

Henry frowned. "What woman?"

"Dolly," Devon mumbled through a yawn.

Henry sat back on his heels. "Come on, Devon. Dolly's crazy about you. Why would you say something like that?"

Devon looked at him, the weight of something unspoken in his eyes. "Do you remember last time we came here?"

"Sure," Henry said. "Easter break."

"I slept with that little white dog."

Henry tried to remember. "What? No, I don't think—"

"Yes, I did. He licked my face after you left the room. Then Louie came in. He slept in your bed. All night."

Henry didn't answer right away. The air between them went still.

"What?" Henry blinked, caught off guard. "No, I—"

"I didn't tell Mom," Devon said quietly. "She doesn't need to know. Do you still love her?"

Henry hesitated. "Devon, that's something we'll talk about later, okay? Let's get inside before you freeze."

"I don't like her, Dad. I really don't."

"Come on, son. It's cold enough to turn your bones to ice."

"I don't want to go back in."

Henry crouched slightly, and softened his voice. "Please, Devon. Do it for me. We don't have to sit with anyone. I'll have dinner sent up to the room. I'll read you the comics."

Devon looked up. "*Alley Oop*"?

"Of course, pal. *Alley Oop* and all the others."

"Can we watch TV too? Will you stay with me all night?"

Henry nodded. "Of course I will."

"Okay."

The snow came down hard in thick flakes. It was blinding. Devon led the way, stiff-legged and uncertain. He nearly slipped more than once. Henry followed close behind. Two figures adrift in a storm, nearly invisible.

Devon tried to find his old footprints, but they'd already vanished under fresh snow. He had to guess where to place his feet.

Reliving the past is like that, never quite the same. Things can shift. Sometimes you can change the way things end. Devon shut his eyes. When he opened them, his father was beside him. The dog was there too. The storm had lifted. The sun was out. It was warm. They walked along, arms linked, singing songs together.

Big Fish

Ruben stood motionless, careful to keep his shadow from spilling across the water. In the dim light beneath the overhanging rock, he spotted the fish. It was a huge one, the biggest he'd ever seen. It lurked in a shadowed crevice. Every spring, when the snowmelt carved pools into the mountain's edge, Ruben Alcola came to look for fish stranded by chance, but this fish was special. He watched in silence, as his heart pounded. He decided then and there to keep it secret.

Ruben lived with his parents in one of the yellow-painted company houses along the old Southern Pacific rail line. There were only three houses on that stretch. The farthest belonged to Felipe Santiago, a leathery old man who lived alone and had taped pictures of naked women to the ceiling above his bed. "They keep me company," he laughed when Ruben asked. Ruben hadn't known how to respond.

The middle house belonged to the Ramirezes. Teo Ramirez was Ruben's best friend. They fought often, sometimes bitterly, but they always found their way back to each other. That's how it was with them. Then there was Teo's sister, Esperanza. Ruben couldn't explain what she did to him. Sometimes he thought he was in love with her, but the thought embarrassed him. What did that even mean, love? How could you ever be sure? All he knew was that he went soft and stupid around her. His stomach knotted when she walked by. When she smiled, he melted into something helpless and ridiculous. He hated how he acted around her, and hated more that he couldn't help it.

Ruben's father, Teo's father, and old-man Santiago worked the line for the Southern Pacific. They kept the tracks clear, replaced rusted spikes and rotten ties, and maintained the snowsheds that protected the rails through the winter snows. They did whatever was needed without some foreman to tell them what to do. They took pride in the work because they understood how much depended on it. Years ago, when the blizzard trapped the *City of San Francisco* streamliner at Donner Pass, it was old-man Santiago who helped rescue over two hundred passengers. A reporter snapped his picture, and it made the front page of the paper.

The stretch of track they cared for wound through pine forests along the mountainside, roughly halfway between Sacramento and Reno, two cities Ruben had never visited. He had only the vague images of them he glimpsed on television sets in the hotel as he tagged along with his mother when she cleaned the rooms.

The hotel sat perched high above the tracks, built on a natural plateau beside the highway. To the west, the road climbed sharply up the hillside on the way to Sacramento. When winter storms rolled in and snow piled deep, cars couldn't make it up the grade, and the hotel quickly filled with stranded travelers.

Ruben's mother, Teo's mother, and Esperanza all worked at the hotel. The rest of the staff came from nearby towns like Colfax, Dutch Flat, Alta, and Cisco Grove, small scattered communities that clung to the edges of the highway. Bear Valley lay on the north side of the mountain. Ruben loved the view of Lake Spalding from the grand dining room upstairs, but even better was the view from the bar patio below. The whole valley spread out like something from a painting. The hotel itself was carved into the mountainside and braced over the drop on massive steel beams, as if it had grown there, half-hidden in the rock and sky.

Ruben was friends with Devon, the boss's son. No one expected them to get along. Ruben lived in a yellow company house with his parents; Devon visited his father up the hill in the big hotel on holidays and summer vacations. His parents were divorced and he lived with his mother in the far-away Sacramento Valley. Their lives were miles apart, but that didn't seem to matter. Together they explored the forests and granite cliffs that surrounded the lodge; they slipped through shadows and ducked behind trees like outlaws in a forgotten land. They played hide-and-seek beneath towering pines, pulled tails off the lizards that hid in the woodpile, and took aim at birds with their homemade slingshots. During the winter snow season, they slid down the mountain on wooden sleds.

They passed secret messages to each other, wedged into cracks between the stone walls along the hotel's walkways. Sometimes they spied on the guests through windows, half daring, half bored. Once, Ruben saw Esperanza through the glass as she helped her mother clean a room. She didn't notice him. His heart dropped like a leaf falling from a branch, limp and sodden.

"Why do you act so weird around Esperanza?" Devon asked later, as he licked the honey butter off his fingers. "Is she your girl?"

They had snuck behind the kitchen to steal still-warm rolls from the cooling racks, sweet and soft and dripping with glaze. Ruben didn't answer. His English faltered in moments like this. He just smiled. Butter glistened on his chin, and he shook his head. Devon smiled too. It wasn't an ordinary smile. It was odd, unreadable. Ruben remembered it later, more than once. It stuck in his mind like a burr in wool.

⧖ ⧖ ⧖

The big fish burst from the shadows of the crevice and snatched a mosquito off the surface of the pool. In a blink, it vanished beneath the water again. Concentric ripples spread across the glassy surface where the insect had been. The air was hotter. Ruben knew the fish wouldn't last much longer as the melt-pool shrank. When the oxygen ran out, it would die and float to the top. The thought made him ache with sorrow.

Behind their yellow company houses, the Alcola and Ramirez families kept sprawling gardens. Old-man Santiago didn't bother with one. Teo's family went further, they kept two pigs and a cow. Ruben's parents wanted none of that. "They stink," his mother said. "Too much damn work," added his father.

Sometimes, Ruben followed Esperanza when she fed the cow or slopped the pigs. He went along when it was Teo's turn too, but it wasn't the same. Esperanza made it more fun.

"We should go fishing," Teo said one warm afternoon as they hauled buckets of kitchen slop down to the pen. "There's gotta be fish in the melt-pools by now." Ruben trailed behind, and struggled to match his friend's stride.

"I'm not going this year," he said.

Teo shrugged. "Suit yourself. I'm heading back to that hole we found last year. We cleaned up there. I'll bet there's a fat one waiting for me."

"I already checked it," Ruben said. "There's nothing in it this year."

He hated lying, but the big fish was his secret. Some things felt too sacred to share.

"Maybe you're just blind," Teo said with a smirk, and flicked his eyes toward Ruben as he tipped the slop bucket over the fence.

Ruben frowned. "What's that supposed to mean?"

The bucket emptied with a wet splash. Two black-and-white pigs barreled over, grunting and squealing as they fought for scraps.

Teo wiped his hands on his pants. "I've seen the way you look at my sister," he said. "You think it's love. That's silly. You'd have better luck with the pinups inside Santiago's cabin."

Ruben clenched his jaw. What did Teo know about anything?

"My eyes are fine," he said coolly. "And there's no fish this year. I already checked. If you want to waste your time, go ahead. Makes no difference to me."

But it did matter. Ruben's fists curled at his sides. He hated that smug grin on Teo's face, hated how easily Teo could twist the knife. Ruben took a breath and held back his anger. No use to swing at shadows. Still, his heart jumped when he thought of Esperanza. Maybe it was love. Or maybe it was something else. Whatever it was, Teo didn't understand. Probably no one did.

"Maybe I'll go, maybe I won't," Teo said with a shrug. "Who cares anyway? Say, why are do you always hang around Devon? You think he's your friend? He just uses you."

Ruben narrowed his eyes. "What do you mean?"

Teo smirked. "He's got a thing for Esperanza. Isn't it obvious? He even asked me to help him get with her."

"What did you tell him?" Ruben asked, his voice tight.

"I told him to run back home to his *mamá*." Teo chuckled. "Let *her* help him."

Ruben tried to shake it off. "So what? Maybe he does like Esperanza. Doesn't mean he's not my friend. He's always been decent to me."

"He doesn't even live here," Teo said. "He drops in for vacations like he owns the place."

Ruben forced a shrug, but the words gnawed at him. He turned, walked away, and pretended not to care. Inside, he burned. He had trusted Devon. Now he wasn't sure what to think.

Once out of sight, he broke into a run, headed up the hill to the rock pool. The water was still and cold under a dim sky. The big fish didn't show itself, but Ruben knew it was there, hiding in the shadows. Two smaller fish hovered near the bottom; they glowed gold in the sunlight.

The sun slipped behind the ridge. He and Teo had fished this pool so many times. They had pulled fish out with hooks, nets, even their bare hands. Sometimes they speared them with sticks. It used to feel like a game. Now it didn't. The fish were trapped. They couldn't escape. They'd die anyway as the pool dried up, but that didn't make it right to kill them.

Ruben stood for a long moment and watched the water ripple gently. Then he turned back toward home, his chest heavy with something he couldn't quite name.

When Ruben stepped through the door, he asked his mother, "How did you know you were in love with Dad?"

She gave him a long, thoughtful look. "Is there something you want to tell me, *hijo?* Have you met someone?"

"No, Mama," he said quickly. "I just want to understand. How do you know when it happens, when you're in love?"

She smiled, but there was seriousness in her eyes. "There's no sign, no announcement. No one rings a bell or hits you over the head. I think I started to love your father the day we met. I watched how he treated me, how he cared, and little by little it just became clear. One moment followed another, and there it was."

"There what was?" Ruben asked.

"Love," she said gently. "Love. I didn't fall all at once. I just… realized one day that it had happened."

Ruben frowned. Fall into love? Like into a hole? That didn't make much sense. Love seemed too slippery, too strange. Maybe there was no clear answer. Maybe it was like that big fish trapped in the melt-pool, stuck in the wrong place, with no way out. The thought unsettled him. He suddenly wasn't sure if he wanted love to happen at all.

⧗ ⧗ ⧗

Just up the road from Ruben's house stood a small one-room schoolhouse. It served all the children who lived nearby. There were never more than a dozen at a time. The student roster shifted often, depending on the hotel staff's comings and goings. It was the day before Easter break. The air buzzed with anticipation. Even the older kids, like Ruben and Teo, were excited about the candy and the egg hunt, though they did their best to act like they weren't.

That afternoon, a sleek car pulled up outside in a small cloud of dust. Ruben stared as Devon stepped out with his father. The trunk was full of Easter baskets, each brimful of sandwiches, sweets, and brightly wrapped presents tied with shiny ribbons. Devon grinned as he handed them out, moving from desk to desk like a proud host.

Ruben received the first basket.

"Here you go, Ruben," Devon said. "I hope you like it."

Ruben mumbled his thanks, suddenly self-conscious. He had nothing to give in return. He watched in silence as Devon made his way around the room and handed out basket after basket. When he reached Esperanza, he held out the prettiest one of all. She took it with a quiet smile, and lowered her eyes so that only her long black lashes were visible.

Ruben felt a chill run through him, then a flush of heat.

Teo shot Ruben a knowing wink. "Told you so."

Ruben shrugged. "What does it matter?"

He pulled a small pocketknife from his pocket and flipped it open. "Look! Devon gave me this. Pretty cool, right?" He forced a smile, but inside he felt the opposite of cool. Something didn't sit right.

Just then, Devon strolled up to them with a grin. "Hey, you guys want to catch a movie in Colfax tonight? My dad said he'd drive us. It's on us."

Ruben and Teo didn't get chances like this often. A trip to the movies was a real vacation.

"Heck, yes!" Teo said without hesitation.

Ruben nodded. "Sure." He wanted to be excited, but a knot of suspicion had already started to tighten in his gut.

"Awesome," Devon said. "Hey, Teo, make sure your sister comes too. We'll swing by around five."

There it was, the real reason behind the sudden generosity: Esperanza.

Devon and his father headed back toward the hotel, leaving Ruben, Teo, and Esperanza to walk the dirt path toward home.

"Hey, guess what," Teo said, nudging his sister. "Devon wants to take us to the movies tonight. You're invited too. We already told him we'd go."

Esperanza hesitated. Ruben watched her carefully. She didn't say anything right away, but he could tell she was interested.

"We'll have to ask Dad," she said finally.

"He'll say yes," Teo replied confidently.

"Devon said five. Don't be late," he added, giving Ruben a quick glance as they each turned off toward their house.

On his way home, Ruben ran into old-man Santiago, who was wiping his hands with a red cloth after finishing his lunch.

"*Hola, Señor Santiago,*" Ruben called out.

"Hola, Ruben," Santiago said with a wide grin. "No school for a whole week now, eh? You must be excited. Sleep in late, fish all day at the rock pools, maybe catch me a big one and we'll have ourselves a *barbacoa!*"

His teeth flashed like the snow that still clung to the mountaintops.

Ruben smiled as he pictured the huge fish, how he put it on the fire, and everyone cheered. Esperanza would beam at him, throw her arms around his neck, maybe even kiss him. The thought made his heart thump.

"Can I ask you something, Señor Santiago?"

"Of course, mijo," Santiago said with a chuckle. "Ask away. I might not have the answer, but I'll try.

Santiago was old but solid. His back was straight as a pine trunk. His thick black hair barely showed any gray, and his arms, corded with muscle, looked like they could still toss a railroad tie over a fence. His mustache was yellowed from cigarettes, but his eyes sparkled like sunlight on water.

"Have you ever been in love?" Ruben asked, a little embarrassed by his question.

Santiago didn't answer right away. He lowered himself onto a pile of cut logs beside the tracks and rubbed his chin thoughtfully.

"Yes," he said finally. "I have. A long time ago. I remember like it was yesterday."

Ruben shifted his weight and stared at his shoes. A breeze passed through, carrying the scent of pine needles and wildflowers, sweet and clean. Beneath it lingered the sharp bite of creosote that rose from the railroad ties.

"How did you know it was love?" Ruben asked.

"At first it was just attraction," Santiago said. "That kind of pull any man can feel for a beautiful woman, but then it deepened. I came to admire her, respect her, and then, boom! One day it hit me like lightning. I could feel her heart as if it were inside my chest. That was the moment when I knew it was love, real love. Magic."

Ruben listened attentively. "Did she love you back?"

Santiago gave a low chuckle and looked down at the ground. "Ah, no. That's the twist. She didn't feel the same. You know what they say, it takes two to tango."

Ruben's chest tightened. It felt like something inside him had collapsed, like a fishhook that tugged in the wrong direction.

"Weren't you sad?" he asked Santiago.

"Sad?" Santiago looked up at the sky for a moment. "No, not really. I was lucky. I got to feel something real. That's the thing, Ruben, it's not about holding on, it's about feeling it at all. I loved her enough to let her go, and that love, well, it never left me."

Santiago stood and brushed wood dust from his pants. His face glowed in the sunlight. Ruben didn't understand. How could someone be happy after they lost the one they loved? How could love survive like that?

"I've got to get back to work," Santiago said, and he pulled up his toolbelt around his waist. "You'll know when it's your time, Ruben. Love doesn't whisper. It crashes in like a wave. When it comes, you'll feel it. You won't have a single doubt."

Santiago walked east along the tracks, his silhouette framed by the golden light. Ruben watched him go, the smell of pine still thick in the air, his heart a little heavier, but also a little more awake.

⏳ ⏳ ⏳

At five o'clock the car pulled up. Esperanza sat in the front seat beside Devon's father, and the three boys squeezed into the back. Ruben knew the road to Colfax well. He had made the trip before with his parents to visit the high school. One of the teachers explained how he would have to take a special English class before he enrolled. He could start after he finished the school at Emigrant Gap. The thought made him nervous, but he told himself it would all work out.

In the back seat, the boys played Rock, Paper, Scissors, but Ruben didn't pay attention to the game. His eyes drifted to the delicate curve of Esperanza's neck where a few short black hairs curled beneath her ear.

Up front, Devon's father talked about the new highway project. They planned to widen the road all the way from Sacramento to Reno. The hotel would be torn down to make way. He would be forced to sell.

"What about all the jobs?" Teo asked, his voice tense with concern.

"I'm afraid they'll all be gone," Devon's father said.

Ruben caught the shadow that crossed Esperanza's face. They all knew what it meant. Without the hotel, there would be nothing to keep the families here. Teo's mother, Ruben's mother, and Esperanza would all be out of work. Santiago might manage alone, but a family couldn't survive on a single income.

The mood in the car shifted, weighed down by the news. By the time they reached the theater, the excitement had faded. The movie, *The Time Machine*, felt eerie and distant to Ruben. While the others seemed to enjoy it, he couldn't shake what he felt in his chest. When he saw Devon take Esperanza's hand in the dark, he quietly got up, slipped into the lobby, and waited for it to be over.

On the ride home, Ruben pretended to sleep, his face turned toward the window, eyes closed but he listened. He heard Teo ask Devon to go fishing over the weekend.

"I know where there's a big one," Teo said, voice full of excitement.

In the front seat, Esperanza slept soundly, head resting against the window.

Before dawn the next morning, Ruben slipped out of bed and crept through the quiet house. He didn't turn on any lights. In the garage he found a large pail and an old fishing net, then stepped outside into the stillness. The sky had just started to lighten. No lights shone from Teo's house or old-man Santiago's.

Ruben followed the tracks to the narrow trail that led to the rock pools. When he reached the big pool, he crouched down and waited silently for the sun. As the first golden rays touched the water's surface, he thought about what Santiago had said: *I loved enough to let her go.* At the time, he hadn't understood, but now he did.

At just the right moment, when the big fish broke the surface, Ruben moved quickly but gently, and scooped it up with the net. He filled the pail with water and lowered the fish inside. Then, without a word, he turned and carried it all the way to the river that flowed west.

He knelt at the river's edge, tilted the pail, and released the fish into the current. Sunlight flashed off its scales as it vanished into the deep water, and for a moment the light was so bright it nearly blinded him, but he didn't look away.

Women Alone

"It was such a shock to all of us," Janet said soberly.

She stood just outside the church steps, waiting with Mrs. P for the Jensen family to emerge. Mr. P had passed away a year ago. Janet was divorced. The two women had become Sunday companions. They met each week at St. Anthony's before Mass. Today, both wore their wide-brimmed Sunday hats, a ritual they both enjoyed.

Behind Janet, her young son, Devon, shifted from foot to foot, bored and impatient. He thought the hats looked ridiculous, almost as bad as the stiff white robes the altar boys wore. He'd never wear something so silly, and he certainly didn't want to be an altar boy. That had been Eric's cross to bear, back when Eric still went to church. Now Eric had escaped to USC, too busy and indifferent to bother with religion. Devon showed up only to keep his mother happy. He didn't believe any of it, but he kept his opinions to himself. With his dad gone and his brother off to college, his mother's life was weighted down enough. He didn't want to add to her burden.

At last, the Jensen family appeared and stepped solemnly into the sunlight. They filed out in perfect order, like ducklings behind their mother, eight children in all; the smallest clung to her hand, the eldest brought up the rear.

"Such a terrible shock," Janet repeated. She tried not to stare, but it was difficult. She was caught in a tangle of pity, dread, and curiosity that she was hesitant to admit. She didn't want to judge, yet part of her couldn't help but wonder if Mabel Jensen, however unintentionally, had played some role in the tragedy that had rocked the quiet farming town of Sugarvale.

Jeffrey Jensen had married well. Mabel was the prize of the Peterson family. The Petersons had farmed in the valley for generations. While Jeffrey's family owned a modest parcel, it was Mabel's inheritance that turned their farm into the largest in the county. How had it all unraveled? Whispers of debt had begun to circle, but Janet waved them off as nothing more than envy. After all, every farmer borrowed against the harvest. There were rumors of another woman. There always were in these situations, but Janet could not believe this of Jeffrey. She had known him since they grew up together. He was not like that. No, it had to be something deeper and darker behind the fall.

Mabel Jensen was a woman apart. She ran the household with grace and steel. Even after eight children, her beauty never dimmed, and her home gleamed with a cleanliness that seemed almost sacred. She cooked, cleaned, and hosted with effortless charm. Intelligent, though always reserved, she let Jeffrey take center stage, until now.

On this somber Sunday, Mabel led the way. Her blue eyes fixed straight ahead, she ushered her children out of the church and into the van with quiet, unwavering purpose. The ride home would be long and lonely.

Devon followed his mother to their car. Mrs. P called out an invitation as they passed: "Come by for a swim." Devon's face lit up. He loved to swim in Mrs. P's pool on hot summer afternoons, but Janet had something she wanted to do first.

"We should stop by Pearl's," she said. "She might leave town for the summer. You should offer to water the garden and keep an eye on the house."

Devon perked up. He relied on side jobs to supplement his grocery-store wages. He worked weekends, squeezed in shifts before school, and put in long hours all summer.

"Every little bit helps," Janet said as she led him out of the church parking lot.

Pearl did not go to church. She lived alone in the sprawling old house across the street. From there she watched the Sunday procession from her front window. Her garden was legendary, an intricate tapestry of color and scent. Rare irises from around the world stood tall beside roses in every imaginable hue, their fragrance drifting across the fence. Bulbs and blossoms bloomed in neat, radiant rows, like the tulip fields in Holland Devon had only seen in books.

Pearl was short and stout; she reminded Devon of his grandmother, but more poised and worldly. The two women were fast friends. Pearl could be blunt. Her stern manner rubbed some townsfolk the wrong way, but Devon adored her, and she in turn trusted him more than most. She even let him tend to her prized irises—an honor not easily won. Devon wasn't a gardener, not really, but he recognized beauty when he saw it. He was steady and respectful, with a quiet attentiveness that older women instinctively appreciated. Raised by his mother and grandmother, Devon understood their ways, their silences, and how to listen.

Pearl's house, dark and cool in summer, was a wonderland of rooms filled with treasures collected during her travels. Devon loved to explore its nooks and corners, the painted ceramics, the carved wooden figurines, the lace-draped tables, the antique vases, and the framed prints from distant lands. Each item had a story, and Pearl was eager to tell them. He imagined her in crowded bazaars, straw hat askew, flannel dress neat and proper, her eyes gleaming as she haggled with seasoned vendors. She claimed she always got the better deal, and Devon believed her. He liked to picture Pearl as she walked through the world with quiet confidence and sharp wit.

Though her health remained good, Pearl traveled less now. Maybe she simply preferred the company of her memories, those dusty, beautiful relics of a well-lived life. "Memories are how you live it all over again," she told Devon. "That way you squeeze the most out of it." She shared those memories with him freely, weaving truth and invention into something richer than either. Devon didn't care what was real. Every story felt like a gift, as the best ones always do.

Pearl once told Devon about a thin veil that separates each of us from reality. "We're on one side," she said, "and everything else is on the other. We live in solitude, each in our own private world. All we have are the five senses, our tools to reach across the divide. At best we just collect impressions. We can't be sure what is really there, so we invent stories and call them truth."

Pearl was strange, yes, but Devon liked her. He didn't mind her peculiar ways. She didn't invite them in. "I'm in a hurry," she said, which might have been true, or might mean she wasn't in the mood for company. Devon was used to it. Pearl had built a shell around herself, and she guarded it carefully. It wasn't wise to press her. People who had tried had come away hurt, some left with scars, not the visible kind, but the kind that made you call someone "difficult" or "severe." Devon understood this without being told. He knew better than to crack the shell.

"I'm sorry I can't talk right now," Pearl added, and stepped back inside. "I could use your help in August. I'll let you know the dates. I appreciate your help, Devon, always. Goodbye. Thank you for stopping by."

She closed the door.

"Well, that was brief," Janet said with a small laugh as they turned toward the car.

"Pearl's just… eccentric," Devon replied. "She lives alone. Sometimes she doesn't want to be around people. That's okay. I still like her."

"I do too," Janet said softly.

A cold breeze cut unexpectedly through the afternoon warmth. Janet shivered. A thought rose unbidden: *Will I she end up like Pearl, old and alone in a quiet house with no one to answer the door?* Eric was gone. Devon would soon be on his way. She slipped her arm around his shoulder.

"I love you," she said.

Devon didn't notice the tear that slid down her cheek.

Across the street, Mabel Jensen and her eight children left in the van that would take them back to the farm, back to the barley and safflower, the rice and alfalfa that stretched all the way to the river where Jeffrey Jensen's truck had been found.

Janet held Devon close, so close he squirmed a little under her grip.

"It was a great shock to us all," she murmured to no one in particular. "A great shock to us all."

⧗ ⧗ ⧗

Mrs. P's pool was little more than a shallow basin ringed with a thin border of concrete, but to Devon it was a paradise. He spent hours swimming, floated on his back, dove to the bottom, and burst through the surface like a porpoise. In the shade of the old olive trees, Mrs. P and Janet sipped iced tea and watched him play. Mr. P had planted those trees decades ago. Now tall and generous, they cast dappled shadows across the patio.

"I wonder what the poor people are doing," Mrs. P said with a wry smile. It was her favorite joke, especially when they lounged by the pool. There were only a handful of olive trees, but the almond orchard beyond them was large enough to bring a modest income. Since Mr. P's passing, their son, Lyle, had taken a job in the city after he finished college. He managed the orchard on weekends.

The family, Italian Catholics, had always lived simply but comfortably. They'd put two children through college and took pride in seeing them build successful lives. Still, after Mr. P died, Mrs. P chose not to follow them into a faster, fancier world. She remained in the humble home her husband had built next to the trees he had tended all his life. She preferred the rhythm of the old ways.

Mr. P could be a hard man. He was kind at heart but frugal and exacting. He was skeptical of indulgence, and his disapproval of small pleasures often loomed large in their household. Mrs. P never complained. She carried herself with quiet dignity. Though her days were in some ways easier now, she would never say so aloud.

"Yes," Janet chuckled, playing along. "I wonder what the poor people are doing." Then her smile faded, and she looked directly into Mrs. P's soft brown eyes. "I worry about Mabel and those children," she said. "Have you heard the rumors? About debt and another woman? I can't believe they're true."

Mrs. P answered from the shade with quiet intensity. "Well, if they *are* true, that man wasn't the Jeffrey Jensen I thought I knew. No one knows, Janet, no one. Lord, have mercy on his soul. What he did was terrible. Mary, Jesus, and Joseph! How is she supposed to carry on after something like that? I can't even begin to think what this will do to the children. Poor Mary Alice isn't even five, and the oldest, Jeff Jr., isn't out of high school yet."

Devon sat at the edge of the pool; his legs dangled in the water, the sun warming his skin like a blanket. He caught fragments of the adult conversation that drifted over from the olive trees, but he didn't try to follow. Instead, his mind wandered. *Was Mr. Jensen's private world filled with shadows? Was it possible for a person to fall so far into themselves that no one else could reach them? Could such a thing happen to me? If it does, what would I do?*

He rolled onto his stomach and rested his cheek on his crossed arms. The golden heat on his back made his thoughts melt into dreams.

"Devon, wake up! Time to go." His mother's voice cut through the haze. Devon squinted his eyes and looked up. The bright sunlight behind her turned her into a silhouette. She was a shadow against the light.

On the short drive home, they went down main street past Dawley's Shell station, the old Sugarvale Theater where his father once worked, now a skating rink, past McFarland's Five and Dime, Tuffy's Bar, Bub Howe's barbershop, Mona's clothing store, and Stinson's Drugs. Just before the bridge that crossed the freeway and divided the town in two stood the faded brick jail behind the old hotel. Every place had a memory tucked inside it.

Devon's grandmother, Eunice, was on the back porch, deep into a game of Canasta with her friend Ida. The two sat at a small table, cards in hand, their banter lively and competitive. It was Eunice and Ida who taught him how to play. Ida played to win, and Devon, a quick study, often beat her, which made her furious. He didn't care much for cards anymore; he had other interests now. He sometimes joined in just to see Ida's scowl when she lost. That made the game worth it.

Life was more magical before Eunice moved in with him and his mother. Devon missed the old house with the worn card table tucked in the kitchen corner, and the antique gas stove that hummed beside the sink. His grandmother cooked the simple things he liked, scrambled eggs and ground beef, round steak with mashed potatoes and milk gravy, fruit cobblers. His grandfather bounded in through the back door after work and towered over him, quiet and steady.

He rolled up his sleeves, and washed his hands at the sink in the bathroom behind the kitchen. He had once been a medical student but gave it up when his family lost their farm in the Depression. Instead, he took a job as a propane truck driver. He never forgot the habits he learned in medical school. He showed Devon the way doctors scrub, palms first, then fingers, rotating one hand over the other, back and forth. From then on, Devon always washed his hands the same way.

Ida was a retired schoolteacher, a lifelong spinster with no close kin, just a few distant cousins in Sugarvale who kept one eye on her and the other on her modest inheritance. When she left the city after retirement, she bought a small house on the outskirts of town and her backyard backed up against the high school football field. As a boy, Devon used to linger in her yard, gripping the chain-link fence to watch the games. Now, years later, he played on the field he'd once watched in awe.

Ida's garden was a lush, shadowed haven, a tangle of exotic shrubs, vibrant blooms that almost glowed, miniature trees, and massive, unruly bushes. It was wild, almost secretive, the kind of place that whispered rather than shouted. In contrast, Pearl's garden was neat, geometric, and basked in full sun, a study in order and intention. The two gardens reflected the personalities of their owners perfectly. Ida was sharp, solitary, cloaked in mystery; Pearl was eccentric but open-hearted, as readable as a seed catalog. Devon was raised by independent women who lived alone and shouldered the world without asking permission. In homes like his, there was no father figure to shape his sense of self; instead, Devon absorbed the rhythms and sensibilities of a matriarchal world. He learned how to cook, how to fold laundry just so, how to keep a tidy space, and how to read the emotions in a room before anyone spoke. He was drawn to art, music, and flowers rather than guns or engines. He preferred a good book to hunting or fishing.

Still, he knew the rules of survival in a world that could be cruel to boys who strayed too far outside the expected lines, so he worked hard at math, cultivated a logical mind, joined the football team, and taught himself to hide in plain sight. He walked through haunted buildings and didn't flinch, stepped on cracks others avoided, and laughed at danger when it counted. He had a girlfriend who took him to hunt deer with her father. He turned out to be better at it than he expected. At church he played the part for his mother's sake, but made sure his friends knew he didn't buy into the idea of a sky-bound father who watched his every move. He refused to be labeled soft. What softer qualities he had, he buried beneath armor stitched from performance and silence.

Ida shot Devon a frosty look, the kind that said she feared he might join in and take over the game. He gave her a warm smile.

"Hi, Ida. I don't have time to play cards today. I wish I could. I've got some chores to handle."

Her expression softened. A smile flickered, faint but genuine, before she turned back to her cup of tea.

Devon stepped out the backdoor. The screen creaked shut behind him. He made his way into the field behind the house. It was his refuge. As a young boy, he'd carved narrow trails through the tall weeds, and played hide-and-seek with the neighborhood kids. He came here now to think, to breathe, and to be alone.

Inside, Janet stood at the kitchen counter and scribbled a grocery list. It was her turn to host the women's group Tuesday night. The theme was Hawaiian. She was determined to make a pineapple upside-down cake. The macadamia nuts she'd picked up during last weekend's trip to The Nut Tree sat in a bowl on the counter. She would transform them into her famous macadamia nut cookies.

Out in the field, Devon paused. In the distance, he spotted Marjorie Jackson watering the flowerpots on her front deck. She was his best friend, Roger's, mother. Nobody talked much about Roger's father because nobody knew who he was. Devon's mother once told him Marjorie got pregnant by a man who vanished before Roger was born. Marjorie's own parents disowned her after she gave birth. She scraped by with sewing jobs. The dresses she made for others were vibrant, full of life, but she dressed herself in simple blouses and skirts and rarely left her porch.

As he drifted back toward the house, Devon slowed near the kitchen window. He heard the low voices of his grandmother and Ida inside. They spoke in hushed tones.

"They say there was a pile of cigarette butts outside his truck," Ida murmured. "Two packs or more."

"Yes," Devon's grandmother replied. "I heard that too. Must've sat there for hours, just thinking, before he finally did it."

There was a long, uneasy silence, then the scrape of a chair and the click of a spoon in a teacup.

⧗ ⧗ ⧗

At the other side of town, Mrs. P sat alone in her kitchen, the refrigerator's hum the only sound. Around this time of day, she would hear Mr. P's boots on the back steps, the creak of the screen door, and then he would be there in front of her, dusty from the orchard. He'd sigh, wipe his brow, and tell her it was going to be a tough season. There would be no money for a trip to the coast again this year. She would nod silently and continue to chop vegetables for dinner while the sun dipped lower.

Now alone, she stood at the window and watched the last light of day melt through the trees, shimmer across the pool, and fade into the rose bed by the fence.

"I wonder what the poor people are doing," she said with a dry chuckle. She took a sip from the miniature can of Coors she allowed herself each night, her one small indulgence to coax sleep.

Across the street, Pearl had no plans and wanted none. She preferred it that way. Solitude wasn't loneliness to her. It was protection. She guarded her privacy the way a dog guards a bone. From her window, she watched the undertaker's car ease into the church parking lot, to prepare for Jeffrey Jensen's funeral.

"Foolish man," she muttered. "Weak. Cowardly."

She shook her head.

"Life's too precious to throw away. What kind of man leaves his family in a mess like that?"

Out at the Jensen farm, Mabel moved through the motions like a ghost as friends arrived, their faces solemn and voices soft. Her eight children had been sent off to the homes of neighbors, surrounded by playmates and distractions, shielded from the weight of grief, but that protection came at a cost. They were spared sorrow, yes, but also the chance to grasp death's shape and meaning. That lesson would come later, and it would come harder.

Mabel, meanwhile, remained untouched by the rituals around her. She didn't step through the veil; she hid behind it, separate, unreachable. She lifted a glass of cold tea to her lips but tasted nothing. She listened to condolences spoken with care, embraced friends she hadn't seen in years and felt no comfort. The comings and goings of cars on the long gravel drive registered as distant motion, like a dream half-remembered. The house still carried the scent of flowers and food, but her senses no longer reached for them. Even familiar sounds, the creak of floorboards, the hum of motors, had fallen silent.

Time didn't pass; it simply stopped. Mable stood alone in her bubble, aware of nothing but the great, yawning absence that now defined her world.

Roger's Secret

The town dump lay west of Sugarvale, a half-hour's drive in our battered old truck. On Saturdays, my mother and I made the trip to toss our garbage. The sour smoke from the fires stung my eyes, and the stench churned my stomach, but I didn't care. I was on the hunt for treasure. I sifted through acres of junk like a miner panning for gold, careful and selective. My mother let me bring home only the "good stuff," and I learned to spot it amidst the worthless.

Sometimes my friend Roger came along. He brought his .22 rifle to shoot gophers. We lit fires in their tunnels to smoke them out, but it never really worked. We didn't shoot a single gopher, but the idea that we might was enough to keep us at it. We lined up cans and old bottles, and sharpened our aim with every shot.

My parents were divorced. I lived with my mother. Roger never knew his father; no one did. My mother once told me Roger was "born out of wedlock," a phrase that meant little to me but carried weight in the eyes of others. Roger's father vanished when his mother got pregnant. When Roger's grandparents found out, they were furious. They insisted his mom go to a home for unwed mothers. When she refused, and vowed to keep the baby, they cast her out. From that day on, she raised Roger alone.

By the time Roger and I were old enough to understand any of it, the story had gone quiet. People didn't bring it up anymore, but for us, the absence of a father brought us together. Growing up without fathers had carved out a bond between us, an unspoken understanding.

Roger and I camped once with the Boy Scouts just a few miles west of the town dump, in a wide valley tucked against the base of the coastal range. The land belonged to Roger's grandparents, who ran a sprawling ranch with cattle, sheep, barley, alfalfa, and fruit orchards. Long before them, Native people had lived there in caves carved into the hillsides. Some people called them "digger" Indians, but they were much more than that. They made baskets, fished, hunted, and traded with other Native peoples all the way to the Pacific coast. Some of those caves were still reachable. Roger and I would squeeze our way through the narrow openings and hunt for arrowheads in the thick, biting layers of bat guano that blanketed the floors. Bats clung to the ceilings like clustered shadows. It was a filthy job, but we couldn't resist the idea that we might find something real, something ancient. My grandfather once found a grinding stone in one of the caves, which made us believe there might be more out there. We were always on the lookout.

The new highway sliced Sugarvale into three parts, the east side, the west side, and the Camp to the north. The Camp was once a World War II prisoner-of-war facility, later converted into low-income apartments and a general store. Roger and I were born not long after German prisoners had been held there. When we were in grade school, one of the old guard towers still stood. We used to play war games beneath that tower as if we were soldiers. We sometimes sneaked into the garage of a house next door where there was an old shortwave radio and pretended to communicate with troops overseas.

My mother told me she and her girlfriends would go out to the camp to watch the prisoners play soccer. Most of the local boys went overseas to fight, and some of the girls flirted with the prisoners even though it wasn't allowed. By the time I was in high school, the camp store had become known as a place where you could buy cigarettes and beer without an ID. I once dated a girl who lived out there. Her family shared a single room where mattresses were lined up on the floor. When I arrived to pick her up, her father offered me a cigarette and a beer. I declined, but that shook me, the sheer weight of poverty in every corner. My mom wasn't wealthy, but we had a house, and I had my own room.

There was a boy in my class named Jerry who lived at the Camp. He died from diabetes. My mother said he got the disease because of a poor diet. That kind of poverty shapes people. It was like that back then, and, I suspect, in too many places it still is.

During the time of the POW camp, some of the prisoners were put to work on nearby farms. Many of the local farmers were German Americans who spoke the language. That helped ease communication. My great-great-grandfather had emigrated from Germany to avoid conscription into the kaiser's army. Now, decades later, his adopted country was at war with his homeland. With most of the young men overseas, farmers were desperate for help, and the German prisoners filled that gap. A few tried to escape now and then, but they never got far. Without money, shelter, or a grasp of English, they were easily caught and returned.

One summer, Roger and I came up with a scheme to hunt deer. Our plan was to dry the meat into jerky and sell it around town. Back then, deer jerky was in high demand. Roger swore there were plenty of deer in the hills behind his grandparents' old ranch. His grandparents had passed away by then, and the land had been sold to some out-of-towners who rarely visited. That weekend we packed up our gear, set up camp on the edge of the property, and spent the next couple of days in the hills, to follow our own version of adventure.

On the first day, we spent hours crisscrossing the foothill trails without a single deer in sight. It was around dusk, and we were about to give up, when Roger froze mid-step and pointed across a narrow stream toward a stand of oaks.

"Shh," he whispered.

I squinted into the shadows. Just visible among the trees was a buck, motionless and alert. Roger held up three fingers to signify a three-point. Before we could raise our rifles, the deer jerked its head, spooked by something unseen, and bounded off into the woods.

"Damn!" Roger muttered.

"Figures," I said. "Too dark to chase him now. Let's come back in the morning, cross the stream, and check the other side."

"It's posted," Roger warned.

"Yeah?" I said. "The owners don't live around here. There's no one to stop us."

We made it back to camp just as night settled in, built a small fire, and ate the sandwiches I'd packed so we wouldn't have to cook.

By dawn we were up again, eager to track that buck, or at least one of his friends. We hiked through dense oak forest tangled with underbrush. The morning was full of movement: quail fluttered low, doves burst from cover, rabbits darted, we even saw a lone pheasant, everything but deer.

After an hour or so, the trees opened into a marshy clearing. On the far side, a cliff rose up sharply from the streambed. An opening near its base caught my eye.

"What's that dark spot down there?" I said. "Looks like a cave."

Roger shrugged. "Who cares? Doesn't look like a place deer would hide."

The stream moved faster here, about twelve feet across but still shallow enough to wade. On the far side, a rocky stretch gave way to a grassy beach that sloped up toward the shadowy patch I'd noticed.

"I'm gonna check it out," I said. "This looks like a good place to cross."

I put down my rifle and pack, then picked my way across the stream. The water was cold and slick around my boots, but the current wasn't strong. On the other side, the beach gave way to tall grass, and nestled in the slope beyond was what I'd suspected, an opening, hidden by years of fallen branches and debris.

"It's a cave!" I called back. "Bring the gear. We can explore the trails from this side. I'll try to clear the entrance."

"You serious?" Roger shouted. "I thought we came out here to get some deer meat, not play explorer!"

"This'll just take a minute. Hey, there's a gap. I can get in!"

I wiggled through the opening and into the cool, musty dark. "Roger!" There's stuff in here. Bring your flashlight! Looks like someone used to live here."

Roger laughed. "The Treasure of the Sierra Madre, huh?"

"Yeah, yeah, hilarious," I said. "I'm serious. There's a bunch of crap in here. Hurry up with that light."

Over the years, the foothills west of Sugarvalc had sparked every kind of rumor, tales of wild men, Indians, hermits, fugitives, monsters, even ghosts. Roger and I never bought into any of it, but we both figured the cave might hold something worthwhile. At the very least, it'd give us a good story to tell.

When Roger flicked on his flashlight, the beam cut through the musty dark and lit up a pile of old junk. Amid the clutter were two weatherbeaten backpacks stuffed with men's clothing.

"Check this out," I said, as I nudged a rotted shirt with my boot. "It's marked with a PW."

We both spoke at the same time: "Prisoner of war!"

Roger's eyes lit up. "Whoa. Maybe this was a hideout. Maybe one of those German prisoners escaped from the camp!"

"My mom always said they caught every one of them," I replied. "Whoever hid these bags probably didn't get far."

"We should tell someone," I added. "Maybe we'll end up in the news!"

"It's wild," said Roger, digging deeper. "Hey, there's a newspaper in this one."

"Careful," I said. "We don't want to mess up anything that could be, you know, evidence."

Roger had already unfolded it. "It's a *Sugarvale Sentinel* from January 4, 1946. That's the year I was born. Headline says: SUGARVALE PW CAMP IS HISTORY. Says they moved all the prisoners to Camp Beale near Marysville." He paused. "Wait, there's something stamped at the top."

When he held it closer to the light, his face went pale.

"What is it?" I asked.

Roger didn't answer. He just handed me the paper. It was old and yellowed, and it was addressed to his grandparents.

"Hey, didn't some of the POWs work on your grandfather's ranch?" I said.

"Yeah," Roger nodded.

"Well, maybe one of them stole this stuff and hid it here. Maybe he wanted to make a run for it."

"Maybe," Roger said quietly. "I'll show it to my mom and see if she knows anything. Just... don't tell anyone for now. I don't want my family getting dragged into something."

"You got it," I said.

We left the backpacks right where we found them. Roger kept the newspaper. The deer hunt forgotten, we headed back to town in silence.

A few days passed. I was excited about the cave, the newspaper, the mystery of it all. When I finally asked Roger what his mom had to say, he shook his head.

"Let's just keep this between us, all right?" he asked.

"You can't tell me what she said?"

"Not now," he said. "Please. Be my friend, just let it go."

I was disappointed. I'd grown up on Hardy Boys stories, and this was my first mystery to solve. This was our chance, but Roger was my friend. I didn't want to cause trouble for him and his mom, so I promised to stay quiet.

Time passed. We started our senior year. Those long aimless summer days faded, and football took over our lives. By the time I left for college that fall, Roger and I barely saw each other, and the secret we shared stayed buried just like those old backpacks in the cave.

Years pass. Old friends drift away, replaced by new ones as life pushes us forward. Work, family, routines blur the past until it feels like it's vanished, but it never really goes away. The past waits in quiet corners, ready to reappear when you least expect it. That's how it was for me.

Through a mutual friend, I found out Roger died. Cancer. The moment I heard, the cave rushed back into my head. It was right there, ready to surface, and I didn't know it. People are complicated. Life is messy. Careers, reputations, opinions, they seem so important at the time, but most of it fades. What lasts are the things you never talk about.

I always wondered what Roger's mother said when he showed her that newspaper. After his death, I figured I'd never know. He did tell me she cried for days and wouldn't say a word about it. We never brought it up again. I gave Roger my word I'd keep his secret, and I did.

At the funeral, his son approached me with a sealed envelope.

"Dad wanted you to have this," he said. "He told me you were his best friend… and that you'd know what to do with it. I didn't open it. He said it was for your eyes only."

I waited weeks before I opened Roger's letter. I was afraid of what it might stir up, memories I'd buried, choices I'd regret. Like most people, I have my share of secrets, and Roger, as my closest friend, knew more than anyone. I assumed the letter might bring one of my secrets to the surface. Instead, it revealed one of his.

Devon,

I imagine you've wondered now and then about what we found in that cave. You never pressed me, and I've always been grateful, but the time has come to tell the story, first to you, and then to my son. Inside, I've included a letter from my mother. It explains everything.

Dear Roger,

Fate led you to that cave all those years ago. You deserve to know what was hidden there and why. The place you know as Alexander's Camp was built originally to house farmworkers. The government intended to grow guayule, a plant that could provide natural rubber needed for the war, but the project failed so the site was converted into a prisoner of war camp for Germans, most of them captured in North Africa after Rommel's defeat.

With local men off overseas, farmers here were desperate for help. That's how prisoners, like your father, ended up working in the fields. My father, your grandfather, was a German immigrant. He spoke the language and became friendly with some of the prisoners who worked on his ranch. We even shared meals with them, though that was against the rules. We kept it quiet, and no one reported it. Your father's name was Alfred Kelmer. He was respectful, intelligent, and deeply kind. I was drawn to him almost instantly. He understood me better than anyone else did, even my parents. His English was excellent, and despite being a soldier, he never felt like a soldier to me. He told me he had been forced into the German army and never supported Hitler or the Nazi party. Like many of the captured young men, he was caught up in something far larger and darker than he understood. Still, there were true believers in the camp, dangerous men who watched their fellow prisoners closely. Alfred stayed away from them. He told me they had punished, even murdered, other Germans who cooperated with Americans.

In time, Alfred and I fell in love. We kept our relationship hidden, but we couldn't hide our feelings. I knew the risks of being accused of aiding the enemy or worse. He knew the risk if other prisoners discovered our bond. Our love grew anyway. When we heard he was to be transferred to Camp Beale and then sent back to Germany, we started to plan his escape. I gathered supplies, clothes, food, anything he might need, and hid them in the cave. It seemed the safest place. The plan was to vanish into the city and start a new life together. But we couldn't get two things: money and an identity for him. Without those, we were stuck.

Then we learned the prisoners would be transferred soon. That's when we made the most difficult decision. If we had a child, we thought Alfred would have a legal reason to return to America after the war. We didn't know if it would work, but it was our best hope, so we tried.

Not long after, everything fell apart. Hardline Nazis at Camp Beale tried to recruit Alfred to help kill a prisoner who cooperated with the Americans. He refused. An argument followed and they murdered your father. I didn't hear the truth for weeks. The army called it a suicide, but I knew better. Alfred would never have left me. He knew I was pregnant with our child. A guard's friend confirmed what really happened. The army kept it quiet. They didn't want to admit what took place on their watch.

Alfred is buried in Section E of Golden Gate National Cemetery in San Bruno alongside other German soldiers who died under suspicious circumstances. I've visited him every year since.

I kept all of this from you because I wanted to protect you, and myself. After the war, anything connected to Germany was met with suspicion and hate. I wanted you to grow up free from that shadow, but now you deserve the truth.

Your father was a good man. He died because he refused to be a part of something evil. He loved you, even if he never got the chance to say it.

That was Roger's secret. Now it was mine.

Devon,
Please share this with my son. Tell him about us and about how we found the cave. It's his choice whether to carry the story forward or let it fade, but he needs to know the truth. I trust you to do this for me.

Roger

Bailey

It's a quarter to five in the morning. The street lies empty, the world hushed before dawn. Yesterday's heat still simmers up from the asphalt in faint waves. Overhead, a full moon floats, luminous and heavy, as the stars begin their quiet retreat.

Bailey steps outside and locks the door to his small apartment. He lights a cigarette, the flame flares briefly in the gloom. It's freight day at the store. Peggy will be there at five to unload the truck. He moves quickly, and expects a long day ahead.

As he passes the school and rounds the corner near the Bettencourt place, he spots Tom Bettencourt's tractor-trailer parked out front. Tom is a force of nature, thick with muscle, and curly black hair that spreads from scalp to chest to forearms like a bear's pelt. His skin is dark and tough like sunbaked leather, his teeth shockingly white. He wears grease-stained jeans and a tattered T-shirt with the sleeves hacked off, the uniform of a man who works with his hands and doesn't care who knows it. He looks like something out of a myth: wild, powerful, and best appreciated from a distance. Bailey struck up an odd friendship with him.

Tom's wife, Oola, is another story. Pale-skinned, raven-haired, with long legs that have fueled more gossip than any scandal in Sugarvale. In summer she strolls the sidewalks in skimpy tops and denim shorts that hug her every curve; in winter, her skirts are sleek, her blouses low-cut, her coat luxurious. The local women roll their eyes when she walks by. The men watch. Tom sees it all. He knows, and that's what makes him dangerous.

Tom and Oola laugh at the gossip, like they're in on a joke no one else understands.

Bailey thought of Oola as he passed the Bettencourts' house. Bailey, a drifter by nature, a solitary handyman, seemed an unlikely match for Tom and Oola's flashy world, but Bailey had a gift with animals, especially the exotic kind. He knew everything there was to know about chinchillas, the soft-furred rodents imported from South America and coveted for high-end women's fashion: coats, jackets, and hats. Chinchilla fur was a rare luxury, and Bailey understood its value. He dreamed of wealth, but a proper chinchilla farm required more than he was likely to ever have. That's how he entered Tom and Oola's world.

Oola wanted a chinchilla coat, but Tom scoffed at the price tag. Bailey saw his chance. He proposed a deal: If they'd help him get started, he'd supply enough fur for Oola's coat. Tom agreed to front the money for the initial stock, and just like that, they were in business.

Bailey arrived at the warehouse behind the grocery store at exactly five AM. The delivery truck was already backed into the alley. Its rear doors yawned open. Peggy stood beside the driver, Lonnie, locked in one of those half-awake conversations that only happen before sunrise.

"Ah, here comes Bailey. Always right on the dot," Peggy said.

"There's no reason for me to show up early," Bailey replied with a crooked grin. "I'm on the clock at five. That's when I start. Let's get to it."

Lonnie chuckled, flicked his cigarette into the gutter, and climbed into the truck. He knew the score. Everyone did. Peggy had arranged for Bailey's modest apartment and paid him a small salary to help out around the store, but it wasn't just business. Lonnie had seen enough to know that much.

Bailey snapped the conveyor belt into place at the back of the truck. Lonnie began to feed boxes down the rollers; their cardboard sides whispered against the belt as they slid toward the warehouse table. Bailey and Peggy moved quickly; they pulled each box off and stacked them in tidy piles across the concrete floor.

Once the last box was off the truck, Bailey would get to work and shelve the freight. He would rotate the stock so the oldest items would go out first. It was quiet, methodical work, the hum of the belt, the scrape of boxes, and the faint rustle of Peggy's clipboard as she double-checked the inventory.

"The moon was something else this morning," Bailey said. "Full and low on the horizon like a harvest moon."

"A real barley moon," Peggy agreed. She wasn't one for small talk. Short and broad-shouldered, she wore her blond hair in a no-nonsense crop. Her thick glasses magnified sharp blue eyes that didn't miss much. Peggy had a reputation in town. Nobody pushed her around.

"Move it, Lonnie!" she barked. "I need this freight in before I open the damn store."

"Yes, ma'am," Lonnie muttered, but his pace didn't change.

"Your ears plugged, Lonnie? You crawl along like a busted lawnmower."

He gave her an awkward smile. "You want the two-dollar speed or the four-dollar speed?"

Peggy cursed under her breath. "Damn union boys. Bleed you dry and call it justice!"

Bailey snickered quietly. "I passed the Bettencourt place on the way here. Tom's truck was still in the driveway. He's late today."

Peggy shot him a look. "How are those chinchillas doing? That Oola's gonna be the death of you. Tom gets jealous easy."

"He's got no reason," Bailey said. "I'm saving him money. A chinchilla coat would run him four, five grand. He can get it done for half that if I provide the fur, and for the record, I stay clear of Oola. I don't want trouble with Tom."

Peggy's eyes narrowed behind the lenses. She didn't like Bailey around Oola. That girl was a menace in silken gloves.

Once the freight was unloaded and stacked, Lonnie slammed the truck doors shut and drove off. Among the boxes were a few marked for Schneidermann's Bakery. Bailey loaded them onto the handcart and wheeled them three doors down the alley.

Felix Schneidermann made the best donuts in the county. His cream blitzes and fruit-filled butterhorns had a reputation all their own.

"Gut morning, Bailey. Dump de flour in de bin, ja? I'm too busy vid zee blitzes," barked Felix without looking up.

"Sure thing, Felix. How's the missus?" Bailey asked as he hoisted the sack.

Felix groaned. "Ach, she talks to the devil, that one. Keeps us out of the grave one more day. Ve're too old for dis job. Vork, vork, vork."

Felix was tall and broad-shouldered, his white apron smeared with fruit preserves and dusted with flour. It looked like someone had hurled pies at a canvas. In contrast, his wife was a squat little storm cloud of a woman: red-faced, fair-skinned, hair in a tight bun that pulsed with tension. She ran Felix like a factory foreman.

Bailey couldn't help but grin. He had this mental image of her barreling down the street like a bowling ball with her arms tucked in, eyes and mouth flashing in a whirl. That image always cracked him up.

"Oh, come on," Bailey said. "You wouldn't know what to do with yourself if you weren't down here at three every morning. How about a dozen donuts, a few blitzes, and some butterhorns for the crew?" he added.

Felix snorted. "You bring me a few boxes and expect de vorld! Always ask, never pay."

"It's not me, it's Peggy," Bailey replied. "You know she can't live without your pastries."

Felix threw up his hands. "Ja, ja. Go before my vife sees you and thinks ve're giving avay de shop."

On the walk back to the store, Bailey slipped a donut from the box and bit in. Powdered sugar clung to his lips. With his curly red hair, pale, freckled skin, and lean frame, he looked something like a leprechaun, or so folks around Sugarvale liked to say.

Bailey was a bit of a mystery. Rumors followed him like smoke: Some said he'd been in jail, others figured he was just another drifter, but whatever his past, he was useful. Handy with tools, good with his hands. He could wire a house, fix a leaky pipe, or build a fence. He was also an expert hunter. He could drop a deer with an arrow from fifty paces and have it skinned and dressed before sundown.

At the loading dock, Peggy met him with a grin. "What'd you bring and what'd you swipe? You've got crumbs all over your face."

Bailey wiped his mouth on his sleeve. "A dozen donuts, a few blitzes, some butterhorns. Old man Schneidermann gave his usual speech about how we robbed him of all his profits, but once I mentioned your name, he clammed up and started packing boxes."

"Profits, my ass," said Peggy. "That old windbag still owes me for last week's supplies. He can bake, I'll give him that, but he couldn't run a business if it came with instructions and a map."

⚱ ⚱ ⚱

It was nine AM. Oola stood naked before her bedroom mirror and studied herself with calm admiration. Her black hair fell over her shoulders, a stark contrast against the pale sheen of her skin. She opened the cabinet and drew out one of the chinchilla pelts she and Bailey had raised. Soft and gray, it shimmered in the light. She traced it along her collarbone, then let it slide across her breasts. She held it against her neck, and gazed at her reflection. A sly smile tugged at her lips. The combination of snow-white skin, dark hair, and silvery fur was arresting. She fingered it there, momentarily entranced, then tossed the pelt back into the drawer and disappeared into the bathroom for a shower.

Meanwhile, Bailey had finished with the freight in the warehouse. The shelves at the store were stocked. With little left for him do, Peggy gave him the rest of the morning off, and told him to check back after lunch. The sunlight hit him hard as he stepped outside, bright and unforgiving. Bailey shielded his eyes and walked home the same way he'd come, his mind empty, and feet automatic. He saw Mag, the town drunk, walk along in the opposite direction on the other side of the street, one sixteen-ounce can of Bud in each back pocket and one in his hand. Everyone tolerated Mag, who didn't cause trouble. He was kind to the kids around town. He always carried a few pieces of wrapped candy in his pockets to pass out.

In the park across the street from the Bettencourt house, Bailey dropped down on the grass beneath a big oak tree and quickly drifted off to sleep. In his dream, he drove a harvester across a wide field of barley, golden stalks rippling in the wind. It was his land, his machine, his labor. He fixed his eyes on a distant point on the horizon and followed it, row by row, each pass as straight and true as the last. It's said Picasso created fifty thousand paintings; Bailey was the Picasso of plowing.

Dust coated his skin. Chaff stuck to the sweat on his arms and neck. His eyes burned, but he didn't care. This was his life, his place. He spotted something small and brown ahead of the blades. He hit the brakes but it was too late. He climbed down and found a rabbit, trembling and broken, one hind leg severed. Its wide brown eyes pleaded with him.

He scooped it up gently and carried it to the seat of the harvester. From his lunchbox he pulled out a towel and nestled the rabbit inside. That evening, he treated the wound as carefully as a parent would tend to a child. Over time, the rabbit learned to move again. It hopped about on three legs. When it was strong enough, he carried it down to the river and let it go. It was a wild thing, after all. He had no right to keep it.

Later, seated on the deck with a pipe between his lips and the sunset at his back, Bailey wondered whether he'd done the right thing. The rabbit might not survive out there. He reached into his pocket and pulled out the rabbit's foot he'd kept for luck. It wasn't just a charm now, it was a memory, a quiet promise to himself.

⧗ ⧗ ⧗

Oola stepped out of the shower. Steam curled around her like fog. As she patted herself dry, she paused in front of the mirror. The towel in her hands vanished. In its place, she saw a luxurious chinchilla fur coat draped around her shoulders. She pulled it close and marveled at the elegant reflection that stared back at her with a sly, knowing smile.

Suddenly the coat began to twitch. The fur rippled. Tiny heads emerged, beady eyes glowed red and black, teeth gleamed. The chinchillas were alive! Dozens of them. Their mouths opened wide and they sank their sharp teeth into her skin. Fire bloomed across her body where they bit. Olla screamed. They clawed at her arms, her neck. The rodents scurried over her, gnashing and biting relentlessly. She spun in a panic, slipped on the wet tile, and crashed to the floor. A vase toppled from the windowsill and shattered on the sidewalk below. Oola's head struck the edge of the vanity with a sickening thud. She didn't move after that.

Downstairs, Bailey was jolted awake by the sound of breaking glass. Disoriented, he stared at the tree limbs above him. The dream still vivid in his mind. Then it hit him. He knew where that crash had come from.

"Oola!" he called out. "Are you okay?"

No reply.

"Oola," he shouted again. Nothing but the soft rustle of wind and the hum of the bees in the honeysuckle just outside her window. Panic seized Bailey. He ran to the front door and knocked hard. Still no answer. He kicked it open and bounded up the stairs.

There was Oola, sprawled naked on the cold tile, her black hair fanned around her like ink, her pale skin stained crimson.

"Oh, my God!" Bailey gasped. "Help! Help! Somebody heeelp, please!" he cried. His voice tore through the quiet morning. A neighbor rushed over, then another. Someone called the police. Bailey knelt beside her and gently draped a towel over her body.

The official police report called it an accident, but the townsfolk didn't buy it. They blamed Bailey.

"What was he doing alone with Oola? asked Mona, who owned the women's clothing store.

"She was naked," muttered the postman, eyes wide with gossip. "You think he tried something?"

Denny Firestone, owner of the hardware and electronics store, told the local paper he'd seen Bailey trailing Oola around town for weeks. "Like a damn shadow," he said.

Tom Bettencourt didn't speak much. He just simmered, and when he did speak, it was only to swear he'd get even.

Bailey knew it was over. Peggy threw him out that night, told him not to come near the store again. By morning he was gone. Vanished. Completely off the radar.

Rumors bloomed. Some said he fled to Southern California to start a chinchilla farm. Others whispered darker things. Tom Bettencourt tried to find him, but never could.

On Saturday nights, after a few too many schnapps, old Felix Schneidermann would lean back in his chair and mutter, "Dat Bailey... I cink he made a deal wid da devil."

Uncle Ned

After my parents divorced, I drew the attention of my meddlesome Uncle Ned. I suppose he felt it was his duty to step in, to teach me the things he thought I'd miss without a father around. I lived with my mother. The split had happened not long after I was born, but I never doubted my father's love. He just wanted his freedom.

I understand that better now that I'm older. My father wasn't heartless. He was just hungry for life. A successful businessman, he was a charmer, restless, and not cut out for domesticity. Still, in his own way, he was a good father. He told me he was proud of my grades, of my skills on the sports field. He even came to one of my football games. I broke my nose when I made a tackle that one time he was in the stands. I think it hurt him more than it did me. What hurt worse was that he left before the game ended. I wish he'd seen me finish. They taped up my nose and sent me back in. A few plays later I ran for a touchdown.

He loved my mother, I'm sure of it. Unfortunately for her, he was a womanizer. He just wasn't the type to settle down. I had to make peace with that, and I did.

Uncle Ned, on the other hand, was the family-man type. He had a soft spot for my mother and started to show up not long after I was born. Mom wasn't having it; she had to deal with sleepless nights and diapers, not romance, but Uncle Ned didn't take the hint. He lingered, always hopeful, always with gifts. As I got older, he was more and more in the picture. I didn't think much about it back then; I accepted what was given and appreciated the kindness for what it was.

The Uncle Ned I remember was in his forties, a towering man, easily over six feet and tipping the scales near three hundred pounds. He was mostly bald and not what anyone would call handsome, but what he lacked in looks he made up for in sheer presence. He had a big voice, an easy laugh, and a kind of stubborn charm that made people listen. He was the kind of man who didn't just enter a room, he filled it.

After my parents divorced, Uncle Ned started to visit more often. We spent time together doing things he thought a boy should learn: hunting, fishing, outdoor survival. These weren't activities I particularly enjoyed or excelled at, but I understood their importance, and so did Uncle Ned. He was determined to teach me what he believed my father's absence had left out. He signed me up for a hunter safety course where I learned the essentials: how to handle a gun, how to store it, load, carry, and fire it.

Not long after I passed the course and got my permit, he took me on my first duck hunt. Uncle Ned and two brothers, John and Jim Ayers, shared a modest duck club tucked against the north slope of the Sutter Buttes. The buttes rose abruptly from the flat valley floor like a jagged scar, dark, and slightly menacing. The club wasn't much, a small one-story house with a garage. There was a living room, three cramped bedrooms, a single bathroom, and a kitchen warmed by a battered wood-burning stove. I loved it. Uncle Ned worked magic on that stove. I can still taste the hotcakes and bacon and eggs he made, simple, perfect and somehow better during the chilly duck season.

Out back, the garage held supplies and tools, and there was a contraption that fascinated me: a homemade feather-plucking machine. Connected to an electric motor was a steel shaft with rubber strips affixed along its length. When powered on, the rubber strips whisked the feathers off the ducks with surprising efficiency, and left the skin and meat intact. I thought it was nothing short of brilliant.

The hunt itself was a ritual of cold, silent anticipation. The ducks followed a popular flyway that passed right over the man-made pond. The Ayerses built the pond to lure them in. Uncle Ned outfitted me in rubber waders and led me through the icy water to one of three camouflaged blinds, small islands hidden in tall grass, each with an oil drum half buried in the ground for cover. It was early morning and bitterly cold. We kept our hands warm over coffee cans filled with burning charcoal. Ice cracked beneath our boots as we walked, and every step was a careful negotiation. A single slip could leave you soaked and shivering before the hunt even began.

I heard the ducks before I saw them, their sharp quacks cut through the ink-black sky. I'd learned to call them down with a wooden duck call, the hollow instrument that vibrated against my tongue as I mimicked the birds' sound. It felt strange at first, like a trick on nature. Uncle Ned gave me a 20-gauge shotgun for my birthday. I practiced how to hold it properly, and learned to track the ducks in flight to lead them just enough before I pulled the trigger. I still remember the first duck I hit. It spiraled down from the sky and crashed into the shallows of the pond where it flapped frantically, not dead, just wounded.

"Get after it!" Uncle Ned shouted from his blind. "Grab it and break its neck!"

The duck's wing was broken, twisted at a sickening angle. I hesitated. Its eyes were wide, terrified. My stomach turned as I gripped the poor creature. Snapping it neck was the humane thing to do, or so I was told, but I'll never forget the look it gave me in its final moment. I turned away and vomited into the pond, careful not to let Uncle Ned see.

"You're a good shot, Devon. A natural," he said when I climbed back down into the oil-drum, limp bird in hand, but nothing about killing felt natural to me. I knew then I wasn't cut out to be a hunter. Still, I went along with it for Uncle Ned, who believed he passed down something important, maybe even essential. Maybe he did. I didn't say otherwise. I didn't want to ruin the moment. We ate the ducks we brought down that day. I wasn't a vegetarian. Nothing went to waste.

Uncle Ned, with his massive frame, always struggled to get in and out of the blind. That morning, I stood in the icy pond as he clambered up, using his unloaded shotgun like a cane. Just as he made it out, he sneezed, a blast from his hay fever, and lost his footing. The gun slipped. Uncle Ned toppled headfirst into the freezing water with a splash.

In their waders, Jim and John sloshed through the muck. We pulled Uncle Ned upright, soaked and snorting, his face red with laughter and cold. John and I guided him toward the car while Jim fished his gun out of the pond.

Even then, as he dripped and shivered, Uncle Ned was grinning. That was Uncle Ned: part buffoon, part mentor, entirely unforgettable.

Poor Uncle Ned sneezed and coughed, then sneezed and coughed again. "My God, what an ass I've made of myself," he bellowed, his face flushed with embarrassment. He sounded like a wounded bull, as he snorted and wheezed to compose himself.

Back at the house, he went straight to the shower without a word. Jim took care of the shotgun, cleaned and oiled it carefully to keep it from rusting. Uncle Ned eventually recovered, but his spirit for duck hunting was gone. Whatever thrill he'd felt had drained out of him with the sneezing fits.

The next morning, I chose to sleep in. After a leisurely breakfast, I wandered out to the orchard beside the house and waited for doves. They darted overhead like gray bullets, far quicker and more elusive than ducks. I found the challenge exhilarating. I managed to shoot enough to take home for a feast. We left the following day.

That final night, the three men sat around the table by the woodstove, shuffling cards and swapping stories. I went to bed, but their voices drifted down the hallway, loud echoes that bounced off the walls. John was in the middle of a tale about a bar he'd visited the week before.

"There was a girl, naked, hidden inside a barrel." John laughed, animated. "You could catch glimpses of her when she jumped up and down," he said.

"Must've been quite the spectacle," Uncle Ned replied.

"Oh, it was," John said. "For a quarter, you could walk right up to the barrel and take a peek."

"I'll bet they made a killing in quarters that night," Jim chuckled.

"No doubt," John said.

As I lay in bed, I thought of a woman, a friend of my dad's, an artist who lived in a beautiful house on the Yuba River. I tried to picture her in that barrel, her hair wild, skin aglow in the dim light. The image stirred up strange pleasant feelings I didn't quite understand but couldn't ignore. I tossed and turned under the weight of it, and finally drifted off to sleep.

On the way home, we stopped to pick up groceries. Uncle Ned was eager to cook dinner.

"The ducks and doves will make a fine meal," he said enthusiastically. "I'll whip up some mashed potatoes with gravy, a crisp green salad, and maybe some artichokes. I've been anxious to try this special recipe for artichokes baked in a mold. You and your mother will love it."

Uncle Ned fancied himself a gourmet chef. He owned a restaurant, but the truth was he didn't actually know how to cook. He'd picked up just enough from real chefs over the years to be dangerous in a kitchen. My mother endured his culinary experiments with forced smiles and quiet dread. She was too polite to tell him no. He'd leave the kitchen a disaster zone, every pot and pan dirty, and never lift a finger to clean up.

I found out eventually why my mother tolerated him: Uncle Ned helped her financially. My father hadn't abandoned us, he just wasn't always reliable. Sometimes the checks came late, and even when they were on time they didn't stretch far enough. Mom worked full-time and took on part-time jobs to make ends meet. I worked summers and weekends at the local grocery, and during harvest season we both pitched in on the almond huller and in the drying sheds for the apricots. My mother never said it, but I knew she appreciated Uncle Ned's support. I didn't see him make a move on her, but I always suspected he wanted to.

One Christmas holiday, Uncle Ned took me to Hawaii along with my half-sister and her daughter Norma Jean. My father had been married before he met my mother. His first wife died giving birth to my sister, who's much older than I am, nearly as old as my mother. Norma Jean is a year older than I am, which always throws people. It's not every day you meet someone who's older than their uncle.

Norma Jean and I got along like siblings. We shared a lot of laughs, and a fair amount of trouble. Uncle Ned never seemed to mind. If anything, I think he found our mischief entertaining.

One time Norma Jean offered to take me out to a ranch near Winnemucca to visit a friend. We borrowed one of the shiny new trucks from her father's dealership. He sold cars for a living. Just as we left the house, Norma Jean's boyfriend showed up in his own car. Norma Jean jumped in with him and told me to follow in the truck. I didn't have a license. My driving experience was limited to backing down the driveway, but I didn't argue.

We turned off the highway onto a dusty backroad lined with nothing but sagebrush. The air was thick with grit, and visibility was awful. I followed too closely. I didn't want to lose them in the dust. When they braked unexpectedly, I plowed right into the back of the boyfriend's car. We got in trouble, of course, but Uncle Ned smoothed things over like he always did.

Another time, we got caught skinny-dipping in the family pool. Norma Jean just laughed it off, but her father was furious. He told Uncle Ned to put me on the first train back home.

Uncle Ned lived in Marysville. The last time we went to visit my sister, we took the California Zephyr through the Feather River Canyon all the way to Winnemucca. The train had a vista dome where you could watch the scenery unfold like a movie. In the dining car, Uncle Ned let me have my first glass of wine, even though I was only sixteen.

That train ride marked a turning point between us. I think Uncle Ned knew he didn't have much time left. He told me stories about his life like a man passing down heirlooms. He told me how he and my dad were raised by Mormons after their parents died. He respected the Mormons, he said, though he couldn't bring himself to believe in their religion, or any religion for that matter. That was the one subject he and my mother clashed over. She was a devout Catholic. I never took sides when she was around, but I agreed with Uncle Ned.

He walked the railroad tracks through Idaho when he was just fifteen. "They gave me a pistol in case of bears or mountain lions," he told me. "I never had to use it, but I would have." He admitted he gambled a little when he was younger. He got burned early and that was it for him. He didn't talk about it except to say, "It's like a disease. Some people can handle it, some can't." He told a story about a friend who lost everything in Reno. I've always suspected that might have been himself.

Uncle Ned had opinions, firm, immovable ones. Some were harmless quirks: "The best-tasting lamb comes from sagebrush country," he'd say, "Grass-fed doesn't hold a candle to it." Or, "*Alley Oop* is the finest newspaper cartoon ever drawn, no contest."

Others ran deeper, rooted in experience. He once told me how he'd been drugged in a bar outside Reno.

"They wanted to rob me, maybe worse," he said. His voice was low, eyes fixed on something far off. "I was lucky to get out alive."

That memory had scarred him. It shaped another of his guiding rules: "Always be on your guard. Never trust anyone completely."

I once asked him what he thought mattered most in life. He didn't pause to think.

"Courage," he said. "Not the reckless kind that charges in blind, but the kind that acts despite fear when the risks are real and high."

He tapped his chest for emphasis. "Then ambition. Without it a person's no different than a sheep, but not stupid ambition like some fool who thinks anything goes. Have a little humility."

He spoke about love too. "Not the easy kind. Real love is to want the best for someone, even if it breaks your own heart."

Last was honesty. "Honesty. That's the bedrock. Your word is your bond. That includes being honest with yourself, especially when you've screwed up."

As I got older and life pulled me away with college and then work, I didn't see Uncle Ned as often. We'd catch up around the holidays, and I'd visit in the summers when I could. One time I watched him shoot a rattlesnake on his front porch. "Never use a shotgun on a rattler," he laughed and shook his head. "Makes one hell of a mess."

When my sister called and told me he'd had a heart attack, I didn't make it in time to say goodbye. I still hear his voice sometimes: "Real love is to want the best for someone, even if it breaks your heart." "Your word is your bond." I know he loved me and my mother, but the family tangle made his life hard.

I think about Uncle Ned sometimes, especially when I remember that duck I strangled and that look in its eyes, full of terror. Something changed in me that day. Something permanent. Some people leave a mark. It's hard to describe, but you know. Uncle Ned left his mark on me.

The Sixties

The Fletchers

My dad preferred to drive his Dodge pickup when we took short trips away from Nyack Lodge, the mountain hotel where he lived and worked. I lived with my mom in Sugarvale, a quiet farm town in the Sacramento Valley, and visited him during school vacations. I always liked the Dodge more than the Cadillac he used for longer drives. It felt more rugged, more like him. Nyack sat high in the Sierras. My friends and I jokingly called them the Nowhere Mountains because bears, mountain lions, and rattlesnakes seemed to appear out of nowhere when you least expected.

At night, the bears came to dig through the hotel's garbage. My dad used to feed them scraps while the bar patrons watched from behind thick glass windows. One night a massive black bear got too close and chased my dad halfway up the rock wall beside the trash bins. The crowd loved it. Dad didn't. After that, he stayed on top and tossed the food down from a safe perch.

He once shot a mountain lion that came around too often. He had it stuffed with its mouth open and teeth bared, then gave it to me on one of my visits. I took it home and donated it to the local Boy Scouts. They used it in spirit dances for years, until the fur wore thin, the head got scratched and dingy, one eye cracked, and a long canine tooth snapped off. Eventually, no one wanted it anymore.

Nyack was near Emigrant Gap, a natural break in the Sierra ridge along the old California Trail, not far from Donner Pass, where a party of pioneers got trapped by snow and resorted to cannibalism to survive. Nearly half of them didn't make it.

My dad used to sing *Riding the Old Donner Trail,* a Jerry Colonna tune he used in hotel advertisements. He'd sing it every time we hit the road together.

To get to Nyack, I'd board a Greyhound bus in Sugarvale, a packed lunch in my bag and a book in hand. Until I got older, my mom gave the driver five bucks to make sure I made the transfer in Sacramento. When I arrived, my dad would be there in the shadows of Nyack Garage, always happy to see me. The garage had three large stalls for auto repairs, and an office. In the winter travelers streamed in to have tire chains installed. Tow truck drivers rescued stranded travelers. The owner had three sons around my age that I'd hang out with when I visited

One spring, I rode with my dad to visit an artist named Fletcher. The cab of Dad's new truck still carried that crisp, leathery new-car scent. It was nice but I missed the old truck. Dad took obsessive pride in keeping things clean and orderly, except his ties. Every one of them bore the record of some forgotten meal: a dot of gravy here, a smear of mustard there. His uniform never changed: wool fedora, starched white shirt, gray sport coat, and pressed slacks. His Nunn Bush shoes gleamed with a spit-shine so bright they looked wet. He bought me a matching pair that I wore to please him even though they pinched a little.

The drive to the Fletchers' took us through the high Sierra, where snow dusted the pine and fir trees and lingered in the shadows where the sun couldn't reach. The Yuba River ran wild beside us; its emerald-green current crashed into granite boulders and broke into white foam and spray. It was like something out of a dream when we arrived at the house. It was constructed almost entirely of glass, perched on steel legs in the middle of the river itself. I'd never seen anything like it before, and haven't since.

Fletcher, whose first name was Thomas, but no one called him that, painted vast minimalist landscapes of the Sierra. His style reminded me of ancient Chinese scrolls, spare and atmospheric, but distinctly Californian. He left wide expanses of blank canvas and punctuated them with bold, intentional strokes in the colors of the mountains: green, red, orange, yellow, brown, gray, black. With a few brush marks, he conjured mountains, rocks, and trees. No people. No animals. The scenes were like riddles; you had to finish the image yourself with your own eyes. I never quite understood why my father loved them so much, but he did.

Lois, Fletcher's wife, painted the opposite: bursts of mountain wildflowers rendered in such lush, vivid detail they seemed to glow. I would stand in front of her canvases, and imagine creatures hidden in the foliage: birds, chipmunks, maybe a fox just out of sight. Her paintings made my imagination reel like I was deep inside a storybook. I half-expected a sprite or a leprechaun to leap from behind a fern. Her pictures opened something inside me I didn't know was there.

Fletcher the minimalist, Lois the munificent, and my father, the unlikely patron who held them in balance. He showcased several of their paintings on the walls of Nyack, and sent guests to their studio with subtle encouragement. Not that he had any real sense for art; he was blind in that department, but he had a keen eye for character. He liked the Fletchers. That was enough.

We parked by the river and stepped from boulder to boulder until we reached the narrow wooden stairway that climbed to the deck that encircled their house. Fletcher met us there and offered a hand.

"Welcome, Henry! And who's this with you? Devon? My God, you've shot up a foot since I saw you last. Come in, come in. Lois has her hot apple cider ready, a perfect treat for a cool afternoon like this. Henry, would you like the usual? Early Times and soda?"

I flushed. I hated those grown-a-foot comments, that brand of grown-up small talk, but the cider sounded good, and Lois, gorgeous and radiant, unsettled me in a way I couldn't yet understand. Even then I knew I'd never forget that day, and she was the reason why.

"Thanks, Fletcher," my dad said, easing into his familiar charm. "A whiskey and soda sounds perfect. Devon's been up for a couple of weeks. Thought this would be a great time for him to see some of your new pieces before he heads home."

I saw the flicker of a smile cross Fletcher's lips. He was already doing the math, but I didn't care about the art or the business. I was transfixed by Lois. I'd forgotten how striking she was, how she seemed to steal the air from the room just by being in it. A soft, persistent fantasy buzzed in my head from the minute Dad mentioned the visit. Now, here she was.

Lois kissed me on the cheek when I stepped inside, her hand warm in mine.

"Sit here beside me, Devon," she said, patting the cushion next to her. "Tell me everything. What have you been up to since we last saw you?"

Her hair was golden-brown, swept into a loose bun with a single tendril that curled down her cheek. She looked like she'd stepped out of a dream. I was tongue-tied and hopeless, and could barely form a sentence.

"I read a lot," I said, and instantly regretted how flat it sounded.

"Oh? I'm a reader too. What are your favorites?" she asked, her voice warm with curiosity. Her nose had a graceful, straight ridge that ended in a soft point. Her oval eyes, deep brown and steady, held me like a spotlight. I couldn't move or think. I felt stripped bare.

"I like Edgar Allan Poe... and Robert Louis Stevenson," I blurted. "For the visit to Dad's, I brought *The Scarlet Letter* by Hawthorne. My voice came out too fast, too loud, propelled by nervous energy.

"*The Scarlet Letter*? At your age? My goodness, Devon, you're growing up fast." Her expression shifted. Her smile turned into an assessment, an evaluation.

Not fast enough to catch you, Lois, I thought, but didn't dare say it.

"Dad thinks it's some kind of trashy dime-store novel," I added, trying to sound casual. "It's not, it's real literature. I'm really into it."

I tried to appear composed, but inside I was a bundle of nerves, adrift in a sea far deeper than I knew how to navigate.

"Literature indeed," said Lois, Her eyes glinted, and her smile sent a tremor through me. She laughed at the mention of my father. "Yes, that sounds like him, but don't let him hear me say so. Read, Devon, as much as you can. With good books, you get to live a hundred lives. They're like paintings: they take you to places you've never been, places you couldn't even dream of."

I glanced down at my legs and froze. There was a bulge in my pants. Heat flooded my face. Had she seen it? Could she know what she does to me?

Across the room, Dad and Fletcher were on their second drink when Lois slipped away to join them. I wandered through the house and pretended to study the paintings, trying to settle the storm inside me. The house doubled as their studio. Fletcher worked in one corner, Lois in another. The entire space was open, a large, airy room with the kitchen tucked into one side. The bedroom was behind it, curtained off but open enough to see the bed, unmade, though the covers had been pulled up.

Paintings leaned against the walls like lodgers lined up for an excursion. In the far corner, a chest of drawers stood slightly ajar. Inside, I saw the edge of Lois's underwear. My pulse jumped. I wanted to move closer, but I didn't, couldn't. Instead, I walked back to the main room and looked out at the river and the woods that lined its bank, and waited for my breath to slow, my body to calm.

From behind me, I heard Lois laugh. My stomach tightened. I forgot to breathe.

By late afternoon, it was clear my father wasn't in any shape to drive. I didn't have my license yet, but I knew how to handle a car. He handed over the keys without a word. Fletcher and I loaded the truck, and carefully secured the paintings in the back.

As we left, Lois pulled me into a warm hug, kissed me on the cheek, and slipped a book into my coat pocket. "This is for you, Devon," she whispered. "Take care of Henry. He's a good man. Come back and see us again, won't you?" Her white teeth flashed in the sunlight when she smiled goodbye.

"I'll try," I said, but wasn't sure I ever would.

The drive home turned out smoother than I expected. After a few white-knuckle turns, I found my rhythm. To my surprise, my father stayed awake, and we talked as the miles slid by.

I asked what had been on my mind all day.

"Why don't the Fletchers have any kids?"

My father's jaw tightened slightly. He was quiet for a few seconds.

"You're old enough to know this, Devon, but what I'm about to tell you stays between us. Understand?"

"I won't say anything. I promise."

"Before Lois met Thomas, she was engaged to someone else. Thomas and Lois had an affair, and she got pregnant. She broke off the engagement, but she was ashamed, humiliated even. She decided to end the pregnancy." He glanced at me. "Do you know what that means?"

"You mean an abortion," I said.

He nodded. "They didn't have the money. Thomas came to me for help. I gave it. That's something you need to understand, son. The choices we make carry weight. Some consequences never go away."

By the time we pulled into the hotel, my father was sober. My hands were pale on the steering wheel, which I held too tightly, my eyes tired from being locked on the road ahead, my thoughts tangled from what he'd just told me.

"I knew a very good doctor," he said quietly. "I wanted only the best for Lois. The procedure was done under ideal conditions, not in some back alley, but..." he paused as he searched for the right words, "there was a complication. Even when everything's done right, things can go wrong. After that, Lois couldn't have children."

A sheen of sweat glistened on his forehead. Maybe it was the remnants of the alcohol working their way out of his system, but I sensed something deeper. Guilt. Not fresh, but still alive. The story had unearthed it.

"It wasn't your fault, Dad," I said. "Don't carry that weight."

I didn't know what else to offer.

At the hotel, Ricky the bartender helped me carry the paintings down to the storage room. My father went to the front desk to check on the new arrivals.

"You want a Coke, Devon?" Ricky asked as we came back up.

"Sure," I said. "And how about the jukebox key?"

He tossed it to me, and I picked out a few songs, Sinatra, a little Brubeck, then took my Coke to a table by the window. Sunlight spilled through the glass and glinted off Lake Spaulding in the distance. Guests began to arrive. Ricky got busy behind the bar.

I sat alone, stared out at the Lake, and my mind drifted. I thought about how the river cut around the rocks earlier that day, the strange beauty of the Fletchers' glass house, the warmth in Lois's smile, the weight behind my father's words.

One of Fletcher's landscapes hung on the wall, large, mostly white, with soft washes of color and brushwork like whispers. I walked over and studied it. The blank spaces were deliberate. They seemed empty but they contributed to the picture in a significant way. I didn't know what they meant, not then, but I knew they were important to Fletcher.

I packed my things that evening and took the bus home the next day.

Weeks later, I found the book Lois had slipped into my coat pocket. I'd forgotten all about it. *Goodbye Columbus* by Philip Roth. I read it in one sitting. I've read it many times since.

Each time my thoughts trail back to the Fletchers' house. I think Lois wanted me to find something in that book, something that echoed the meaning of those white spaces in Fletcher's paintings. A quiet message: *Don't tie yourself down too soon.* Maybe that was it.

Lois's paintings were harder to read. Bold in color, seemingly complete, but the longer you stared, the more you sensed an absence. You'd expected life to be hidden in the shrubs or skim across the water, but there was only shadow. A presence implied but never shown, like one of those optical illusions where the image shifts depending on how you look: a rabbit, then a duck. A young woman, then an old crone. There and not there.

Lois painted a world suspended at the edge of something irrevocable. The world that defined her life. A world both full and hollow. What you saw depended on what you wanted to believe.

The next time I saw Lois was at my father's funeral. She and Fletcher had moved to a small town in North Carolina, close to her family. Fletcher died of cancer not long after the move.

"I'm so sorry, Lois. No one told me. If I'd known, I would've been there," I said. She looked as beautiful as I remembered, older but just as graceful.

"I know you would have, Devon," she replied gently. "Your father was a dear friend to both Thomas and me. He believed in our work, and he was incredibly kind during a very difficult time. I hope he's found peace."

I knew she meant the abortion my father had quietly paid for, but I didn't let on that he'd ever mentioned it.

"Thank you," I said. "I hope Thomas rests in peace too. Dad thought the world of both of you."

A tear slipped free before she could stop it.

"The world moves so fast, Devon. You've grown into a man, and I've grown old."

"You're not old," I said. "Not even close to middle-aged. While things might feel dark right now, most of your life still lies ahead. You'll see."

When Lois turned her deep brown eyes on me, I was struck again by how infatuated I'd once been with her, and how that feeling hadn't entirely faded.

"I've often wondered," she said, "what you made of that Philip Roth book I gave you. Did you ever read it?"

I read it several times," I said. "I guess it taught me to slow down, to keep perspective. Maybe it was your way to tell me not to get swept up in that wild puppy love I had for you." I blushed.

She smiled softly. "That was part of it, yes. But what did you think of the little Black boy at the library and his fascination with Gauguin?"

"Of course," I said, a bit sheepishly. "You're an artist. I should've realized Gauguin meant something personal to you. I'll have to read it again and look at it through a different lens."

"It's so good to see you again, Devon," she said, glancing at her watch. "I'm sorry, but I've got to run. My plane leaves in an hour. Come visit me sometime in Beaufort. It's the kind of place Gauguin might've loved, if he'd been born in a different time."

She kissed me lightly on the cheek and disappeared into the crowd before I could answer. I stood there for a moment, dazed, overcome by the same emotions her paintings always stirred in me, mysterious and unnamable.

That old wedding rhyme came to mind out of nowhere: "Something old, something new, something borrowed, something blue." Then, I remembered that enigmatic painting by Gauguin: *Where Do We Come From? What Are We? Where Are We Going?* His masterpiece.

Lois.

Oh, Lois.

After all these years, I'm still under your spell.

Twenty-Dollar Bill

Roger decided it was time to change his life. That kind of thing wasn't unusual after a divorce. If his wife, Brenda, could pack up and head to Argentina with her lesbian friend, then surely he could do something too, and not just anything, something that mattered. He could, and he would.

His wife's list of grievances had been relentless: She was tired of picking up after him, tired of cooking his meals, tired of cleaning *his* house, tired of dragging herself through one mindless routine after another. They had nothing in common anymore, she said. He had his hobby, building meticulous models of planes, ships, and cars. She had nothing, nothing but exhaustion. Exhaustion with men, with marriage, with monotony. So she left.

Good, Roger thought. *She's gone.*

His wife did one thing he admired. She made a decision. Now it was Roger's turn. He was free. Alone, but free.

They sold the house. He took early retirement. Everything was split fifty-fifty.

"Goodbye."

"Goodbye."

What did *he* need to do? Reinvent himself. But how?

Roger's social circle was sparse; certainly no one he could picture running off with to Argentina or anywhere else. He found a small apartment on a month-to-month lease to test the waters. He threw himself into his models.

I've built a good collection, haven't I? Some of these are rare. They're difficult to assemble. Precision work. I'm good at it. I might even call myself a professional.

After a while, though, the models lost their appeal.

"I'm bored," he admitted aloud one evening. "I need to get out and see the world."

He tried bars and bistros. He went to a major league baseball game. Museums. Art galleries. A rock concert. Even the theater. One outing after another, but none of them stuck. None gave him what he looked for. They were noisy, crowded, expensive, and left him feeling more alone than before, so he stopped.

Maybe nature will do the trick. Fresh air. Flowers. Trees. Wild animals. That kind of thing.

He wandered through city parks. He took up hiking. He bought fishing gear and gave that a whirl. He joined a group of bicyclists. He built and flew remote-control planes. None of these were bad choices, but none of them were transformative either. He couldn't make a connection. Nature didn't speak to him. It just wasn't his thing.

Roger thought having a roommate might help.

It'd be good to have someone to talk to. The extra room is going to waste, and a little rent money won't hurt.

Roger should've been more selective. The guy he found was a disaster. The renter turned out to be a slob. He left dishes everywhere, and didn't clean up after himself. Roger couldn't trust him near the stove. He hogged the television and blasted it day and night. Roger couldn't stand the constant noise.

One day, fed up, Roger yanked the TV off the stand and pawned it.

The roommate went ballistic: "What the hell am I supposed to do now?

"Why don't you go to Argentina?" Roger snapped.

The roommate took the hint and his bags and left without paying the overdue rent. Roger was back where he started: alone, broke, and frustrated.

He hadn't budgeted well. The rent money mattered more than he realized. His retirement funds had thinned fast, and his expenses were higher than expected. Roger was many things, but a planner was not one of them.

He decided to find work.

Luck was just around the corner. A hobby shop nearby needed help. They sold exactly the kind of model kits Roger liked to build: planes, ships, cars. It felt like fate.

"This is heaven," he said after his first day.

He was great at the job. Customers who didn't know where to start came in, confused. Roger guided them patiently. They left smiling, with kits and glue and a little confidence. The owner was thrilled with the boost in business. He himself didn't know much about the models he sold. He was lazy at heart. Roger was happy, but something still gnawed at him, loneliness.

One day, Brenda called. She said she wanted to come back and start over. She said she'd made a mistake.

Roger didn't hesitate. "No! Absolutely not. That door's closed."

Two days later, she was on his doorstep.

They argued. Brenda pleaded. Roger held his ground.

"You made your choice," he said. "You've got the life you wanted, and I've got mine. Let's keep things like they are."

She slapped him hard on his face. Before he could think, he struck back.

She fell, hit her head on the doorframe, and collapsed.

Roger called 911. He rode in the ambulance all the way to the hospital, blood on his hands. It was too late.

Roger was arrested and charged with involuntary manslaughter.

"I didn't mean to hurt her," he told the detective.

"That doesn't matter," the cop replied. "You're in deep."

At trial, the jury watched Roger closely. He didn't cry or apologize. In fact, he showed no emotion at all as photos of Brenda's body were displayed. When asked if he felt remorse, he said simply, "We didn't love each other."

His lack of remorse turned the jury against him. He was found guilty, and sentenced to five years and a fine. He didn't appeal or speak when the guards took him away. His silence was his protest.

Later, in his cell, Roger had time to think.

I blew it and got crushed. When I get out of here, I'll do better. I have to.

Roger's life changed irrevocably. All that remained was the slow, bitter work of acceptance.

His only visitor in those long, silent months behind bars was his former boss from the toy and model shop.

"I'll handle things while you're locked up," the man said casually, like it was a favor. Grateful and naïve, Roger signed over power of attorney. Two years early, he walked out on parole for good behavior only to find out the shop was gone. His boss sold everything and vanished with the money. He left Roger penniless and betrayed.

There was still a small bank account where the pension money had trickled in, but most of it had been drained to pay court-ordered fines. The rest barely kept him afloat. He was nearly broke. Soon, he would be homeless.

He drifted through the city in a daze. With nothing for a deposit and no steady income, he spent nights on benches or curled up in alleys. When he could scrounge enough, he might splurge on a cheap motel room, but that was a rare luxury.

Roger searched for work, anything at all, but no one wanted to hire a man who'd been to prison, especially one who killed his wife, even if it had been ruled an accident. His only skill, building delicate models with patient hands, was worth little in a world that had no use for hobbies. He didn't drink or use drugs, but despair has a gravity of its own. It pulled him under slowly, until the man who once had a hobby and a job and a life learned to panhandle, to sleep on cardboard, to dodge the cops and raid dumpsters, to survive in a society that had written him off.

He adjusted to the life but not to the shame. That never dulled. Parents whispered to their children to steer clear of him. Strangers either ignored him or made fun of him. The police treated him with contempt. Worst of all was the self-loathing that came each time he looked into a mirror.

His health eroded. His mind, once quick and careful, lost its edge. Some nights, buried in a sleeping bag on cold concrete, he would cry quietly, ashamed of the tears but unable to stop them. He had no reason to go on, and yet, he did.

One afternoon at the park, Roger noticed a young boy who stood alone by the water's edge and watched other children sail their toy boats across the pond. The boy had no boat of his own, just empty hands and a quiet ache in his eyes. Roger recognized that kind of longing. He'd known it too well himself.

With what little money he had left, Roger bought supplies: a small motor, a simple remote, balsa wood, paint. He worked on the boat for days, sanded and glued in the shadows of doorways and beneath streetlamps. When it was finished, it was a sturdy little craft: elegant, fast, and unsinkable.

The next time Roger saw the boy at the park, he walked up and placed the boat gently into the boy's hands. The child's face lit up with pure joy, but the moment was short-lived. The boy's parents arrived and quickly intervened, their expressions hard and suspicious.

"Stay away from our son," the father said coldly.

Roger didn't argue. He nodded once, left the boat behind, and walked off in silence. A few blocks away, Roger settled into his usual spot near the corner convenience store. He unfolded his sign—SPARE CHANGE, PLEASE—and placed his paper cup on the sidewalk. Most passersby ignored him. A few tossed in coins. One man, with a smirk, dropped a single penny into the cup and said, "Change comes from within," then walked off laughing.

Roger didn't even look up. *Maybe he's right. Maybe it's too late for me.*

He felt a tap on his shoulder.

He expected a police officer, but when he turned it wasn't a cop. It was the boy from the park and his father.

"Did you build that boat, mister?" the boy asked.

"Yes," Roger said quietly. "I built it."

"It's awesome," the boy grinned. "Will you teach me how to make one?"

Roger hesitated. "I used to build boats. Cars and planes too, but not anymore."

"You built this one," the boy said.

Roger looked at him. For a moment, he almost believed he could build again.

"It's the last one," he said. "Now, go on. Stay with your dad. I've got work to do."

He turned away, picked up his sign, and raised it without looking back.

As they walked off the boy's father paused. He reached into his wallet and placed a twenty-dollar bill in Roger's cup without a word.

Roger didn't thank him. He just held the cup steady and watched them go, the boy clutched the little boat Roger had made and disappeared into the park.

The Barula Ching

The bar is narrow and dim, a slit in the city's ribs. On the left, a row of stools leans against a burnished bar top. On the right, seven tables hug a smoke-darkened sandstone wall, etched with grooves too worn to read, remnants of hands, elbows, lives. The air hums with a luminous alphabet, an ancient script born of the Canaanites, that flickers like phosphorescent fireflies. The letters drift, rearrange themselves midair into words, only to dissolve again into syllables and silence.

At the back, behind a battered door that opens into an alley, there's a bathroom and a second door with a broken lock.

Péra sits at his usual table, where he can watch everything unfold. The place is cool, and still, and conducive to writing. He scribbles notes about a former life, when Batu Khan, grandson of Genghis, stormed the Caucasus with fire and steel. Péra was born inside a story: *The Little Cow Barula* by Clara Winlow-Vostrovsky. When Vostrovsky went blind in her final years, he sneaked through the fissures of her fading vision and escaped the story. The thought-police have been after him ever since. Everything has its time and place. They noticed the anomaly. They had to put him back where he belongs. His presence here is a danger to the empire.

The world has changed. Where once there were many small, independent states, now uniformity is sacred. There is no room for difference, no space for dissent, no tolerance for exceptions to the natural order. The thought-police are the keepers of that order.

Péra comes to the Barula Ching because the bartender understands the rules: no questions, cash only, the usual drink, and silence about the pile of pages beside his glass. The bartender was once a scribe for a local therapist. Now, he decodes drinks instead of dialogue. Each cocktail is a translation, each pour an interpretation. Behind the bar, glass jars shimmer with alphabet dust, the phonemes and graphemes of conversations long since disassembled.

Péra writes about Batu Khan's horrors: the sacking of villages, the casual murders, the livestock mutilated for sport. He writes of Serbia. Today it's Vietnam. Same war, different era. War gives ordinary men permission to become monsters. Péra tired of war, so he left the story, but there is no getting away.

The bar serves popcorn, hardboiled eggs, and greasy piroshky. Péra doesn't eat here. He craves Mongolian beef, but not for its flavor. He craves its memory. Memory is everything, the only thing.

Salmon sits at the bar and reads a folded newspaper. Péra watches him over his glass. He recognizes him from the Great Book. He too is an escapee, like Rahab, whom he waits for. The front door creaks open, and Rahab enters. Her golden scarf veils her chestnut hair. Backlit by the sun, her floral dress turns sheer. Her hips sway, and her feline green eyes are sharp enough to pierce skin. She slides onto the stool beside the Salmon. They whisper. They kiss. They engage in spirited conversation.

Péra returns to his notebook. He writes a poem.

He reads it back, grimaces, and crumples the page. The knot of poetry and war is always tangled, always intimate. He lifts his empty glass. The bartender is on the phone. Péra clears his throat to get the bartender's attention. Without a pause in his conversation, the barman decodes another drink. Péra slides some bills across the bar. The refill arrives.

Cha-ching.

On his way back to his table, Péra picks up an abandoned newspaper. Péra offers it to Salmon. He waves it off. He and Rahab continue to discuss their cataclysmic future, Kings, Saviors, as if it will make a difference. The bartender serves them Golden Cadillacs, the preferred drink of the new age.

The newspaper carries an obituary for Clara Winlow-Vostrovsky.

Stanford graduate. First Czech-American woman to earn a college degree. Fluent in six languages. Former head of the Los Angeles Public Library's foreign language division. Died at ninety-one.

Under the harsh bar lights, Rahab and Salmon speak about a house with no walls, no floors.

Péra feels the butterflies of hunger in his stomach.

Cha-ching. Salmon pays. On the way out he stops by Péra and says: "Inside out, upside down, everything is ready. Go to the Mongolian Café. Buy a dinner to share with Rahab. Have them secure it with a scarlet bow, and you will be safe."

When Péra's mother died, she left him a cow named Barula. His stepmother loathed him. She banished him to the barn with the cow. He loved that cow. When she ordered Barula slaughtered, Péra grabbed the cow's magical horn, leapt on her back, and fled. They rested in a deer meadow where Barula grazed. This enraged the deer, and they attacked. To escape, Péra broke off the horn and ran. Inside the horn was a flood of animals: horses, pigs, ducks, sheep. Suddenly Péra was wealthy. He married the czar's daughter, and when the czar died, Péra became the czar, imprisoned in the walls and the floor of the palace

As the day dims, the bar fills: lovers, prophets, exiles, and linguists. A woman weeps quietly in the corner, vowels gather like dew in her hands, fragments of the first breath that dared to become language.

In the Barula Ching, language is not decoration. It is the atmosphere, the currency, the soul. You don't just drink here. *Ideas and fornication are the reason and the rhyme.* Péra tears up the article on Vostrovsky and drops the shreds into his empty glass. If only he could wash away the past and brighten the future as easily.

As Péra walks out the door, he asks the bartender, "Is the Mongolian Café open?"

"It's always open," the man replies.

Péra steps into the night.

"Who is that guy?" someone asks.

"Says he's the Czar of Serbia," the bartender says.

Two soldiers enter. The bar goes still.

Rahab observes them. Her teeth gleam like secrets. One soldier points to the painting above the register.

"That damn cow!" he says.

The other soldier slips out the back door with Rahab.

A couple at the bar finish their drinks and head to the Mongolian Café. They arrive just as Péra leaves with a white bag tied with a scarlet string. Steam curls from its knot.

Back at the Barula Café, the soldiers pay their bill. Cha-ching.

Rahab orders another Golden Cadillac.

"One soldier says to the other as he pulls up his pants, "She told me he's left the gates of the city. Let's hurry!"

The two soldiers run past the Mongolian Café.

The patrons roll their eyes.

Outside, storm clouds tumble across the sky. The weeds tremble.

Péra walks quickly back to the Barula Ching. The steam from the meal warms his hands. Everything is in place.

Back at the bar, Rahab welcomes him with a smile. They share the Mongolian beef.

"Are you ready?" she says.

"Ready," he says.

Cha-ching.

Thunder.

The walls of the city fall.

Somewhere, the great khan turns in his unmarked grave.

The Last Time

"Do we have to keep this up?" Felicia said, her voice low and frayed. "I'm so tired, Bert. And guilty. It didn't used to get to me, but now I can't even sleep."

"Don't go soft on me, Leesha. Not now. We're so close. One more, that's all we need. Then we're done. Mexico, white sand, golden sun, the easy life. You want that as much as I do. We earned it."

"Yes," she said. "More than anything. I want to leave this place, and the person I've become."

She turned from the window where she had rested her cheek against the cool glass. She moved to the middle of the bed, hands folded in her lap like a peasant girl in a Waterhouse painting. From the Saint Francis, Union Square looked like a miniature world, too small and too fast to matter. She picked up her new passport. For the first time, the name inside was real.

"I've had so many names I can't remember the one I was born with."

Bert shrugged. "You're not wrong. I've started to lose track myself."

She looked at him. "Do you ever think about all the lives we've wrecked? Does that bother you at all?"

"They weren't saints, Leesha. They made their own mistakes. Greed, lust, power, we just gave them the nudge. If anything, they got more than they lost."

"What about us, Bert? Did we gain more than we lost?"

"We're still here, aren't we? We've never been taken, have we?"

"It's not the theft. I know they can afford that. These rich folks always have some offshore stash. I mean, you know, what happened after...." She hesitated. "Forget it."

Bert turned back to his old Smith Corona. The steady tap of the keys grated on Leesha's nerves. She cradled her new passport, she stared at the name, her real name: Felicia Fairchild. *Can I ever be that girl again?* she wondered.

"So, what the hell, Leesha," Bert said, and looked up. "You're worried about the sad ones? The strays? We gave them a story. They were bored, numb, already half dead. We lit them up. For a while, they were alive. Isn't that better than to live a long boring life and die in your sleep?"

Felicia stared out the window again. The people below looked like bugs in business suits, looping their endless, deluded circuits.

"You might be right. Maybe we did give them something. But sometimes... I can't forget the faces."

Bert tapped the keys as if he didn't hear her.

Felicia slammed her fist against the window frame.

"Must you pound on that infernal thing all afternoon?"

He looked up, feigned a pout. She laughed despite herself. Bert dropped to his hands and knees and crawled toward her like a dog, eyes round and pleading. She slid from the ledge and into his arms. They collapsed together, kissing, laughing, tumbling. Clothes came off. Then stillness. Then more undressing.

Felicia had never met her birth parents. She was adopted, as was her older brother Maurice. The Fairchilds died in a car crash when she was three. She and Maurice were separated and never saw each other again. She missed him terribly at first, but time eroded even that. She floundered until she met Bert at a Project One concert. He took control, wrote her life like a script, and she went along.

Bert Cameron came from money. Trouble stuck to him. Once, in a fit of rage, he sent pornographic letters to his father's clients. His father disowned him. Bert cleaned out the old man's account, stole a hundred grand, took off in his mother's Mercedes, and headed for Mexico. He blew the money in a month. It didn't matter. He always landed on his feet.

The sun had gone down. They woke in darkness, wrapped in sweat and city noise.

"I'm famished," Felicia said, as she stepped out of the bathroom in a terrycloth robe two sizes too big.

"Let's not go out," Bert said. "Order in. I want to go over the plan again. It has to be perfect. I'll have the lobster pizza." Felicia scanned the menu, then dialed room service. She ordered a chicken Caesar, a lobster pizza, and a bottle of Iron Horse champagne. Bert was already back at the typewriter.

"It's all set," he said. "This last one, our masterpiece. I sent the ticket last week. He confirmed. He'll be at the theater. The room next door is reserved. The switch is ready. You work your magic tomorrow night. When he's out, we make the swap. Roger Hamilton disappears, a new Reese is born."

Bert leaned back, satisfied. *You just have to know what you want. Leesha's been useful. She's bright, beautiful, cooperative, but she doesn't have the distance. Not like I do. She feels too much.*

"So, what's he like, this Reese?" she asked.

"You don't need to know. The less the better. You can handle him. That's all that matters."

"You're right. Easier that way."

She drifted to the window again. Lights flooded the square. She picked up the binoculars, scanned the crowd.

"Oh, my God. Look at that poor old man who just came out of El Prado. He looks... broken. Rags and dirt. He probably stinks. I've seen people like that up close. It gives me the creeps. That could be us, Bert. I've dreamt it. I swear, I wake up with the shivers."

"You out of your goddamn mind?" Bert bared his teeth. "That will never be us. I know how to survive. Those people gave up. They're human refuse. They should be cleared out like rats before the whole damn country falls apart."

Felicia stared at him.

"How can you be so callous? I just made an observation. Anyone can get down on their luck."

"Luck is for children. Adults make choices. Nature doesn't give second chances. You want to save every poor soul, go join a convent. Don't bring it in here. Not now."

He stood up. Towered over her. Eyes wild.

"Leave me alone!" she snapped. "I pull my weight. I never complain, but maybe I'd like to see you feel something once in a while."

"I keep my emotions where they belong," Bert said flatly.

A knock on the door. A waiter wheeled in their food and champagne.

"Will there be anything else, sir?" the man asked.

"No," Bert said, curtly.

The waiter stood there and stared at Bert for a few moments before he left.

"He wanted a tip," Felicia whispered.

"They add it to the bill. Sit down. Let's celebrate."

"How can I celebrate when I know what's coming tomorrow?"

"Don't think. Just get through it. After this, it's over. We'll be in Mexico. The sun will bleach away every bad memory. All we need is this one last job.

"When the heart's involved, it's not so simple," she said. "Don't you have any room in your heart for anyone, for me?"

"The only thing I share with humanity is my drive to take what I deserve and crush whatever gets in the way."

She looked at him closer than ever before.

He softened. "Of course I love you, Leesha. You know that."

"Happiness isn't everything," she said. "We have responsibilities too."

This was going sideways fast. Bert knew he needed to reel it back in.

"You're right. We have obligations. Mine is to you. After tomorrow, we walk away. Start over. Maybe even start a family."

Her eyes lit up. "A family? Do you mean that?"

"Sure I do, baby. Let's celebrate."

⌛ ⌛ ⌛

Reese hesitated. A free ticket to a play he'd never heard of wasn't exactly enticing. Still, it might be fun. He hadn't made any real connections since he'd moved to San Francisco. If he really wanted to start over, he needed to get out, see people, important people.

Theatergoers, he told himself, probably fit that bill. What did he have to lose? Just time, and he had plenty of that.

Inside the lobby, he flipped through the playbill. *The Misunderstanding* by Albert Camus. He recognized the name, some kind of French existentialist, if he remembered right. Reese hoped the play wouldn't be too heady. Surely there'd be others who hadn't read it. People often came to these things just to be seen. If the play was any good, it would speak for itself.

The theater was ornate and close. He felt suffocated. Heavy velvet curtains, the faint scent of cologne and mildew, voices that bounced off marble and goldleaf. It made him dizzy. Reese pushed through the crowd until he reached the usher: a red-faced man in a tight black suit, his neck bulged against a collar two sizes too small, freckles scattered across his pale hands like static.

Resse's seat was in the middle of an empty row. He sat, conspicuously alone. As the house filled, the presence of others calmed him. Laughter, chatter, rustling coats. The crowd anchored him. The seat next to him remained empty. Just as the lights dimmed, a young woman slipped past him and took the vacant seat. She brushed his knee. A whisper of perfume, jasmine, maybe. Her hair caught the light: soft brown, glossy. She smelled like sunlight and clean skin.

"Sorry," she said, she leaned in close, her voice slow and low. "I hope I didn't disturb you."

"Not at all," Reese said, surprised by the ease in his voice. "I'm alone. It's nice to have company."

She smiled, and it was radiant. Her breath was clean, her teeth bright. She looked eerily familiar, though he couldn't imagine why.

The lights went out. The curtain rose.

The play confused him at first, half comedy, half something else. It was dark, philosophical, full of long, sharp exchanges between a mother and a daughter who ran an inn and murdered unsuspecting male guests. There were moments of humor, but an unshakable bleakness ran beneath everything.

Reese stole glances at the woman beside him. She didn't shift or fidget. Her focus was total. Once, she turned to him and smiled. He leaned in.

"Strange play," he whispered.

"Yes," she murmured. "The girl's so... cold, just like the mother says. I don't like her much."

"That's to your credit," Reese said, and she gave a soft laugh.

Leesha didn't laugh inside. The play's story hit too close to home. A mother and daughter who killed for money—it wasn't just fiction to her. As the dialogue deepened, so did her unease. She felt the urge to shut her eyes, cover her ears, retreat into herself, but didn't. She sat still, and tried to breathe.

Reese, though he didn't know it yet, had just brushed shoulders with a past darker than anything Camus could conjure.

The play dragged on. Reese found it hard to concentrate. His thoughts drifted to the woman beside him. He wondered what her voice sounded like outside the hush of the theater, without the stage lights and solemn silence pressing down on them. *Maybe I'll catch her at intermission,* he thought. There was a flutter in his chest, like he'd swallowed feathers laced with heat. *This is silly, I don't even know her.*

Once, he glanced over and thought he saw the stage light catch a tear on her cheek, but when she turned toward him, she was composed. Poised. *I probably just imagined it like everything else that's going through my brain.*

Finally, the houselights came up. His eyes took a moment to adjust. People began to shuffle out of their rows; some stretched toward the bar, others toward the bathrooms.

Reese leaned toward her. "Would it be too forward if I offered to buy you a drink?"

She smiled without hesitation. "Not at all. A white wine would be lovely. I'm Leesha, by the way. I just need to run to the ladies' room. Go ahead and order. I'll meet you at the bar."

"Reese," he said, as she disappeared into the crowd. "See you there."

She had him. Just like Bert said she would. Too easy. The play rattled her. The dialogue, the dread... *it's too familiar.* She needed air, needed distance. If she stayed in her seat any longer, she'd break.

Bert would never forgive her if she messed this up, but this one felt different. Reese felt different. It wasn't just the play. Or was it?

As soon as she was out of sight, she ducked into a service hallway and phoned Bert.

"Jesus Christ, Leesha," Bert's voice snapped through the line. "Get a grip. You've never cracked like this before."

"I know." Her voice trembled. "But maybe we can wait a day? Just one day?"

"A day? Are you kidding me? We've got the room ready, the papers, the timing. Think of Mexico—white sand, golden sun, no more lies. We're almost there. You have to finish this."

She closed her eyes. "All right. He's at the bar. I've got him hooked, don't worry. I'll... I'll buck up."

She ended the call and took a breath. *You can do this,* she told herself. *Just get your head on straight.*

Back at the bar, Reese scanned the room. His eyes flitted toward the bathrooms. He didn't see her anywhere. She touched his back, lightly but deliberately, and he turned to see her smile and a shimmer of blue eyeliner catching the light. Her touch lingered just long enough to make him wonder.

"Oh. Hey. Here's your wine."

"Thanks, Reese." Her smile disarmed him, and she knew it.

He stared at her for a beat too long. "Have we met before?"

"I don't think so." She tilted her head, a tease. "Do you live here, or is this a visit?'

"I hope to settle here," he said. "Just getting a feel for the city."

She laughed softly. "Getting the lay of the land?"

"Yeah, I guess." He smiled, a little sheepish. "I'm from Chicago."

She looked around the room, scanned the faces, then returned her gaze to him. "So, what do you make of the play?"

"I've never read anything by Camus," he admitted. "It's slow. A little creepy."

"Not my cup of tea either." Her laugh was nervous this time. She sipped her white wine, eyes on his. *He's thinking about sex,* she thought. *It's written all over his face.*

"You know," she said, "I've got a cold bottle of champagne back in my room at the Saint Francis. We could skip the second half of this, go find some music, maybe have a dance. Have some fun. What do you say, Reese?"

He almost choked on his wine. Was she serious? She couldn't be, but the look in her eyes said otherwise. The bells rang for the next act just as they stepped into the cold night outside the theater. Union Square glowed ahead, a scatter of city lights blurred in the fog.

They were nearly at the hotel entrance when Leesha froze. A man stood in the shadows—grimy, gaunt, familiar.

"That's him," she whispered, and she gripped Reese's arm tightly. "The man I saw last night. He gives me the creeps."

Reese paused. "Just a sec." He approached the man, pressed a few bills into his palm, then returned to Leesha.

"We all need a break sometimes," he said to Leesha and grabbed her hand.

That simple act shook her. To see him do that, so casually, so sincerely, twisted something inside her, twisted it back toward who she used to be, before the midnight terrors, before the masks.

Upstairs she let Reese into the room. The lights came on. She stood close enough to feel the heat of his skin. Their eyes locked. They kissed.

Something was wrong.

She pulled away.

"I'll get the champagne ready," she said, and vanished into the small kitchen.

Reese wandered to the window. Outside, the cold was deeper than before. *Leesha,* he whispered to himself. *It sounds like a nickname. I wonder what her real name is?*

She returned, tray in hand. From behind, she watched him framed by the window. His shoulders were squared, his hands on his hips. Something about his posture stirred a memory she couldn't grasp. Then it slipped away. The drug was in one of the glasses. She stepped forward. But, when Reese turned to her, she nearly dropped the tray.

"You okay?" he asked. "You look like you've seen a ghost."

"That glass is cracked," she lied. "Take the other one."

"He examined it. "I don't see a crack."

"I'll get a new one." She fled to the kitchen, put the doctored wine in the fridge, poured a fresh one for herself, and returned. She just wasn't ready to do it. Not yet.

"I'm feeling a little strange, Reese. I know it was my idea to come here, but now... I don't want you to get the wrong idea."

Reese nodded. "If you'd rather I leave, just say so. I'm not here to push anything."

"No, stay. Please. Let's talk. You go first. Tell me something real."

She didn't know why she said it. The job had unraveled. Her resolve was gone. She didn't want to be alone, but didn't want him dead either.

Reese studied her. *Something's off,* he thought. *But all right, I'll talk.*

Leesha sat on the edge of her chair, unsure of her own motives.

"I never knew my real parents," Reese began. "I bounced through the system. Eventually, I found someone who looked out for me. I built a business, sold it a few months ago. That's why I'm here. Time to start fresh."

"You didn't have a family?" Her voice trembled. Something clicked.

"Well, I had a sister. We were split up when she was three. Her name was Felicia."

Leesha bolted upright. "Oh, my God... oh, my God! You're Maurice! You're Maurice! I knew it. I just felt it. You're my brother."

It hit him like a body blow. The idea had lingered on the edges of his thoughts, but it seemed too unlikely. Now it was real. She was his sister, his Felicia.

When the shock wore off, Felicia told him everything, about Bert, the scam, the plan to take him out. Time was short. Bert was on his way. She had to act fast.

"Do you think this'll work?" Reese asked.

"It will. I know him inside out."

She dialed Bert. "It's done. He's out cold. I've got the wallet and the cash. Come celebrate and then we'll finish."

Bert arrived quickly, twitchy and tight-jawed.

"That call from the theater nearly gave me a heart attack," he said.

"It's over now," she replied. "This is the last time. You promised."

He slouched into a chair. She handed him the chilled glass, the drugged one. They toasted.

"To Mexico!"

"To Mexico," Bert echoed, downing it in a single gulp.

"Let me see the wallet."

As Bert pored over the cards and ID, a satisfied smile crept across his face. Everything aligned. He replaced the originals with fakes: Reese was now Roger Hamilton, a man who didn't exist. In a few hours, "Roger" would be found dead in a hotel bed, cash and cards gone, no ties, no one to claim him. Bert's masterpiece.

Felicia watched as Bert slipped into unconsciousness, a strange serenity softened his features for the first time she could remember.

She called out. Reese emerged. Together, they restored the contents of the wallet and swapped out the license.

"When he wakes up," she said, "he'll be Roger Hamilton. Broke, alone, and forgotten. Just like he planned for you."

"Yea, well I wasn't supposed to wake up," Reese muttered.

"No. But we're not like him, Maurice. I never killed anyone. I set the trap, yes, but I didn't pull the trigger. That was always his part. It's over now. The nightmare's over."

Reese looked at her for a long time. "Let's never speak of this again, Felicia. Time to move on."

⏳ ⏳ ⏳

Bert's skull pounded when he woke up, but that was nothing compared to what came next. The real headache hit when he realized he'd been outplayed.

He was no longer Bert Cameron, the slick operator with a plan. He was Roger Hamilton, broke, stranded, and legally toxic. The paper trail he'd so carefully engineered led straight to bankruptcy. Bert Cameron? That name was scorched. Warrants. Investigations. No going back.

She hadn't left him a dime.

Downstairs at the hotel restaurant, he tried to keep up appearances.

"I'm sorry, Mr. Hamilton," the waiter said. "There seems to be an issue with your account. We can't charge this to your room. Cash only. Please see the front desk."

Bert forced a smile. "Well, that's unexpected. I'll just run up and grab some cash, be back before you miss me."

The waiter didn't buy it. As soon as Bert turned the corner, the man was on the phone to the front desk.

Bert didn't hesitate. He ducked out through a side exit and walked away. There was no going back for his things. All he had were his passport and the tickets, but tickets to what? To where? With no money, they were just paper.

He walked faster. Sweat collected under his collar. Around the next corner, he nearly collided with a homeless man whose dead-eyed stare stopped him in his tracks. For a moment, Bert just stood there. Paralyzed.

Then he muttered, almost to himself:

"Exterminated... just like rats."

He kept on, no idea where he would go or what he would do, swallowed by the hard white glare of morning.

In The Clover

Money changes everything. It can lift you up or drag you down, but it never leaves things the same.

When Bill Marsden opened the letter, he assumed it was either a scam or an elaborate prank by one of his students. He crumpled it without reading past the second line. "I'm no fool," he muttered, and dropped it in the trash.

One week later, on a foggy Friday afternoon, a man in a tan double-breasted suit, gray fedora, and two-tone wingtips appeared on his doorstep with a leather briefcase. Without much ceremony, the man removed a cashier's check for $1 million and handed it over.

"We sent a letter," the man said. "You didn't respond. Mr. Fishbeck insisted we deliver it in person. No strings attached."

Before Bill could find his voice, the man turned and walked back to the black limousine that waited out front. It pulled away and vanished into the fog.

Attached to the check was a single sheet of heavyweight bond paper:

> The enclosed check for $1,000,000 is a bequest from the estate of Albert Fishbeck. All applicable taxes have been paid. Please deposit the check into a personal account at the Pine Grove Savings and Loan. Arrangements have been made. The funds must remain there until withdrawn for use at your discretion.
>
> Very Truly Yours,
> Jonathan Fishbeck, Executor

Bill stood incredulously and blinked at the check.

"Well," he whispered to himself, "I'll be a horse's ass. Who the hell is Albert Fishbeck?"

As a high-school math teacher, Bill was used to being the butt of teenage jokes: his chalk-dusted ties, the hilarious notes on Fibonacci sequences, his weekly lectures on the poetry of numbers, but this? This was beyond senior prank territory.

That weekend, he launched a quiet investigation. He made calls, scoured obituaries, rifled through archives at the public library, even called funeral homes. He told no one. He wasn't about to let himself be played.

Nothing. No Albert Fishbeck. No Jonathan either.

"Someone's messing with me," he growled. "I'll get to the bottom of it. Mind what I say."

Bill was a man of routine, known for his moral backbone and love of the arts, always in the audience, never on stage. He lived alone, and kept his life neat and restrained. The sudden influx of a million dollars didn't sit right.

Still, on Monday morning, he walked into Pine Grove Savings and Loan with the check and shaky hands. The branch manager confirmed the funds. The check was real.

An account was opened. The manager asked if Bill would like investment advice.

"No," said Bill firmly. "The instructions were clear. It stays in the account."

The young teller leaned forward from her window. "Would you like to order checks, Mr. Marsden?"

He hesitated. "Yes, I suppose I would."

She handed him a form. Their fingers brushed. A flicker of something passed between them, an electric jolt that ran from the base of Bill's spine to the back of his skull.

"Thank you," he said, and he studied her nametag.

DIWANNA LOVE. The name sounded absurdly poetic.

"When will the checks be ready, Miss Love?" he asked, careful to keep his voice even.

She blinked. "You... know me?"

"Your nametag."

Diwanna glanced down at her blouse, which puckered slightly as she did. Bill caught a briefly accidental glimpse of skin.

He looked away, flustered.

"It usually takes about two weeks," she said with a broad smile, "but I can put a rush on it if you'd like."

She had long red hair, and freckles like constellations across her nose. *Cute. Damn cute,* he thought. *New vistas lie ahead.* He couldn't fit her into any mathematical equation he was aware of.

When Bill walked out of the bank, that strange electric pulse hit him again. *Did she feel it too*?

He still had a mystery to solve. Who was Fishbeck? Why him? He hadn't touched the money yet, but now he had the means. He also had a reason to linger around the bank a bit more often, he pondered as he felt a quiver between his legs that he promptly stifled.

Bill was cautious with money. A lifetime as a teacher had taught him thrift. His father's savings had evaporated in a market crash decades ago. He had no appetite for risks, financial or otherwise.

"Smart old Fishbeck," he murmured. "Told me to leave it in the bank." Then he remembered, "banks can go bust too."

Late that afternoon, Bill ran into Tom Foresight, a fellow teacher from the English department.

"Hey, Bill. Where'd you disappear to this morning?

"Had some errands. Did I miss anything?"

"Same-old, same-old. I guess you haven't heard." Tom raised an eyebrow.

"Don't tell me," Bill groaned. "They killed the music program again."

"Dropped the guillotine," Tom said. "Redirected the funds to football, new gear, new uniforms. Real flashy stuff. You should've been there to fight against it. Wouldn't have done any good though."

"Of course they did," Bill mumbled.

"The arts always play second fiddle, or third or fourth. Maybe we can find a sponsor, get someone to fund it privately."

Tom chuckled. "Even if you could, they'd find a way to reroute the money to the gridiron. Old-man Grissom would twist the rules to make it happen."

Bill frowned. "They can't do that, not if it's earmarked."

Tom just shook his head. "Grissom finds a way. Every time. Good luck, though. I've got a mountain of essays to climb." He waved and walked off.

Bill stood there, his mind raced ahead. *Maybe I could fund the program. Anonymously. That check could do more than change my life. It could save the one thing that makes my job worthwhile.*

⧗ ⧗ ⧗

At home, he grabbed a beer from the fridge and sat on the couch, surrounded by scattered papers and unanswered questions. Two weeks had passed, and he still hadn't uncovered a single fact to explain the check. Nothing about Fishbeck. No records, no obituary, no online trace. It was like the man never existed. *I guess these rich folk can hide better than the rest of us.*

While Bill thumbed through his paperwork, he was startled by a knock on the door. When he opened it, he had to catch his breath. Standing there was a woman with an easy smile and confident posture. It took a second before he recognized her.

"Well, Diwanna Love! To what do I owe the honor?" She looked worlds away from the professional he'd seen earlier at the bank, casual and radiant.

"Hello, Mr. Marsden," she said smoothly. She noticed the way his eyes flicked over her, the small hitch in his breath. *Good,* she thought. *He's off balance already.*

"Wow. Uh, come in. Sit down. What... why are you here?"

"I brought your new checks," she said. She pulled a thick envelope from her oversized leather purse. As she leaned forward to hand it to him, her skirt slipped just slightly apart, revealing a flash of leg.

Bill blinked and swallowed hard. "You came all the way out here just to drop those off? On a Saturday?"

"It's a beautiful day," she said with a shrug. "My Aunt Sally lives nearby. Figured I'd kill two birds with one trip." Her smile was a delight. It totally brightened his day.

"Well, I appreciate it," he said as he regained his composure. "The least I can do is buy you dinner. Give me a chance to put these new checks to good use. Your Aunt's welcome to join us."

He surprised himself with the offer.

"That's very sweet," Diwanna said, her voice warm as syrup, "but my Aunt is bedridden. She hasn't left her house in years. I'd love to go, though. I'll come back after I spend some time with her. Is seven okay?"

"Perfect," said Bill. "I'm sorry about your Aunt."

"Don't be. She has her stories and her window. That's enough for her." Diwanna smiled and extended her hand. "See you at seven."

Her touch lingered. When she left, the scent of her perfume stayed behind. Bill stood transfixed for a few minutes, then reached for his inhaler.

When Diwanna left, she headed off to shop. The Aunt Sally fabrication gave her some time to get prepared. *I'm not really a bad person*, she repeated to herself over and over as if to justify what she knew was coming. *I'm just going to play him a little, have some fun, and move on. There's nothing so bad about that, is there? He'll get some fun out of it. I'll make sure of that.*

Bill looked around at the wreck of his living room and laughed. "God, what a mess." He picked up his papers and stacked them neatly on the desk. He rearranged the furniture and fluffed the pillows on the couch, then went and cleaned up the kitchen. No way he would let her see him like this again.

Dinner that Saturday night started something that changed everything. One dinner led to another, week after week, until it became routine. Before long, Diwanna moved in. It surprised Bill how naturally it all happened. He'd never had a serious relationship before. Truth was, he didn't know what hit him.

"She's living with you already?" Tom asked over coffee in the teacher's lounge. "Isn't that a little fast? Where'd you meet her?"

"At the bank," said Bill. "She helped me when I went in to cash that big check. Can you believe it? I still can't."

Tom raised an eyebrow. "She's a hell of a catch. No offense, but this isn't like you. You sure you know what you're doing?"

Bill smiled, more calm than confident. "I know how it looks. It's time I changed my life, Tom. She's not a gold digger, if that's what you mean. I've been in a rut far too long. She makes me happy. I'm ready to make some changes in my life."

"I'm just saying you should be careful," said Tom.

"I'm no fool, Tom. My eyes are open. We get on so well. It's like we were made for each other. She hasn't asked for anything or even mentioned the money. She has a job and does fine on her own."

Tom didn't press. He just nodded, though something in his expression said he wasn't convinced.

⧖ ⧖ ⧖

School was out for the summer. Bill had nearly two months to himself. Diwanna floated the idea of a European vacation.

Why not?" Bill said. "I've always heard my family came from somewhere in northern England. Lancashire, I think. It might be nice to trace the Marsden roots."

Diwanna lit up. "I've got relatives in Edinburgh. That's not far at all. We could do both."

Bill was pleased, unaware that the trip was something Diwanna had planned all along.

They flew to London. Bill picked up a walking guide and they explored the city on foot and by subway. Diwanna found Portobello Road a shopper's paradise.

"I could take weeks to rummage through these stalls," she said. "The Smithfield Market, though, not so much. Ugh! All the blood and dead animals? I can't handle it."

Bill, meanwhile, was entranced by the city. The highlight was the Tate. Seeing William Blake's work in person felt like a pilgrimage. Blake had been a personal hero since high school. Tom liked him too. Bill bought a book to take back to his friend. The only hiccup was Diwanna's new boots. They left her with blisters. She ended up on a bench, and gingerly pulled the boots off. A museum guard immediately approached. "You can't remove your shoes in here, miss. Please put them back on."

Bill caught the scowl Diwanna shot the guard, and read the profanity on her lips. It was the first time he'd seen that side of her, and it unsettled him. They left the museum early.

Diwanna had a taste for the finer things. She steered Bill toward chic restaurants and storied hotels. The Savoy Grill, Rules, anywhere with a bit of prestige and a heavy bill. He spent more than he should have, but he didn't want to let her down, and he had to admit that he enjoyed a taste of extravagance. He told himself the expenses would taper off once they headed north where the countryside might be gentler on the wallet.

On their last night in London they visited the Salisbury Pub, a moody old place with stained glass and history in the walls. Oscar Wilde had once held court there. That meant something; Wilde was Tom's favorite writer.

They traveled by BritRail which proved to be cheap, scenic, and efficient. Bill loved it. They made stops in Cambridge, York, and Leeds, then detoured to Blackpool and Lancaster. In Lancaster, Bill dove into the local archives. He traced the Marsden name back to the twelfth century. He found no living relatives, but the lineage itself gave him a quiet thrill.

"All right," he said after a few days. "I've done what I came to do. Time to meet your family."

On the train to Edinburgh, Diwanna's mood changed. She grew distant, quiet. Bill chalked it up to exhaustion and let her be, while he fascinated himself with the countryside that passed by outside.

Their first morning in Edinburgh, Diwanna pulled him aside. He sensed she was uncomfortable. It was the first time since they'd been together that Bill felt distant from her.

"I want to see them alone first," she said. "It's been a while, and the last time didn't end well. I don't want to drag you into a potential fight."

Bill hesitated. "That's... understandable," he said, though the explanation felt a little off. "I'll take the day to explore. I've always wanted to see Adam Smith's grave and the castle too. I'll wander around the Royal Mile and sight see on my own."

She kissed him on the cheek. "Thanks for that. It might be a long day, so enjoy yourself."

As she walked away, Bill couldn't shake the feeling that something was being kept from him, and not just a family quarrel.

If Bill knew Diwanna's thoughts, he'd have realized his suspicions were justified. Diwanna was not an evil person but she'd been dragged into an evil plan. Since she'd been approached by Jonathan Fishbeck, her world had been turned upside down. Something strange had happened to her. To her surprise, she'd grown to like Bill more than she ever expected. At first, she just went along with the plan for the money. Now, she needed to find a way to satisfy Fishbeck without ruining a relationship she hoped to keep. It wouldn't be easy.

The day went surprisingly well for Bill. He relaxed and grew less anxious about the money. Whatever he spent, he told himself, was worth it if it brought Diwanna joy.

After a modest lunch of fish and chips, he took a long walk to settle his stomach and clear his head. Eventually, he wandered onto Ann Street, a quiet, tree-lined avenue flanked by stately old mansions. As he turned a corner, he stopped cold.

There, at the grandest house on the block, stood Diwanna, deep in a tense exchange with a young man on the front steps. Bill froze, confused. She hadn't told him about anyone in this neighborhood.

He ducked behind a hedge of tall heather and watched. Their conversation was animated; the young man gestured sharply while Diwanna held her ground. After a few minutes, she turned and walked away, her pace brisk and tight. The man disappeared into the house.

When Bill stepped out from behind the bush, he collided with a woman walking a small dog.

"Pardon me," he said, as he recovered. "That house, do you know who lives there?"

The woman followed his gaze. "Oh, that's Mr. Albert Fishbeck's residence. He's one of the wealthiest men around. Surprisingly kind, for a man of his means."

"Fishbeck?" Bill's stomach tightened. As they spoke, the young man he had seen with Diwanna stepped out of the house and walked away.

"That's Jonathan, his son," said the woman. "Quite the disappointment. No warmth, no compassion. Nothing like his father."

"Thank you," Bill said absently. The woman nodded and continued on her way. His mind spun at the news. Bill crossed the street and climbed the mansion's stone steps. He rang the bell. A stately butler opened the door.

"May I help you?"

"Yes. I'd like to speak with Mr. Albert Fishbeck regarding a one-million-dollar check received at my home in Pine Grove, Pennsylvania."

The butler's brows lifted. "Please wait here." He gestured toward a carved oak chair in the entryway.

Bill sat, surrounded by old oil portraits, stern men and elegant women in antique frames. One painting caught his eye. It was unmistakably the same young man who'd argued with Diwanna.

After a few minutes, the butler returned and led him to a large upstairs bedroom. There, propped in bed, was Albert Fishbeck. He was old, frail, and whitehaired. His gravelly voice was barely audible behind an oxygen mask.

"What's this about a million-dollar check?" the old man asked.

Bill explained, and carefully went through the events from the mysterious delivery to his failed attempts to trace its origin. Fisbeck listened, his eyes sharp despite his age. He paused occasionally to breathe through the mask.

"You say you placed the money in a savings account?" he asked.

"Yes. I used only a small portion for this trip. My plan was to track down the source, but I ran into dead ends... until today."

"That's not your fault," Albert said. He pressed a call button. A nurse entered instantly.

"Sofie, send for Callum. Tell him to bring the account book."

"Of course, Mr. Fishbeck."

Albert turned back to Bill. "We'll get to the bottom of this, Mr. Marsden. You were right to safeguard the money. I'm sorry it had to be such a mystery."

A few minutes later, a sharply dressed man arrived with a leather-bound ledger.

"Bill, this is Callum, my accountant," Albert said. "Callum, Mr. Marsden claims he received a million-dollar check bearing our name. Can you verify that?"

Callum flipped through the book. "No check issued to a Bill Marsden," he said, "but there *was* a withdrawal of one million dollars from our US HSBC account."

"That's the same bank listed on the check I received," Bill added.

Albert's eyes narrowed. "Why wasn't I informed of that withdrawal, Callum?"

"Jonathan said it was approved by you, sir. I assumed—"

"*You assumed?*" Albert's voice was brittle with fury. "You know better."

"I'm deeply sorry, sir. It won't happen again."

"It certainly won't," Albert muttered. He leaned back and closed his eyes. Bill waited, uncertain. Seconds passed. Then minutes. The old man lay still. Bill began to worry Albert had fallen asleep or worse.

At last, just before Bill was about to speak, Albert opened his eyes. They were cold, alert, and filled with purpose.

"Here's what we'll do, Mr. Marsden," Albert said, his voice calm but resolute. "You and Callum will freeze the account immediately. I understand this might put you in a bind, so I'll have Callum set up a separate cash account for your use without restrictions. I'll handle matters within my family. I'm afraid my son, Jonathan, cannot be trusted. I believe he intended to steal that money. Once I've resolved things on my end, the full amount will be yours. I appreciate your honesty, Mr. Marsden. I wish you well. Good day."

Before Bill could reply, the door opened and Callum ushered him out. True to his word, Callum handled everything swiftly. A taxi waited downstairs to return Bill to his hotel. When he arrived, he took the elevator to the sixth floor. As he stepped into the hallway, raised voices leaked from the room next to his. He froze. One of the voices was Diwanna's.

"I can't Jonathan," she said, panicked. "I don't want any part of this. I did what I was supposed to do. Just pay me and let me go before it's too late."

Bill knocked on the door. The argument stopped. He knocked again, harder this time. Jonathan opened it, tense and flushed.

"What the hell is going on?" Bill demanded, as he pushed past Jonathan and confronted Diwanna. "What is this all about?"

"I can explain," Diwanna began.

"No, you can't," Bill snapped. "I know that man is Jonathan Fishbeck. He's Albert's son. He's concocted a plan to steal from his own father, and now I find you here with him? Are you in on it? Were you in on it from the start?"

Tears welled in Diwanna's eyes. "No, it's not like that. You don't understand. Please listen to me."

"Don't touch me," Bill shouted, backing away. "You used me. I trusted you, and you made a fool of me."

Jonathan had been silent until now, jaw tight and fists clenched. Then, suddenly, he lunged. The two men grappled. Bill stumbled backward, off balance, and crashed into the window. The glass shattered. A split second later, Bill was gone, six stories down.

Diwanna screamed, falling to her knees.

"Oh my God, Jonathan! You killed him!"

Jonathan stood, frozen. His chest heaved as he stared at the broken window. "It was an accident," he said. "He charged at me, I moved, he went through the glass. That's what happened, Diwanna. That's what you must say. Otherwise, we both go to prison."

⌛ ⌛ ⌛

"I'm sorry, Jonathan," Albert Fishbeck rasped, as he sat up in bed, his voice brittle with fury. "What you've done is unforgivable. Accident or not, you're no son of mine. I won't leave you a damn thing!"

He scowled, then slipped the oxygen mask over his face and drew a slow, shuddering breath.

Jonathan stepped forward, desperate.

"Come on, Albert. This Marsden guy is a fraud. He conned you, took advantage. I can fix this if you'll just let me."

Albert pulled the mask away. His eyes burned. "Don't insult me with more lies. I know everything. You embezzled my recent contributions to the Fishbeck charitable foundation and tried to steal the money for yourself. All you've ever done is wait for me to die."

"It's our family money," Jonathan snapped. His hand trembled as he reached into his briefcase. *Now,* he thought. *End it here, end it now.*

From a hidden compartment, Jonathan withdrew a small vial and syringe. He pretended to adjust the IV bag, and injected the poison into the solution. His mouth curled into a crooked smile.

Albert caught the expression. That smile. The cold satisfaction. It crushed what remained of his hope. *I failed you son, utterly,* he said under his breath.

"Your plan won't work, Jonathan," he said, voice low but clear. "You're too late. The will's been finalized. Not one penny will go to you."

Jonathan's eyes narrowed as he watched the tainted fluid inch down the IV line.

"Then rot in hell, you bastard! You've never loved me, never given me a chance. I had to look out for myself because no one else would."

Albert tried to speak, but it quickly turned into a coughing fit. He hit the nurse's call button. Outside the door, a nurse and police officer waited. They heard it all.

"You couldn't wait," Albert wheezed. "Now you will get what you deserve."

The nurse rushed in, calm and efficient. She unhooked the IV line. Albert's arm had never been connected, he knew what Jonathan was capable of. The nurse swapped the bag for a fresh one. The officer stepped forward and snapped handcuffs onto Jonathan's wrists.

"Greed always brings out the worst," Albert said, and shook his head. "What you did to Bill Marsden was vile. He had nothing to do with our family, yet he did his best to do right by me. One of my bequests will support the arts and music program at the school where he worked. In Bill's name. I hope that gives him some peace.

The nurse and officer escorted Jonathan from the room. Albert lay back, exhausted, and the tension drained from his face, but not the sorrow in his heart.

Months later, in Pine Grove, Tom Foresight hammered a brass plaque onto the door of the new arts building.

In Honor of Bill Marsden
Champion of Music and the Arts

"I tried to warn you," Tom muttered under his breath. "But you wouldn't listen. You got what you wanted, old friend. Too late for you to see it, but you got it. You were in the clover... but now you're under it. I'm sorry, my friend, dreadfully sorry."

The Seventies

Ribeauville

Devon sat alone in the town square. His hands trembled as he read the letter. Tears slid silently down his cheeks. He felt more distant from her now than he ever had, more than in those early days at Stanford when he was young, uncertain, and adrift. He shut his eyes, and the past came flooding back, uninvited but vivid, like a tide that never fully recedes.

Back then, while his classmates planned Friday-night dates or trips for quarter break, Devon ironed their shirts and typed term papers for extra money. At his one and only fraternity rush, he ended up in the kitchen with a Black cook, and watched how she made rice in industrial-sized pots. Meanwhile, a stripper entertained the pledges in the living room. They asked him to join, but he declined. Instead, he moved off campus with an unlikely roommate: Jerry Fleishman, a red-haired, freckled New Yorker from an absurdly wealthy family.

Devon had a conflicted relationship with money. He knew he needed it to survive, but his interest was elsewhere, in art, literature, and the long sweep of history. He envied his rich classmates' carefree disdain for their privilege. He didn't have that luxury. He would have to earn his future. That's why he'd chosen to major in mathematics and economics, practical subjects, steppingstones to a stable life in education or business.

It was Jerry who introduced him to Monica. Meeting her stunned Devon almost as much as the day Jerry's father gifted them a limited-edition Kandinsky for their apartment. "Start your collection early," the old man advised. "Art appreciates just like a good education." Years later, Devon read in the news that Jerry Fleishman donated several million dollars' worth of rare paintings to a private university. Old man Fleishman knew his stuff.

The advice didn't stick with Devon. Monica did. She and Devon became friends, unlikely, but enduring. Monica was everything Devon had dreamed of but knew he could never have. There are different worlds on this earth, and each of us is assigned only to one. Monica belongs to the world of gallery openings, foreign summers, and family wealth so vast it feels mythical. Devon came from a world where Kandinsky was a museum object, not wall décor.

Monica and Jerry met at an art show in San Francisco when she was a student at Berkeley. He and Devon were at Stanford. Devon got in on a scholarship, one of those gifts from the high tower of elite guilt, with the unspoken caveat that he'd better make good on it.

At first, Monica struck Devon as another moody rich girl, theatrically melancholic when it suited her, but the more time he spent with her, the more he realized she wasn't a fake. The darkness she carried wasn't performance, it was real, raw, and deeply rooted.

She had piercing green eyes, jet-black hair, alabaster skin, and lips the color of crushed berries. There was something devilish, almost unreal, in her beauty. If there was one flaw, it was her emaciated frame; she was fragile in both body and spirit.

Devon was sure she knew the effect she had on him. He wondered if, behind closed doors, she laughed about him with Jerry. She moved through the apartment like she didn't quite belong in her own skin, handled objects with a strange detachment, inspected, replaced, then drifted on. What he didn't realize at the time was that this wasn't a performance. Monica was just as uneasy, just as uncertain, as he was.

For Jerry, Monica was a pastime, one of many. She didn't know it, but Devon did. He saw past Jerry's charm and through to the cold machinery beneath. Devon assumed they were involved, at least temporarily. He kept his distance, watched from the sidelines, content to glimpse another universe. Jerry had befriended Devon out of convenience. Devon knew that, and he used Jerry in return, though for different reasons.

Monica was different. She was a riddle Devon could never quite unravel. She pulled him like a magnet though he knew full well how it might end. He stayed close, but not too close, not close enough to self-destruct.

Jerry and Monica planned a long weekend in France.

"You'll take notes for me and catch me up on what I miss, right?" Jerry asked.

Devon gave a half-smile. "Of course. Won't five days in France cost a fortune?"

"Just say you'll cover for me, okay?"

"I said I would. You know I will."

When Monica visited, she was always on stage. She'd mastered the performance, knew the effect she had on Devon, and for all his awareness of it, he still fell under her spell. She treated him kindly enough. He enjoyed her company, he couldn't deny it. It was a quiet transaction, both aware, both amused in their own way.

A few weeks after the trip, Jerry was out at class. Devon found himself alone with Monica. He sat across from her, awkward, unsure how to act. The silence stretched, became brittle.

"So," he said, "how was France?"

Monica didn't look up from her magazine.

"France is France."

"That's not an answer," he said firmly. "I've never been. Never even left California."

At that, Monica looked up, startled. "Oh, you poor boy," she said, half-serious, half-smiling. "We were only in Paris for a day. We stayed on this tiny island in the Seine, Île Saint-Louis. It's like a country village that floats in the middle of the city. Roosters, children, music that echoes off the river, the bells of Notre Dame. It felt out of time. Baudelaire lived there."

"You like Baudelaire?" Devon asked. "*Fleurs du Mal* always felt... heavy to me."

"Of course it's heavy," she said. Her eyes lit up. "Beauty grows out of pain. Baudelaire tried to kill himself once, you know. He failed, he lacked the strength. Some of his poems are dark, even grotesque, but others..." she paused, her voice softening, "others are transcendent. He wrote about how a poet is like an albatross: majestic in flight, clumsy on land. And then there's this: *He whose thoughts, like skylarks, soar into the morning sky... who understands with ease the language of flowers and of silent things.* That's real beauty, Devon. The kind you only reach through pain."

"I understand he admired Poe," Devon offered.

"Another great poet with a taste for gloom," Monica laughed. "I thought you were an Econ guy?"

"I am. Doesn't mean I don't read poetry. Shelley had some wild economic ideas. Keynes ran with Virginia Woolf and the Bloomsbury crowd. Art and money aren't strangers even if they rarely sit at the same table."

Monica stretched, feline and lazy. "I love cities. The real ones. Filthy, electric, alive. I saw a woman in Paris stand on the back of a truck and shave her pubic hair as if it was a hedge. You don't see that even in San Francisco."

Devon's cheeks flushed. He wasn't sure if it was the image or Monica's cool delivery that rattled him.

"The problem is Jerry," she continued. "He drags me to places where the rich people go. We ate at Le Coupe-Chou; supposedly the Beatles once dined there, but I'm not there for the Beatles. I'm there for the street, for the real sights, for the weird stuff."

"You like the shock factor," Devon said, his face still aglow.

"I like the ordinary too, people doing everyday things, but yes, I love the strange. The freakish. The dangerous. There's something that thrills me about it. When you stare down something totally bizarre and it doesn't shake you, that's when you know you've won."

"Won what?"

"The game," she said. "Life is a game. It's everything at once. It's love, grief, wonder, and terror, all turned up to full volume. That's the point, isn't it?"

Devon didn't know how to answer. Monica leaned toward him.

"I'm going back to France soon. My brother's in Alsace. I want you to come with me. I'll show you a new world, or the old one."

Devon was stunned. "What?"

"I'm serious," she said. "Jerry's got family stuff in New York. He can't go."

It took Devon a minute to find his voice.

"But... Jerry's your boyfriend."

Monica laughed loudly. "That doesn't mean you and I can't travel as friends."

"I can't afford it," said Devon.

Something in Monica's expression disarmed him, the way her green eyes caught the light, the casual tilt of her shoulder toward him, like they already shared a secret.

"Jerry knows I can't travel alone," she said, her voice soft but deliberate. "I told him I needed someone dependable. A strong shoulder. He said you were the obvious choice, and that he'd cover everything."

Her lashes fluttered. Devon wasn't sure if it was nerves or strategy.

"You're joking."

"I'm not."

"It's awkward," he said, and glanced away.

"Awkward how?"

"Jerry. He's my friend. My roommate. This whole thing, it feels wrong."

"Jerry and I are just friends," she said breezily. "Do you speak French?"

Devon frowned. "I think you're more than friends."

Monica gave a short laugh. "Don't be silly. So, do you speak French or not?"

"I took a year here at Stanford. We read *L'Étranger*. I'm not fluent. I'd probably just slow you down."

"You read *The Myth of Sisyphus?*"

"No, just *The Stranger.*"

"Well, then," she said, undeterred. "Don't sell yourself short, Devon. I'm not as worldly as you seem to think. We'll manage. You'll have plenty of time to explore on your own. I'll be tied up with my brother most of the time. I don't want to go alone, and I definitely don't want to bring some creep I barely know."

She leaned in, eyes alight. "Come with me. Please."

Devon hesitated. In one way he was thrilled about it: Paris, a change of scenery, the chance to shake off the weight of his routine, but the idea of Jerry footing the bill unsettled him.

"I can't," he said flatly. "Jerry's my friend. I won't run off on some European... thing, and especially at his expense. It would be humiliating."

Monica threw her head back and laughed again, louder.

"A *tryst?* Is that what you're worried about? No one's asking for a scandal, Devon. You'd be my bodyguard. My chaperone." She giggled, clearly enjoying his discomfort. "He trusts you to look after me. The money? It's nothing to him. His family's loaded. He already bought the tickets."

Devon stared at her, caught between instinct and desire.

She smiled. "Come on, say yes."

⧗ ⧗ ⧗

Devon sat on the weathered bench in the town square, Monica's letter open on his lap. He glanced around at the changed face of Ribeauville. The once-quiet Alsatian village had transformed into a bustling tourist hub, and now proudly claimed to be the inspiration for Disney's *Beauty and the Beast,* a fairytale that managed to romanticize the idea of arranged marriage. Devon closed his eyes and the past came rushing back.

France, Europe, had been a long-held dream, now realized. Devon knew this might be his one and only chance, so he prepared like a man embarking on a pilgrimage. He read Fernand Braudel and Henri Pirenne for a sweeping view of European history, but that wasn't enough. Perhaps it was Monica's influence, or a desire to impress her, that led him to Baudelaire, Camus, and the strange poetry of disillusionment. He discovered that Goethe had earned his law degree in Strasbourg, where he began *Faust,* and even wrote a novel in Alsace about a young man undone by love for a married woman.

Once they arrived, Monica spent most of her time with her brother, Max, as promised. Max lived in Colmar. Devon was left to wander on his own. He strolled through storybook villages that seemed plucked from another century. His budget was tight, but he found ways to make it work: He'd sometimes slip into elegant restaurants, order modestly, nurse a drink for hours. He listened, observed, and later shared his impressions with Monica. She appeared fascinated by his accounts, though Devon wondered if it was real interest or just a way to flatter him. In any case, their conversations wove a quiet intimacy between them.

One afternoon, with Max occupied elsewhere, Monica asked Devon to show her around town. They found themselves back in the square beneath a sky brushed with spring. Overhead, a pair of white storks circled and settled into their great nests.

"I've seen them before," Monica said softly. "Today they feel different."

"They used to migrate from Africa every spring," said Devon. "Over the years they stopped. Lost the instinct. Now they live here year-round."

She tilted her head to watch the slow arc of wings. "Why the black tips?"

Devon brightened. "Ah, that's a legend that goes back to Charlemagne. After his death, legend has it there was a brutal dispute over his lands. Violence broke out. The storks, heartbroken by what they saw, flew up to God and begged him to stop it, but God gave man free will, so he refused. Instead, he told the storks to dip their wings in black to mourn what they couldn't change."

Monica moved toward him, her green eyes darker now. "Do you think it helped?"

"You'll have to ask the storks," Devon said, with a faint, sad smile.

"Tell me another story," she said. "I knew I'd be bored and lost without you."

Devon couldn't pinpoint the exact moment he'd fallen under Monica's spell, only the sensation it left behind: the hot, churning weight in his gut whenever she was near, the way his normally steady thoughts turned to vapor. She scrambled his reason, reduced him to instinct.

"Have you read Goethe?" he asked.

"Of course. Everyone's read *Faust*," she said breezily.

Devon smiled. *She has no idea,* he thought, *how most people live, or what they read, or how they think.*

"He lived here once," Devon said. "In Strasbourg. He fell in love with a village girl, Friederike, but it didn't last. He left. She waited for him for the rest of her life. She kept the poems he wrote her. There's one I remember. *Wild Rose.* It stayed with me."

Monica leaned into him. "Recite it."

"I only remember the last few lines," he said.

> ...the impetuous boy plucked
> the wild rose from the heather;
> the rose defended herself and pricked him,
> but her cries of pain were to no avail;
> she simply had to suffer.
> Wild rose, wild rose, wild rose red,
> wild rose in the heather.

Quietly, Monica began to cry. Devon froze. He wasn't used to tears, not like this. He held her without saying anything, gently, as if words might break whatever was between them. He knew he didn't belong in Monica and Jerry's world. He might play the part, but he would always be a guest in their kingdom, never a citizen. Still, no amount of reason could undo what he felt. She'd trapped him, whether she meant to or not.

They walked back to the lodgings in silence, her shoulder brushed his now and then like a thought half-formed. That night she came to his room. They made love, quietly, without ceremony. They never spoke of it after, and it never happened again, but the memory stayed, like the line of a half-forgotten poem, buried somewhere deep and still burning.

⧗ ⧗ ⧗

It was Max who called to tell Devon that Monica had taken her own life.

"You were her one true friend," Max said quietly.

"I should have seen it coming," Devon replied. "I feel so damn guilty."

"We all saw it coming in some way," Max said. "None of us could stop it. Don't carry that weight. You gave her what happiness she could bear."

Jerry didn't attend the funeral. He had long since cut ties with Monica and disappeared into his world of wealth and fame. After the service, Devon took a leave from work. Max handed him a note Monica had left behind, a final request: She asked Devon to return to Ribeauville, the little town where their strange, beautiful connection had first come alive. He booked a room at the same hotel they had stayed in years ago. He wasn't surprised when, upon arrival, the concierge handed him a sealed envelope.

Monica had planned it all.

She said once that life was a game, a comedy, full of missteps, pretensions, and misunderstood lines. She laughed easily, captivated friends with her clever, sideways observations, but beneath the charm was a far more fragile creature who ached for approval, terrified of being truly known. Sadly, Devon doubted she ever figured out who she really was.

What he and Monica shared was never quite a relationship, at least not in the traditional sense. It was mostly long-distance, late-night phone calls, letters, fragments of truth wrapped in riddles. In recent years, she had opened up more, often spoke as though only he could be trusted with her secrets. Sometimes she would fall silent for long stretches. Devon never knew if she wanted a response or just hoped he'd sit in the silence with her, which he did.

She trusted him for his honesty, his mind, maybe even his steadiness. He should have seen the signs: the oscillation between giddy brilliance and bottomless despair. But he hadn't, or maybe he'd refused to. Love can soften the edges of truth until they no longer cut.

There had been signs. Her approach to sex, for one, unapologetically promiscuous, yet strangely detached. "If you do anything enough," she once told him with a weary sigh, "you just want to do it more." For Monica, sex was less about desire and more about the intimacy that came after, the vulnerability of a post-coital conversation, the truths whispered in the dark. People opened up to her because she had that gift: the ability to listen. Ironically, she could never truly open up herself, not even to Devon.

She wore her strength like armor. What he failed to grasp was that people often choose to die not out of weakness but in a final act of control. He remembered what she said of Baudelaire, "He tried to kill himself, but he was too weak." Monica was stronger than Devon realized. Now it was too late. He had failed her and failed himself.

He unfolded the letter she'd left for him. His hands trembled as he read. Once again, Monica spoke to him, only this time it was too late.

> Dearest Devon,
>
> I knew you'd come back to the place where it all began for us. You always were the faithful one. You must know by now you were my one true love. I never had the courage to say it aloud. I've never been brave, especially when it came to love. Love is strange, isn't it? To know, but not know, to want, but not want. Illusions shared and truths deferred. Do you remember when I asked you to be my bodyguard? You took that role so seriously, as if love and protection were incompatible. Maybe that's why we were never lovers in the ordinary sense. Or maybe I was wrong. Could we have truly been together? I've asked myself that question more times than I care to admit. Camus said life is absurd. Still, he asks us to be happy. I tried, Devon. God, how I tried, and yet I don't even believe in God. Why do I invoke Him now?
>
> Please don't blame yourself. You were never the cause. You never abandoned me. As a bodyguard, you were the best. More than I deserved. More than I could understand.
>
> Birth, sex, death, they follow like scenes in a play. Anticipation, climax, silence. The mystery continues, but not for me.

There's one last thing I've never told you, one thing I couldn't carry with me into the grave. That night, our night, we conceived a child I didn't allow to live. I carried that guilt like a hidden wound. I never found the right moment or the right words. I don't know if this confession hurts you. That's the last thing I'd want. I only know, I had to tell you.

Forgive me, Devon. Forgive me for everything.

Your wild rose,

Monica

Emma of Whiterashes

So, it's come to this.

I've decided to end my life; I've thought about it more times than I can count, fleetingly at first, in the way a shadow eclipses the sun. I'm serious this time. There's a plan.

I'm in London on business. Money, success, they came easily to me. Meaning, purpose, and love are another story. I was born with a skeptic's soul. Even as a child, the bright seed of hope never took root. It's no surprise that life turned out to be the mess it is.

Dinner alone at Inigo Jones. The food was exquisite, the silence unbearable. Waiters lingered just out of view, refilled my water glass after each perfunctory sip like silent sentinels of the void. Last night it was Rules, elegance draped in dust. Elderly women sat on each floor with calculators and quiet judgment, ready to tote up the bills. A friend suggested the Salisbury Pub. He neglected to mention that Oscar Wilde once held court there. Had I known, I wouldn't have been so startled by the boy in the chiffon scarf who watched me with eyes too old for his face.

Tomorrow, I leave London and head to Edinburgh by train. Then, I'll trek northward to Aberdeen and finally to Banff. A friend waits for me there. He knows the purpose of my journey. We've rehearsed it all.

The train crosses Berwick-upon-Tweed. The sea cliffs are blunt and gray. Smoke lingers above the trees. Outside, the world is silent and heartless, crystalline in its indifference. Inside, my chest tightens with a kind of anxious nothingness.

In Edinburgh the castle looms above The Royal Mile like a stone fist. Mary gave birth here to a boy who would rule England.

They rewarded her with a blade across the neck. History abhors a vacuum.

⧗ ⧗ ⧗

At last I'm on the bus to Banff in the final stretch. I've sent word. He'll meet me at the station.

A girl of four or five tender years catches my eye. She sits between her parents near the front of the bus. She stands on her seat and turns toward me. Our eyes meet. She smiles with her ruddy cheeks and full-fleshed face and bright eyes.

Outside, snow drifts down. Farmers in weathered tweed coats wade through winter fields. They tend their sheep and cattle, indifferent to the cold.

The heat on the bus is oppressive. The windows fog with breath and exhaustion. That little girl, her life still unshaped, doesn't know what the world will take from her. She smiles at me for no reason at all.

⧗ ⧗ ⧗

He was a kind man, patient, respectful, never dismissive. He answered her questions without making her feel foolish, and always found time to help, even though she wasn't really his client. She was, technically, but it never felt official. He gave generously of himself. She was grateful for that.

They had never met in person. She only ever spoke to him over the phone, called his office when the need arose. This time, the secretary answered.

"He's out at the moment. Would you like to leave a message, Emma?"

She hesitated. "No, thank you. I'll try again later."

Only after she hung up did it strike her that she hadn't said her name. Somehow the secretary had known.

"Emma of Whiterashes," she told the man on the bus so long ago. It felt right to add the place, as if it added weight or poetry to her small existence. Now the memory struck her as faintly ridiculous. Whiterashes, a name from another life, yet here it was again, circling back. She set the receiver down, leaned into the chair, and gazed out the window. Snow fell, soft, slow, and silent, like white butterflies might tumble through air, wings that flicker in no hurry, as if lost in time.

⧗ ⧗ ⧗

A little girl steps into a darkened room. She hesitates. The air is heavy, thick with a smell she doesn't understand; something sour and strange, like the scent of something gone. It's the smell of death, though she doesn't yet know what death smells like.

Her mother lies on the bed, propped up by pillows, her face pale and quiet. Thin bands of sunlight from the hallway stretch across the floor and slant over her face, turn it into patches of shadow and light.

"Come here, Emma. Take my hand."

Her mother's hand reaches out, slowly, painfully. Emma doesn't know how much it hurts. Her mother's face remains calm, the way it always did when she wanted to protect Emma from the truth.

It has been a long time since Emma has seen her mother. They haven't let her in much lately. Grown-up whispers and closed doors is all she's heard or seen. The moans and cries that come from this room at night sound like the monsters she used to fear beneath her bed. Now they live here, in the corners.

"Don't be afraid, love. Come to me."

Emma moves forward, carefully. She doesn't look up. She doesn't want to see. She places her small hand in her mother's and feels the brittle bones shift beneath the skin, the way autumn leaves crackle underfoot. The hand tightens gently around hers.

"Look at me, Emma. Look into my eyes."

"I can't, Mummy. I don't want to see.

"That's all right."

With the last of her strength, Emma's mother draws her daughter close. Emma lays her head against her mother's chest. She hears it there, the soft, uneven beat of a frail heart, like a bird tapping behind glass. She closes her eyes and tries to hold it all in place.

She remembers before the illness when they walked together through the woods, how she darted back and forth around her mother's legs. They sang silly songs. They laughed. They gathered wild orchids, lady slippers, pink and white, with petals like tiny shoes, soft and cinnamon-scented.

"Do you remember, Mummy?" she whispers. "Do you remember the lady slippers?"

There is no reply. Her mother's breath has gone quiet. Emma stays very still, and listens. Her mother is asleep.

⧗ ⧗ ⧗

The bus lumbers through the snow-covered pastures between Aberdeen and Banff, a white silence stretches out on either side. Now and then, a lone farmer trudges through the drifts, his silhouette dwarfed by the bleak expanse and the sheep that follow him like ghosts. I watch and wonder: What's the point? What's the point of any of this? Life unravels like a frayed thread, random, absurd, and ends in the same cold, dark earth for everyone. It ends as a lump of rot in a final silence. Meanwhile, we shuffle through the days, perform the same tired rituals, pretend they matter.

Across the aisle, the young girl stares out the window at the frozen fields. Her father dozes off, his chin falls to his chest. The mother looks ill, hollow, her body wrapped in an amber woolen coat like a bird buried in its own plumage. The girl's coat is plaid, warm with its blocks of black, red, brown, orange, and gray. Her name, she says when I ask, is Emma ... Emma of Whiterashes.

The hum of the bus lulled me to sleep. My plan changed.

Life isn't a straight line. It's a tangle of threads that converge only in hindsight, if at all. Before they step off the bus, I scribble my name and address on a scrap of paper and quietly slip it into the mother's coat pocket. A note for Emma's parents, if they find it and dare to read it.

My friend awaits me at the station.

We walk together past the cemetery on the way to his office, our boots crunch through the frost.

"Picked out your plot yet?" he asks, his tone dry, the smirk not unkind.

"Change of plans," I say.

I've got it figured out.

☒ ☒ ☒

The next day, Emma called the solicitor again.

"Oh, hello, Emma. I expected your call. I have some news, good news, I suppose."

"I'm confused," she said. "I don't understand why someone I never met would pay for my college and everything else. It's too much. I don't feel right about it. Honestly, I want it to stop. Is this even legal?"

There was a pause on the line.

"Hello?" she said. "Are you still there?"

"Yes, Emma. I'm here. Everything is legal, you have no worries on that account. I'm afraid it can't be stopped now. The arrangements were finalized some time ago."

"What arrangements?"

The solicitor's voice softened. "A friend of mine met you many years ago. You were just a child then, on a bus between Aberdeen and Gardenstown. Your mother was still alive. You likely don't remember."

Emma said nothing.

"My friend had plans to end his life. He had nothing to live for. He'd arranged everything, even the burial. On the bus everything changed for him. He said you gave him a reason to keep going. In his words, you saved his life."

Emma's chest tightened. "What do you mean? What did he want from me?"

"Nothing," the solicitor said gently. "It was just your presence that gave him what he needed, a reason to live. He passed away last month, from natural causes. He's buried here, in Gardenstown."

Emma stared at the wall, stunned. She didn't say goodbye. She simply hung up.

Once the initial shock subsided, Emma began to grasp the weight of the trust and everything it entailed. Others might have reacted with indulgence or extravagance, but Emma had grown up with nothing. To her, wealth wasn't freedom, it was responsibility. She felt a moral obligation to handle the fortune wisely. Real estate, stocks, tax codes, she studied them all, determined not to let the government, or her own inexperience, squander the gift this stranger had left her. At the very least, she owed him that much. Didn't she?

Emma dreamed of marriage, of children one day, of giving them the kind of life she never had, but that all changed. She became cautious, wary, consumed. Money distorts everything, even friends. Especially friends. Silence became her shield. She kept her thoughts to herself. She learned to listen more and speak less, and to trust no one completely.

Years passed. The trust multiplied. She doubled it. Tripled it. She built businesses, sold them, and started others. She was proud of her success. She was sharp and principled, an honest but formidable negotiator.

She was very good at making money, but at night, alone, she felt a quiet emptiness she couldn't explain. Something had slipped through her fingers, something vital but nameless. One day, with the force of an explosion, it all became clear.

Now I understand why he wanted to end his life, and what he saw in me, and why he did what he did. He saved himself. He handed me the weight he couldn't carry, the weight that nearly destroyed him. He gave me that burden.

The realization came too late.

She had no husband, no children, no life, only obligations. It was an arranged marriage. He had married her to wealth, and wealth grew on its own, like her mother's cancer: silent, relentless, and deadly.

She was a servant to the trust. What she lacked and yearned for was real trust, the kind that lives in friendship, love, and family. She was a brilliant machine, nothing more. Built to manage money, but not to feel, not to live. *Wealth is a drug. Once it owns you, you don't get to go back.*

She felt what that man on the bus felt: his despair, his desire to be free from it all. She understood his final act. It was not her salvation, but a transfer of his burden so that he could be free.

⧗⧗⧗

In Aberdeenshire there's a town tucked so deep beneath a sheer cliff that the sun rarely touches it. Emma stands at the edge of that cliff; the wind tugs at her coat as she stares at the relentless sea. Below, a small fishing boat rises and falls with the chop; its hull glints briefly in the gray light.

Behind her, a young boy walks hand in hand with his parents. They weave through the grasses and gather wildflowers. As they approach, the boy steps forward and offers Emma a fistful of blossoms, their colors soft against the bleak backdrop.

She curtsies playfully and accepts. "Thank you, my prince," she says with a smile.

"Please," she adds to the parents, "let me send something in return. May I have your address?" They tell her they're from Edinburgh. She writes it down. They walk on, their laughter trails behind them in the wind.

Emma stays at the edge. She looks down at the rocks and the waves. A spray of foam rises up and nearly hits her.

It's not too late.

Not yet.

⧗⧗⧗

The solicitor blinked, stunned. "You want to transfer *all* the proceeds of the trust to this boy's account in Edinburgh?"

"Yes," she replied without hesitation. "Every last penny."

⧗⧗⧗

I jolt awake as the bus jerks to a sudden halt at the station.

Through the window, I watch the little girl in the plaid coat step off with her parents. Moments later, they vanish into the crowd.

If only, I whisper to no one. *If only.*

I see my friend in the crowd as I exit the bus.

It's time.

Lois

Two kinds of people attend public meetings: Those who raise their hands, and those who don't. Lois belonged to the latter. It wasn't because she was afraid; quite the opposite, she was on a mission, but long ago she learned that it was best to stay quiet until the time was right. It wasn't fear that held her back. Nothing rattled Lois. She had to lay the groundwork first.

She knew real change didn't happen at the front of a room where the two sides shouted into the wind. It happened quietly, person to person. She had a skill, a practiced charm that could turn minds like a locksmith works a pin tumbler.

Persuasion, after all, was a kind of dance. Lois moved minds with the grace of a young Isadora Duncan.

"Why? Why, Lois, wudn't you speak up if you had sumpin' ta say?" Armand snapped shut his Colonel Littleton leather binder, the one embossed with AMH—Armand Maxwell Haverfield. He liked to say it stood for "Are Man in Havana," like in the movie, not realizing the euphemism.

Lois tilted her head; her chestnut hair fell out of its bun and flowed gently down the sides of her face. Her velvet voice was soft but firm. "Armand, you know as well as I do, they don't listen to people like me, but they do listen to *you*. You're a pillar in this community."

She batted her eyelashes, aware how it affected him. Her brown eyes sparkled with mischief. She stepped closer, close enough that her words warmed his chest. "Aw, now, you give me too much credit," said Armand. His cheeks blushed the soft hue of poached salmon. He liked the sound of her flattery.

"Now, Armand, don't pretend. You've got a gift. This town's a mess of factions: hippies still caught up in Woodstock; shop owners who'd vote for a rock if it balanced the books, and the holier-than-thou folks who won't sneeze without asking God's permission. You're the only one who can talk to all of them. You're the bridge."

She's right, Armand thought. *I can de-thorn a cactus if I set my mind to it, but mediators burn just as easily as matches. One must be careful what one gets mixed up in.*

"I'll think on it, Lois. I really will, but next time, *you* speak up, ya hear? You'd be surprised who might listen."

Armand was vain. Lois knew this, and she knew how to use it to her advantage.

"Thanks, Armand. I need your help. Do put some thought to it." She gave his hand a squeeze. "I'll be in touch."

Her perfume lingered in the room long after she'd left, wrapped itself around Armand and unwound him.

The town was fractured, sure, but Lois knew how to get things done one person at a time. She and Fletcher had discussed this, and she couldn't let him down. His untimely death made his last wish even more important. Lois and Fletcher were artists. They were not among the wealthy movers and shakers of their small seaside community, but an artist is never poor. An artist has the ability to see beyond the mundane.

As Lois made her way home, a green Chevy Cheyenne with oversized tires slowed beside her. Rich Dexter was behind the wheel. Casey, his wife, leaned across the passenger seat, window down, her voice already sharp.

"I can't believe you really want to go through with this," she said.

The Dexters had money, new money, that hung on them like an ill-fitted suit. Everything they owned was oversized and gleamed too brightly. They dropped the names of celebrities, and confused fame with greatness, familiarity with substance, and novelty with depth. Casey used Lois to tip her toe into the artworld. Rich fantasized a more physical relationship.

Lois didn't break stride. "Going through with what?"

"Oh, come on," Casey said. "You know what."

Lois smirked. "Don't believe everything you read in the *Beaufort Times.*"

Rich kept the truck crawling along beside Lois. His hands gripped the wheel, his eyes locked on the road ahead.

"I don't," Casey said. "But seriously, do you actually think it's a proper thing to do? Your plan is blasphemous. I thought Pastor Mike spoke out against it pretty effectively."

Lois stood still, and Rich stopped the car. Lois leaned toward the window and looked directly at Casey. Rich still wouldn't look at her.

"Cat got your tongue, Rich?" Lois said sweetly, with a glint of mischief. She remembered that Rotary Club banquet, just the two of them in the kitchen, Rich's hand on her hip like he owned the place.

Casey turned to her husband. "For heaven's sake, Rich, can't you at least say hello?"

"Hello, Lois," he muttered but kept his eyes ahead.

Casey pressed on. "So, you'll give up the idea, right?"

"I always thought you two were free-market types," Lois said. "To each her own. No nanny-state rules? Have you suddenly become Democrats?"

That landed. Rich finally glanced at her.

"Hell no," he said.

"Well, that's good to know," said Lois. She gave them both a nod and veered off the road onto a wooded path.

Casey called after her, not ready to let it go.

"See you tomorrow night," Lois said over her shoulder. "I've got places to be."

Casey turned to her husband. "What is it with you and Lois? She always manages to get under your skin."

Rich stared ahead, jaw tight. "She's not wrong about the government."

"Oh, sure," Casey scoffed. "What next, you going to start driving on the wrong side of the road?"

Rich didn't answer. Some things were better left unsaid. *That Lois,* he thought, *too damn mouthy, but she has nice tits.*

⧗ ⧗ ⧗

The next morning, Johnny Johnson invited Lois over for coffee. The weather was perfect. They sat outside on his deck and soaked up the sun. After a few sips, Johnny pulled a joint out of his shirt pocket.

"Wanna toke?" he asked.

"Why not?" said Lois. "Go ahead, light up and pass it over."

She knew what was coming. She was ready for it.

Johnny lit up and exhaled a flawless smoke ring. "So... I guess you've heard the rumors."

"Rumors?" Lois played innocent. She liked to watch men sweat.

Johnny shifted in his seat. "Are you really going through with it? I mean, I think it's kind of badass, but is it even legal?"

Lois grinned. "Since when has legal ever stopped you, Johnny?"

The weed had kicked in. Lois looked radiant, and Johnny inched closer.

She caught the look in his eye. *Time to exit gracefully.*

"Don't answer that," she said with a laugh. "I'm feeling a little lightheaded. Better go get ready for the big event."

As she stood, Johnny called after her, "What's the environmental impact?"

His eyes sparkled with genuine curiosity.

He's into this, she thought.

"Don't worry, sweetheart. Taxidermy's carbon neutral," she called back over her shoulder.

Back at home, Lois sat on the edge of her bed and honed her plan. She wasn't worried about the conservatives or the liberals, they were predictable. It was those God-fearing Christians who had the biggest objections. Casey was right about Pastor Mike. He was a force to be reckoned with. That's where Mel came in. Mel was a seasoned actor with a gravel voice and a crooked smile. He'd once been described as the meanest, toughest son of a bitch in town.

Religious folks love a macho man, but they don't like uppity women. Lois needed to play it smart. She'd let Mel take the heat. He and Armand could be her front line. They were an unbeatable duo.

Lois lay down for a quick nap; she needed to sober up before she made any big moves. When she woke in the late afternoon, her plan was fully formed.

She called Armand.

"Hey, I'm coming over to run a few things by you before the meeting."

"What do ya mean, 'run a few things by me'?" said Armand. "Ain't you gonna stand up and speak your piece like I told ya?"

"I'll explain when I get there," said Lois.

When Lois arrived, Armand paced around nervously. He poured two glasses of wine, Bordeaux, naturally, and waited until she was seated before he spoke.

"I take it you've got a plan," he said. "Because I'm having second thoughts."

Lois leaned in. Her lashes fluttered like fans and her soft brown eyes disarmed him as usual. "You *do* support me, don't you, Armand?"

Armand sighed, and swirled the wine in his glass. "My dear, this whole idea is absolute madness."

That wasn't the answer Lois expected.

She blinked, just once.

"There's no precedent," Armand continued. "You're my granddaughter, Lois. Of course I'll help you, but what you propose will shock this town's sensibilities."

"That's why you need to get Mel onboard," she said.

"Mel? That sanctimonious zealot? Why in the name of all that's holy would *he* support this?"

"He owes you, doesn't he?" Lois said coolly. "Besides, there is a precedent, one that Mel will absolutely eat up when he hears it. Ever hear of Jules Verreaux?"

Armand frowned. "Who the hell is Jules Verreaux?"

"Sit tight. This is going to sound...unusual. Just trust me." She took a sip of wine. "The short version goes like this: Verreau was a bold French adventurer. He was a man's man, Mel's type. He ventured deep into Africa to collect, let's say, *specimens,* for museums. He brought back a stuffed African warrior." Armand's eye grew wide. "Yes, *stuffed,* Armand. Taxidermied. Verreau toured the museums of Europe for decades with his African warrior."

Armand choked. "Lord Amighty!"

"I know," Lois said with a smile. "Mel will love it. He'll take on the role of Verreaux's disciple, a great white savior. All you have to do is tell him the story. Juice it up a bit. I'll handle the rest."

Armand stared at her for a long moment. "You are a marvel," he said.

"I know," she said with a satisfied smile.

She leaned forward, voice low and conspiratorial. "Here's how we play it. You present my proposal to the council. Appeal to Rich Dexter's libertarian streak to get him onboard; that'll secure the business folks. Next, pitch it as an eco-friendly solution to pull in the liberals. My neighbor Johnny will back me just to get me into bed. That will take care of the space cadets. Finally, stroke Mel's ego. Tell him he will be as famous as Jules Verreaux. He'll bring in the Christians. Game, set, match."

Armand refilled both glasses. "Well, seems like you've thought of everything."

"I'll be ever so grateful, Armand. I'll be in your debt forever."

"One question."

"Shoot."

"How exactly do you plan to taxidermy him?"

"My dead husband?" Lois asked sweetly.

"Well, you don't have another one lined up, have you?" Armand chuckled.

"Don't worry," Lois said. She raised her eyebrows and grinned. "I've been reading up on it."

Reclaiming Willard's Trophies

(Apologies to Richard Brautigan and Mikhail Bulgakov)

Before the operation, the dog had a haunted look, if dogs can look haunted. Then the scalpel cut not just flesh but something deeper, something cosmic. It was as if the surgery tore a hole in the fabric of the universe. Boundaries unraveled. Dogs, humans, time, memory, everything got scrambled.

Elim bolted upright in bed, and rubbed the dream from his eyes.

"Jeepers," he gasped. "Something's wrong in my head."

"What now?" his mother asked. She didn't look up from her book. Patricia Valentina, unshaken by her son's outbursts, turned a page and blinked slowly; her indigo lashes cast flickers across the room. "Don't tell me is that damn dog again."

Elim squeezed his eyes shut. "The knife. I hear it. Slice, slice, slice. Over and over."

"Let it go, Elim. Dog gone. You boy now, not dog. I had dog, now I have son. Trade made. Done." She waved a hand and went back to her book.

Elim collapsed onto the bed, his eyes fixed on the ceiling.

"People of zee worl... relax," croaked a voice.

"What bird said that?" Patricia muttered.

Willard, the papier-mâché bird on the dresser, gave Elim a wink.

"Why do we have that bird?" Elim asked.

Patricia Valentina ignored him. If she answered, it would spiral into a conversation, and she was knee-deep into the zipless fuck chapter in *Fear of Flying.* She wasn't about to put her book down for a bird debate.

"I can't just let my dog nature go, Mom," Elim murmured. "Before the operation, I made eye contact with a beautiful little bitch. We understood each other. She was Russian. We spoke in Russian."

He added the last part just to needle her. Patricia Valentina, who claimed to be the secret lovechild of Frida Kahlo and Leon Trotsky, tolerated no questioning of her complicated lineage, no matter how absurd.

Mierda, she thought. She hated interruptions during good sex scenes, even fictional ones, but when she saw the pain flicker behind Elim's eyes, her artist's heart softened.

"Dog gone," she said gently. "But you still here. Come. Put head in my lap. I rub the hurt away."

Elim rested his head on her legs and sighed.

"Maybe this is all the butterfly effect," he said after a moment.

"What is?" Patricia asked. She thought of her mother's butterfly paintings gathering dust in a closet, but couldn't see the connection.

"You know, Mom," Elim said. "Chaos theory."

Patricia Valentina blinked. "Chaos is theory? Life is chaos, sure. What this got to do with butterfly?"

"It's the idea that a butterfly flaps its wings on one side of the world and it starts a hurricane on the other," Elim explained.

"Ah," said Patricia Valentina, nodding sagely. "You mean like gossip."

She reached up. One of her press-on nails had migrated into Elim's hair.

"No, Mother," Elim snapped. "It's science."

"Science schmience," Patricia Valentina exclaimed, not entirely sure what she meant, only that Elim's tone disturbed her. Something was wrong. She made a note to text Victor, her professor friend, in case a... recalibration was in order.

"You worried about bowling trophies again?" she asked, and instantly regretted it.

Elim stiffened. His face shifted through a spectrum, pale, then flushed, then an odd shade of cautionary orange. Something was off. Very off.

"I don't want to talk about the trophies," he said darkly.

That look, half troubled, half eager, gave Patricia pause. She'd seen it before. It was a prelude to something. Something Elim couldn't stop.

"I know, my precious," she said gently. "I sorry, Elim. I not mean upset you."

Patricia Valentina looked at Willard, the looming papier-mâché bird who stood three feet tall in their living room like a forgotten idol. His long black legs and tricolor plumage, red, white, blue in no recognizable pattern, seemed more mournful now. His eyes, those big round things, stared past her, and his belly sagged with theatrical grief. Willard's beak, elegant as a stork's, jutted forward accusingly.

Everything had changed since the trophies vanished. Willard used to be surrounded by them. They'd given him a kind of power, a makeshift shrine. Now he just stood there. Empty. Less than he'd been.

"That damn Richard Brautigan," thought Patricia Valentina. "Why he bring Willard into it?" Her thoughts slipped, as they often did, toward sex. The trophies always reminded her. That husband of hers, and his... preferences.

The bowling trophies have no mercy. The bowling trophies are a super race.

That's what Richard Brautigan wrote.

Elim went silent, and focused on Willard.

Patricia Valentina gently ruffled his thick, doglike hair, the way she did when he was a small puppy and couldn't sleep. When his shoulders finally relaxed, she plucked her rogue fingernail from his curls and carefully reapplied it. Maybe a change would do him good.

"I think we find you a job, Elim," she said, as she noticed the chipped polish on her toes. She'd have to call Jen Li for a pedicure.

"Job is good, right?"

"Maybe," Elim murmured.

She nodded, satisfied.

Yes, this is good thing for Elim.

⧗ ⧗ ⧗

Elim woke up late the next morning. He looked better, more present, to Patricia Valentina. Before she could say a word, he brought it up."

"You were right, Mom. A job wouldn't hurt. With Mr. Logan's boys in prison, I bet he needs someone at the garage."

Patricia beamed. She'd just come back from the hairdresser, her hair now a bold spiced cherry red. The color made her feel electric.

"Yes, Elim. Your father told me this morning, Mr. Logan needs someone for the night shift." She gave a little shiver at the thought of having her evenings to herself. This, she thought, would be good thing.

Elim squinted at her. "What happened to your hair?"

"A little surprise for your father," Patrcia laughed, pleased he'd noticed. She hoped John would, too. He was a filmmaker, always surrounded by gorgeous, wide-eyed girls with tight clothes and looser morals. Patricia knew she had to keep her edge. Things between them had cooled ever since John returned Mr. Logan's bowling trophies.

Spoiler Alert

Mr. Logan was an ace mechanic, a transmission whisperer, the proud owner of a garage along Highway 80 somewhere between Sacramento and Reno. He had three sons, clean-cut, all-American types, and champion bowlers. Their proudest possessions were their bowling trophies, which they displayed like sacred relics.

One night, the boys came home from a movie and found their shrine empty. The trophies were gone.

Something inside them snapped.

What began as a search turned into a rampage. They crisscrossed the country in a fever of revenge, transformed from golden boys to violent maniacs. They would stop at nothing to recover their trophies: break and enter, torture, kill.

There were three Logan sisters too, but they're not relevant in the story.

By some cosmic accident, the trophies ended up in Marin County. John, husband to Patricia Valentina, discovered them in the trunk of a rusted-out car. He didn't know whose they were. He thought they would look good around Willard, his papier-mâché bird. He brought them home and arranged them in a little tableau that, for reasons we won't get into, radically improved his and Patricia Valentina's sex life.

Weeks later, the Logan boys received a tip, from an Eskimo, that the trophies were inside apartment 1 of a certain nondescript building. Acting on that tip, they burst into the home of Bob and Constance, upstairs neighbors of John and Patricia Valentina.

Unaware they had the wrong apartment, the Logan boys gunned Bob and Constance down in their sleep. It wasn't hard, they were already half-dead inside. Constance had contracted a venereal disease during a drunken one-night stand with a washed-up lawyer, and Bob hadn't touched her since.

Unbeknownst to the Logans, the trophies were downstairs in apartment 2, but John, ever the prankster, had swapped the apartment numbers weeks earlier: 1 was now upstairs, 2 downstairs. The boys didn't question it. That was their mistake.

"You're one smart cookie," Patricia Valentina whispered to John that night. "You save our lives."

They made love as Johnny Carson laughed in the background.

The Logan boys were arrested and sent to prison. That's the gist of it.

Richard Brautigan wrote about all this a long time ago. The butterfly effect was probably at work somewhere, but we won't go into that now.

Patricia Valentina longed for a child. John, her husband, was barren, something spoken of only once, softly, like a prayer gone wrong. In his place, she had Pucho Pequeño, a scrappy street mutt the color of dried tobacco leaves. With a wry smile, she named him "Little Pudge," though he was lean and nervous and watched everything. A dog could ease loneliness, yes, but her heart ached for a son, something deeper, something final.

She asked Victor one evening, between drinks and half-revealed desires. "Is there a way," she murmured, "to turn a dog into a boy?"

Victor hesitated, but only for a breath. He'd once confessed, during a fevered night in her bed, that he experimented with the boundaries between species, fringe science whispered into her ear like foreplay. It had excited them both. Patricia, a Spanish teacher with an eye for drama, called it *una fantasía profunda.* Victor, always helpless before the lilt of Latin vowels, hummed "From Granada to Seville... in the quiet of the night..." whenever he got aroused.

"*Sí, señora,*" he said now with a sly wink and a trace of arrogance.

When John was away, Patricia indulged herself. "What's good for the goose is good for the gander," she said aloud one afternoon, adjusting her lace push-up bra in the hallway mirror. Victor took her right there on the kitchen table. He moaned like a beast, drooled across her chest with the hunger of some monster uncaged.

In the living room, Pucho Pequeño lay curled in a shaft of sunlight, unaware of the spell the two conjurers spun around him, but not everyone was oblivious. Willard, the papier-mâché bird perched above the mantel, listened closely. He always listened. No one thought he could hear, but Willard had been trained on TV, on sitcoms, soaps, and late-night dramas. He knew what sex sounded like, what betrayal meant.

Willard also knew what mattered most to him: the bowling trophies. Fifty of them gleamed in their crooked rows, untouched by dust, and they became the only things Willard had ever seen that he truly cared for. They were gone now, and that stuck in his craw.

Victor didn't like the bird. "You should get rid of that creepy thing," he muttered afterward, as he buttoned his corduroy pants. "I can't perform with it in the next room. It's a total turnoff."

"Willard is an acquired taste," Patricia said. She fluttered her eyelashes as she reclined in the afterglow. "In this great land of America, the bird and the trophies are part of the package."

Victor grimaced but said nothing more. He was too deep in now, and besides, he had to admit, sometimes, the stranger things stirred him more than he cared to admit.

He told Patricia Valentina she'd have to wait until fate smiled on them to make the transformation. Fate smiled sooner than either of them expected.

⧗ ⧗ ⧗

Victor had friends who dealt in corpses, no questions asked. They wanted the bodies gone, and Victor needed parts. Organs were his to use as he pleased, but the rest had to vanish without a trace.

The day after his fevered night with Patricia Valentina, Victor received a knock at his lab door.

"When did he die?" Victor asked. His pulse rose in anticipation.

"Three hours ago," his friend answered.

Victor didn't hesitate. He called Patricia.

"Bring your dog to the lab. Now."

Within minutes, Patricia arrived, clutching little Pucho to her chest. Victor operated with the precision of a seasoned surgeon, though his doctorate was in mathematics. His hands moved with the confidence of someone possessed, methodical, unshaken.

Then they waited.

Days passed in a haze of worry and silence. One morning, the impossible happened.

Pucho stood on his hind legs... and laughed.

Patricia fainted.

The next day, Pucho spoke. Haltingly at first, then fluently, with the oily charm of a practiced politician. His tail dropped off soon after. The fur thinned. His face changed, and molded into something eerily familiar. Not just human, but something between John and Patricia, the way couples begin to look like one another after years of sharing breath and bed.

Within a month, he passed for a boy. Almost. His face still bore sharp lines, and his snout never quite disappeared.

"You must be careful what you say around him," Victor warned Patricia one evening. "I don't know what memories lie dormant in that brain I stitched together. They could be dog, they could be man, or both. A memory, or something worse, could resurface. Something he saw. Something he felt. If it does, he could unravel. You need to guide him. Watch him closely. Don't let him slip back."

Patricia's eyes glistened with fervor.

"I understand what it means to be mother," she said, and stomped the floor for emphasis. "Is my dream, Viktor. I no screw it up."

She named the boy Elim after her grandfather. It meant *strong.* She bathed him, clothed him, brushed his dark hair into a part, and whispered prayers over his bed. This act of creation, of mothering, made her feel alive. It made John love her a little more.

One night, from the living room, a voice echoed.

"What's that noise?" Elim called, startled to hear himself speak.

"Don't worry, my precious," Patricia purred from the bedroom. "Stay out there with Willard and his trophies."

John was pleased with the name. "Elim suits him," he told Patricia. "The boy and the bird, they're a team now."

"Team? What you mean, 'team'?" Patricia asked, and narrowed her eyes.

John gestured to the wooden bird. "Willard's expression changes sometimes. That's not a trick of the light, it's craftsmanship. Pucho's face used to shift the same way. And now Elim's does too."

"I don't notice this," Patricia whispered. The words stayed with her. Something about it didn't sit right.

There was something else inside the boy.

Something... bird.

"Damn fool," she whispered. "Victor got some bird in the boy."

⧗ ⧗ ⧗

Elim hesitated. Should he ask Mr. Logan for a job? His thoughts began to churn, mechanical and deliberate, like one of Mr. Logan's old transmissions grinding through its gears. Just as his decision started to take shape, his mind was hijacked, jerked sideways into a memory of the operation.

He slipped backward into fur and instinct. He wasn't Elim anymore; he was the dog again.

A voice spoke in his head, low and familiar.

"Operations are dangerous."

Elim spun around. Empty street. No one.

What the hell? Are there voices?

"Not voices, just me. The dog you used to be."

"Dogs can't talk, and you're dead. That's a fact."

"Not dead. Transformed. By a kind of equation. A new identity. You still smell like me. Like a dog."

"Why would I believe that?" Elim's heart knocked against his ribs. This wasn't just memory; it was something else, something deeper. "I'm not crazy."

"You know the truth," the dog said." When I walk, I read the ground like a history book. Piss, shit, sweat, rust, the whole world's written there. That's what dogs do. You remember."

Then, silence. As sudden as it had come, the voice was gone.

Elim stood still for a moment, to let the world return to normal. No voices. No fur. Just the faint smell of oil and old rubber from the shop behind him.

Fantasies can be your undoing. That was what Victor once told his mother during one of his professorial visits. Elim never forgot it. Especially now.

⧗ ⧗ ⧗

Cars tore down the highway like lemmings, bound for Reno—*The Biggest Little City in the World.* They'd be back again soon, after they'd saved enough to lose all over again. Gambling was a disease, but for the garage, it was good business.

"The hours are ten at night to six in the morning. Think you can handle that?"

Elim nodded. He already knew he had the job; his mother told him. Mr. Logan visited her sometimes when Elim's father was off somewhere shooting a movie. John didn't know Patricia Valentina was sleeping with Mr. Logan. If he had, he wouldn't have returned the boys' trophies.

Elim hated secrets, but that was just how things worked.

Willard missed those trophies. His parents missed them too. Elim heard them talk about it one night, after a movie. It must've been before the operation. His ears had flopped over and he'd barked in reflex.

Mr. Logan needed someone to watch the place at night. Someone who wouldn't scare easy when the road got strange, when the misfits drifted between Reno and Sacramento under the neon moon.

"I can handle it," Elim said. "The hours, the job. Sure."

He didn't know *how,* exactly, but as he stood there, a plan started to form, one that might bring the trophies back. He had good memories from those days. When they were all together.

Mr. Logan looked him over, his expression unreadable.

"You sure you're up for the people who show up this late? They aren't like folks you meet at the grocery store."

Elim peeled back his lips, showed his teeth, raised his eyebrows. "I can handle them. But I'm not a mechanic, Mr. Logan. I can pump gas, check oil, clean windows... but engines? No."

"You don't need to fix anything," Logan said. "That's my job. You just handle the basics. If someone needs real work, they can sleep it off until I roll in."

"Fair enough," Elim said, and turned to go. "See you tonight."

"One more thing," Mr. Logan added. "This place is dead-center nowhere. Halfway to Reno. Weird stuff happens. We've got a panic button under the counter. Use it if you have to, but I'd rather you didn't."

"No problem," said Elim. "You can count on me. I'm as dependable as Argos."

He regretted the line immediately. Why had he said that? Hopefully Mr. Logan hadn't read *The Odyssey.*

The kid looks a little like that dog Patricia Valentina used to have, Mr. Logan thought as he watched Elim leave. *I wonder what happened to it.*

"Well," Logan called after him, "It was good of your father to bring the trophies back. My boys'll be glad to have 'em if they ever get out. I think you'll do just fine."

Elim felt his back prickle, like it did when the hair rose. He ignored it. The urge to wag his tail struck him hard, but his tail was long gone.

"Our pleasure," Elim muttered, then barked quietly under his breath.

He didn't need much sleep, afternoon naps were enough. Old instinct. And the money would help. He already knew what to do with the first paycheck: a subscription to *Eves,* that women's magazine his mother lingered over at the liquor store while buying her favorite white wine.

It had pictures of naked men in it. They made her smile, and when she smiled, she laughed. Elim liked that.

On his first night at the garage, Elim found a key that unlocked the office. Inside was a drawer stuffed with cash. He started to skim, just a little each shift. Mr. Logan never seemed to notice. The office also held Willard's bowling trophies, stashed like afterthoughts. Elim figured he'd reclaim them when the time was right.

His duties were simple: pump gas, check oil, fill radiators, test batteries, inflate tires. Routine stuff. He had plenty of downtime to plot the retrieval of those trophies.

Sometimes customers drove off without paying. The security cameras caught their plates. Mr. Logan handed the footage to the cops.

Most shifts were quiet, until one early morning when a man stumbled into the garage.

"Call an ambulance," he said. "My friend shot himself. Don't call the police."

He reeked of liquor and stared straight through Elim.

"You better check on your friend," Elim said calmly. "I'll call the ambulance right now."

The man went back outside. Elim picked up the phone and dialed the police.

"There's a man who's been shot," he said. "Send an ambulance too. Hurry."

When the cruiser rolled up, the man's face twisted with rage, but there wasn't a thing he could do. The ambulance arrived moments later.

"You did the right thing, kid," one officer said. "Man's dead. Friend says it was self-inflicted. Doesn't add up. They'd been drinking; we found the empties. Friend claims the gun just went off when he pulled it from a holster. Sounds like crap to me. We'll run forensics, but my guess? There's more to it. Good instincts, kid."

Elim growled softly and wiggled his butt against the cold concrete.

The man in the back of the cruiser glared at him as they pulled away. Elim felt electrified. He dropped to the floor and writhed in a euphoric spasm. His ears drooped, and drool slid down his chin.

Later, he called home.

"I'm sorry I put you in danger, Elim," his mother said. She was in bed with the professor. Elim could hear Victor's damp, wheezy breathing.

"You should quit that job. Come home."

In the background, a voice sang: "From Granada to Seville...."

"No, Mom. I want to stay. I like it here."

"You are not safe, Elim. This is bad," Patricia Valentina said.

Elim had already hung up.

Victor pulled her back into bed. By morning, she had forgotten all about it.

Elim sometimes worked on cars even though it wasn't part of his job. *If I can help someone out and pocket a little cash, why not?* he figured.

One afternoon, a family pulled in with a busted fuel pump. Elim had seen the big repair manual in the office, dog-eared pages filled with diagrams and step-by-steps. He knew the part was in inventory, so he rolled up his sleeves and got to it, following the instructions like a recipe. Replacing the pump was no harder than flushing a bird from the brush.

He didn't tell Mr. Logan. The customer paid cash. Elim slipped the bills into his pocket. *Mr. Logan'll never miss one lousy fuel pump,* he told himself. *I earned it. I did the work.* Over time, he picked up a handful of simple fixes and made decent money on the side.

One night, a stocky Puerto Rican man rumbled in on a motorcycle, a much younger Filipina woman sat behind him. They wore matching leather jackets with red, white, and blue stars, loud and proud. The man looked to be around fifty. The girl, maybe twenty.

"Can you fix a fouled-up carb on a bike, kid?" the man asked.

"There's no mechanic here until morning," Elim said. He didn't want anything to do with motorcycles, too much trouble. Plus, the girl had caught his eye. Something stirred in him he hadn't felt in a long while.

"Hmph." The man glanced around the office. "You got any food in this joint?"

Elim had a sudden impulse to bark, but held it in. "The restaurant's closed, but I've got some sardines and saltines in the back. You're welcome to them."

"Wepa! I love sardines and crackers." He turned to the girl. "Sit your ass down, baby. We'll wait for the mechanic."

"Might be a few hours," Elim said.

"No problem. We'll camp out. I'll take those snacks if you don't mind. I'll pay."

"No charge," Elim said, eyes drifting to the girl. She noticed. She didn't look away.

"I'm Big Tony," the man said. "That's Olga. Best girl I ever had. Think she's gonna stick. Sometimes shit goes sideways on a bike, kid. When I see it comin', I yell 'Jump!' Olga's the only one who actually does it. That's why she's still here."

A few beers and two sardine tins later, Big Tony passed out in the corner. Olga locked eyes with Elim, then led him to the storage room. What happened there felt familiar, like something from another life. He liked it. She seemed to, too.

Days passed. Elim found more ways to line his pockets.

One afternoon, two mob types showed up with slot machines.

"Here's the deal," one said. "You set these up, find some folks to play, and we cut you in. We come back end of the month to settle."

"Okey dokey," Elim said, something he'd picked up from Olga. After they left, he barked twice under his breath, then checked to make sure no one heard.

He remembered guys like this. He knew the type, knew the angles. He found an old storage building and filled it with the machines. Word spread fast. Soon, locals came from miles away and pumped in quarters like addicts at a church bingo night.

Elim stuffed the cash into his pocket. His plan was simple: vanish before the wiseguys came back. That meant picking up the pace.

The next few days passed quickly.

Then Olga showed up, out of nowhere, just like that.

"Hey, there," she purred. Her eyes glittered as she flashed a grin full of perfect white teeth.

Elim started to pant like a mutt who'd just caught a whiff of steak. "Hey. What's goin' on?"

"I can't stop thinking about you."

He blinked. "What about Big Tony?"

"I left him. He was dead weight. Had some cash stashed. I took it while he was passed out drunk. Fair exchange, considering what I gave him." She stepped in close, hands on her hips, chest out, with a smile that dripped sugar and venom. "I know a place we can go. Off the map. You in?"

Elim gave a low growl. "Ruff, ruff."

Tempting didn't even begin to cover it.

"Yeah, I'm in, but I need a couple days to wrap things up."

"What kinds of things?"

"Just things." He glanced toward the gravel road. "I've got a cabin not far from here. Quiet. Lay low there while I tie up loose ends."

She narrowed her eyes, with fire behind them. "This isn't just a warm bed and goodbye, is it?"

"No, no. I got a stash too, and I can score us a ride. Just need a little time."

She gave him a slow once-over. He was still that eager puppy she remembered. That's what made him irresistible in the first place. "All right," she said. "But if you screw me over, I'll find you and tear your balls off."

Elim laughed. "You're a hot tamale, Olga. Here's the cabin key. I'm off in an hour."

Meanwhile, something gnawed at Mr. Logan.

He couldn't prove it, but the numbers weren't right. Cash from the register had started to vanish, just a little at first, like a slow leak. Inventory too: parts gone without a trace. Like most small-time bosses with big secrets, he'd skimmed and hid the real books, but now someone was stealing from him.

There was only one likely culprit.

Elim.

That made things complicated.

Mr. Logan couldn't risk exposure, not with his side thing with Patricia Valentina. If his wife found out, well, if she were a transmission, he could replace her, but she wasn't. She was jealous and dangerous.

He picked up the phone.

"Patricia, I think your Elim's been stealing."

Her voice exploded like a lit match in a gas can.

"You say my Elim is thief? *¡Ay, caramba!* I cut off your *cojones!*" *Click.*

Mr. Logan stared at the receiver.

Yeah... better think this through.

Rash moves get men killed.

The next morning, as Elim hosed down the tow trucks, a woman staggered through the garage's backdoor. She wobbled like a marionette cut from its strings and collapsed on the oil-stained floor.

Elim rushed to her side. The acrid tang of cheap booze hung around her like a curse. He jogged out back and spotted a new Ford truck parked crookedly against the chain-link fence. A man was slumped inside, passed out cold. His mouth hung open.

This is it, Elim thought.

He unlocked the storeroom. Inside were the weapons the Logan brothers used to kill Constance and Bob. There was also a worn copy of *The Greek Anthology,* a battered paperback of *The Story of O,* some comic books, a leather belt, and a bundle of rags.

None of it meant anything to Elim. What he wanted were the bowling trophies and the cash.

He knew it was wrong, but he also knew what it meant to ignore a gift horse. The habit of taking what wasn't his was baked deep into the clay of his past. He took what he wanted, locked the door again, and slipped the key back into its hiding place.

He tied up the man and woman with bungee cords and left a note pinned to the man's jacket:

> I made Elim steal. You will not find me. Do not look.
> I'm that attorney who loved Constance, the woman your
> boys killed.
> This is payback for your SOB sons.

Then Elim and Olga loaded the trophies and the money into the truck.

"What's the deal with these trophies?" Olga asked, as she squinted suspiciously at the pile.

"They're Willard's," Elim said. "We're dropping them off before we hit the road."

Across town, Patricia Valentina had cooled off from Mr. Logan's ugly accusations. Her rage had pivoted; now it was Victor she wanted answers from.

She called and told him to come over immediately.

Victor, ever the romantic optimist, hummed a tune as he strolled to her front door.

"From Granada to Seville..." he sang softly, already half-aroused by the thought of reconciliation.

The door flew open.

"*¡Sinvergüenza!*" Patricia screamed. "My son is defective! What have you done to me?"

At that moment, Elim and Olga arrived on the doorstep, trophies in tow.

"*¿Quién eres, señorita?*" Patricia demanded in a high, piercing voice.

Olga flashed her pearly smile. "Me? I'm going to marry your son."

Victor's jaw dropped. "Oh, dear God," he muttered. Then to Olga: "Come, girl. We need to talk."

His eyes danced. His trousers twitched.

"To the banks of the sacred Nile..." he hummed as he pulled her into the back room.

When Olga emerged, her makeup was ruined and her pride had taken a beating.

"You beast," she said, glaring at Victor. Then, when she turned to Elim, her mascara streaked like warpaint: "Don't ever speak to me again."

As she ran out the door, her heels clacked like pistol shots.

Elim tried to follow, but Patricia blocked him.

"Where do you think you go?"

"I- I'm..."

"Shush, *mi precioso.* Professor has to make changes."

She pulled him inside.

Soon, Victor had Elim sedated on a makeshift operating table in the garage. Willard sat nearby; he cradled his bowling trophies like holy relics, and smiled as if nothing in the world could ever go wrong again.

Later, Patricia Valentina called John to explain that things had spiraled beyond her control.

After the operation, she sat with Victor, nursing a tumbler of rum.

"It's damn shame," she said, wiping a tear. "Must be dog heart."

"No," Victor replied. "The real horror is that he had a human heart. That was our mistake. We've gone too far. We must learn to live simply. Seek tranquility. Abandon ambition."

"Easy for you, maybe. Not for me."

She stared at her fingernails, chipped and ruined.

Jen Li can fix this, she thought, but then she saw the truth. It wasn't her nails. It was her hands. She was getting old.

"Bark, bark, bark!" echoed from the operating table.

"Victor! *¿Dónde está? ¿Dónde está, Victor?!*" she cried. She spun in panic, but Victor was gone.

"¡Mierda!" she snarled. "He went after that Olga creature. Must be damn butterfly effect."

When she finally calmed down, she noticed Elim was no longer on the table. In his place, Pucho Pequeño snoozed peacefully on his rug. Willard was there with a wide smile, trophies all around.

Is end, thought Patricia Valentina. *Oh, well. Was fun while lasted.*

She wandered into the kitchen and made herself a turkey sandwich: white meat and an irresponsible amount of mayonnaise.

After The Accident

After the accident, the wind howled for five days without rest. Then the sun burned and scorched the earth until the rocks glowed like embers. Birds crossed the sky in long, determined lines, orderly as ants. Maria's grandmother gave birth, not to a baby but to a full-grown man. Her husband, Abelardo, lost his faith entirely, and vanished into the mountains to live among the beasts.

For two weeks, every dog in the village disappeared. After that, order and silence returned, broken only when the sea hammered the cliffs.

Nocensio was infatuated with Maria's underwear. He adored the gentle pastels, swooned at the black lace, but one afternoon, when he arrived unannounced, she wore a pair ablaze with red roses scattered over a sea-blue triangle. The sight overwhelmed him. He collapsed in her arms. She revived him with cold water from the terracotta jug she kept beside her bed.

Weeks passed before Abelardo emerged from the mountains. His hair had grown long, his beard wild, his body thin as a reed. The villagers mistook him for a ghost. He claimed he had learned to speak with the animals, only to find they were fools. They gossiped and repeated themselves, and none of them had wisdom. Crestfallen, he returned to church. He refused communion, though, because a vegetarian could not, in good conscience, consume flesh, even symbolically.

The man-child, born of the grandmother, proved useful around the house. Still, Abelardo distrusted him. Abelardo set traps, small, clever ones, to catch the man-child in some mischief, but the man-child never stumbled. One day, the man-child left the house and wandered into nearby villages, where he preached to crowds. Some said he was wise. Others claimed he performed miracles. Debate spread quickly.

Abelardo was respected by everyone in town. Apart from the priest, he was the closest the people had to a leader. Had the tiny village been more than a forgotten seaside hamlet, Abelardo would have been the mayor. Everyone accepted his grandson, Nocensio's, strange ways and chalked them up to mathematical genius. Nocensio claimed his infatuation with Maria was the solution to a mathematical conundrum he called David and Bathsheba, a puzzle that confuses addition and subtraction. No one could follow his logic. The priest said that would require the wisdom of Solomon.

Abelardo argued with the priest. Was the man-child a sign? A prophet? God himself? The priest consulted an ancient Bible buried deep in the church archives and concluded that the man-child was indeed a messenger. The prophecies had named this very time, this very place. Abelardo scoffed. "He never went through puberty," he muttered. "Don't insult God." Then he told the priest to lay off the sacramental wine.

One morning, a large wooden box arrived in the village. The neighbors gathered, curious, but Abelardo would not let it be opened. "Not yet," he said, and set it on his porch. Passersby would ask, "Is it time?" and Abelardo would answer, "No." As they left, they whispered and shook their heads.

Later, Nocensio visited Maria again. This time, she wore nothing underneath. He was stunned, but not in the way he had hoped. Disheartened, he left without a word. He walked through the night, and by dawn reached the next village, where he found a lingerie shop. Beneath the stars, he saw something sacred in their geometry. Inspired, he bought three pairs of cotton panties: one with red triangles, another with blue circles, a third adorned with yellow lines, green dots, and orange squares.

He walked all the way back and tossed them through Maria's window, and then he waited.

Moments later, the panties fluttered back out and landed at his feet.

He looked down at the scattered shapes, then turned and walked away very slowly.

It broke the symmetry of his heart.

The day finally came when Abelardo decided to open the box. He invited the entire village. Everyone came except Nocensio who was mathematically exhausted.

Nocensio couldn't bear to be near Maria, not after what had happened. Instead, he stood alone at the edge of the sea and stared at the horizon. It had been so long since the accident that the village moved on. Life, supposedly, had returned to normal; however, Nocensio had discovered an error in his calculations that foreshadowed the apocalypse he believed was to come.

Only he, Nocensio, had seen what really happened. He had done his best to fix it but he was thwarted by the incompleteness theorem.

No one else believed him. Some whispered it had all been a dream. Others thought it was grief, but Nocensio knew. He had seen Maria's grandmother struck by lightning: a single, blinding bolt from a clear sky, white as judgment, that pierced her belly and fractured into every color in the universe. Her eyes had been shut tight. No one else had noticed. Not even her.

When Nocensio closed his eyes, he could still see her face in that moment, serene, unknowing, incandescent.

Back at Abelardo's, the villagers gathered outside his house, abuzz with curiosity. Everyone was there, everyone but Nocensio. Maria searched for him in the crowd. She scanned the faces in earnest, but he wasn't among them.

Then came the sirens.

A fire truck barreled into the village; its red lights spun, its bells clanged. Children screamed and ran to their parents. A round man in a tight red uniform sat behind the wheel, grinning like a madman. A police officer followed on foot in a wrinkled blue suit, out of breath and out of tickets. Then, as if reality itself snapped a seam, Maria's grandmother's man-baby raised his pudgy arms, lifted off the ground, spiraled upward into the sky, and vanished into an infinite regress of clouds and light.

The villagers were so stunned they forgot all about the box.

Nocensio watched from the beach as the man-baby disappeared into the horizon. A wild part of him wanted to follow, but he knew it was too far to swim. That realization settled like stone in his chest just as the explosion hit.

A sharp crack split the sky. He turned. Color poured from the rooftops in great shimmering sheets. Paint, in every hue imaginable, rained down on the town like a second miracle.

Abelardo made a mistake. He'd misjudged the timing. The box hadn't waited for him. It had opened on its own. Inside were a hundred cans of special paint, sealed tight, stacked together, heated by the sun. The pressure had built, then ignited. By the time Abelardo understood what had happened, he was covered, his shirt, pants, even his face, spattered in bursts of violent color.

The next day, Maria's grandmother, tired of cooking nothing but vegetables, convinced Abelardo to have a lamb butchered. He agreed. They hosted a barbacoa for the whole village to celebrate survival or whatever it was that had just occurred.

Everyone came. They brought food and stories and laughter. Lupita arrived with her famous iguana tamales, still wrapped in plantain leaves now stained red from the explosion. The fishermen brought tacos speckled with green. The fat man from the firetruck passed around bottles of mezcal, each with a yellow worm curled inside like punctuation. Doña Morales stirred a great vat of sweet atole.

There were bowls of rice and beans, baskets of warm tortillas. Every guest was spattered and streaked with pigment. No one minded. They wore it with pride.

The priest arrived to bless the poor, unlucky goat. Abelardo cut its throat with practiced grace. He caught some of the blood in a bowl. He would carry it back up the mountain to the little altar he'd built from stone and bone, where he'd prayed so many times before. Since returning home, he had climbed that trail over and over. He drug along the stubborn hope that the animals might one day listen, that they might finally come to their senses and stop their mad babbling, but God, so far, had stayed silent.

They rubbed the goat with dried chilies, wrapped it tight in avocado and maguey leaves, and lowered it into a pit to steam over hot coals. For twelve hours it cooked, slow and secretive, while the ocean wind dragged its scent across the village like a spell. All night long, the smell kept Nocensio from sleep. By morning, it had worked into his bones.

When the meal was served, Nocensio couldn't bear it any longer. He went to Maria's grandmother and asked if he might eat alone, behind the house where no one could see him. He said he would wait until everyone else had their fill.

Maria's grandmother told Abelardo, and Abelardo told Maria. Abelardo knew the truth: that Maria and Nocensio loved each other. Nocensio was too proud or too afraid to be seen after he fell victim to the incompleteness theorem. Abelardo thought the boy was a fool. Maria smiled and said, "It's just geometry. Nothing to worry about." She said she would take him the food herself.

When she approached Nocensio, he stood to leave.

"Stay," she said. "Eat with me. I want to show you something."

They sat together in silence, and chewed slowly, as if to delay what was coming. Then, Nocensio heard the voice, thin and high, like a child's attempt to mimic a man. It was the man-baby that whispered in his head. *Ye who have seen me yet fail to believe are a fool.* He tried to shut it out, but the voice stuck in his head like a whisper caught in a seashell. It told him to speak, to tell Maria what he had seen the night of the accident.

Frightened and unsure but determined to solve the David and Bathsheba puzzle, Nocensio spilled the beans. He told Maria everything.

"I know," she said quietly.

Nocensio blinked. "How could you know?"

"I was there too," Maria said. "Hiding right behind you."

"You saw it? The white light explode into all the colors of the universe?"

"I did."

"The colors were beautiful," he said. His voice trembled. "They were like rays from rainbow stars."

"I know."

He couldn't think what to say after that. He sat and stared at her, and thought of the underwear he had brought to her, the ones she threw away. They had geometric patterns, absurd and lovely. He had imagined her in them more times than he cared to admit.

"Come," Maria said, and rose to her feet.

They walked to her room. On the bed, the panties were laid out in a neat row. Dried globs of paint from the explosion the day before were scattered over them like the aftermath of a cosmic storm.

A smile broke over Nocensio's face when he realized the solution was right there in front of his eyes.

"They're more beautiful than I ever imagined," he said. "I love you, Maria."

"I know," she said. "I love you too."

The Eighties

The Dead Man

The ceiling fan purred lazily above the bed, but did little to cut the heavy heat that filled the room. Puerto Vallarta overwhelmed him, humid, unmoving, so unlike the brisk, indifferent chill of San Francisco he'd left behind. Albert had come alone, ten days carved out to think, not work.

He stepped out onto the small deck of his third-floor room at Hotel Roger. The view gave him the street below: narrow, sun-faded, alive. He'd showered, shaved, dressed early for dinner, and now waited. The sun was still up, but sinking slowly. The heat, however, wouldn't leave. Not even the night offered relief. Darkness here only mimicked coolness, like a trick played by the air itself.

A procession wandered down the street. Some people carried decorated crosses; some were dressed like they'd come from a wedding, others like carnival performers, most in whatever they'd worn that morning. Brassy music tangled with drumbeats and the insistent honk of cars that tried to push through the slow-moving crowd. A small knot of onlookers stood and watched in half-amused confusion. Across the street, a more solemn group gathered at the door of a house wedged between a gift shop and a restaurant. Black clothes. Rosaries. A wake. People arrived in quiet clusters of whole families, parents, elders, and children, and slipped inside to pay respects. Albert assumed a man had died. The woman who greeted the mourners wore a black veil.

Vaguely unsettled, Albert watched the scene. Death still seemed distant to him, but the sight of it, especially in this quiet, Catholic way, made it feel suddenly plausible. He turned and went back inside.

The room had old charm: windows that welcomed bright sunlight during the day; a large bed with tarnished brass posts; a tall armoire, and a small wooden desk. Beside it sat a crooked green-shaded lamp on an ornate metal base. Albert unpacked slowly and placed each item in drawers as if to ground himself.

He had come to see Gomez, an older man he'd met a couple of years ago. They were never close, just occasional drinking companions, but Gomez had been sharp, full of strange, compelling stories that stayed with Albert long after the glasses were empty. He wasn't sure what he wanted from the man now, maybe just a sounding board, someone to help him clarify the decision he hadn't quite admitted he was here to make. They had agreed on a time and place to meet, but Albert hadn't heard from Gomez since. *That's just Mexico,* he thought, and shrugged it off. *Gomez will show.*

Out on the street, the children continued to play and dart between the feet of the somber adults. Inside, the room where the dead man lay was dim, but Albert thought he could make out the coffin through the open door. He unpacked the last of his shirts and closed the drawer. There was nothing left to do but wait.

A truck pulled up and sent a ripple through the street. It idled just outside the dead man's door. When the pallbearers emerged with the coffin, the neighborhood children scattered like birds startled from a wire. A few lingered, the braver ones, but the box was sealed. There was nothing to see.

Albert watched from his window, the view as clear as if he'd stayed on the rooftop deck.

The hour of his meeting with Gomez crept close. He locked his room and descended the cast-iron spiral staircase. The black metal treads groaned and flexed under his steps. Outside, the noise hit him all at once, a thick, loud pulse that had only been a murmur from above. He was jostled in the crowd, bodies pressed from every direction, all flowing toward the parade. He pushed against the current, elbowed through until he reached the corner. He turned, and slipped onto the next street. It was quieter there, almost deserted. The rest of the walk to the bar was smooth sailing.

Inside, by the window where Gomez usually sat, a man hunched over a beer. Albert approached, uncertain.

"Gomez?"

The man looked up. The beard was new, a wild, snow-white thing that made his face harder to read. But the eyes, brown and sharp, were impossible to mistake.

"Ah?" the old man said.

Albert smiled. "Hello, my friend. I think I'll grab a beer. Can I get you another? Tonight's on me."

Gomez nodded faintly, lips curled into the ghost of a smile. Albert went to the bar and ordered a Negro Modelo for himself, and another Pacifico for Gomez. He carried the bottles back and took the seat across from the old man.

Neither spoke. Minutes passed like hours. Gomez sipped while Albert waited. That was always Gomez's way, measured, unfazed, elusive. It was that patience that had drawn Albert to him in the first place.

"What's wrong?" Albert asked. "Cat got your tongue?"

Gomez tilted his head, his eyes narrowed slightly as he sucked on his lower lip. His mustache, thick and unruly, twitched with the motion. From outside came the distant thump of drums and brass. The parade was circling back; it echoed off the narrow walls of the street.

Gomez remained quiet. That didn't bother Albert. The two of them had always operated in a space between words. Spanish, English, it didn't matter. It was the pauses that spoke to Albert, that gave him the space to answer his own questions.

The music surged just outside. The bar door flew open. A costumed couple stumbled in, she in a tight catsuit and mask with long white whiskers, he in a rumpled academic's jacket with devil horns. They scanned the room, decided instantly it wasn't their kind of place, and vanished again. The bartender, expression unreadable, followed them with his eyes, then looked down and wiped all memory of the couple off the bartop.

Gomez drained his beer and raised the bottle. The bartender brought another Pacifico and gestured at Albert's half-full Modelo.

Albert shook his head. One was enough. He needed to think clearly. He had important things to say and wanted to focus. He looked up and caught his own reflection in the bartender's glasses.

The bartender chuckled softly.

Albert shifted in his seat. "What was that about?" he asked Gomez.

The old man lifted his shoulders in a shrug.

Albert leaned forward. "I'm sure you've wondered why I wanted to meet."

Gomez straightened, chin out. It was a signal that he was ready to listen.

"I've got a decision to make," Albert said. "A big one. Life-changing, maybe. I came here to work things out. I thought maybe you could help me."

Gomez looked puzzled. He took a long sip of beer, then tilted his head to the side, slowly nodded, as if he agreed to something unsaid.

Albert gave a curt nod. "Good. Okay. Here's the situation."

He drained the last of his beer. The bartender didn't notice or didn't care. His eyes were glued to a soccer match on the TV above the bar. With a quiet sigh, Albert got up and returned with two fresh beers, slid one in front of Gomez.

Gomez smiled, nodded his thanks.

"You're welcome," Albert said. "Now, here's the situation—"

The words caught in his throat. Instead, an image surfaced: the wake he'd passed on the way here, the open casket, the too-still body.

"You know... there's something else," he said.

Gomez burped and quickly muttered an apology. It was odd and out of place. Albert glanced at him sideways. Was he already drunk? He let it go.

"As I walked over, there was a wake across from my hotel. It gave me the creeps."

The bartender turned from the game and looked in their direction.

"I don't put much stock in signs or omens, but it struck me as strange," Albert continued. "On my first day in Puerto Vallarta I walk right into death. Then, out of nowhere, a parade goes by. What the hell was that about?"

The bartender walked over. "*Día de la Santa Cruz,*" he said. "Holy Cross Day. We dress up, carry flower-covered crosses, march in the streets. The wake you saw, *señor,* that was for Gomez. Your friend. He died last week. I'm very sorry. Gomez was a friend of mine too."

Albert froze. He turned toward the man beside him.

"Then... who are you?" he asked quietly.

The man smiled. "Hector," he said. "You thought I was Gomez? It happens. Americans come and go, I lose track. Honestly, I wasn't sure if we'd met before."

The bartender reached into his apron and handed Albert an envelope. "Before he died, Gomez asked me to give this to you if you ever came looking."

Albert took it, the weight of it suddenly immense.

"I should go," he said. "Thank you for the letter." He turned to Hector. "You could've said something sooner."

Hector gave a small shrug and a crooked smile. "Maybe you didn't give me the chance."

Albert laid some pesos on the table and left without another word.

Back at the hotel, he paused at the front desk. "Got a cigarette?" he asked the young clerk. "I don't smoke, but I thought it might help."

The clerk vanished into a back room. Before he returned, Albert was already out the door.

When the clerk reappeared, cigarette in hand, the lobby was empty.

Albert stood in his dark room, and watched the quiet house across the street. No lights. No movement. He figured the family had gone to dinner or dispersed with relatives for the evening.

He stayed at the window, alone with his thoughts. Death could come anywhere, any time. That was the truth. He didn't fear it exactly, but he felt its nearness now, like a shadow in the room. He remembered Gomez's cough. The way he lit one cigarette after another. Maybe he had cancer. It makes sense.

Stupid habit, Albert thought.

He clicked on the green desk lamp and opened the letter.

Albert:

I'm sorry I missed our meeting. By now, you'll know why: death intervened. I've asked a friend to help write this letter in proper English so it might be easier for you to read. You said you had something important to tell me. I regret that I won't be there to listen.

I have my own story to tell, something I've never told before. I write it now in the hope it might mean something to you. Please don't share this with my friends or family. It's too late for me, but maybe it isn't too late for you.

Albert, I lied to myself my whole life. Right up until the end. Only now, with everything slipping away, do I feel the hunger, the desperate, late hunger, to see, to hear, to experience the world, but it's too late. I look back in disgust, not because I was evil or cruel but because I was afraid. Because I was lazy and took the easy way out.

We pretend to admire self-awareness, but in truth, we run from it. I lived with self-doubt like a shadow on my back. It made me small when I might have been brave. It made me modest when I should have been bold. Modesty, it turns out, is easier than honesty, because honesty demands action, and I always chose the easier path.

You'll understand what I mean: We spoke of these things once, when you visited. I wanted, in the race against death, to complete something I had failed to do in life. I was just an ordinary man, but even ordinary men can do something. Instead, I chose a small, safe life. I was too afraid to fail.

Now that it's too late, it tortures me. Since we last spoke, I've turned it over and over in my mind. I wasted so much time. I should have lived intensely. I don't want to die, but worse than death is dying full of regret.

We lie to ourselves. Mexico, beautiful, seductive Mexico, makes it easier than anywhere. It coddles illusion, it lets us drift. Illusions have a cost. I know that now. Eventually, the truth finds you. I wish I had faced it sooner.

This is what I would have said to you, my friend, if I'd made our meeting. Don't hold back. Go for your dream. Live life to the fullest. Maybe it will mean something to you. I wrote it for your benefit, but the truth is, this letter gave *me* peace. I couldn't say these things to those close to me, but I can say them to you.

With gratitude,

Gomez

Albert folded the letter carefully, overcome with emotion. It humbled him, being the one Gomez chose for this final confession.

Yes, we squander time. That part rang especially true. The excuses are endless, the diversions seductive. Albert loved Mexico, in part because it still allowed that old-world luxury, to simply sit and watch and think, yet even here, Gomez had managed to drift through life. It can happen anywhere.

The beer on an empty stomach made Albert light-headed. He wandered back into the street, and looked for a restaurant. The parade had passed, but the streets still swelled with life: people talked, shopped, laughed. They were like the characters in a novel where all you could know of them came from the brief impressions the author offered: the way they moved, the tone of their voices, a gesture, a face. Maybe that's all we ever *can* know of others, even of ourselves.

Should he want more? Gomez's words echoed.

Albert believed he was in control, but self-deception, as he saw now, was a quiet yet powerful force. A liar in the mirror. Life doesn't follow a script. You try to shape it, but fate always carves out its share.

He found the small fish house he remembered from his last trip. He sat by the front window where he could see the street, and ordered a glass of wine. The waiter left a menu.

He ordered the sea bass and asked for another glass. A young girl stepped inside the restaurant with flowers for sale. She looked to be around ten. Albert bought a red rose. She wrapped it in damp newspaper, then ran back to her family who sat on a bench sharing a meal beneath a mango tree. She was beautiful. The whole scene, simple and golden in the evening sunset, felt like a painting.

Should I have been an artist? Albert wondered. *I chose a job with a steady paycheck. Was that a mistake?*

It was good to be alone. To think. Maybe it wasn't too late. Maybe he could still drop everything and travel. He could write travelogues and make documentaries. There's a market for that sort of thing. He could write if he made the time. *Would that be a better life?*

The wine warmed Albert's chest. His fiancée would be in London by now with her sister. They had agreed to take time apart, to see if marriage was really what they wanted. They'd lived together for over a year, but still, who really knows? Everything is a gamble.

A man outside took a photograph of the family on the bench. Albert thought of his favorite photographer, Dorothea Lange. A camera demands that you look closer. That you *see* what others ignore. Lange said once that if she'd chosen a practical career like teaching as her mother advised, she'd never have been a photographer. *Was there a truth in that he needed to hear?*

Albert made a good salary as a salesman. He liked the options money gave him. He wasn't anxious to disrupt the life he'd planned: a steady job, a bright future, marriage, kids. *There would be time to fill in the blanks later, wouldn't there?*

He thought of the letter from Gomez. An unease set in, an emptiness in the pit of his stomach. *I'm probably just hungry*, he thought.

There was rice in the saltshaker so the crystals wouldn't clump with the humidity. A black ant crawled out of the centerpiece rose and wandered across the table, aimless but determined. *Even ants must make decisions.*

At the next table, a young woman frowned at her plate.

"This fish is full of bones," she complained. "It's not cooked through."

That's my life, thought Albert.

Outside, the flower girl moved farther along the street. The restaurant filled steadily. There were more customers now, and more chatter. When the waiter brought his fish, Albert ate slowly, and savored each bite. He finished and ordered another glass of wine. As the waiter set it down, Albert spotted Hector on the walkway.

"Hey, Hector! Join me!" he called.

Hector paused at the window, his beard wild, his eyes lively.

"I cannot, señor. I must get home. It's time for my mother's supper."

"Another time, then. I enjoyed our afternoon, even with the mix-up."

"So did I, señor. Thank you for the beers. Next time, I pay."

Hector waved and went on his way. Albert stood abruptly and leaned out the window.

"Hector! One question!"

Hector glanced back.

"Yes?"

"Should I get married?"

Hector squinted. "What do you *want* to do?"

"I don't know."

"Then wait until you do know."

Albert wanted to ask how he'd know, but Hector was too far away. He paid the bill and walked back to his room. He undressed and sat on the bed between its brass posts. He thought about the couple who'd entered the bar in costume earlier. Choosing the right costume is important, but it's just a costume. It's you inside, always you, the one you can't escape. Except in death. He fell into a shallow, restless sleep and he dreamed.

Men loaded a casket into a truck, then opened it. They looked around, furtively, and began to remove things from inside, piece by piece, until only a naked body remained.

"As he came forth from his mother's womb, naked shall he return… and shall take nothing of his labor, which he may carry away in his hand. Amen."

Albert strained to see the face. His heart jolted—it wasn't Gomez.

It was his own face.

They closed the casket and darkness fell with the lid.

Albert woke early. Downstairs, he asked where to make a long-distance call. He walked to a money exchange that rented phones and had them dial London.

"Hello, it's Albert. Is Elizabeth there?"

There was a rustle, then her voice.

"Albert? Are you all right?"

"I'm fine. Listen, I'm not ready, not right now."

He heard a loud cry, then a scream, then a click, and the line went dead. Behind the counter, the girl in the exchange threw her hands in the air and muttered something in Spanish. He didn't understand.

Albert stepped out into the sun. People sipped coffee at the café next door. A boy teased a dog in the street.

He felt strange. The absurdity of it all caught him off guard, and he started to laugh. First a chuckle, then louder. Heads turned. He laughed still louder, giddy and wild.

"I'm not him!" he shouted. "I'm not the dead man!"

Children stared. He didn't care. He had no time to explain. As he walked along the street, he spoke to himself. People mocked him with wry smiles, and stepped out of the way.

"No more lies! No illusions! I've killed them, all. But now what? How can I walk without sure footing, without a path? Gomez. Gomez! Where are you now?

The Backpack

A thick fog clung to the road like a bitter smell. It was late, too late for traffic. No headlights to blind him, no taillights to follow. Just an empty road that wound through the redwoods to the coast. He eased off the gas, and took care on the curves, aware how quickly things could go wrong.

The forest finally thinned, and the road leveled out before it rose toward the coastal highway. Though the fog still pressed, it was easier to see now without the dense trees that hemmed him in on each side. A small shape darted across the asphalt, probably a shrew mole or a fieldmouse, gone in an instant.

Near Mendocino, a handful of lights glimmered through the mist. Most of the town was asleep. He turned off at the first entrance. Something flicked past the edge of his vision, a blur near the driver's-side window. He turned to look and squinted through the murk. He could see nothing distinct. Then, he heard a loud thump, and the car jolted.

His pulse surged. *Christ. I hit something!*

He braked hard. In the rearview mirror, the fog churned like smoke. His heart pounded as he stepped out onto the street. Behind the car, sprawled across the pavement, lay the crumpled body of a young man. His head was crushed.

He staggered back. "Holy Jesus," he whispered.

The silence was absolute, just fog, salt air, and the faint hiss of the sea. He turned in slow circles and scanned the empty street. There was no movement and no witnesses. He hesitated, and for just a second thought about driving away, but he couldn't. He wouldn't.

A single house down the block had a light on. He ran toward the light.

His knuckles rattled the door. "Call 911! There's been an accident and someone's dead!"

The wait for the police felt endless. When they arrived, he answered everything honestly. He passed the sobriety test. There were no traces of alcohol or drugs. It was just bad luck compounded by the fog.

The ambulance came and took the body.

"You're free to go," said the inspector. "We've got your information. If anything changes, we'll be in touch. Expect the official report in a month. You'll get a copy, along with any next steps."

"That's it?" he asked.

"For now. It looks like an accident, but if we find evidence of negligence, you could still be charged."

"Negligence?"

"It's unlikely," the inspector said. "I wouldn't worry about it."

He drove home. He forgot to stop for the mail. The sun broke over the Big River Bridge in a riot of pink and gold. By the time he pulled into the driveway, the fog had lifted.

The house wasn't his. He was the caretaker for an out-of-town family. He tried to sleep, but his mind spun in circles. He gave up, made coffee, sat at the kitchen table and retraced every moment.

His stomach churned. He rushed to the bathroom and vomited.

Everything had changed. Nothing would ever be simple again.

Three weeks later when he received the official report, he had calmed down. He'd already scoured the news articles: LOCAL TRANSIENT KILLED IN UNFORTUNATE ACCIDENT. He was relieved they hadn't named him as the driver. The transient was identified as J. B. Knot, known locally as B-Not. In the official report the unnamed driver was fully exonerated. "Tragic accident, transient in dark clothing ran in front of car. The autopsy found enough cocaine in Mr. Knot's system to fuel a horse."

A month passed. He tried to forget the whole thing but it was impossible. He thought about it day in and day out. He avoided the street where the accident happened. He kept to himself. By now everyone knew he was the driver of the car. It was a small town. There were no secrets. Something would happen sooner or later. He knew it.

☙ ☙ ☙

He sat on the deck in back of the house to have a smoke. As the fog descended from the treetops, he smelled the ocean. The fog took him back to that night. He figured out what he'd seen out the window. It was just a blur, but he was sure someone was ahead of B-Not on the other side of the street. Was he running away from B-Not or running with him? Who was he, and why were both out at that late hour? He ran these questions over and over through his head as he sat and smoked in the dark night.

The owners of the rental had two German Shepherds, Verna and Myrna. They sat inside the door to the deck behind him. Their growls alerted him that something was up. The fog made it impossible to see the fence at the bottom of his meadow, but he heard the gate open. He sat up, suddenly alert, and looked for a weapon but he had none. A man emerged out of the dark. The dogs barked as the man walked toward him.

"Who are you? What are you doing here?" he asked in a panic.

"No worries, man. Just want to talk."

As he got a better look at the man, his concern for his safety diminished. He recognized him as one of B-Not's loose group of friends who hung out around town.

"Talk about what?"

"Your accident. B-Not was my friend."

"I'm sorry. He ran in front of me. There was nothing I could do."

"We'll see about that."

The man hauled himself up onto the deck and dropped into the empty chair. His hair hung in greasy strands, uncombed, and his beard was patchy and wild. A fresh gash split the skin above his eyebrow. He stank of sweat and liquor.

The dogs, tense at first, settled down. It was quiet again.

The man grinned and held out a hand. "Name's Billy. I know who you are, Mac. You wash dishes over at The Frolic, right? I've been through there a few times."

Mac eyed him cautiously.

"Okay," he said slowly. "But I don't know what you want, and I'm not in the mood for bullshit. I still have nightmares about the accident. I feel awful about it, really."

Billy leaned forward, and his voice dropped. "B-Not and I were working a deal that night. Heavy stuff, real expensive. Dangerous people on both sides. You don't want their attention, believe me. B-Not had the goods in his backpack. I want that backpack, Mac. I know you've got it."

That stopped Mac cold.

"What do you mean, dangerous?" Mac asked, suddenly alert. "I don't know anything about a backpack. All I got from that night is a heap of guilt."

Mac studied Billy carefully. The cut on his head, the stink, the desperation. He wasn't a threat, not on his own, just a street rat in over his head, but the people he was mixed up with? Mac had heard enough to be scared. Gangs worked these backwater coastal towns like parasites. You didn't tangle with them unless you had a death wish.

"I know you have it," Billy insisted. "Cops didn't find it. Neither did the EMTs. That's been checked. Come on, Mac, give it up. If you don't, those guys will come after both of us."

The dogs snapped back to attention, barked and scratched at the screen.

"I don't have your damn backpack, Billy," Mac said. "Whatever this is, it's *your* mess, not mine."

Billy's eyes flicked past Mac, toward the side of the house.

Mac turned, and his gut clenched. Three men moved in the narrow space between the house and the fence. There was no time to think.

Mac shot to his feet and flung the door open. The dogs burst out, snarling, and lunged at the intruders.

He and Billy sprinted into the house, tore through the front, and dove into Mac's car. Tires screamed as he plowed through the front fence. In the rearview, Mac saw them: three shadows piled into a dark SUV and gave chase.

He slammed the accelerator.

The fog was thick, but Mac knew these roads better than his own name. Every curve, every dip, every stretch of gravel. The SUV loomed in the mirror, getting closer.

Mac punched it.

Up ahead, the road forked. This was the move he'd counted on. At the last second, he jerked the wheel, veered hard onto an unmarked side road. The tires skidded; the car fishtailed. Behind him, the SUV missed the turn and slammed headfirst into a redwood with a sound like a bomb going off.

Mac didn't wait to celebrate. He doubled back toward the house.

He slammed on the brakes, threw it in park, and looked at Billy. "End of the line. If I were you, I'd get the hell out of town."

Billy stared at him, hollow-eyed. "You really don't have it?"

"Hell no," Mac said. "But I'm not gonna stick around to prove it. This town's lit up now."

Mac knew it was time to leave Mendocino. Those guys would be back, and he wasn't about to be here when they did. He threw his gear in the car, headed south, and never looked back.

An hour later, his nerves jangled, he pulled off at a coastal lookout. The Pacific churned below, hidden under a thick fogbank. He lit a cigarette with shaky fingers, stepped out, and leaned against the car. That's when he saw it, something jutting out from beneath the rear bumper.

He crouched down and peered beneath the chassis. Wedged tight between the axle and the back tire was a filthy, battered backpack. He drew his knife, sliced it free, and unzipped it.

Drugs. Packed tight.

Mac stared at the contents for a long moment.

"Well, I'll be fucked," he muttered.

He zipped the backpack back up tightly and carried it to the cliff's edge. The drop was sheer. There was no guardrail, no second chances. He hesitated only a second, then heaved the thing into the void. It vanished into the mist, silent until a distant splash broke the stillness.

He took one last drag, flicked the cigarette into the wind, and walked back to the car.

⌛ ⌛ ⌛

Several months later, Mac went back to the Frolic Café. The boss hired him back. He asked his friend, Rafan, who also worked there, if Billy was still in town.

"Billy's dead, Mac. Something about a drug deal gone wrong. After you left, a couple of gang members caught up with him. There was a witness to his murder, so those guys split. No one's seen them since."

"Jesus! That's cold," Mac said. "I'm glad they're gone. You think they'll be back?" He didn't say anything about the backpack or about the discussion he'd had with Billy. He wanted to be done with it. He felt bad for Billy, but he'd told Billy to split. It was his own fault that he didn't.

"Doubt it," Rafan said. "Things have changed. Some local guys have a lock on the business now. Something really weird happened though."

"Oh, yeah," Mac said and his heart jumped. "What's that?"

A couple of kids on that beach north of Point Arena found a backpack with bricks of cocaine inside," said Rafan. "They didn't know what it was, so they took it to their father. Turns out the bricks were still good. I guess they were packed really well. The stupid guy didn't turn them over to the police like he should have. He tried to sell them instead, and got caught. He's in jail now. The clinker is that those bricks were marked with symbols that tie them to the gang that killed Billy. That's odd, don't you think?"

Mac's stomach churned. "Yea, really odd," he said. He didn't know what else to say or do. It was too late now. He thought he solved his problem, and maybe he did, but he created two more. That damn backpack wouldn't leave him alone. If he'd taken it to the police when he found it, Billy might still be alive and the father of those kids wouldn't be in jail. The truth will set you free, they say, even an inconvenient truth.

"I wonder how that backpack got all the way down there," said Rafan.

"Yea, I wonder too," Mac said. Then, he unloaded a rack of clean dishes and carried them into the dining room.

Seduction

Graham handled all the logistics. I was tied up with another project and barely had time to skim the basics, let alone do our usual obsessive prep. Still, I felt ready. I'd spent most of my short life obsessing over B, read everything he wrote, everything written about him. I knew him, or thought I did, better than anyone alive.

B, the famously elusive author, had vanished into Oaxaca years ago. A Mexican J. D. Salinger, people said. He'd published one brilliant, wild novel, followed it with a clutch of equally enigmatic stories and a second, quieter book, and then he was gone. It was not a publicity stunt or a breakdown. It was a refusal, but unlike Camus's revolt, it was a deliberate attempt to fade away.

I first discovered him in college. Our literature professor, a rogue academic with a motorcycle and a chip on his shoulder, devoted a semester to five new authors he swore were destined for greatness. All five hit, but it was B that hit me hardest. That professor eventually ditched academia for a cabin in the Northwest, a jogging trail, and a legal battle over banned books. He won the case, then he vanished too. It seemed like everyone touched by B disappeared.

B's first novel sold quietly, steadily, year after year, enough to keep him afloat without compromise. Like many obsessed readers, I made the pilgrimage. Most were turned away at the door or ignored entirely. I waited months. Then came a terse note:

> I don't know why people think I'm a cold fish. I don't mean
> to offend. I just value solitude. Come if you must. I'll speak
> if I feel like it.

When I arrived at his ramshackle house on Reforma Street, it looked exactly as I'd imagined: tired, overgrown, and quiet. He could've lived anywhere, but he chose this, to hide, to shed the bullshit. He loathed small talk and hated most of his fans, especially the ones who raved.

A small, frail woman opened the door. She looked ancient. She was B's legendary housekeeper. She'd been with him since childhood. She looked like parchment held together by wire, but her movements were sure and swift. She hoisted my pack like it weighed nothing, and led me through a strange, skeletal entryway of rusted beams and angles that seemed one bad weld away from collapse.

Inside, the air shifted to cool, dark, and silent. I lost sight of her in the gloom. Then my eyes adjusted, and the walls came alive.

There were murals on every surface, vast and feverish. The ceiling swirled with imagery. A blazing orange goat head with black eyes and jagged white fangs glared down at me. Behind it, Christ drifted into a night sky full of tiny comets, his gaze turned away as if he was about to abandon mankind. Below, surreal sea creatures writhed in an oily green ocean. One wall showed a tiger mid-leap toward an elephant-headed man perched on an alligator's back. Another was dominated by a white skull, with flames that curled from every orifice. A jinn with a green face and razor teeth glared from the shadows, and in the corner, a brown-skinned woman watched over it all, her bare body bathed in a soft glow, her jeweled headdress faintly glittering. I knew that face, or thought I did, from one of B's stories.

The room pulsed with the same confusion and wonder that haunted B's writing. Just when you thought you understood, the ground shifted and the meaning dissolved. Incense clung to the air. I breathed it in and felt fully awake, but I wasn't sure. I stood there alone, a little afraid, a little awestruck, and tried to take it all in.

A door creaked open, and a burst of sunlight struck me full in the face. For a moment, I was blinded; then, slowly, a figure resolved in the glare, a man, framed by the doorway.

"Welcome," he said. "I see you managed to find your way. I hope the journey wasn't too rough."

He was not at all what I had imagined. Given the visceral nature of his work, I'd pictured someone more essential, more physical. Instead, he looked worn out in the way people do when they've lived alone too long. He wasn't exactly disheveled, but close. Unshaven, though not bearded. Long, black hair streaked with gray hung limp around his face. There was a calm about him, a kind of gravity that contradicted my expectations.

B's work flirted with the obscene, but always held something just out of reach, something magnetic, maddening. His stories didn't so much conclude as they lingered, like an itch in the mind you couldn't quite scratch. That itch was what had brought me here. I'd come to find the man behind the mystery. I hoped to close the distance between art and artist.

"I've found your house," I said, "but what I'm really want to find is you."

His expression changed, just slightly, but enough. I knew I'd said the wrong thing. A chill of doubt crept in.

"I'm sure you do," he said at last. "You have a reputation for being thorough. That's why I agreed to see you. Come. Let's sit in the courtyard and get acquainted."

That's how I met B, infamous, elusive B, driven into self-exile in Mexico by a swarm of critics and journalists desperate to crack him open. No one knew anything definitive about his life. My job was to gather what fragments I could. To build even a sketch of the man would be a notable accomplishment. That sketch would make headlines. I'd be published everywhere, I could feel it. The problem was, so could he.

The courtyard garden was unexpectedly lush and serene. Bougainvillea spilled over a crumbly wall, jacarandas bloomed purple overhead. It was a world apart from the dry, forsaken dead garden outside his door.

We sat across from each other at a small iron table. A maid appeared with two wide clay cups of warm atole, thick, sweet, and flavored with chocolate. As she handed me mine, her fingers brushed my hand. The sensation was subtle, strange, an echo of the disquiet I felt reading B's prose. It was almost erotic like one of those visual riddles: the old woman, the young girl, both at once, neither entirely true.

B took a sip and fixed his gaze on me. "If you read my letter, you know I only agreed to meet. I didn't promise an interview."

His eyes penetrated the space between us, paternal in their scrutiny. In spite of his distant nature, I felt strongly he had a lesson to teach me like a father to a son.

"You know how famous you are," I said. "You have readers all over the world yet no one knows a thing about your life, your origins, your influences, how you became who you are. People want to know. They want to hear your voice. This, here at this table, is what they dream of."

"They think I'm a recluse, an eccentric, but I only want to protect my work and myself. I've found peace since I stopped publishing. I still write, of course. Maybe someday I'll release something small, a breadcrumb or two, but for now, I'm content. As for those who want to know more, everything I have to say is already in my books."

"No, it isn't. Your books will be better understood in context. That's what your readers want, some context."

He raised an eyebrow. "Context? Whose context? My stories stand on their own."

"No they don't, not entirely, not for those who care deeply. Your readers want to know more than your work. They want to know *you*."

"That's a dangerous assumption," he said, his tone sharp. "What do you mean by me, my Wikipedia page? Be careful. None of us, myself, you, anyone, is exactly what we think we are, and we're certainly not what others make of us. Everything is in flux, as Heraclitus told us. What I believed at twenty is not what I believe today, and what I believe today will not hold tomorrow. Try to put that on a Wikipedia page."

A sound broke my focus, a shuffle or scrape in the far corner of the courtyard. I turned toward it instinctively. Something moved behind a low wall, too quick and indistinct to make out. An animal, maybe, or a person. I couldn't tell. Later, I wondered if it had been a ruse, staged to draw my attention away. Maybe that's just paranoia, but when I looked back at B, his chair was empty. He had vanished, quietly and completely. No farewell, no trace, just absence. I was disoriented, but perhaps that was the point. Maybe it was his way to express his desire to be left alone, the importance he attached to solitude.

The maid arrived and gestured silently for me to follow. We walked along a narrow hallway lined with closed doors. At the very end, one door stood open. "Your room," she said. My backpack lay neatly on the bed inside. I stepped in. She closed the door behind me without a word.

A note awaited me on the desk, written in B's hand:

"I will consider the interview. I will let you know in the morning. Sleep well."

It was written on faded stationery that bore the ghostly image of the same woman I'd seen earlier on the mural in the dark room.

Exhaustion overtook me. I lay down and sank deep into the mattress. Within minutes, I was asleep. It crossed my mind, later, that the atole might have been drugged. My friends say what followed sounds like a hallucination, but it didn't feel that way. It felt real, more real than waking life, like I had stepped into a story not of my own making, one in which I moved of my own will, yet under the pressure of a hidden narrative. I will describe it exactly as it happened.

I awoke to the sound of soft, unfamiliar movements. The room was dim, lit only by a single candle burning in a far corner. In its flickering light, I saw a figure seated in a chair: a man wearing a deer mask with a full, regal rack of antlers. He faced slightly away, his body lean and powerful, clad only in a pair of gray shorts with a jagged Zapotec design. His dark eyes were fixed on something in back of me.

Behind him was another man, motionless, in a jaguar mask. His face was expressionless, his gaze unfocused and upward, as though entranced. A black cap sat atop his head, and pointed jaguar ears poked out from either side. He wore a long-sleeved blue shirt, sleeves rolled up to the elbows, the collar open just enough to reveal a priest's collar beneath. His hands rested on the shoulders of the seated man, still as a statue.

I sensed two women behind me, one on each side of the bed. They came forward in jaguar masks, their bodies otherwise unclothed. Their long, silver-gray hair shimmered in the low light and cascaded past their shoulders.

The woman closest to the deer-masked man approached him, slipped her hand beneath his shorts, and stroked him with quiet reverence. Slowly, she mounted him, and eased into a rhythm that was both ritual and release.

The other woman turned her attention to me. Her breasts hovered over my face, full and glowing in the candlelight. I felt her touch, not just on my skin, but through it, as though she had pressed herself into every cell of my body. Her scent enveloped me: soft, humid, floral, and animal. I breathed her in, and she entered me in a way I can't describe except to say it was total.

She climbed atop me, and guided me inside her with a deliberate grace. My body responded before my mind could catch up. We moved together. A current pulsed through us like electricity. Her hair draped over my face as I kissed the heat of her breasts. Her nails dug into my shoulders as she trembled, our bodies locked in a crescendo of sensation. We moaned, we gasped, we collided, and then, like an explosion, we climaxed together. It felt like every atom in our bodies erupted in a single blinding release.

All the while, the man in the jaguar mask stood still as stone, and watched silently.

The last thing I remember before I lost consciousness was a reflection of B's housekeeper in the mirror on the wall.

When I awoke, daylight pressed faintly through the heavy curtains. The room was exactly as it had been the night before. The candle was gone. The chair was empty. I was alone.

"The interview has been declined," said the housekeeper with a wry smile. "You have learned all there is to know," she said as she lead me back out the way I came. At the threshold, she paused and smiled; something perceptive in it, something final. Around her neck hung a mask, half jaguar, half deer.

Later that day, back at my hotel, Graham wired me.

"What have you got?" he asked. "We're going to press."

"Nothing," I said. "I've got nothing."

A week later, our rival published an exclusive: an elaborate, glowing interview with B. Every word of it was false. It was later copied word for word onto B's Wikipedia page, where it remains to this day. I was disappointed, sure, but I let it go. I had other authors, other interviews to chase.

Months passed. One day, a package arrived from Oaxaca. There was no return address and no note. Inside was a mask, half jaguar, half deer, and a book, untitled, unauthored. One empty page after another flew past as I flipped through the pages.

I still don't know what actually happened that night. I only know what I saw and what I felt. Whether dream or reality or some drug-induced combination, it has stayed with me ever since. I've come to believe that it was a ruse staged by B to teach me some lesson. I've mulled it over again and again without ever cracking the nut in any satisfactory way. For B, as for his favorite philosopher, Heraclitus, or his favorite poet, Blake, human nature and life itself depend on melding together opposites that are constantly in flux like the opposite poles of two magnets.

Years later, when B died, he left everything, his estate, his papers, and his money, to the housekeeper. She vanished without a trace.

There are moments when I'm alone, when I see her face in that mirror and laugh. I hear her raspy voice: "You have learned all there is to know."

Indeed. I will leave it at that.

She Raven

---

*The eye that mocks a father and scorns a mother— ravens
of the valley will pluck it out; young eagles will eat it.*
—Proverbs 30:17

I've seen lots of ravens lately. If I were superstitious, I might
be nervous. People have all kinds of names for them: death birds,
demon birds, shepherds of the dead. Some say ravens carry the souls
of the unburied, the murdered, the damned. Legend has it that if
two ravens fight at a wedding, the marriage is doomed, and if seven
ravens battle in the sky, war will come.

For every omen there's an opposite belief. Newton's Third Law
for the soul.

To the Indigenous peoples of the Pacific Northwest, Raven is the
Creator, a trickster who brought light to the world. The Norse god
Odin kept two: Huginn and Muninn, Thought and Memory. Ravens
are prophets in feathers. The old Viking warriors believed a raven
could shield them in battle, that its feathers were magic; that a stone
from its nest could make you invisible; that it could unlock anything,
even someone's heart.

Maybe they're all true. Life is full of incompatibilities, at least
mine is.

Ravens have been good to me. They're clever and cunning
survivors. That's why I watch them. That's why I trusted one. A raven
changed my life.

Back when I was young, beautiful, and innocent, selling coke wasn't
my plan. It just happened. I had the knack to get things others couldn't

get as easily. My friends asked me, one after another. I didn't even charge at first, but if I had to risk jail, I figured I might as well get paid. It was just supply and demand, standard capitalism, or so I told myself.

My edge was a bird: my pet raven, Parakeet. Don't ask. It was the first name that came to mind, and it stuck. He spoke like a parrot and was smart as hell. He brought me presents: buttons, bones, shiny rocks, bottle caps arranged like jewelry. That's what drew me in. He'd fly in with a pine sprig strung through a soda tab like it was treasure. I was charmed. That's how I got the idea.

Cocaine usually comes in boring baggies or paper folds, bad for the environment, disposable. I started to wrap mine in ornate boxes, little ceramic jars, origami envelopes, something you'd want to keep, something with a little wonder attached.

Word spread. The product was good, but it was the packaging that caused the chatter and the sales.

Freddie was my supplier. He had cartel ties. I stayed clear of that. It cost more, but it kept me safe. Freddie liked me. I paid cash, up front. I never flaked or owed a cent. I was a customer, not a partner, and that kept me alive.

"The fishermen bring it in," Freddie told me once, his voice low. "CIA's running shit down in Nicaragua. Frogmen smuggle bricks through the Bay. I shouldn't even say."

He pressed his finger to his lips like a bad movie. Sunlight caught the diamond on his ring, and it sparkled like it had a message.

He didn't get it. "You mean you sell more at higher prices just because it looks cute? That's crazy. Where you get that idea?"

"Branding," I said. "It's basic marketing. I learned it from my raven."

Freddie blinked. "You got a pet raven?"

"Yeah. I call him Parakeet."

He laughed. "Why you call him that?"

"Because he talks. He's a big black parakeet that can speak." I flashed him a grin.

"You got beautiful teeth," he said, with that crazy laugh of his.

"I treat my raven well," I told him, "and he treats me well. He brings me gifts."

"No way," said Freddie.

"Yep," I said. "That's how the whole idea started. I thought, what if I made the coke feel like a gift, something personal? My customers trust me. They feel like they get more than magic powder; they get something extra special."

Freddie's eyes darted left, then right, like he was solving a riddle he wasn't sure he wanted the answer to. "Damn! We should call you 'She-Raven.' You smart like the bird."

"Thanks," I said. "Listen, keep that nickname to yourself, all right? This is my game."

He held up his hand, palm out. "No worry, She-Raven."

I knew then I'd screwed myself. Secrets don't stay secret, not when money is involved. Nothing that flies that high stays untouched forever.

These were the days when drugs were in the air like pollen, everywhere, unavoidable. People moved like souped-up machines, all gas and no driver, chasing a high with nothing to steer with but impulse. The first thing you'd hear when someone walked into a room was "Who's got the blow?"

My name made the rounds fast. Word of mouth, still the most potent marketing on earth. People get wild on drugs, no question. Some lose their minds, some lose their lives, but not my clients. Mine were there for the buzz, the glamour, the scene, and were in control, or thought they were. I got swept up like everyone else. The easy cash sparkled, and sure, I won't lie, I liked being wanted. Still, I always kept my head down.

The whole "She Raven" thing blew up faster than even Freddie could've hoped. Suddenly I was the name people whispered when they wanted something clean, discreet, and chic. I had to move smarter. The way I packaged the dope became part of the brand. My packages became a collectible. Some clients flipped the boxes for more than the coke inside. The product still mattered, of course. Everybody wanted to get skied, but the package was the gimmick, the hook for the high-end crowd. Whether rich kids, trust-fund brats, or business types, it was a cocaine couture, and they couldn't get enough.

Jail was the nightmare, but honestly, the risks were low. The cops were busy chasing real violence. Some of them were even on my list. If you did get pinched, first-time offenders usually walked after a month or two and maybe a rehab stint. The real cost wasn't legal, it was losing your pipeline. That's what I feared. I liked the lifestyle and I'd gotten used to the money, and the money was serious: two, three, sometimes five grand a week, untaxed, untraceable. Freddie liked me because I never begged him to front me. I kept it professional. That got me everything I needed. I only served the top-shelf crowd; no street deals, no desperate junkies. Upscale joints: bars, theaters, hotel lobbies, concerts, arenas. I checked out every buyer, and I never sold to strangers.

What's most important, I didn't use, ever. That's rule one in this game. Don't shit where you sleep. I watched plenty of dealers crash and burn because they couldn't follow that rule. I didn't need a drug house or a crew. I prepped everything myself in a hidden nook behind my closet. Nobody knew. I only carried when I had a drop. I usually tucked a stash under my bra or disguised in a charm bracelet, sometimes hidden ahead in a spot I knew I'd circle back to. I never held the stuff longer than necessary.

Discipline kept me sharp and discretion kept me free.

I kept a low profile in my personal life: no drama, no headlines. When it came to business, especially with the top-tier clients in the high-end hotels and velvet-draped theaters, I dressed for the part. That meant heels, designer dress or a tight skirt suit, hair done up, and full makeup: the whole illusion. The men didn't care about the quality of the coke half as much as the image it bought them. Most weren't even real users. They wanted the drugs to impress the young women they brought along, girls they wanted to party with, sleep with, show off for. A girl dealer added panache.

I could've cut the product and padded my margins, but reputation was everything. In that world, speed and safety were worth more than purity. Clients wanted clean, quick deliveries; some of them were already high when they called, desperate to get their next bump before the crash hit.

"Coke and sex addiction go hand in hand," one girl told me. "Middle-aged guys snort lines with college girls and escorts. It's like they've forgotten how to have normal sex."

I didn't tolerate violence against women, but the truth is, most of the women were willing participants. They chased the high as much as the status. They liked the glow, the glamour, the illusion of power that came with hanging off the arm of a well-dressed man with money to burn. I told myself it was better than the chaos of the crack houses, where desperation stank in the walls and violence was always one bad deal away. These girls were going to score somewhere; better from me than from some street shark with a switchblade and a grudge.

High-quality coke brings in cash, sure, but it's not the purity that sells, it's the immediacy. Having it right there, ready, when the girls walk through the door. These men liked to have perfect white lines lined up on a mirror before the party even started.

The circles I moved in were loose and loud: rich kids mostly, young men who ran in packs of four or five, wild for the weekend; party animals with too much money and not enough fear. I had female clients, too, Many of them preferred buying from a woman. There was a comfort in that, I think. A little less risk.

Every city has its saints and sinners, its sanctuaries and shadows. I learned how to navigate both. Most bar owners looked the other way as long as the deals stayed in the bathroom or down some dark hallway. They understood the economics. Cocaine meant more drinks sold, longer nights, looser wallets and looser tongues. Bars are where people go to forget themselves, or find someone else.

My clientele ran the full spectrum: lawyers, doctors, college kids, teachers, mechanics, bartenders, secretaries, you name it. When I wasn't dressed to kill, I kept it casual but sharp: tight jeans, a snug top, tennis shoes, but my hair and makeup were always done. Appearance was part of the hustle. I never looked like a street pusher. People felt safer buying from someone who looked like they had something to lose. They appreciated the tamper-proof packages too; little things go a long way.

I didn't feel guilty, not then. I didn't deal to kids. I wasn't some monster. My clients were adults who made their own choices. I just gave them a safer way to make the wrong ones. There's a constant battle between the desire to sin and the need to feel righteous. Anyone with eyes can see it. I spent a lot of nights at a bar called the Butcher Shop. Things got rowdy there, lots of noise, lots of stories. One time, a tourist watched it all unfold and asked the bartender, "So what do normal people do around here?"

The bartender just smiled and poured her drink.

Coke was social. That's how Tina, one of my regulars, put it.

"I only ever do it with alcohol," she said, as she swirled her vodka tonic. "Me and the girls hit the restroom, chop up a couple lines on the tank lid, and boom, back to the bar like nothing happened."

"Yeah," laughed Theresa," and then we're out on the dance floor, eyes twitching in every direction like strobe lights."

"Snorting's an art form," chimed in Rebecca with a giggle. "Like sex. You either learn it the hard way or get a good teacher."

"Sure," Tina nodded. "But you've gotta stay cool or some asshole's gonna grab your ass."

"Those brainless creeps," Rebecca added. "And the people that complain, they don't realize their favorite musicians and comedians are riding the same snowdrift."

But things didn't always stay fun. Cocaine kicks in fast, fades faster. Fifteen minutes and you're itching for more. The high? It's big, bigger than most people are built to handle, which makes the crash worse. It grabs hold like alcohol but with sharper teeth.

"Colors looked brighter," Alice once told me. "Everything felt electric, but then the crash hit, and it was unbearable. Two snorts and I'd be up again. Just to avoid the comedown."

When I suspected someone was stealing to feed their habit, I cut them off. If I thought they were going too far, I told them straight: Get help. That didn't always stick. One woman I knew burned a hole the size of a quarter clean through her septum. Got part of her face rebuilt. Switched to freebasing after that, stuff I didn't deal. She vanished into rehab not long after. I never heard from her again.

I avoided the serious users. My regulars were weekend warriors, bored and restless. They'd start on Thursday, ride the wave through Sunday, and disappear come Monday. The hardcore crowd? They came crawling on Tuesday. I didn't serve them.

Insane deals went down in those barrooms, fueled by coke-induced bravado. I watched a guy buy the bar he was in, then sell it the same night, coked out of his mind. Real estate, startups, brand-new LLCs, they spun out of control on powdered wings. Half the market would collapse if these fools had to go sober for seven days. I didn't sell to that crowd. Too wild, too reckless, too dangerous.

There's nothing *real* about cocaine. It's a mirage. A glittering trick of the brain. A fast-forward fantasy of happiness. It feeds egos, not souls. Cokeheads don't care about truth or consequences, they want to feel godlike for ten minutes. Meanwhile, it's burning down rainforests, funding wars, collapsing families. It's killing people, quietly and loudly, every day.

I played a part. I told myself it wasn't my fault. People chose to use. There are alcoholics and shopaholics and workaholics. Nobody blames bartenders or CEOs or the Walton family. I floated on that denial for a while. I told myself I was clean because I'd never snorted, not once.

I knew deep down I wasn't clean. I was caught in the web.

I didn't have a private life. I was always on-call, always on edge. Then crack exploded, coke cooked with water and baking soda, turned into hard rocks you could smoke. Straight to the brain, fast and devastating. The streets were flooded. Everyone was high, all the time. There were too many dealers, no boundaries. The whole game changed. What worked for the few fell apart for the many.

It was time to quit. Quitting isn't easy when you're addicted to money so I hopped along a while longer.

One night, my parrot, Parakeet, flew out of his cage and came at me. He pecked my face to ribbons and clawed at my eyes. He'd never done anything like that before. I don't believe in omens, but I took it as one.

That night, I stopped cold. I let Parakeet fly free into the night. Then I grabbed my stash of cash, packed up, and vanished. No goodbyes. I knew too much to stick around. I changed my name, changed my life and disappeared.

Would I do it again? If I could go back, knowing what I know now?

I want to say no. I should say no. But the truth is I don't know. When you're young and hungry and clueless, chasing something you can't name, you mess up, sometimes fatally. Somebody always pays. Maybe it's you, maybe it's the user, maybe it's the planet. Maybe all three.

Eventually, I settled into a new routine. Years later, I heard someone started a company called She Raven Designs. They sell gift boxes now, no coke, just candles and tea. Go figure.

The next wave was Oxy, basically heroin in pill form. Of course, corporate America wanted in. I'm lucky I stayed clear of that. Kids are lacing coke with fentanyl now. One dust mote too much and you're dead. I wouldn't be surprised if someone starts calling coke a gateway drug, like they did with weed. Then the poor folks go to prison, the prisons overflow, and maybe coke gets legalized too.

Whatever. It's not my problem anymore and hasn't been for a long time.

I'm old now and gray, and tucked away in the quiet corners of a society falling apart from the inside out. Do I carry some of the blame? I suppose I do. We all go down on the *Titanic*, trying to guess which stairway is up.

I lost myself in that cocaine daze, but I found my way out before it was too late. I'm thankful for that. She Raven still lives on but it's someone else's worry now and nothing more than the same old materialist shit that powers the American economy into environmental overload. God help us.

Don't Explain It Away

Strange things happen when the fog rolls in.

Reality softens. Edges blur. It gets harder to tell where the world ends and your thoughts begin.

John and Blake sat on the deck with bourbon in plastic cups as the gray mist swallowed the sun.

"I'm working on something new," Blake said, and he swirled the amber in his cup. "Might be onto something big this time."

John had heard this before. Blake said it every few months, always with a flicker of the old fire, but it had been years since he'd published. One breakout novel after college, critically adored, prize-winning, optioned for a film that never materialized. The early success turned out to be more trap than springboard. Since then, the world spun on without him, and Blake grew bitter. He hung out at the Frolic Bar where he relived his one success over and over to anyone who would listen.

"What's it about?" John asked, his voice light.

"I don't want to jinx it," Blake said. "It's too early for me to give any details."

Morgen and Catherine were busy in the kitchen. They moved around each other easily, tossed a salad, boiled pasta. Randall, John's neighbor, had dropped off a fresh salmon earlier that day, one of his many quiet offerings. He worked at Rossi Building Materials but fished every chance he got, especially when he knew Morgen would be around.

"I think Randall's got a crush on you," John teased when Morgen put the fish in the frig. She laughed, but he could see the faint blush. Randall's rugged, untethered charm wasn't lost on her.

They'd invited Blake and Catherine for dinner and told Randall to swing by after work. He always brought good energy and better stories.

Blake finished his drink. John grabbed the bottle and tilted it toward him.

"Top off?"

"Why not?" Blake said. "Bourbon's the only defense we've got against this cursed fog. That's why we call it 'Fogust' around here, I guess."

"It's getting cold," John said. "I think we'll have to eat inside."

He peered through the kitchen window just as Randall arrived, arms wide. Randall hugged Morgen and Catherine with that easy warmth of his. John tapped the glass and waved him out.

Randall stepped outside. "You guys started without me, huh?" He took the cup John offered and nodded to Blake. "How's it going, man?"

"Blake's started a new book," John said.

Blake winced. "Don't listen to him. Just scribbles, really. Probably nothing."

"Didn't you just say you were onto something?" John asked, eyebrow raised.

Randall laughed and deflected. "You need help with that salmon?"

"I've got it. The girls are at the door now. I'll throw it on," John said. "Hey, babe, can you set the table inside? It's getting cold out here."

"Already done," Morgen said. She smiled as she passed Billy.

"So, Blake," Randall said, as he leaned on the railing, "what's this mystery project? Spill it. What's it about, any of us?"

Morgen laughed. Blake flushed a deep red.

John poured another round and emptied the bottle. He ducked inside to grab a second one. Just as he returned, the lights flickered and went out.

"Here we go again," Randall muttered as the house went dark. "You guys really ought to get a generator."

"What's with all these blackouts lately?" Morgen asked as she reached for the candles. "Good thing we're prepared. I'll light the tapers and switch on the battery lights."

"I've got it," Randall said, and trailed her inside. John and Morgen had a small forest of battery-operated LED shimmer trees. They were festive; slightly tacky, but surprisingly useful. Randall had snagged them on discount through work. They gave the dining room a soft, twinkling glow.

Out back, Catherine held a flashlight steady while John tended the salmon on the grill.

"I wish you hadn't brought up my book," Blake said, as he cradled his bourbon. "I hate to talk about stuff that isn't finished. Besides, publishers aren't on the hunt for straight white male writers right now. Even if I wrote something brilliant, no one would touch it."

"So, now you're a victim of diversity?" John smirked. "Sexist and racist. That's quite a combo."

"You're about one wisecrack away from pissing me off," Blake snapped. He drained his glass and poured another.

"All right, boys," Catherine said coolly. "It's Friday night. Let's not start a war."

John pulled the salmon off the grill and brought it inside. They gathered around the table. He poured wine for the girls and passed the platters around.

"C'mon, Blakey," Morgen said. "Tell us what it's about. I want to know. It sounds exciting."

Blake exhaled sharply. "I've had enough of this," he said loudly. "It's not about *any of you*." He glanced around the table, piqued and sheepish at the same time. "It's about... ghosts."

"Ghosts?" Randall echoed, as he lifted a forkful of salmon to his mouth. He wasn't as drunk as the rest.

"Wait, real ghosts?" John arched an eyebrow. "You mean like the Winchester House, right? That kind of thing?" Practical to the bone, John didn't believe in the supernatural. Attorneys rarely did. "Nobody buys into real ghosts anymore."

"I do," Randall said. "I've seen them, out on the ocean. When I'm alone."

Morgen reached across the table and touched Randall's hand." So have I," she said softly.

Even Catherine brightened. Usually reserved, she became excited. "I've seen things at the hospital. Not apparitions, exactly, but presences. Human essences. There's something there that we don't have the words for but it's real."

John groaned. "You've all gone nuts. I need another drink."

Outside, the fog pressed in, and swallowed the view of the garden and the forest beyond. It was as if the world had shrunk to the glow of flickering candles and bourbon-soaked voices.

Blake let the silence linger. He let their attention stretch around him. He topped off his drink.

"Even if I finish the damn book," he said, "I'll never find a publisher. Good agents are as hard to find as unicorns. The industry wants easy sells. Trendy garbage. Not stories that actually mean something."

John slammed back his drink and poured another.

The conversation picked up speed and heat as the alcohol flowed. Suddenly, the power blinked back on.

"Jesus," Blake flinched. "Way too bright. Kill the LEDs, John. I like the candles better."

"Fits the ghost story vibe," John muttered, as he flipped the switch.

"You would never understand," Blake said. "Not from that concrete world you live in."

"I made a cake," Morgen suddenly said, to ease the tension. I'll get plates. You can cut your own slice when you're ready."

"None of you have actually seen a ghost," John said. He ignored Morgen's comment about the cake. He couldn't abide the idea that anyone could believe in ghosts. "I mean really seen one. I certainly haven't."

"You wouldn't," Morgen whispered.

John didn't catch it, but Randall did. He chuckled to himself.

"I'm serious," John went on. "People see things like reflections or tricks of the eye, and the brain fills in blanks. It's basic psychology."

"What I saw wasn't a trick," Randall said "It was out there. Real. Call it what you want, but it wasn't something ordinary."

"Exactly," John said, as if that proved his point. "It was something your brain couldn't explain, so you made something up to explain it. It's not supernatural, it's neurological."

"You always do this," Morgen snapped. She set the cake down, her voice tight. "You can't stand the idea of mystery. Not everything needs to be dissected and debunked. There are things science hasn't figured out yet. Is that so hard to admit?"

She sat beside Randall and folded her arms.

"I think we're here for a reason," Catherine said softly. "If we don't fulfill it, maybe some part of us lingers and tries to set things right."

John scoffed. "Maybe we're just meat. Nature doesn't give a damn about us. Hurricanes, earthquakes, cancer, random as a coin toss. People die, the world shrugs. Ghosts? Superstition. Religion needed an afterlife to hook the masses, so it made one up. Where did that get us? Crusades. Extremism. Abuse."

Morgen's cheeks flushed. "What about love?" she asked. "What about connection? Maybe ghosts are reminders that not everything can or should be explained."

Blake leaned forward in agreement. "Yes. Exactly. The ghosts that matter aren't the ones that float in the attic, they're inside us, the selves we bury, the lives we don't live."

John snorted. "You want to talk about love? Fine. But brace yourself. People talk about soul mates like they're fate. Bullshit. If your 'one true love' dies, you mourn, sure, but eventually you meet someone else. We're wired to attach. Whom we love? It's as much chance as anything else. Circumstance. There isn't anything mystical about it."

Morgen's face turned crimson. "Well, I guess you rolled snake eyes, John." She stood, grabbed her wine, stepped outside, and vanished into the fog.

Catherine rose. "I'll go. She's hurt, John. You can be brutal sometimes."

"What the hell did I say?" John threw up his hands. "I made a point. That's all. I didn't say I didn't love her."

"No," Blake said, "you said love isn't real. That it's just another ghost."

"I didn't say that. I said soul mates aren't real. Love is fine. It's just... fluid. Contextual. One person or another. There's a random component to it."

"That's not something most women want to hear," said Randall.

John turned sharply. "What the hell do you know about women, Randall? You even have a girlfriend? While we're at it, quit hovering around my wife. You're a little too friendly sometimes. She's married."

Randall's face closed off. "Got it. Thanks for dinner." He walked out the front door.

"C'mon, Blake," John said, as he poured another drink. "Let's have one more. Let the girls freeze their asses off out there."

Blake stood. "I'm good. So are you. Catherine and I need to head out. Thanks for the meal."

"Bullshit!" John slammed the bottle down. "Go on, leave me like the rest. Screw your damn book. Screw your precious ghosts. All you do is whine about how hard it is to put a few words on a piece of paper. Real writers pump out books year after year. Success builds success. Failure builds failure. That's life."

He poured another bourbon and knocked it back. He knew he'd had too much. Something in him cracked open. He took another drink, grabbed his coat, and shoved the bottle into his pocket. He held his hand against the wall to get his balance, then stumbled outside onto the deck.

The fog hit him like a curtain.

"Morgen?" he called, but his voice came out thin and small. "Please. I'm sorry."

Silence.

He moved down the steps, into the trees. His eyes adjusted slowly as he followed a narrow deer trail. The woods were warped, tangled; trees leaned, deadfall cluttered the ground, leaves hid shallow dips that caught his feet. He tripped, sliced his hand on a jagged limb.

"Dammit!"

He pushed forward with no clear reason why.

In the distance, a faint light flickered. He moved toward it, but it kept its distance. *Must be the moon,* he thought. *Or some kind of reflection.* He looked around but saw no simple explanation.

"Randall?" he called out. "Hey, I didn't mean it. I was drunk. I shouldn't have run my mouth off. We're friends. I'm sorry, man."

No reply except from the trees that swayed with the wind.

He kept going until exhaustion stopped him. He dropped to the ground, leaned against a tree, and pulled out what was left of the bourbon.

Jesus, he thought, *I guess I screwed up. Pissed off every one of them. Why do people, especially women, get so caught up in all this paranormal bullshit? Beats me.*

"Blake!" he shouted. "I'm sorry, man. I want to hear about your story. Really. Forget what I said about ghosts. Tell me. I'll bet it's really good."

Nothing.

He took a final swig. The light still hovered ahead, but he'd lost interest. He flung the bottle toward it. It landed short with a dull thud. He curled into his coat and fell asleep.

Morgen found him at dawn.

"For Christ's sake, John. We looked everywhere. How the hell did you end up out here?"

He blinked at her, groggy and hungover. "Huh?"

"Come on. Let's get you home." She reached for his arm.

"Thanks, Morg." He turned back toward the woods. His eyes narrowed.

"What is it?" she asked. "What are you looking at?"

"Nothing," he muttered.

She tugged at his arm and he followed.

"You know I love you, right?" he said.

"Yes, John," she replied. "I know. Let's go home."

Margaret

The summer fog twists around the redwoods, thick as smoke and just as quiet. Pale light filters through the canopy, and slices the dark green stillness, a silence so deep it feels sacred. No bird sings or tries to sing. The fog settles around me like a second skin. In this pocket of isolation, untouched by sound or motion, time holds its breath. Whether it's madness or peace, it only holds for a moment until the world rushes in.

Drip. Drip. Drip. Condensation slides from branches to the forest floor. A foghorn bellows from somewhere far off. A raven croaks once, rough and abrupt. The outside seeps in and bleeds into my solitary space, a silence that, for a moment, was everything, was enough.

Two men emerge through the fog like evil personified. They walk toward me down the hill. Tall, dark-skinned, they carry fishing poles and plastic buckets, like they'd stepped out of a bad dream with a cheerful mask painted over it.

"Any luck down there?" one calls out.

"Just mussels," I say. "I'm making spaghetti sauce."

"They're toxic this time of year."

"I'll take my chances."

We stop a few feet apart, like warriors before a fight. The tall one, Louie, speaks. His brother, Billy, watches like a mute, not dangerous but unsettling.

"You oughta come watch the parade from our deck," Louie says. "We'll get drunk. Billy and I will fry the fish. You can bring that toxic spaghetti of yours."

"I'll pass. I'm gonna sit it out at home this year. You guys have a good time. See 'ya around."

I turn to go. I know they'll rattle me if I stay.

"Suit yourself. Margaret will be there."

That wolfish smile on Louie's face beneath his thick black mustache goads me, but I don't take the bait. Billy giggles on cue.

Golden hair. Ivory teeth. Eyes like robin's eggs. That was Margaret.

"Tell her hello," I say as if I don't care.

"She'll be sad if you're not there, Randall. Don't be a jackass. Drop by around two. What else you got goin' on? Who sits home alone on the Fourth of July?"

"Yeh, what else you got goin' on?" Billy parrots.

"If I'm there, I'm there," I say. "Don't count on it."

I walk away. Behind me, they descend toward the surf and slither like eels into the shallow surf. The moment I saw Louie, I knew the day was lost, that my peace was gone. Margaret got into my head again. It's a damn shame.

Time crawled by like a wounded deer limps through the meadow. I rinsed the mussels and stuck them in a bowl in the fridge. I cracked a beer, sat at the kitchen table, and stared out the window. There were apples on the tree, but they weren't ripe yet. They wouldn't be ready until September. I'd be gone by then.

I was done with this place. It was no longer the place I grew up in. I had a job in Port Angeles. Jake set it up. He was a carpenter, same as me. Said they needed hands. After that, I'd decide, head up to British Columbia, maybe. I'd heard it was beautiful. I didn't know a soul there and that was the way I liked it.

I popped the top off another beer. A robin tugged a worm from the soil beneath the apple tree, swallowed it in jerks. I watched the worm disappear down the bird's gullet and made up my mind: no way I'd go to Billy's. I didn't want to see Margaret. That chapter was closed a long time ago.

She chose Tom and the city. She chose the life she thought she wanted. It didn't work out, but that wasn't on me. I didn't owe her. I couldn't get pulled back into her orbit, not again.

We were together a year, maybe two. It's hard to remember now. Then, Tom showed up. Fast-talker, sharp-dresser, money, charm, the whole kit. He swept her off her feet like dirt into a dustpan. I warned her. I saw what he was, but she was already gone. She was gone from me, and gone from who she used to be.

Maybe he loved her. She was easy to love. I seriously doubt it, Tom only loved himself.

I remember when we walked the bluff above the sea. Tall grass, sun on our backs, the crash of waves below. There was a look in her face that day, something wild and clear and new. We made love for the first time there, under the open sky. I told her I loved her. It was a mistake to say it. She wasn't ready to hear it. That was the beginning of the end.

I knew it was over the day I saw her on the porch, curlers in, mouth full of red fireball gum, phone clutched to her ear. I didn't need to ask who was on the other end. Her face gave it away. The blush. The smile. It was Tom. She was gone.

I couldn't believe it. Not then. Maybe not even now.

Goddamn it, Louie, why'd you have to say Margaret would be there?

Once, we were in my car and she said she wanted to see the snow. Just like that. No coats, no money, just the impulse. We drove straight to the mountains, no plan, no hesitation. We threw snowballs till our fingers burned from the cold, and we laughed like kids, until we dove back into the car to feel our skin again. She did that to me. She spun me around without warning. She made the world feel tilted, reckless, alive.

A rabbit nosed through the grass in the empty lot across the street. That was it. All the action was in town where they geared up for the Fourth: barbecues lit, flags out, music amped up. I heard a few firecrackers snap in the distance like nervous fingers. Louie and Billy were probably back by now. The parade would start in an hour.

I opened another beer. I won't go. That's final. I wandered the house in silence, room to room. It was tidy, always had been. Even when I was a kid living with my grandparents, I kept my room in order. That was my world, my own small kingdom. I scooped up the dirty laundry, started a wash, congratulated myself that I remembered the bread for dinner. French bread and pasta. I got everything set up, then took my beer outside and settled into a chair.

The fog lifted but the sky stayed gray, thick as wool. It felt like winter even though it was July. That's how the coast is, sweltering inland, damp and cool here. When I miss the heat I take a drive over to the valley just to soak it in, sit under the stars, and feel it on my skin like firelight. Sometimes I stay and sleep. I've even slept out under the sky, just to remember I could.

The town will be packed. Everyone will come for the parade. In a place like this, it's the main event. Floats decked out on flatbeds, log trucks pass by with redwood trunks as big as whales. Old-timers and toddlers play cowboy on horses. Marching bands stomp and blow and bang while baton-twirling girls lead the way in shorts and sequins. The fire department brings out their rigs, everyone's in full gear. The weird crowd comes too: dyed hair, piercings, the whole show. Politicians show up to woo the voters. Most folks come just to feel a part of something. Announcers rattle off names from loudspeakers, judges take notes, winners are crowned. People leave with smiles. I won't be there. I don't want to be. I go back inside.

I add cheap white wine to the water in the pot and drop in mussels and bay leaves. Garlic sizzles in a pan. I add tomatoes, saffron. When the mussels pop open, I strain the broth, add salt, pepper. The aroma makes me hungry.

Time rushes past faster than I expect.

I switch to red wine and drink the first glass like water. I put on the pasta.

I hear a knock at the door.

The fog had burned off completely. The sky looked painted, a white cloud with a golden glow. The sun was buried behind the cloud like a secret. A breeze moved the leaves outside. It was chilly again. I couldn't see her face against the light, but I didn't have to. I already knew it was her.

"Hi."

"Hi."

"I heard you made spaghetti. You always make too much. Mind if I join? I brought a decent red."

What was I supposed to say? *I don't want to see you. I wish you hadn't come.*

"Thanks. Come on in. Spaghetti's almost ready."

"Hold on. Let's catch up first."

Three years, I thought. *How do you catch up on three years?*

I turned off the burner, poured two glasses of the cheap red, and kept hers for later.

"No girlfriend?" she asked, as she glanced around. The silence in the place must've answered for me.

"No point. I'm out of here soon."

"Leaving? Where?"

"British Columbia. Next month, probably."

A bee landed in my wine. I fished it out with my finger, and it flew off, dazed but alive. Jays screeched in the trees. She watched me with a look I couldn't name. Her hair still caught the light like spun gold. Her eyes were the same shade of trouble. Her smile didn't quite hold though, and she'd lost weight.

Her glass was empty. I filled it, then topped mine off.

"You know," she said, "my father told me I should've married you, not Tom. I was so blind, Randall. What a mess."

"That was a long time ago. I'm sorry things didn't work out."

"Yeah."

She looked down.

"British Columbia. That's far. For good?"

"For good. I've stayed here too long. Nothing left for me. How's San Francisco?"

"Lonely," she whispered. "I'm really lonely, Randall. Oh, God, I can't do this."

She started to cry, came over, and sat beside me. She laid her head on my shoulder.

"Oh, Randall. Hold me. Just this once. Please."

What could I do? I put my arm around her. She folded into me like no time had passed. I could smell her hair, feel her skin. My heart fluttered the way it used to. Then, surprisingly, I realized my feelings for her were gone. I felt only emptiness inside.

I sat there, hungry, and wished she'd leave.

"I guess I'll make the pasta."

She didn't move. It was like a sleeping child when you're scared to move, scared to wake it. Ten minutes passed. My arm went numb.

She rose at last. She knew. No words were needed. She left without a word.

I wanted to say something, God knows what. I opened my mouth. She put a finger to my lips.

"Shh."

I didn't see her again for ten years. Funny how memory works. I spotted her in a mall with a man who looked like Tom but wasn't. She looked older, thinner, tired, but I knew it was her.

She didn't see me. I didn't make myself seen. I stepped into the sun and walked away.

Last year, I was back in Mendocino and ran into Louie and Billy at the bar.

"Hey, Randall, you back?" Louie said.

"Just passing through."

He still wore that slick little grin. Maybe it wasn't evil. Maybe it was just his face.

"Remember Margaret?"

"Sure."

"You really pissed her off, man, not showing up that day."

That smile *was* evil. Everything about Louie was evil.

"Yeah," Billy added. "She just packed up and went back to the city. She's a high-priced hooker now. Rich clients only."

"Oo-ee! Fancy lady!" Billy crowed.

I knocked him out cold. Louie pulled a knife; I kicked it from his hand and broke his nose.

The bartender called the cops, but I was gone before they showed.

I'm back in British Columbia. I've got a little cabin tucked into the cove. I fish. I do odd jobs to make a little dough. I don't need much.

I've let my beard grow. My hair's wild. No one bothers me. That's how I like it.

Sometimes I close my eyes and let it all vanish. I do that a lot.

Hell, Margaret wouldn't even recognize me now.

Henry's Woodpeckers

In East Mendocino, we're known for our woodpeckers.

We're a quiet little enclave tucked just inland from the more famous Mendocino Village. Tourists often pass us by, which suits most of us just fine. Locals here are a strange and colorful mix: hippies and loggers, artists, carpenters, fishermen, small business owners, government workers, and the occasional escapee from city life. For the most part, we get along. The woodpeckers and the humans have worked out a kind of truce. We stick to our routines. So do they.

Our biggest and loudest neighbor is the Pileated Woodpecker, a foot and a half of red-crested fur with wild yellow eyes and a shriek that could wake the dead. It hammers away at redwood snags and towering firs, sends drumbeats echoing across the forest like a warning. Its sharp beak carves out holes the size of a man's fist. You don't forget the sound once you've heard it.

Then there's the acorn woodpecker, a little joker with a face like a painted mask. You'll see them in gangs, working the oaks, stashing acorns into hundreds of tiny holes they've drilled into trees, fence posts, even telephone poles. We've also got downies and hairies, flickers, sapsuckers, and Nuttall's. Their plumage flares like tiny beacons against the forest's backdrop of green and gray.

The woodpeckers that put us on the map though, they aren't the ones that fly and drill. They're Henry's.

Henry was, well, let's call him eccentric. He lived on a rundown spread just beyond the last paved road, and he had a thing for woodpeckers. He wasn't satisfied to just watch or listen to them. His passion was to stuff and preserve them. He mounted them in lifelike poses on the trees around his house.

People came from all over to see Henry's collection, especially kids. I was one of those kids. The real woodpeckers came too. They'd flutter around the woods, call and hammer, then freeze in their tracks when they caught sight of one of Henry's birds. They were curious, sure, but never fooled. Henry's woodpeckers didn't move. They didn't eat or fight. They didn't fly in that trademark up-and-down rollercoaster way. They just hung there, silent and stiff.

Sometimes, when the forest was still, it was hard to tell the difference. You'd see a flash of red or yellow cling to a tree trunk and say, "That one's real," but if it didn't twitch, didn't tap, didn't even breathe, it was one of Henry's.

Real woodpeckers go quiet sometimes, but they never go *dead*. That's the difference. Birds don't linger around corpses. People, some people, are drawn to dead things. They gawk. They photograph. They make up sensational stories.

Henry didn't speak much. He charged a small entrance fee and pointed you toward the trees. That was it. No guided tours, no friendly chatter. His house was a mystery. The barn was always locked. Locals said he lived with his wife, two children, one dog and one cat. No one was quite sure. Nobody ever got invited inside.

He let the dead birds speak for themselves.

One day, Henry's family vanished, all of them, even the dog and the cat. There was no warning and no note. One morning they were there, the next they weren't. People in town waited for them to come back, as if it was some kind of break or misunderstanding, but Henry's family didn't return.

Rumors filled the vacuum.

"He chased them off with that strange behavior of his," said the town barber.

"Maybe his wife ran off with someone else," speculated the checker at the grocery store.

"How could that be?" said the owner of the bookstore. "He never let them out of the house."

Eventually, the gossip died down. The questions stopped. Henry didn't explain, and no one dared press him.

Henry turned to his birds.

He filled his property with feeders to lure in the local woodpeckers. He stocked the feeders with the suet, seed, and fruit he knew they liked. He wasn't a birdwatcher; he was a taxidermist. He trapped and stuffed them, and arranged them in lifeless displays that filled the forest like grim trophies, but the live birds never gave his stuffed ones so much as a glance. Woodpeckers, unlike some birds, know the difference between dead and alive, especially when it comes to mating. Ducks might try, but woodpeckers? Never.

The same old Pileated Woodpecker returns each spring. It hammers away at a redwood snag at the edge of Henry's overgrown meadow. He's a big one, flame-red crest, yellow eyes, and a scream like a banshee. He probably knows more about Henry than Henry knows about him. My grandfather once said if you see a woodpecker it means someone's going to die. The fire chief swore their red heads were omens of wildfire. Indian Joe, whose ancestors were Pomo, says the sound of a woodpecker drumming is the heartbeat of the earth. If they vanish, so does the planet.

The old woodpecker doesn't seem to care about omens or fate. He braces himself against that snag with two toes forward, two back, his tail propped stiff for support. Then he goes to work. Kyuk, kyuk, kak-kak, kyuk, kyuk, kak-kak, a rhythm as old as trees. He's not worried about death or prophecy. He's on the hunt for carpenter ants or maybe trying to impress a mate. He's a worker, a craftsman, a sculptor who chisels perfect rectangular cavities high in the snag, year after year. Beneath the tree, a soft pile of wood shavings marks his industry.

Woodpeckers will drum on anything that echoes: tin roofs, gutters, hollow logs, metal signs, anything but glass or painted walls. They have no use for plastic, mesh, or wind chimes. Henry knew this, so he built his house to be woodpecker-proof, no music, no invitation.

The birds prefer the margins anyway. They haunt the edges of orchards, tangled grapevines, berry thickets, and the rotting trees where insects breed. They're good for orchards. They eat what harms the fruit. Their scarlet crests flash in the sun as they dart from limb to limb. You rarely see more than a blur.

Watch one at work on an apple tree: It stops, listens, taps, then drills. Something inside the bark, a grub, perhaps, could kill the tree from within. The woodpecker can't see it, but hears it as it chews. The insect, disturbed, scurries deeper, trying to escape. The woodpecker hammers faster, tongue ready. When the time is right: wham! The woodpecker's barbed tongue strikes like a harpoon. He pulls out the grub and swallows it whole. His tongue, nearly four inches long, coils around his skull when not in use. He saves the tree by doing what he does best: find the rot and tear it out.

Sometimes I think about Henry when I see that old bird at the snag. Maybe he hears what's hidden under the surface. Maybe he expects someone, or something, to claw its way back to light, but all that's left now is the drumming.

Most of Henry's apples went into his cider. Tart, crisp, and always in demand. he sold it at the local stores. Aside from that, his only income came from the modest admission he charged to visitors eager to see his famous woodpecker display. Rumor had it Henry inherited a small fortune from an eccentric uncle, a man even more unhinged than Henry himself. The uncle believed he *was* a woodpecker. He strapped on a pair of homemade wings, flung himself off a cliff, and plummeted into the sea like Icarus. Henry hadn't taken flight, not yet anyway.

He had brochures printed for the display: Glossy paper filled with facts about each bird, some real, some invented. His orchard, he claimed, doubled as a "living classroom." Once, a state inspector came by to check for permits. Whatever paperwork was required, Henry must have produced it, because the inspector never came back.

Henry liked kids, especially local schoolchildren. I visited his orchard once the same year the high school basketball team disappeared. They were headed down the coast in a van to play an away game. Never made it. A massive search turned up nothing, no wreckage, no bodies, no tire tracks. The official story was that the van slid off a cliff and sunk into the Pacific. Everyone agreed it was a tragedy. Henry, who rarely left his orchard, joined the search. Later, he donated one of his stuffed woodpeckers for a community auction to raise money for the families. People said he may have been weird, but he had a good heart.

After my visit, I got it into my head to sneak back and check out Henry's barn. Something about the place felt off. I dared a few friends to come with me. We went just after dark. The fence wasn't hard to climb. We crept through the orchard to the barn, which was locked. There was a high window at the back. I suggested we lean a board against the wall and climb up. They chickened out, but my curiosity got the best of me. I got the board in place and scrambled up.

What I saw through that window froze me in place. I slipped and crashed to the ground, bruised but lucky. My heart hammered all the way home. The next morning, I went to the police station and told them everything. It felt good just to say it out loud.

The very next day, the sheriff and his deputy showed up at Henry's place.

"Hey, Henry," the sheriff said. "How've you been?"

Henry smiled and handed each of them a cold glass of apple cider.

"One of the local kids told us quite a story," the sheriff added as he drank.

Henry didn't flinch.

"Mind if we have a look inside the barn?"

"Of course," Henry said pleasantly, and led them there himself.

Inside, the walls were covered in birds, hundreds of them, stuffed, mounted, posed mid-peck or mid-flight, but at the back of the barn, the deputies stopped in disbelief.

It was a tableau of domestic bliss.

Henry's wife and children sat with both sets of grandparents. The kids played on a rug. His wife stirred a pot of cider. The grandparents played cards. The cat napped beside the dog. All of them perfectly preserved, taxidermied and dressed in their everyday clothes, posed like they'd never left.

The missing state inspector was there too and so was the basketball team and the coach.

Henry watched them sip his cider and waited for the poison to kick in.

Later, when the sheriff and his deputy failed to return, a search party went out. Their cruiser was found down a ravine off Comptche Road, twisted and abandoned. No bodies, no clues, just more unanswered questions.

Authorities returned to search Henry's property. They found the barn empty except for a few dusty woodpeckers. No cider press, no family, no visitors.

In time, the mystery faded like fog at dawn. The tourists found other diversions and the locals stopped asking questions. Henry's woodpecker display gained notoriety. The orchard remained open. People said it was quaint, a bit strange, maybe, but harmless.

So, what really happened?

Some things, folks around here say, are better left unexplained.

Occasionally, I think back to what I saw in Henry's barn. I've done my best to forget, but the memory won't let go. People say it was a dream, a hallucination, a psychotic break, anything but the truth. No one believes me; not the doctors, not the few friends I still have. That moment wrecked me. If I could go back, I'd never climb that warped board or peek through that dusty window again.

Henry's been dead for years now, but his stuffed woodpeckers still dangle from the twisted branches of the old apple trees, and sway like strange fruit in the breeze. The new owner still makes cider, and folks still come by from time to time, but it's not like it was when I was a kid. The buzz faded. The rumors, though, they never quite died.

I don't go near Henry's orchard anymore, not since the voices started. I hear them in the soil, whispering from under the roots. I know what's buried there: Henry's family, the county inspector, the sheriff, the vanished basketball team. People say I'm insane. Maybe I am. But the woodpeckers know. They're the only ones who still listen.

That big Pileated Woodpecker returns each year to the same redwood snag at the edge of the property. I swear he drums out the truth in bursts of Morse code. Just before Indian Joe passed, he told me he heard the voices too. After that, there was no one left but me to listen.

The Nineties

Money Chase

When I first met Riley Gulick, I had no idea one day I'd chase him halfway around the world to recover the money he stole from our clients.

We met at an investment conference in New York; two small-town boys who'd found our way into big money. We both jogged at dawn, ran successful financial-planning firms, and had built reputations as trusted advisors. On a crisp fall morning, as we jogged around the pond in Central Park, we decided to team up.

Our client bases overlapped in interesting ways. I worked mostly with farmers: rice growers, orchard owners, cattle ranchers. My background was academic; I had ties to university economists, policy wonks, even a couple of Nobel laureates. Riley came from a glitzier world. His niche was sports and entertainment. One of his clients was the family of rock-and-roll legend Bill Haley, who'd once lived in Riley's hometown of Harlingen, Texas.

At one of our quarterly meetings when I was having trouble staying awake, Riley leaned over and said, "Jer, I know how much you hate the administrative bullshit. What if I took that off your plate?"

"You don't hate it too?" I asked.

"Of course I do, but I've got a crack admin team just sitting around half the time. You're a client guy. People trust you. Let me handle the back-end drudgery. You can focus on new accounts. We'll grow our book way faster that way."

I hesitated. "I don't know. I like to keep an eye on the engine, to know how things run under the hood."

"Oh, come on, Mr. Jerry Fleishman," Riley said, with a smirk. "You think I can't handle it, or is it that you don't trust me?"

"It's not that," I said. "I know my Adam Smith. Division of labor makes sense, but I owe it to my clients to maintain scrupulous oversight. Due diligence isn't just a checklist, it's a mindset."

"Right," he said. "I get it."

"Let me think it over," I said. "Give me a couple of weeks."

Together, our firms managed half a billion in assets. I saw the upside: if I could offload the administrative grind, I could easily double that in a few years, but the devil was in the details. I convinced myself that quarterly reports would keep me in the loop, that I'd be able to catch the red flags, if any, in time. I was wrong.

I wanted the growth, wanted the win, and when I chased the money, I ignored the actual discomforts in my gut. It was a rookie mistake, and it came back to bite me hard.

Riley stood about six feet tall, with wavy blond hair, blue eyes, and the kind of pretty-boy face that made people look twice. Some guys win the genetic lottery. Me? I'm five-eight on a good day, with red hair, freckles, and a face people forget five minutes after they meet me. You might think I'd be the numbers guy and Riley the people person, but life doesn't always read the script.

Turns out, I had the charm, the quiet kind that connected with clients who'd built everything from nothing. My family was wealthy, but I didn't play that card. They trusted me because I didn't try to dazzle them. Riley, on the other hand, came across a little too slick for the self-made millionaires. That should've warned me, but the money blinded me. I wanted to prove to my parents I could make my own fortune, and I was in too much of a hurry to see the risks. Riley dropped the names of rock stars and athletes like they were poker buddies. I let myself get dazzled just like his clients.

A few weeks into our partnership, something caught my eye on the client reports.

"Hey, Riley," I said over the phone. "What's this Charter Income fund? We've got a pretty big chunk parked there."

It would have been better if I'd asked in person; I like to read faces when the stakes are high, but I was buried in meetings and couldn't spare the time to fly out.

"Jer," he said, "you know stock prices are through the roof. Charter Income's a safe fixed-income play. Keeps us in the game without the risk of getting burned in a market pullback. The fund manager's a close friend. Solid track record. He's delivered market-level returns with minimal downside for years. We're lucky to get any allocation at all given the herd of advisors that want in."

He kept up with the praise: Charter had clients in Hollywood, pro sports, old-money dynasties. The best advisers in the country trusted him. He served on an industry oversight board. He was the real deal.

"Sure," I said, "but I've read the prospectus. Their models don't make sense to me. The returns look too good to be true."

"Trust me, Jer," Riley said. "I know the guy. We went to school together. He's a mensch. We'll ease in, just a small allocation to start, okay?"

"Fine," I said. "Next time I'm in town, I want a face-to-face meet with their team. Set it up."

"Will do," he said. "They're swamped right now. Let's not rattle the cage. Give me a couple months."

"As soon as you can," I said. "I don't want some invisible bug to bite us in the butt."

"Neither do I," Riley said. "I've got my finger on it. I'll double the oversight."

I didn't know it then, but that was the last time I'd ever hear Riley's voice.

⧗ ⧗ ⧗

A month later, I got the call that cracked everything wide open.

"Jerry, I don't even know where to begin," said Lorna, Riley's office manager. Her voice trembled, like she already knew this would be the worst conversation of her professional life. "Riley's gone. Just disappeared. He flew out for some due diligence meeting and promised to stay in touch. He called once or twice... then nothing."

I felt the hollow spot in my stomach.

"There's more," she added. "Charter Income has been marked to zero across all our client accounts. Turns out it was a Ponzi scheme.

Riley was involved, deeply. I hate saying this, but it looks like he's a conman, a crook. All last week the feds tore through our files, and they're still at it."

"How bad?" I asked, though I already knew the answer wouldn't be survivable.

"Fifty million, split equally across the board."

I sat down hard. "Jesus Christ. That's going to bury us."

She lowered her voice. "We'll have to wait for the auditors' report. From what they've said so far, you'll likely avoid criminal charges. Civil suits are bound to come. Your E&O insurance won't cover everything given the policy limits."

My voice cracked. "He vouched for them, Lorna. Told me he *knew* the Charter guys. I brought it up a month ago and he brushed me off. Now I know why."

"I'm so sorry, Jerry. I can't believe it either."

"Call me when you know more. I've got clients to notify."

By late afternoon, the SEC padlocked my office and froze all client accounts. Just like that, my business, my income, and my reputation were gone. The investigation swallowed my assets whole. I wasn't bankrupt, but everything I'd built professionally was in the deep freeze.

The one piece of good news came weeks later: No criminal liability. I was officially exonerated from the fraud itself, but that didn't mean I was off the hook. They hit me with "insufficient oversight." That meant I'd be tied up in civil court for years. Until the case closed, I was barred from the industry.

With no business left to manage, I turned to the only thing that made sense: I vowed to track Riley down whatever it took. It wasn't just about revenge; I wanted justice, I wanted answers, and I wanted to claw back as much of that money as possible for my clients, even if no one else seemed to care. The feds had already moved on, another dead end for their caseload. They passed it to the asset recovery program, which meant the trail would go cold, unless I followed it myself.

I started with a guess. Riley had mentioned a Dutch girl, Anika Visser. He told me about her once. She was from Harlingen. "Same name as my Texas hometown," he laughed once, "but with better coffee and better sex." He was head over heels in love.

If Riley ran, Europe made sense, and if he was hiding out with Anika, then the Netherlands was the place to start. Even if I didn't find him, I figured Amsterdam would be a good place to lick my wounds: Van Gogh, Rembrandt, canals and tulips, and the city's darker pleasures. They were exactly Riley's speed.

I booked a flight.

⧗ ⧗ ⧗

I landed at Schiphol Airport with no real plan, just a backpack, a guidebook, and a vague idea that I might find answers in the Netherlands. From the airport, I caught the NS train to Centraal Station. It was late, the station buzzed with travelers and the kind of fatigue that hangs in the air after dark. I stood under the harsh fluorescent lights and flipped through hotel listings, unsure where to go next.

That's when she approached me.

"Hi, there," she said, in flawless English. "Do you need a place to stay? I run a small B&B not far from here. It's cozy, affordable, and includes a big breakfast. Easy access to all the tourist spots. Much better than some anonymous hotel."

She was blonde, maybe in her late twenties, with a warm, confident smile and the kind of presence that puts you instantly at ease. She was professional, a charmer, and I quickly relaxed just enough that I didn't second-guess her pitch.

She handed me a bus ticket. "Take this to Marco Polostraat. It's about twenty minutes. Walk to the end of the street; someone from my team will check you in. I'll meet you there after I pick up a few more guests."

I glanced at the ticket, then at her. It was a gamble, but at least I wouldn't be stranded in the station all night. I took the ride.

That turned out to be one of the best decisions I've ever made.

The next morning, I joined the other guests at the breakfast table. It was a spread worthy of a magazine: cheeses, meats, fresh pastries, cereals, and enough coffee to fuel an army.

Across from me sat an Israeli couple. The woman, Talia, grinned as her husband dug into the buffet like it was his last meal.

"They call him the little elephant back home," she said with a laugh. I could see why.

Around the table were a pair of young Americans, two Moroccans, and a French couple. Everyone was younger, but I was welcomed in that easy European way.

After breakfast, I had coffee with Tara, the owner.

"So," she said, stirring her cup, "you plan to hit the usual sights? Canals, museums, the Red Light District?"

"Not exactly," I said. "I'm here to find someone."

That got her attention.

"I need to start in Harlingen. There was a waitress there, Anika, who worked at one of the harbor restaurants. I think she may be involved in something bad."

"A girlfriend?" Tara asked, eyes narrowed with curiosity.

I hesitated, then told her everything. The Ponzi scheme, Riley's disappearance, the missing millions. I told her about Anika's possible involvement, how she and Riley might have run off together, possibly under new names. How I wanted answers, closure, maybe justice.

She listened without interruption, just nodded, her face impenetrable.

"That's awful," she said finally. "I can't believe your friend turned out to be a thief."

She paused, then leaned forward. "I have an idea. My B&B's full for the next few days, and my staff can handle things. Let me drive you to Harlingen. I'll help you look."

I blinked. "Seriously? You'd drive me and help me ask around?"

She laughed. "Jerry, don't look so stunned. Not all Dutch people are standoffish. Besides, I have the time, and I like a good mystery. It's a long drive, three, maybe four hours, but we'll check out as many harbor restaurants as we can, and maybe we can find out something about your partner."

She stood up and grabbed her keys. "Fifteen minutes. Be ready. We'll make a day of it."

⧗ ⧗ ⧗

Harlingen was a beautiful, historic city, but we didn't see much of it. Instead, we trudged from one restaurant to the next along the waterfront. We interviewed owners and staff, but time after time, we hit dead ends. I was ready to call it quits when fortune smiled unexpectedly.

A customer in one of the seaside cafés overheard Tara's questions and approached her.

"I knew Anika well," the woman said. "She used to wait on me every time I came in. Haven't seen her in a while, though. I heard she left with some American man. Anika said she had a brother, an organ grinder who works in the main square of Den Burg, on Texel. Maybe he knows more."

As we stepped outside, I turned to Tara, suddenly reenergized. "Bingo! So, where's Texel?"

"It's an island north of Amsterdam," she said with a grin. "We can go tomorrow. It's an easy trip."

"You sure? You don't have to chauffeur me all over the country."

Tara gave me a curious look. I couldn't tell if it was a tease or something more. "Of course I'm sure, Jerry. This is fun. Like hunting for the colored eggs *de paashaas* hides on Easter Sunday."

Her hand found mine. I felt a subtle shift, something beyond the search for Riley and Anika.

"Paashaas?" I asked.

"The Easter hare," she said. Her eyes sparkled. "Like your bunny."

The next morning, she drove us to the ferry and we crossed to Texel. In Den Burg, we parked near the main square and wandered through the cafés, souvenir shops, and vendor stalls. When I stopped to buy a sandwich from a sausage stand, I noticed an organ grinder nearby, who churned out nostalgic tunes.

Tara walked over and waited for a break in the music. I watched as she approached the man. He looked wary at first, but when she laughed, flipped her hair, and pulled out a small notepad, he seemed to soften. They spoke quietly. She jotted something down, kissed him on both cheeks, and slipped him a few coins for a song.

When she returned, I could see the excitement in her stride.

"He didn't want to talk at first," she said as we walked back to the car, "but I won him over. I told him I worked with Anika at the restaurant and was headed back to the States. I said I had some of her things to return and needed a mailing address."

I grinned. "You're a natural detective. What did he give you?"

"An address in Leiden. He told me to send the package to someone named Anna Guffey. He said she'd get it to Anika."

"Well," I said, "our next step is to find out who Anna Guffey is."

"Leiden's not far," Tara replied. "We'll go tomorrow. But tonight, tonight we celebrate."

"You're enjoying this, aren't you?"

She didn't answer. Instead, she took my hand again, still cool to the touch, and looked straight ahead as we passed Vondelpark. Two girls lay sprawled on the grass, their long legs glinted in the sunlight.

"First," she said softly, "I want to show you the part of my house that isn't the B&B."

Tara told me she'd inherited the house from her father. She'd turned it into an inn, just a few rooms, quiet, tasteful. The income kept her afloat, but it was more than just business.

"I like to share this place with interesting people," she said, as she handed me a glass of wine. "I live upstairs, in the part that overlooks the garden. That view, especially in the mornings, makes it all worth it. The furthest beds are vegetables, the nearest ones flowers and shrubs. You can probably tell which are my favorites."

"It's beautiful," I said. "Like something out of a fairytale."

We didn't make it to dinner. One glass turned into another, and the evening took a turn.

"You're my dinner," Tara laughed as she pulled me into bed. She was ravenous.

We slept late. After a quick breakfast, we drove to Leiden. The search had begun.

Anna Guffey lived in a grand villa on the Herengracht canal; white shutters, wrought-iron gate, the kind of place with history written into the brickwork. We parked nearby and waited for a glimpse of anyone who might give us an edge.

Eventually, a woman stepped out and strolled along the canal.

"That's got to be her," Tara said. "She's headed to one of those cafés we passed."

"Looks like her," I said. "I wonder if Riley's inside."

"I'll find out," Tara said.

She walked up to the front door and knocked. No one answered. She knocked again. She heard footsteps, and a maid appeared.

"Is Anna home?" Tara asked.

"You just missed her," the maid replied. "She's gone to Elsa's Café."

"What about her husband? Is he in?"

The maid paused. Her face stiffened. She raised a hand to her mouth. "Oh... you haven't heard? Mr. Guffey... Roger... he's dead. Murdered. Stabbed on the De Vliet bridge. It was awful."

Tara stepped back, visibly shaken. "No," she whispered. "I hadn't heard. That's... terrible. Did they catch who did it?"

"No clues," said the maid. "They think it was a robbery. He was known to carry cash. Far too much, if you ask me."

"I- I'm sorry. I can't—" Tara turned away, overwhelmed.

"Miss!" the maid called after her. "Who should I say came by?"

Tara was already gone. She got in the car without a word, and we drove off in silence.

⏳ ⏳ ⏳

Several months have passed since we uncovered Anika and Riley's hideout. I turned over everything I'd learned to the authorities in the U.S. and Amsterdam. Anika was charged with conspiracy to defraud for her part in Riley's investment scam, but she was never extradited. She was arrested first in Amsterdam for her part in Riley's murder. The man who carried it out was caught and confessed. Most of the money Riley stole was recovered and returned to his victims. At last, I was in the clear, but I had no further interest in a career in finance.

I became a permanent resident of Holland. For now, I help Tara with the B&B. I like it here; I revel in the contradictions.

Choice and fate are separated by the thinnest of lines. Walk through the Red Light District and you'll see it: prostitutes and transsexuals, dominatrices, Chinese and Eastern Europeans, each with their own carved-out domain. Motorcycle gangs crowd the coffee shops and bars. All of this chaos encircles Oudezijds Voorburgwal 14, the old headquarters of the Dutch Salvation Army, founded by Alida Margaretha Bosshardt the very year I was born. Saints and sinners, cheek by jowl. You make your bargain with the devil or with God.

Fate weaves a web with meticulous care, but there are gaps in the strands, narrow escape routes for the bold. A door cracks open, unbidden. You leap, throw yourself into the wild, and, against all odds, survive. There is a passageway between the threads where reality thins, where the ghost of the possible speaks, and where time doubles back. There are second acts, believe me, I know.

How Was Yelapa?

"

One more thing: when you get there, take the water taxi straight to Yelapa. Skip the tourist beaches."

"Wait, seriously?"

"Dead serious. Don't mess around, girl. There are dragons out there."

"Dragons?"

"Yeah, giant fire-breathing reptiles. '*Los Demandos.*' The Dumbo crowd. You know—overcooked tourists in tiny swimsuits who think elephants can fly."

"Is this a joke?"

"Nope, swear on a stack of guidebooks. You think I'd joke about this? Want the whole story?"

"Obviously. I'm hanging on every word."

"Don't get snarky. I'm trying to help you."

"Fine, I'm all ears."

"It started at the airport. Total chaos. Strollers everywhere. Crying babies get to board first, then come the fatsoes, "passengers who require assistance," aka the ones who sweat through their shirts before takeoff."

"Don't say that. It's rude."

"Look, one third of Americans are clinically obese. That's not rude, it's a statistic."

"You're impossible."

"You're in denial. Anyway, I make it to the gate, and what do they announce? Crew delay."

"What's a crew delay?"

"Means someone forgot to schedule the actual pilots. Like, oops! So, they fly in a crew from Palm Springs. Hour wait, minimum."

"No way!"

"Yes, way. We finally board and then sit on the runway for another hour while they 'fix the cooling system.' Spoiler: they didn't."

"Brutal."

"A three-year-old next to me goes full Mortal Kombat on the seat in front, with actual combat boots on his feet, no less. The guy whose back gets kicked is some retiree in a Hawaiian shirt. He shouts out that he's gonna pee his pants. The flight attendants fail to notice."

"What did you do?"

"What could I do? I popped in earbuds and tried not to scream, but that was just the beginning."

"Oh, my God, did he seriously pee himself right there in front of you?"

"Uh, you think? They opened the bathroom door and it was boom, like the dam broke. A herd of hippos waddled down the aisle to drain their bladders. Within minutes, the whole plane smelled like a frat house after beer pong night."

"Ew, TMI. So, you finally took off, right?"

"Jesus, let me finish. Takeoff was fine, but the second we hit cruising altitude, the plane started to pitch and roll like a busted carnival ride. It was the worst turbulence I've felt since I had sex with Dick."

"You didn't."

"Didn't I just say I did?"

"No way. Not Dick."

"Cross my heart, hope to die. Want to hear what happened at the airport, or are we still stuck on who I banged?"

"Fine. Tell me about the airport."

"We land, like five planes at once. It was a total human stampede. Mexican immigration's like a zoo, baggage claim's a brawl, and Customs? Picture a Chinese dragon parade made entirely of sweaty tourists that winds back and forth for miles."

"There it is again, the dragon thing."

"Oh, bite me. Anyway, I finally get to Customs and there she is, Miss Hoochie Coo, caked in mascara and lipstick thick enough to qualify as insulation. She bats her lashes and tells me to 'press the button.'"

"Hold up. What button? Is this some weird flirtation thing?"

"It's the random inspection machine. Welcome to Mexico. Green light, you go. Red light, you get pulled aside for the full pat-down by Officer Grabbyhands."

"The *full* search?"

"Let's just say it involves rubber gloves and dead eye contact, but only idiots get red. I got green, thank God."

"So that's it? You're done?"

"Hardly. Next, you get funneled through a gauntlet of hustlers, angry Americans in vacation T-shirts, shady dudes that push VIP rides, tequila samples, discount condos, and candy that'll keep you glued to a toilet for the rest of your stay."

"Let me guess. More dragons?"

"Chill. This is for your own good. Wanna hear it or not?"

"Okay, okay. Go on."

"If you somehow survive the torture chamber they call Customs, you'll find yourself in desperate need of a taxi. Surprise! You need a ticket, and the ticket booths are all the way back where you just came from. You're about to throw a tantrum when, like magic, a slick young guy materializes."

"If you can pay *just a little extra,* the taxi driver, says the dude who's eyes ogle your chest, would be *delighted* to take you wherever you need to go. A little something for Mr. Slick would also be appreciated. *Por favor.*"

"Meanwhile, the same herd of passengers who clogged the jet bridge lumber toward the taxis like a flock of geese. You mutter, "*Gracias, amigo. Vámonos,*" and toss him the *pesos.*"

"Turns out your driver can hook you up with "free" tequila and "whatever else you want." You decline, obviously."

"Obviously."

"He then launches into his backstory about when he was a racecar driver in Mexico City and Baja. To prove it, he floors the gas and lays on the horn. He whips past the luxury hotels, Walmart, and the cruise terminals that teem with more plus-size Americans in sweat-stained tank tops."

"You scream down the Malecon through Old Town and the *Zona Romántica*. He exchanges honks and dirty jokes with other cabbies, flirts with a tourist policewoman, and invites her into the cab like he's about to audition for *The Bachelor: Puerto Vallarta Edition*."

"By now, you're completely disoriented."

"Here's the kicker: When you reach *Playa de los Muertos* (yes, 'Beach of the Dead,' not exactly subtle), *do not stop*. Grab the first water taxi to Yelapa. Don't look back. Don't pass Go. Don't mess with the tourist beaches. Stay in Yelapa till it's time to fly home."

"You make it sound like a nightmare."

"Oh, it wasn't half as bad as that woman in the news who got arrested midflight for lighting up in the bathroom, the one who smashed the smoke detector, and screamed she was going to "fucking kill" everyone aboard."

"Let me guess, Virgin America?"

"Nope. Southwest. Flying Southwest is a bitch."

"So... Yelapa? Was it worth it? I mean, *really,* how was it?"

"Yelapa? Yelapa was heaven, barefoot-on-the-beach, jungle-paradise heaven. Glad you asked."

Maya

"Súbeme paso a pasito. No quieras pegar brinquitos."

Climb me step by careful step. Don't try to leap.

—From *La Lotería, La Escalera* (The Ladder)

Female. Single. Elderly. Lonely. Wealthy.

Bailey had the demographic dialed in.

He sipped his coffee from the corner table, eyes on her, ears tuned. She sat across from a sharp young man in a tailored jacket, her financial advisor, judging by the posture and portfolio. He was the gatekeeper. Bailey would have to work around him.

She barely touched her fruit and yogurt, more occupied with memory than appetite.

"I'm so lonely, Sam," she said, her voice soft but clear. "I miss James terribly. I don't want to keep him waiting too long."

"Come on, Maya," the advisor replied. "James wouldn't want you to pine away. He's got all the time in the world now. He'd want you to live."

"I know you're right. James always wanted me happy, but what's the point anymore? I don't have children, and my family's all gone. I've outlived them all." She sighed and shook her head. "Sorry to ramble on like this. That's not why we're here."

Sam leaned in and spoke quietly. "You want me to draft the trust, right?"

She nodded. "It's been sixty years, Sam, since James married me in Mexico. My family hated the idea, him, the dusty ranch up on

231

the coast, but we built it up from nothing. We logged just what was needed to raise money for livestock and plant the vineyards. It took years, but it paid off. Then Jerry—you remember Jerry—persuaded us to go into equities. When James got sick, we sold most of the land and put it all into one of those startups. The money poured in like I never imagined. Now I'm too old to enjoy it."

Bailey pretended to read while he poked casually at his potatoes. From behind his newspaper, he listened carefully to every word.

"Keep it down," Sam whispered. "Let's not broadcast your business."

Maya didn't lower her voice. She glanced out the window, then back toward Bailey in the corner.

"I've got so much space out on the ridge. Too much for one person. I need a live-in caretaker, someone for company and to help out around the place. It gets awfully quiet up there."

Sam followed her gaze, suspiciously. The man in the corner seemed occupied, but Sam wasn't fooled.

"I'll get the trust started," he said. "We'll meet again next week. The only thing I need is your list of beneficiaries. Give that some real thought."

"I have a few ideas," Maya said with a smile that didn't quite reach her eyes. She knew the townsfolk gossiped about who might inherit the ranch when she died. Sometimes she even suspected Sam hoped for a piece.

Sam stood, fished out his wallet, and dropped a few bills on the table. "I've gotta run to a court date in Ukiah. Call my office when you're ready."

He leaned in and kissed her lightly on the forehead.

"You're my favorite girl, Maya."

She laughed. She knew flattery when she heard it, but it still worked. "Thanks, Sam. You always cheer me up."

Sam gave Bailey one last look before he left. Something about the man didn't sit right. Maya could handle herself, but he made a mental note to remember that face.

⧖ ⧖ ⧖

At night, on the ridgetops east of Mendocino, the stars blaze like silver fire in a coal-black sky. Streams full of salmon wind upstream through groves of redwoods. Creatures found nowhere else thrive in this quiet pocket of the world. It was here that James and Maya Rafferty lived out their lives.

Maya was seventy-five now. She met James sixty years earlier when he visited Mexico. Her family warned her about "the soulless gringo." They pleaded with her not to go, but Maya had always been stubborn. Fiercely independent, she followed James north to Mendocino, where they raised sheep and cattle, planted vineyards, tended the forest, and left beauty wherever they went. In time, even her family had to admit she was right to ignore their concerns.

Then, without warning, James died.

Loneliness settled in like a second skin, just as lethal as the cancer that took him.

That afternoon, after she met with Sam, Maya left the market, her cart piled high, bags threatening to topple. As she reached the curb, a man stepped toward her.

"'Scuse me, ma'am. Looks like you could use a hand."

Just as I planned, Maya thought, and caught the cart before it slipped off the walkway.

"Oh, jeez, I didn't mean to scare you," the man said. "Sorry, ma'am."

Maya's face softened. She laughed. "You're the one I saw at the Frolic Café. New in town?"

"Been here a few weeks," he said, as he lifted her bags. "I'm still getting my bearings."

He looked around forty, but Maya knew better than to trust appearances. He had a decent face, fit build, no signs of hard living. She studied him closely. He wasn't a drunk or an ordinary drifter, at least not obviously.

"Where are you holed up?" she asked.

"I have a room at the Art Center, but I've gotta clear out next week when classes start."

"You're an artist?"

He chuckled. "I can paint, but not like that. I'm more of a handyman. Carpentry, plumbing, that sort of thing. They're giving me the room in exchange for some work around the place."

Maya nodded as if this were new information, but she knew exactly who he was.

Thera Maddox, a close friend of hers, had warned her. Poor Thera, conned out of ten thousand dollars. The man used charm and some trick with online banking to clean her out. "With these damn computers, they can do anything," Thera said through her tears. "I'll never trust a bank again. I'm so ashamed."

Of course, Thera couldn't prove it. These types of scams rarely leave a trail, but she knew it was him. Maya had planned ever since. She'd watched and waited, and now she had him. This was her first move.

Thera refused to tell the police. She didn't trust them, not after that traffic accident when someone ran a stop sign and pinned the blame on her. He was young, local, and well connected. She was an old woman. They took her license. She never forgot it.

"Well," said Maya, to break the silence, "thank you for the help. What's your name?"

"Bailey, ma'am. Bailey Stevens."

"You got any references, Mr. Stevens?"

"References?"

"If you check out, I might have some work for you. Maybe even a place to stay."

Bailey's face lit up. "That'd be swell! I'm sure the director of the Art Center would vouch for me. The owner of the Frolic Café knows me. I did a bit of work for him. Before this, I lived in Santa Rosa."

He reached into his pocket and pulled out a dog-eared card. "This is my last landlord's number. I always paid on time, and I left the place better than I found it."

"I'll make some calls," Maya said. "If I like what I hear, I'll leave a note for you at the Art Center."

"I'd really appreciate that, ma'am. I like to stay busy. I'm good with tools. What's your name?"

"Maya," she said. "Maya Rafferty."

⌛ ⌛ ⌛

Bailey sifted through stacks of old issues of the *Frolic Beacon* at the town library and paid a visit to the historical society's dusty museum. It didn't take long to confirm what he'd overheard at the café: old-lady Rafferty was sitting on a pile of money.

Two days later, he found a handwritten note on the nightstand in his room at the Art Center. Maya invited him out to her ranch to discuss a possible live-in caretaker job. She included directions and a number to call if he needed a ride. He didn't.

When he pulled up to the Rafferty place, he knew right away he wanted in. The house, though weathered, was elegant in its bones. A few outbuildings leaned slightly into the hills, nestled among apple trees and overgrown vegetable beds. Acres of redwoods and pine stretched in all directions. A stream cut through a meadow thick with wildflowers. The place needed work, years of it, by the look, but to Bailey, that was part of the charm. Neglect meant opportunity.

Maya met him near the porch. She wore a long, floral dress, her gray hair tied with a ribbon that matched. No jewelry, no pretense. Her skin was deeply lined, sun-burnished. Unlike most women her age, she hadn't thickened. On her feet, a pair of crisp red tennis shoes stood out, unexpected, almost playful.

"You can live here," she said, her voice gravelly but strong, "as long as we get along and your work is up to snuff. No drugs. No women. A drink now and then is ok, but don't overdo it. Nothing works on arthritis like a good whiskey," she laughed. Her eyes flashed as she spoke. It was the first of many warm smiles to come.

"I'll give you a list of what needs to be done. The place went to hell after James passed. If you see something that needs fixing, run it by me first. You're on your own for meals. I'll call you up to the house when I've got extra. Dinner is at six tonight. Get yourself settled. Walk the land. Learn the place."

With that, she turned and left. She didn't wait for him to answer.

She sized him up quickly. The accent said Midwest, probably farm stock. His hands, battered and calloused, fit his story. A man who knew tools, knew how to kill and clean an animal if it came to it. If it weren't for the situation with Thera, Maya might've have considered him long-term, but this was a short con, for her friend's sake, nothing more.

Bailey unpacked, took stock of the cabin, then set out for a walk. He noted a broken fence line, a tangle of oak logs half lost to weeds. He tested one with his boot, still solid. He registered that they'd make good firewood. He plucked an apple from a low branch and bit in. Too early, still tart. Another week or two, and they'd be perfect. He could already see there was plenty to keep him busy here. That suited him.

Patience, he reminded himself. Let it simmer.

At six on the dot, he knocked on Maya's door and joined her for dinner. Conversation was light, the food plain but good. She seemed relaxed, maybe even pleased. Bailey thought he was off to a good start.

He didn't have a plan yet, not exactly. She was lonely, worn down, that much was clear. He'd seen marks like her before. Sooner or later, an opportunity would show itself, and when it did, he'd be ready.

⧗ ⧗ ⧗

Two weeks passed in a blur. Maya kept Bailey busy with a long list of overdue chores around the property. She found that she relied on him more than expected. She actually liked him. That surprised her. She had to remind herself not to lose focus. She had a plan.

She knew Bailey kept a checking account with a decent chunk of money. She'd seen him write checks. One afternoon, while he was off in the woods, Maya slipped into his cabin. It didn't take long to find what she needed. Foolishly, he'd tucked his online banking login and password into his check binder. She jotted everything down. The keys to his kingdom. This would be easier than she'd thought.

Despite her age, Maya was no stranger to technology. She was meticulous with her finances. Sam, her financial advisor, was used to her relentless questions. She read every quarterly report, every prospectus, every piece of fine print. Pen in hand, she circled inconsistencies, underlined concerns, and expected Sam to have the answers. Most of his clients tossed those documents unread, Maya mined them for red flags.

When the time came, she logged into Bailey's account and transferred $10,000 to Thera.

"Is that legal?" Thera asked when Maya called.

"Was what he did to you legal?" Maya replied. "He stole ten grand from you, honey. We just stole it back."

She laughed, but there was no humor in what Bailey had done. Elder abuse wasn't a joke. Even if she had started to like him, Maya couldn't overlook the harm.

Bailey noticed the missing money within days. The bank confirmed the transaction had been made from his own IP address. That's when he realized he'd been outplayed by Maya. Furious and humiliated, he marched up to the house to confront her.

"Yes," she said calmly. "I did it. Why don't you tell me why you stole from my friend? How many others did you fleece, Bailey? You thought you could steal from me too, didn't you?"

Bailey stood there, seething, but also a little in awe, and ashamed. He'd been caught, and by someone older, smarter, and richer than he'd imagined possible.

"I have no excuse," he said. "One lie turned into another, then another. I didn't stop."

"How many women?" she asked.

"Six," he said quietly. "About fifty thousand dollars total, not counting Thera. I knew it was wrong, but it was so damn easy. Now it's gone. I'm a fool."

"No," Maya said, her voice sharp. "You're not a fool, you're a crook, a lousy one, but we can fix this. You have to pay those women back, every cent, with interest. Then you're gonna go straight, no more tricks. You must give me a reason to like you, because I want to."

That shook him. No one had ever said any such thing to him before. He wanted her to like him. More than that, he wanted to like himself.

"How?" he asked. "How do I start?"

"One dollar at a time, kid. You'll work for me until your debt is paid."

So she said and so it was. It took two years.

During that time, Bailey's admiration for Maya grew. He earned her trust, her respect. He proved he was more than a charming scam artist. He laid water lines, rewired cabins, rebuilt what James had left in shambles. He fixed fences, roofs, foundations. He became indispensable.

Dinners at the main house became routine. They got to know each other.

"Don't call me Mrs. Rafferty," she told him. "James is gone. Like Sam says, I'll see him soon enough. Just call me Maya."

"What was your name before you married?" he asked.

"Maya Azul," she said. "Because of my eyes. Blue eyes were rare where I grew up in Mexico."

She'd been a baby during the Great Depression, but she remembered the struggle. Bailey saw how deeply those memories shaped her view of money and work. She wasn't a child of the '60s, but the spirit of the era had touched her. She hated war, mistrusted power, believed investments should yield social good as well as financial return. To Bailey's surprise, she smoked weed. He found that out the day he made his final repayment.

"Let's get high," she said. "The wicked witch is dead."

Bailey laughed. He didn't know what to make of her. She could be a mother, a sister, a friend, a lover, a daughter, sometimes all at once.

"Let's go to town," she'd say with a smile. "I want to show you off to my friends. Don't be a schmuck. Dress up. I want you to look good for me."

She introduced him to *Lotería,* the Mexican version of bingo. Her favorite card was *La Escalera*—The Ladder. Each card had a saying. That one read: *Súbeme paso apasito. No quieres pegar brinquitos* ("Climb me step by step. Don't try to hop up.").

Step by step, they won each other over.

"It's a match made in hell," Maya joked when people asked.

Bailey never argued.

Maya lived to a hundred. Bailey didn't make it that far. He died long before she did. It broke her heart almost as deeply as when James died.

After he died, Maya went through Bailey's things. He had never mentioned a family, but tucked among his belongings she found evidence of a wife and two sons in Illinois. He had walked out on them and never gone back. That explained the dark moods, the bouts of silence.

She asked Sam to find them.

The boys were now in their twenties, both out of college. The wife had never remarried. Bailey sent them money whenever he could. That's where most of his earnings had gone. Just before his death, he sent them everything he'd saved. Maya had no idea about this other side of his life.

"I didn't really know him at all," she told Sam.

She instructed Sam to include Bailey's sons in the trust, the JBM Trust: James, Bailey, Maya. She left the rest of her estate to local charities. She appointed Sam the trustee.

"Distribute it a step at a time," she told him. "No one gets to hop up all at once."

Nahual

But ask the beasts, and they will teach you;
the birds of the air, and they will tell you.

—Job 12:7

You have scratched the jade;
you have torn the quetzal's feather.

—Aztec metaphor (trans. Thelma D. Sullivan)

Devon and Brin bought their first *alebrijes,* a lion, an iguana, and a rhinoceros, from Pepe Santiago in San Antonio Arrazola, a small village just outside Oaxaca. The figures, hand-carved from copal wood, were vivid with brilliant color and life.

"They come from dreams," Santiago told them. "They live there. They guide our spirits. Some say they're *nahuales* or protectors. The ones who have certain powers can become a *nahual* at night. But me?" He shrugged, a glint in his eye. "I've never seen such things myself."

Devon smirked, half-skeptical, but when Santiago's expression shifted, when his brown eyes turned sharp and strange, Devon felt a jolt.

"I see your nahual, my friend. I see..." Santiago's voice trailed off.

"You see what?" Devon asked.

Santiago paused. "Nothing," he said abruptly. "*Vaya con Dios.*" With that, he vanished into his workshop.

That was more than twenty years ago.

Since then, the Jennings' collection of alebrijes had taken on a life of its own. Their country home had become a jungle of painted wood and houseplants. Birds with serpent tails perched on shelves beside snarling tigers with dragon wings. Friends joked, "Visiting you is like a trip into the Amazon."

Devon, born and raised in a dusty Sacramento Valley farm town, had long since abandoned his faith. He left behind churches, mystics, and anything that hinted at magic. He had no patience for gurus or incense sellers. "Hippie-dippy nonsense," he called it.

There was something about the alebrijes, though, that drew him. It wasn't a matter of belief, it was his respect for art and tradition.

He told himself he liked them for the craftsmanship, the cultural memory, the artistry. Their colors, derived from natural dyes. The carvers used green for empathy, red for passion, blue for calm, yellow for joy. This made sense. Color, after all, shapes perception. He'd learned that when he owned a restaurant. Paint the walls red, and people eat faster. Green draws the health-food crowd. Brown is the best color for coffee shops. Wine tastes richer under a warm light. These were facts, not fairytales. He'd seen this work with his own eyes. He didn't want to admit it, even to himself, but he wasn't quite ready to dismiss the "power" of the alebrijes. Whatever it might be.

Math had once seemed like the straight path to truth, but then came Gödel, Cantor, chaos theory, fractals folding in on themselves, matrices expanding into infinite space. He shifted to physics, but quantum theory pulled the rug out from his hope of certainty. The universe, it turned out, was less like a machine and more like a trickster.

He didn't actually accept the idea of a spirit animal, but the idea appealed to him. It made him feel good even if it was childish. He had come to believe, grudgingly, that mystery lies at the core of everything. Thought itself is metaphor. Truth, if it exists, hides behind astonishment, behind awe. How could neurons and cells grasp the infinite? We're flesh animated by something strange. Molecules that dream.

"Devon?" Brin's voice pulled him back. "You're lost in one of your daydreams again. Lunch is ready."

"On my way," he said. "Do you hear the birds? They're out in full force today."

"Careful," she teased. "You'll end up like that monk who got lost in birdsong and woke up fifty years later."

Devon didn't answer. "I like how the same ones come back each spring," he said, "like old friends."

"Yes, I hear those noisy ospreys," Brin agreed as she watched him out on the deck. "That family's nested here as long as we have. Fifty years. How many generations is that?"

"At least five, probably." Devon walked into the kitchen. He slipped his arms around her waist and reached for a snow pea from the pan.

Brin swatted his hand. "Don't you dare! We'll sit at the table like civilized people. You carry the fish and wine. I'll plate the vegetables."

He laughed and obeyed.

They ate outside on the deck. The early afternoon light painted long shadows across the field below. A flock of wild turkeys wandered past; they pecked at the soil for insects and worms, moved with that odd mix of caution and entitlement that always made Devon laugh.

"Those turkeys are the most awkward birds in nature," he said.

"I don't know about that," said Brin. "Remember the albatross we saw in Monterey? They call them gooney birds."

After lunch, with a glass of wine in hand and the warmth of the sun still on his skin, Devon decided to float one of his more unusual thoughts.

"I've been thinking about my *nahual*," he said and waited for Brin's reaction.

Her aquamarine eyes, cool and searching, met his brown ones. He loved those eyes. When they faded to a misty gray like now, it usually meant trouble: she had a rebuttal.

"You don't actually believe in that stuff, do you?" she asked.

Devon grinned. "Just rattling your cage. He paused, then added, "If anything, we should be *their* guardians, right?. We're the ones who've destroyed the environment."

Brin raised her glass. "Yes, well, cheers to the ravens that rip up my garden, the deer that devour my roses, the foxes that massacre our hens, and the bears who think our trash bins are their buffet." Her voice was playful. She got a kick out of the banter.

He sighed. "It's only because we've destroyed their natural habitat. If we keep it up, the only thing left for our grandkids will be strip malls and concrete."

She didn't answer, but her expression softened. Then, quietly, mysteriously, something stirred in the meadow.

It was subtle at first. A shimmer in the air, a shift in the birdsong. Slowly, one by one, animals began to emerge as if summoned by the conversation: a bear, some deer, a mountain lion, all hidden in the tall grass. An osprey and a raven and a woodpecker. A possum, a raccoon, and more turkeys.

Devon blinked in bewilderment. "Do you see what I see? Why are all those animals out in the meadow?"

Brin noticed a strange glow in his eyes. His speech sounded off-kilter. "Devon, are you okay?"

"No. Something's off. It's something to do with those damn alebrijes."

Brin leaned in closer, and tried to gauge if he was serious or teasing. "Maybe it's your nahual," she said gently, to lighten the mood and bring him back.

"It's a jackrabbit," he blurted out. "My nahual."

He didn't know why he said it. It was as if something had taken him over.

"That's a good one," Brin said. "There's been a lonely jackrabbit around since we got back. He must be after you. Tell me, if your nahual is a jackrabbit, why don't you hear me with those big ears?"

"You're right," he laughed. "Maybe I've shapeshifted into something else."

"Are you pulling my leg?" Brin said.

"No," Devon said. "It happens. I read up on it. Some people can change their nahual."

"I didn't think you believed in these things. Either you've lost your mind or some kind of fluke has taken it over."

"What's a fluke?" Devon asked.

"A fluke is a bug that takes over your brain and makes you do silly things. I heard about it in a TED talk." Brin said.

Devon looked up just as a turkey buzzard coasted silently overhead.

"I don't know," Devon said. "You're right. I don't believe in this stuff. I'm not sure why I brought it up. It's like something beyond my control. Like a fluke, yea." Devon looked wobbly on his feet.

Brin narrowed her eyes. "Are you on drugs?"

"God, no. I haven't touched a joint in weeks. Just wine. Well, maybe a touch of mezcal."

"They say mezcal can make you crazy. Maybe that's it," Brin said.

"It's possible," Devon admitted. "Nature is more than it seems, though. I don't mean in some traditional *spiritual* way. There is at the heart of things something opaque and mysterious that we can't completely understand. Our minds are built in a certain way based on our senses, and that limits us."

Brin rolled her eyes. "Here we go again. Philosophy o'clock. Are you sure everything is okay?"

"Sure," Devon said quietly. "But, don't you ever wonder why we're here?"

"We're here to eat and screw," Brin laughed. "You think too much. You're not a jackrabbit, Devon. You're more like a mule. Drop it. All this gobbledygook is giving me a headache."

She shook her head and went inside for more wine.

"Brin," he whispered, but she wasn't there. "Out in the field. Look."

She didn't answer, but that didn't stop him.

"They're everywhere," Devon said. He could barely breathe.

There were dozens of animals that didn't belong: monkeys, storks, iguanas, bulls, crabs, spiders, a horned sheep, dragons, strange insects, and an armadillo that strummed a guitar.

"Oh, that," said a strange voice. "It's just the alebrijes. They wander sometimes. I thought you knew that."

Devon was confounded. "You mean... they're alive?"

"Of course they are," the voice said. "Did you really think they just sat on shelves and waited for you to look at them?"

Devon couldn't figure it out. Who was this? Something brushed against his leg.

He looked down.

A serpent had curled around his ankle. Scales shimmered like old coins. Its eyes locked onto his, and then it spoke.

"I'm Coatl, your nahual," it hissed. "I've chased that damned jackrabbit forever. Normally I wouldn't bother you, but I need that rabbit. He has something of mine."

The snake coiled tighter around Devon's legs.

"Help me, and I'll help you."

"What the hell?" Devon struggled. "How did you get here? We don't have snakes in this area, and last I checked, snakes don't talk."

"Name's Coatl," the serpent said. I'm the seven-times-great-grandson of Quetzalcoatl, the feathered serpent, creator god, wind walker, cosmic mover. They say I'm as fast as a thought, but that damned jackrabbit is always ahead of me."

"Well, I haven't had much luck with him either," Devon muttered. "Can you loosen your grip a little? My legs are going numb."

"No problem," Coatl replied, and he eased up, just a bit.

"That jackrabbit is one the Centzon Totochtin, the four hundred rabbit spirits of drunkenness. Mischievous, wild, and unstoppable, like the Gremlins, only drunker."

"Okay."

They wander around Mexico, and show up uninvited to parties, and leave hangovers and epiphanies in their wake. Each one represents a different shade of intoxication. The Christians call it communion. I just call it Tuesday."

"Why are you telling me this?"

"It's all about that damn jackrabbit. Catch it and I'll slither off and leave you alone. You get your tidy little reality back. If you can't help me out, well..." Coatl grinned, revealing a forked tongue and far too many teeth. "You're stuck with me."

"Devon! Devon!" Brin's voice cut through the dream.

Devon was sprawled on the deck, out cold.

"Wake up, honey! Oh, my God, are you okay?"

He groaned and rubbed his head. "What happened?"

"You slipped on that loose board, and knocked yourself out. I thought I'd lost you. Should I take you to the clinic?"

"No, I'm fine," Devon said. He blinked against the sunlight. "Maybe a shot of mezcal would help. You know what they say: *Para todo mal, mezcal; para todo bien, también.*"

Brin let out a breath of relief and shook her head. "I'm pleased to see your sense of humor's back. Before you passed out, you went on and on about the meaning of life, the big questions. Did you get any answers?"

"Yeah," he said, as he leaned against the railing. "It turns out my nahual is a snake. Can you believe that? I'll take that glass of mezcal now, please? I still feel a little wobbly."

Brin headed inside and mumbled to herself, "A snake. That man's cracked his skull and now he thinks he's the serpent king."

Devon shifted on his feet. Something moved beneath them.

"Fuck off," he whispered into the empty air.

Out across the meadow, he saw nothing but weeds blow in the wind.

Suddenly there was a flurry of activity in the tall grass. A jackrabbit stood up and flicked its ears toward the cobalt sky.

Devon opened his mouth to speak. Too late.

The jackrabbit vanished in a blur of motion. There was a sharp rustle in the brush, and a squeal. Devon heard the cork-pop of the mezcal bottle. Then silence.

The 2000s

Madge

Madge and Walter lived in a cramped apartment not far from the office. Most days, they shuffled through town. Madge power-walked with purpose while Walter lagged behind in a slow tangle with Senior, their drooling Basset Hound.

Walter looked like a heart attack waiting for a green light. Pale, sagging skin, gut hanging over his belt, he carried himself with the same carelessness that marked his rumpled clothes. His personality was no improvement, equal parts vulgarity and self-pity. He spent most of his time glued to his computer screen, watching porn. When he did show up at the office, he'd lean in close and whisper, "Women are only good for one thing, and you know what that is," followed by a conspiratorial wink and a grin. I ignored him. He was a fossil of everything I disliked. Madge, on the other hand, never reacted. Whether it was indifference or she was just used to it, I couldn't say. Why she put up with him was anyone's guess.

Madge was practical, kind, and steadfast. She'd come in regularly to deposit checks into two college savings accounts, for her granddaughters, she said. She'd never gone to college herself, and she wanted better for them. What struck me was that she and Walter lived on Social Security. Their budget was tight, yet, like clockwork, Madge came in every couple of weeks with a check for two or three hundred dollars at a time.

"There's no use to write a check for peanuts," she'd say, as she settled into the chair across from my desk. She'd glance at Walter, who usually sat nearby, eyes half-shut, and he nodded on cue.

The accounts grew slowly. Walter got lazier, heavier, and increasingly glassy-eyed from all the screen time. When Senior died of some intestinal issue, Walter no longer walked with Madge. He didn't come to the office again. She didn't bring him up, not even when he died. I only found out through the obituary. Heart attack, just like I'd figured.

After that, Madge's circumstances visibly worsened. Without Walter's Social Security check, she moved to a smaller apartment. I heard through town gossip that she scavenged bottles and cans from trash bins on her morning walks. The image haunted me. I wanted to ask her if she was okay, but I never found the words.

One afternoon, I tried to ease into the subject.

"You know, Madge, you've put away a lot of money for those granddaughters. You must love them dearly. Do you see them much?"

She smiled faintly. "Oh, they're not my granddaughters, they're Walter's. They don't even know I exist."

I blinked. "Then why—?"

"I made him a promise," she said. "A promise is a promise, even if he's dead."

I was speechless. I nodded. I didn't know what else to do.

Time passed. Every two weeks, she'd come in, and I'd split the deposit between the girls' accounts. I forgot about it, until one day I realized it had been a long time since I'd seen her.

I called the manager of her apartment complex. He told me Madge had moved to Seattle. I checked the accounts. Sure enough, the mailing address had changed, but the deposits hadn't stopped.

I found Madge's new number in the account records and decided to give her a call.

"Hello, Madge. I see you've moved. Those accounts you set up for your granddaughters are doing quite well. I noticed you're still making deposits. Do you have any questions? Is there anything I can help you with?"

"They're Walter's granddaughters," she said flatly. "I'm fine. No, there is nothing to do. Just keep those accounts on track. College isn't cheap. Thanks for the call."

That was the last time we spoke. There was no need for further communication, and I had other clients to look after. A few years later, one of the granddaughters called me.

"How do I get the money out of that account?" she asked.

"I think you should know," I told her, "Madge scrimped and saved to fund that account. She wanted to help with college expenses. I hope you'll use it the way she intended."

"Who's Madge?"

I hesitated. "You don't know her? Your grandfather Walter was married to her before he passed."

"We don't talk about Walter. I have no idea who this Madge is. If she stole my money, there's going to be trouble. Just send the check."

She hung up before I could respond.

That call stayed with me. Madge's Social Security checks weren't large, definitely not enough to explain the size of her deposits. I'd always wondered, but I let it go at the time. Now, my curiosity got the best of me.

Before I released the funds, I tried to reach Madge. That's when I found out she had died. She'd been living with her sister in Seattle.

"Oh, that Madge!" her sister said, surprised but warm. "She was an angel. She worked her whole life to make sure those girls had a shot at college."

"Worked? At her age? I didn't know she had a job."

"It wasn't exactly a regular job," her sister said with a chuckle. "She did very well though. She left over a hundred thousand dollars to the battered women's shelter here in Seattle."

"A hundred thousand?" I was stunned. "How on earth did she earn that?"

"She made me promise not to tell, but I suppose it's all right now. You were her advisor, after all. Walter and Madge were business partners in... well, a gentlemen's club."

"A strip club?" I nearly dropped the phone.

"She inherited it from her father. Kept it quiet. None of her friends knew. Walter, of course, made a mess of things. He got two of the dancers pregnant. Madge turned the business over to a management company that ran several clubs. They mailed her checks regularly. She never spent a dime on herself. She said it was dirty money, only good if it went to something clean. She and Walter lived off their government checks."

I was quiet for a moment, as I absorbed it all. "The girls really weren't her granddaughters?"

"They weren't. Madge treated them like they were, although they never knew each other. Should you send them the money even if they don't use it for college? I guess it's theirs to do as they wish." Her voice cracked. "She really believed in giving them a chance."

There was some noise on the other end of the line.

"Hello? Are you still there? Everything okay?"

"Yes. Sorry. That's just Junior, Madge's Basset Hound. He's a mess. Slobbers on everything. Doesn't bark when strangers come to the door, just drools on their shoes. You want him? He's yours."

"I thought Junior died years ago."

"Oh, that was Senior. Junior's his pup. Madge got him after she moved up here; said he reminded her of Walter." She laughed softly. "She walked him every day to Pike Place Market. She had him fixed and put him on a diet, but it didn't make a dent. A Basset Hound's a Basset Hound, fat slobbering pigs, if you ask me."

"Thanks, but I'll pass on the dog," I said. "And thank you for your time."

After I hung up, I sat in my chair and thought about Madge and what her life must have been like. Then I arranged for the funds to be sent to the girls, no strings attached.

Later that day, I walked across the street to Patterson's Pub and raised a glass to Madge. One for Walter too. And one more for Junior, although I've never been much of a dog person.

García García

The parakeets chirp wildly out on the patio, their tiny chests flutter with each heartbeat. They sense the change to come. Rain is on the way, and they want to be moved beneath the eaves, to safety. It's strange to think that by tomorrow morning I'll be gone from Mexico, this time for good. I return in shame, in quiet defeat, to a place I've never loved and to a life drained of the hope and courage that once brought me here alone. I was young then, and naive. My friends warned me to stay away from the famous painter, but I was irresistibly drawn to him. As I close my eyes, that year returns, vivid, intact, as if no time at all has passed.

"Yes, miss. Your bags are checked through. Immigration and customs will be in Oaxaca. No worries in Mexico City, just a change of planes."

Excitement doesn't begin to describe what I felt that day. It was bliss, pure unfiltered bliss. I had a vision. I wanted to become a great painter, as Mariana Yampolsky had become a great photographer, by force of will alone. I left defiant, buoyed by a confidence that silenced the chorus of doubt from family and friends. All but Uncle Cole, he alone stood by me.

"'The heart has its reasons, which reason knows nothing of,'" he said, quoting Pascal as he kissed my cheek and slipped a hundred-dollar bill into my hand. "Buy something beautiful. And follow your dream, Brin, even when it seems impossible. I'll always be here for you."

I still remember the day I first saw García. He arrived with his entourage, regal in white linen, his long black hair falling loose, his face rugged, unshaven, alive with charisma. The event was a tribute to Oaxaca's painters and their cultural legacy. He was the star. I pressed close to the walkway, hoping for a glimpse. Then, impossibly, he stopped. His eyes locked on mine. For a heartbeat, he smiled.

"I must paint you," he said.

"No," I answered, and trembled at my own daring. "I'll paint you."

He laughed, full and loud. "We'll see about that."

Then he was gone, swept forward by his admirers. That brief exchange, electric and absurd, eclipsed the rest of the night. Nothing else mattered, or so I believed.

He had me out of my clothes within a week. I was bewitched. He first painted me with his eyes, then with his hands, and at last we painted each other, skin to skin. In that sense, we both kept our promises. Later, I picked up a brush and pressed it to canvas. That, finally, is the story I must tell. The world deserves the truth. So many rumors, each less true than the last. It may be a lost cause; people prefer their fantasies, but the truth is all I have left to reclaim my sanity and my pride.

Without sanity or pride, what else in life matters?

García García founded *La Hacienda de los Pintores* as a retreat for young aspiring artists. I was the only American, and the only woman, among them. That fact, along with my relationship with García, made me a magnet for curiosity and jealousy. I was the punchline to their whispered jokes. Still, those early weeks were enchanted. Loneliness drove me to create a world of my own, a world richer and more forgiving than the one I'd left behind. My art became a lifeline, something noble, something mine.

Outside of García, there was only one other person I had any real contact with: Michael Lawrence, the Englishman. I met him by chance when I wandered through the courtyard. He was old and round, and clung to the tattered edges of his once-sharp mind, a nostalgic academic with a mezcal in one hand and a bowl of peanuts in the other. The peanut skins clung to his chin, his shirt gapped open over a bloated pink stomach, and saliva pooled in the corners of his mouth. He told me a story, one I'd come to learn he told to everyone, always the same.

"My first visit to Oaxaca," he said, "I arrived in the darkness just before dawn. I walked to Monte Albán alone to watch the sun rise over the ruins. The colors stole my breath, but there was something else, something in the silence. It was a presence that frightened me, a kind of doom. It's in the blood of the locals, I think. Their eyes, they see too much."

He paused to drink, his shirt straining at every button.

"I lived for a year in the mountains with the Indians. I went native, and for a short while, I lost my grip on reality, but now I dream of going back. I want to die in those mountains and never return to this world."

He was one of the many ghosts orbiting García: burnouts and believers, men who dwell on what they once were or could have been. I should have taken his words as a warning, but I was young and hopeful, and too sure of myself. I dismissed him as a drunk who chased shadows of the past, and believed I was nothing like him.

There was something about Lawrence that unsettled me. I couldn't grasp it then, but now I know what it was. He was broken inside. He functioned out of habit, no longer animated by inspiration or emotion or whatever force through the green fuse drives the flower like the poet said.

"Are you a painter?" I asked to steer the conversation away from his ramblings.

He gave a dry laugh. "There are no painters here, my dear, only ghosts and skeletons, their blood sucked dry and their skin peeled away."

I excused myself and turned to leave, but he wasn't finished.

"You won't find answers in this place," he called after me. "These walls echo with false hopes and questions no one dares answer. If it's wisdom you seek, go into the mountains. If you want to become a great artist, go home. There is nothing but desolation here."

His hand trembled as he raised his glass to take another sip.

García García was rarely at the hacienda. Fame had made him a phantom, his name whispered in galleries from Paris to São Paulo, his movements charted only by gossip and the occasional magazine spread. No one understood how he managed to produce a masterpiece every month, each more provocative or technically astonishing than the last. His success was not only prolific, it was enigmatic in its diversity. He had no signature style, no recognizable palette or recurring motif. He painted across styles and subjects as if possessed by the spirits of many artists. His method remained a mystery, but his magnetism was undeniable; those who knew him spoke of him with reverence, as if his talent and charisma bent reality around him.

As the months passed, my relationship with García deepened, and with it, the tension in the hacienda thickened like fog. The others watched us. He came and went without notice; sometimes arrived in the middle of the night, and knocked softly at my door like a secret. I told myself it was my work that drew him in, that he saw something in my canvases, something raw and promising. He praised me, rarely but meaningfully, and never seemed to offer the same attention to the others. I needed to believe it wasn't just my body that caused him to return. That hope was the only thread that held me together during his long absences, when the rest of the residents shut me out like a pariah.

It was during one of those twilight weeks, when García was gone and the silence pressed in on me, that Lawrence, the Englishman, offered a slurred warning.

"Christ, that snake..." he mumbled, eyes glassy with mezcal. "Don't slither... mocks God, 'e does, walks on borrowed feet. Mind my words, young lady. Go back. Go... back."

I felt pity for him, but little else. We never became friends. Lawrence seemed half-forgotten, half-feral, like an old cat the house couldn't bring itself to kick out. He was always there, planted in the courtyard, muttering nonsense to no one. I no longer listened. His presence faded into the stonework. Occasionally I caught him at work, but he shielded his canvases with a strange protectiveness. I made note of it then, but only now do I understand.

Time passed routinely at the hacienda. People came and went with a rhythm I didn't question until much later. One day, I realized with mild astonishment that I'd been there longer than anyone except Lawrence. The newcomers began to treat me like a kind of oracle. They asked what to expect, confided their insecurities. It gave me an odd sense of stature I hadn't sought but quietly accepted.

One day, without warning, Lawrence was gone.

He vanished as quietly as he'd lived. I knocked on his door for days, worried that he might be sick. One afternoon, the young director, who barely concealed his disdain for me, saw me outside Lawrence's room.

"Señor Lawrence, he leave two days ago," he said with an indifferent shrug.

I was stunned. No goodbye. No note. Then I realized: I had given him no reason to think I'd care.

A few days later, García returned. The sky was heavy with rainclouds, the air electric with storm tension. I told myself not to expect anything, but when he didn't come to my room or even acknowledge me, it stung more than I'd imagined it would. At dinner, he sat with the new arrivals, laughed and gestured grandly, and ignored me as if we'd never shared anything. I sat in silence, watched the performance, then slipped away.

Back in my room, the tears came. I hated myself for them, and tried to compose myself, to believe I was stronger than this. It wasn't that late, he might still come, and if he did, I would tell him exactly what I thought.

Then there was a knock at the door. I rushed to answer it, heart aflutter like a child on Christmas morning. Unable to help the smile that formed, I anticipated the brush of his hands, the warmth of his voice.

It wasn't him.

A woman stood there, poised, unfamiliar, and utterly composed.

"I'm Yvonne," she said. "I know you've been involved with my husband. That doesn't concern me. I'm not here to accuse or to moralize. He's always needed his little distractions. I've long since accepted that, but I fear you may be in danger. You don't know him like I do. That's why I've come to warn you. You must leave now, for your own sake."

I stood frozen, stunned, embarrassed, and confused. I didn't know this woman, but I knew García, or thought I did. I wasn't some *little distraction.* I had convinced myself there was something real between us, something more than physical. We were artists, muses to each other. He believed in my work; at least, I needed to think that he did. That thought had become my anchor. I held it so tightly I was willing to blind myself to everything else.

"I don't know what to say," I stammered. "This is... awkward. I appreciate your concern, and I believe you mean well, but I can't leave. García and I, our connection isn't just personal. It's creative. We bring out the best in each other. If I leave now, I'll lose everything I've built. It will be the end of me."

She studied me for a long moment, then spoke with quiet conviction. "You're very young, and very gifted, more than any of the others. I've seen your work, watched it evolve, but believe me, you are in danger. You must go."

So, he had shown her my paintings. I should have been outraged, but instead I felt an odd flicker of pride.

"Thank you," I said. "Truly. I'll think about what you've said. You've been remarkably kind."

Without another word, she turned and walked away.

The next morning, I learned García had left the hacienda. Just like that, without explanation. I didn't know what to feel. Human emotions are so fickle: you meet someone and think you are soulmates, only to wake up one morning repulsed by the sound of their voice. Part of me was relieved he was gone. There are days when I crave intimacy, but just as many when solitude feels like salvation.

I buried myself in my work. The weeks that followed were the most productive, and the happiest of my time in Oaxaca. Each day, I walked beyond the hacienda to sketch and gather ideas. I painted from dawn until well past midnight, so consumed I often forgot to eat, to change, or even look in a mirror. When I finally did, I was startled by the woman who stared back: unkempt, pale, paint-smeared, but alive in a way I'd never been before.

I had absorbed Mexico's wild extremes and smelted them into shape and color. The heat, the chaos, the beauty, it all flowed through me. I painted not with discipline but with instinct. I had become my paintings.

They say the breakdown happened about a month ago. I have no memory of it. They sedated me, confined me, and took everything.

Every one of my paintings vanished. Yesterday, they told me I was well enough to leave. My flight was arranged.

What no one knows is that I secretly saved one of my canvases, the best.

Before they could take it, I painted over it. I used a layer of crude pigments, easily removable. to hide the work beneath. On top, I scrawled nonsense: wild, chaotic marks, the kind a disturbed girl might make in the throes of madness.

García looked at it before I left. He frowned, suspicious. I thought he might see through my disguise. He looked at me, looked into me, with the eyes of the man who once held me, who once called me gifted, then turned away.

He muttered something to the director. "Let her take this mess. It's worthless. Her family will see she was never talented; just another girl broken by delusion."

He left me there in the courtyard. A newspaper lay folded on the chair he'd occupied. The *Sunday Observer.* I picked it up, and there it was:

Famed painter Michael Lawrence disappears in Mexico along with all the unseen work of his final years....

The parakeets chirp frantically out on the patio. Their tiny bodies tremble as they sense a shift in the weather. They want to be moved, sheltered from the storm.

It hardly seems real that I leave Mexico tomorrow. No one suspects the secret I'll take with me. The truth.

I will go home. I will wait. When the time is right, I will show the world the painting I saved. Not just a portrait, not just a piece of art, but the truth about García García.

Zihuatanejo

They forced him up the steps of the pyramid, each one a mountain to his drugged, trembling legs. His knees barely lifted, his balance faltered, his vision swam in a kaleidoscope of color, mescaline, peyote, as some ancient psychedelic coursed through his veins. The air throbbed with the sound of drums, conches, flutes, and guttural chants, and spiraled into a wild cacophony that seemed to come from the very stone itself.

At the summit, plumed warriors spun in ritual motion. They waved fan-like insignias before a grotesque stone idol that towered over the crowd, the god of war and sun, his obsidian eyes indifferent and eternal. Four priests, naked but for leather loincloths and grotesque masks, seized his limbs and pinned him to a round altar of cold stone. A fifth priest emerged, cloaked in black, hair spiked like a crown of thorns, eyes wide with holy frenzy. He raised a jagged, obsidian knife, and drove it beneath the ribcage, twisted, then wrenched free the still-beating heart.

A flash of white light, and then total darkness.

Randall awoke drenched in sweat, as the hammock swayed beneath him. His body trembled while his breath shallowed. It took minutes to orient himself, to recall that the nightmare was rooted not in imagination but in memory, a vivid echo of his visit that morning to Xihuacan, the archaeological site at *La Soledad de Maciel,* or *La Chole,* as he had first known it ten years earlier.

Back then, the ruins were little more than grassy mounds buried in the jungle, surrounded by sun-scorched fields where local farmers raised corn, beans, and tobacco. Manuel had insisted: "You can feel the energy, man. It's spiritual. You gotta go there."

Now the archaeologists ruled the land. One of the pyramids had been reconstructed. The ancient ballcourt was restored, the site of ritual games once played not merely for sport but as cosmic theater, a symbolic clash between the lords of the underworld and the radiant god of the sun.

A guide showed him the spot where signs of human sacrifice were discovered.

"It was the loser who was killed?" Randall asked.

"No," the guide grinned, eyes agleam. "The *winner!* To be offered to the gods, to have your heart raised to the sun, was the highest honor."

Randall stared at the altar, the very stone where so many hearts had been torn from living chests. *Maybe we're not so different,* he thought. Christianity celebrates a sacrificial death, Abraham was ready to kill Isaac; Jephthah sacrificed his virgin daughter; Agamemnon offered Iphigenia to appease Artemis. Beneath the thin veneer of civilization, the history of humanity is steeped in blood.

Randall rents a modest space at Bungalow del Sol, a ramshackle outpost that clung to the hillside above *La Ropa* Beach. It sits across from *Casa del Sol,* Mary's main house, where she charges premium rates for tourists who want air-conditioning and the illusion of charm. The bungalow isn't much: the kind of place with cockroaches that scatter like spilled beads when you flick on the bathroom light. Geckos patrol the stucco walls like miniature sentinels. The deck boasts an outdoor shower and what was once a view of the sea, now eclipsed by a gaudy, half-finished hotel built with dirty money, always empty, always silent.

Mary's husband lives in Los Angeles. She spends most of her time in Zihuatanejo, running LoLo's, one of the town's trendier restaurants. She's a refined woman with a taste for luxury; dyed black hair set in a flawless bob, nails lacquered and tipped in gold, silver rings glittered on her fingers like tiny suns. Randall once asked her why they didn't fix up the bungalow. She shrugged. The title was murky. No one could untangle the paperwork. "Anyway," she said, "if we upgraded it, I'd have to charge more. You'd have to go somewhere else." That ended the conversation.

In the mornings, the jungle bursts to life. Chachalacas, large and loud like small turkeys, flap through the canopy, squawk and screech with a glorious din. In the old days, they were offered to the gods in place of human hearts. Now, they're fattened alongside turkeys for the feast days of *Independencia* and *Navidad*. Randall has seen women in embroidered dresses walk home from the *mercado*, turkeys upside down in their hands. The birds flapped helplessly, resigned.

After a shower, Randall walks down the hill to *Los Arbolitos,* a beachside joint popular with locals and strays like him. The high-end crowd stays up the way at The Mediterranean, a glossy resort with a swim-up bar and zero contact with anything resembling real Mexico. Farther north, in Ixtapa, an entire gated city of opulence exists for the all-inclusive set—sun, sand, booze, and nothing that might provoke introspection.

Los Arbolitos is owned by the wealthy Rios family. Their eldest son, Alejandro, manages the restaurant. Everyone knows Alejandro is gay, though his parents forced him into a marriage to save face. His poor wife, Marta, is usually at the bar, earbuds in, eyes empty. Randall slides onto the stool beside her and nods.

"Hola, Marta," he says, ordering a beer.

She doesn't look up. "Hola, Randall."

Three young women stroll the shoreline, lesbians, all of them. Randall recognizes them from Mary's place, where they swim nude in the pool. They're stunning. *What a waste,* he thinks, immediately ashamed of the thought.

Hector, a crusty old drinking companion, once told Randall that *Zihuatanejo* means "place of women." Warrior goddesses or shriveled hags greeted the first Spanish ships while the men hid in the jungle. Pirates, Hector claims, used the bay to ambush galleons, and spoke in awe of the fierce women who ruled these shores. He speaks with a beard full of sea salt and breath full of tequila, hoping for free drinks. There's probably some truth in the stories. The place *does* belong to women.

Mary herself is bisexual. Her husband, old, rich, and absent, lets her be. The women in her orbit come and go: elegant types with practiced poise, or wild ones, who chase the dreams of the '60s. Then there's Carla, the town's queen bee of gossip and grit. She runs her own shop and doesn't take handouts. No sugar daddies, no trust funds, just callused hands, sharp eyes, and street smarts. She was never tamed and never needed to be.

Alejandro's wife is barely more than a girl; tiny, fragile, no older than eighteen. Her kinky black hair frames a face that rarely lifts. She moves like a ghost, sways gently to the music in her earbuds, a private refuge in a world that overwhelms her. Her submission is total, her fear of Alejandro's family palpable. Her parents sold her for a handful of pesos. Randall watches her from time to time and wonders what she thinks of Mary's crowd.

Alejandro, forty and thickening despite his attempts to stay lean, plays a different game. When he needs money, he fakes his own kidnapping, and splits the ransom with the pretend abductors. Kidnapping is common in Mexico, everyone knows someone. His family always pays. It's about appearances, about honor. They know the truth but pretend otherwise. Once, the con became real, and he lost two fingers. That earned him a different kind of respect.

On the sand, a wild-eyed urchin teases a red-and-green parrot tethered to a coconut tree by a rusty chain. She dances just out of reach, and shrieks with delight. Her parents sit nearby at a plastic table, faces buried in plates of eggs, beans, and rice. Across the beach, an elderly American couple, their skin burnt and sagging, huddle under a thatched roof and regale younger tourists with crude jokes. Buckets of beer arrive at regular intervals. White plastic chaise lounges line up like tombstones in the sun.

The three girls Randall saw disappeared at the far end of the beach. "I never have luck with women," he says to Marta, who doesn't hear him, doesn't understand English, and keeps time to her music. Randall sips his beer and considers the rest of his day.

South of Los Arbolitos, a narrow river empties into the sea, the tail end of an estuary fed by mangroves. Caimans live there. Sometimes they slip down the river to hunt fish or, once in a while, a careless swimmer. A wooden walkway traces the water's edge all the way from the beach to the highway. Randall walks that way at night. He likes to watch the *luciérnagas* (fireflies) glimmer among the trees. Sometimes he sees the moonlight ripple across the ridged back of a caiman as it glides, like a living fossil, through the dark.

Something elemental pulls Randall back to Zihuatanejo year after year. He can no longer take the winter cold in Canada. He doesn't have close friends here, but he feels tethered nonetheless. "The ocean has no memory," Tim Robbins said in *The Shawshank Redemption*. He and Morgan Freeman ended up on this very beach. Randall dreams of staying for good, but he never does.

He downs another beer. An old man naps against a coconut tree, head tilted toward Randall, an empty plate balanced on his chest like an offering. *Chac Mool*. Randall relives the Carlos Fuentes story about the statue that wakes and takes over its owner's life. A chill prickles his spine. He's never been religious, but the power of ancient idols, especially those that demanded human sacrifice, both repel and obsess him. To kill and eat another person so the sun can shine, so the rain will fall, it's grotesque, yet he can't look away. The old man's plate becomes a symbol, a plea: more life. Always more. Why must death be the price of truth?

Alejandro is tall, dark, and handsome, but there's something off about his face, an arrogance you catch right away. The boss's son, a mama's boy, a man who smokes cigars like they're credentials. Inside Los Arbolitos, he has a walk-in humidor, his sanctuary. Randall considers cigars obscene, always has. There's a smugness to cigar lovers, a performance of masculinity that disgusts him.

He drains the last of his beer, then slips out the back of Los Arbolitos to a gravel road that winds up to the two-lane highway. There he waits for the rickety bus that rattles its way into *El Centro*. Once a sleepy fishing village, Zihuatanejo has swelled into a patchwork town that spills from the waterfront into the surrounding hills. From *La Playa Principal*, the main beach and port, the sprawl climbs unevenly, stitched together by dusty roads and new concrete. When a waiter once caught Randall looking at the hills, he offered a quiet warning: *"Bandidos live there. Don't go, stay away."*

At one end of the beach stands a modest pier where cruise-ship passengers disembark, just steps away from a Mexican naval post. Nearby, local fishermen drag pangas ashore and sell their catch along the *Paseo del Pescador,* the Fisherman's Walk. Restaurateurs, market vendors, and the occasional housewife hover, eager to buy bonito, *huachinango,* or shimmering *dorado.* On rare occasions, a deadly puffer fish appears on a vendor's table, its flesh a gamble only the skilled chef dares to prepare. Across the walkway, tourist restaurants cater to sunburnt visitors. Near the middle of the walkway, crowds gather around the town square, which centers on a basketball court flanked by hand-painted posters for *Jesucristo Superestrella,* scheduled to be performed that night under the open sky.

Randall jumps off the bus near Carla's shop. Mary's friend, she's a folk-art dealer with a laugh like a bleating sheep and skin leathered by years in the sun. Her gruffness could be off-putting, but Randall likes her. He gets along well with older women. It's the younger ones that always give him trouble.

Carla's shop is a curated chaos of folk relics and seaside oddities: delicate carvings in deer antler; black onyx jars etched with indigenous symbols; glass hourglasses; tourist trinkets, and some truly arresting pieces: a line of life-sized tin soldiers inspired by the Terracotta Army, crafted by her business partner Manuel. Among the clutter, Randall spots a necklace: a carved face of a Mayan or Tarascan king. On the reverse, glyphs are etched in neat lines. Manuel says they refer to *Two Blue Bird* or *Double Bird,* the ancient Mayan king of Tikal. Randall buys it. He doesn't wear jewelry, but he's impressed with Manuel's story.

He asks Carla about a bed-and-breakfast in Troncones he visited a few years earlier. Carla recounts the sad story. "Atlantis sank to *Xibalba,*" she says, her laugh echoing like a goat's cry.

"Xibalba?" Randall raises an eyebrow.

"Mexican hell," Carla explains. "The Federales raided the place in the middle of the night. Patricia's husband was jailed. They said the land title had problems. Patricia went to Morelia to fix it, but the judge had been bribed. She never stood a chance."

Life in Mexico resists simple understanding. Salvador Dalí said he couldn't bear to live in a country more surreal than his art. Randall knows what Dali meant. In some ways the chaos appeals to Randall. Beauty and violence exist side by side, interlocked like puzzle pieces.

The ancient world still breathes just beneath the surface. At the museum in Xihuacan, Randall saw the stone bust of a woman, mouth agape, eyes wide with awe, or terror. The expression mirrored his own feelings about Mexico: wonder tinged with dread.

Violence is woven into human history. In Mexico, tragedy clings to beauty like a shadow at noon. That paradox, that haunting, inexplicable pull, is a force Randall has reckoned with all his life. He doesn't fully understand it. He's not sure he ever wants to.

Randall walked down to Joey's next, a beachside restaurant along the Paseo del Pescador. He wanted a few cold beers, a place to watch the crowd and wait for the rock opera to begin. *Jesus Christ Superstar* blared over the speakers and soon blended with his dream of the priests at the ruins of Xihuacan, both fragments of the same ancient dance, humanity's desperate attempt to deal with the inexplicable. *Xihuacan* means "place of the people of the turquoise," a metaphor for those who claim to control time. Two Blue Bird fit right in with the rest of the mosaic. He fingered the necklace around his neck as the waiter approached.

"I'll be back in a Mexican minute," the man said, and vanished like time itself after he took Randall's order.

Joey's was one of six family-run businesses along the strip, prime beachfront real estate: a Oaxacan rug shop, a boutique that sold intricate alebrijes, two folk-art stores, Joey's restaurant, and an espresso bar, inherited from the matriarch who split her real estate among her six children. The eldest brother's young wife was gorgeous and wild. Her name was Natalia, which means "born on Christmas Day." She vanished and left scandal in her wake. The goddess who turned into a witch. Randall saw her once after the disappearance. She walked up out of the sea and sat beside him at Los Arbolitos, told her sad story, smiled, and was gone. Her beauty still haunted him. People whispered that her husband had her killed. Randall didn't believe it. Still, she'd never been seen again.

The day wore on. Morning fishermen hauled in their nets and stowed their gear. The afternoon crew gunned their motors and headed out. Lovers claimed shady spots along the sand, held hands and kissed beneath hats. Mothers and grandmothers perched on benches like sentinels. A beggar shuffled by, hand outstretched. A man walked along with a bucket of Oaxacan cheese. He spun a piece into a perfect ball for a customer. Children pestered a giant iguana that lurked in the brush between the path and the sea. On the basketball court, actors rehearsed lines:

Jesus Christ Superstar... Do you think you're what they say you are?

Far off in the Sierra Madre, tourists rattled along the tequila trails, unaware they shared the road with modern-day bandits. It wasn't just the tequila that made the journey dangerous.

Legend has it that one priest at Xihuacan, before the tsunami in 1350 destroyed the city, wore the same black robe for years, painted himself in a mixture of spider venom, scorpion oil, and rubber sap. He never cut his hair or nails and his hair reached his ankles. His claws curled like talons. The blood rituals are gone now, but the air out there still hums with the residue of sacrifice. Every year locals return to pray for rain, for crops, and fertility.

Randall wiped sweat from his face. Too many beers on an empty stomach. The late-afternoon heat clung to his skin like cellophane. He knew he should eat something before heading back to his bungalow. He ordered Joey's signature pizza, the Italian Stallion. True to promise, the waiter returned in a "Mexican minute."

His friend Reuben walked toward him on the walkway.

"¡Hola, Reuben! ¿Qué tal?"

"I'm good, *gracias a Dios*," Reuben said, and settled into the seat across from him. "Are you here for the celebration of *Nuestra Señora de Guadalupe?*"

"That explains the crowd," said Randall. "No, I just came for the pizza. Joey really piles on the meat. Sit down, have a slice. How's Yvonne?"

"She's fine, but I had to escape. Her to-do lists never end," Reuben laughed. "When are you getting married, Randall? Yvonne's got friends. I could set you up."

Randall didn't answer. A wave of dizziness hit him. Reuben noticed, but said nothing. He knew Randall guarded his privacy.

After the pizza, Randall didn't feel well. His lungs were tight, his arms heavy, his head pounded with heat and something else he couldn't name.

"I'm headed back to the bungalow," Randall said to Reuben. "Catch you later."

Reuben studied Randall's face. "You all right, amigo? You've gone pale."

"I'm fine," Randall said, though his hand went to his chest. "Probably too much of that salty meat on Joey's pizza. My heart's racing. I just need to lie down for a bit."

"I'll go with you," Reuben offered. "Forgot my camera anyway. The parade's always good for a few shots."

Randall usually preferred to walk alone, but today he was glad for the company. They caught the bus to La Ropa. By the time they stepped off, Randall felt steadier.

"Let's grab one more beer at Los Arbolitos," he said. "Get your camera. I'll wait for you there. Afterwards, we can take the walkway through the mangroves. I love that trail."

"You sure you're up for it?" Reuben asked, as he eyed his friend.

Randall nodded. "Yeah. I'm good."

"You should move here," Reuben said when they left Arbolitos. "I'll help you find a place. Yvonne's mom is a realtor, and Yvonne's also got her license. We'd take care of you."

"I know you would," Randall said and tried to smile. "I'm not ready yet. Can't afford it."

"There's always a way," Reuben insisted. "You'd be happier here."

"Maybe," Randall murmured. "But not tonight."

When they entered the mangroves, the air was thick and still. Halfway in, Randall stopped. A wave of dizziness hit him like a tide. A pain, sharp, sudden, and unbearable, seized his chest. He gasped, tried to speak, but the world slipped away.

He turned to Reuben, but in that instant, it wasn't Reuben he saw.

It was the priest at Xihuacan in his black robe, obsidian blade raised high. The knife came down, pierced through his flesh and into Randall's heart.

A total darkness consumed him.

⧗ ⧗ ⧗

Randall woke in a white room, the steady beep of monitors surrounded him like a soft metronome. At the foot of the bed sat a woman, elegant, luminous, and familiar. He knew her face, but the memory was just out of reach.

"Welcome back," she says.

"Where... where am I?" Randall pushes himself upright, scans the room.

"You're in the hospital."

"What happened?"

"You had a heart attack. You blacked out."

His pulse quickens. "Am I... dying?"

Her turquoise eyes lock with his. "No. Not yet. It's not time."

"Not time for what?"

She smiles. "Don't worry. I'll be back."

Before he can say anything else, she's gone. A doctor steps in, clipboard in hand.

"Randall. Good to see you awake. How do you feel?"

"Strangely good... considering. Did I really have a heart attack?"

"Yes. Your heart is still traumatized. We need to run some more tests."

Randall nods, still disoriented. "So, will I be okay?"

"Your friend Reuben got you here quickly. That's the good news, and the alligator didn't get you, but you are still in danger."

Randall blinks. "Alligator?"

"In the estuary. People say it's gotten more aggressive. You're the third case this month with injuries near the mangroves."

Randall exhales, half-laughing. "So, I dodged death twice."

"For now," the doctor says as he packs up. "This is serious, Randall. No more cigarettes, watch the drinking, and maybe skip the Italian Stallion next time."

"Got it."

The monitor starts to blink rapidly.

Outside the room, Reuban stands, arms open.

"Hola, Randall. You look better. Gracias a Dios."

"You saved me," Randall says. "I owe you."

"You were lucky. What now, amigo?"

"I've decided," Randall says with quiet certainty, "to move to Zihuatanejo."

Reuben grins. "Good. It's time. How do you feel?"

Randall smiles, something flutters in his chest. "Happy."

As they turn to leave, he sees her, Natalia, on the stairs. Her name flashes in his mind like a candle relit. Christmas. Born on Christmas Day.

"Wait here, Reuben. I'll be back in a Mexican minute." He runs off: "Natalia! Wait!"

⧗ ⧗ ⧗

The doctor pauses at Reuben's side, when he leaves the room.

"We lost him," he says softly. "I'm sorry. We did everything we could."

Two Oysters

"I think it's your shell."
"My shell?"
"Yeah. Everything's got one."
"Everything?"
"Clams, mussels, scallops, armadillos..."
"You've seen an armadillo?"
"No, but I've read about them."
"That's hearsay. Doesn't count."
"Fine. Beetles. They've got shells you could crack walnuts with."
"Do humans have shells?"
"Yes, invisible ones. Only psychologists can see them."
"What are psychologists?"
"They study human shells. It's a medical specialty."
"What have they learned?"
"That if you live inside your shell all the time it's unhealthy."
"What if it's a camper shell?"
"Depends. Airstreams are okay. Winnebagos, questionable."
"You sound like a liberal."
"Guilty as charged."
"So, what are you trying to tell me, that my shell's the problem?"
"Exactly."
"That's news to me. I like my shell."
"You're too deep into it, too out of touch with society."
"Says who?"
"Psychologists. I would imagine your family agrees."
"Leave my family out of it. You think I should open up?"
"Just a little. Let some light in."

"For my sake?"

"Of course."

"You just want to pry me open with an oyster knife and poke around."

"Don't be absurd."

"I'm cautious, it's safer in my shell."

"I'm concerned about you."

"You want me to wear my heart on my sleeve?"

"No, just don't lock it in a safe."

"You want me to open my shell?"

"Yes."

"And that would make me... what, enlightened?"

"Happier."

"I thought we were supposed to turn on, tune in, drop out."

"That was the sixties."

"A golden age as you should know."

"Some think it was a misguided detour."

"Doesn't that conflict with your chakra or something?"

"Can we stay focused? This is about your shell."

"What's wrong with a little introspection?"

"Navel-gazing. It's a trap. Shell game, shell shock, shell out... the word screams 'problem'."

"What about shellfish?"

"They're the exception."

"To what rule?"

"To the rule that I want to help you with."

"You're no help. This is a misdiagnosis. My shell isn't the problem, it's my sanctuary. I read there and think."

"Aren't you lonely?"

"Sometimes. Aren't you?"

"Well..."

"Don't you ever just want to disappear for a while? No noise, no drama, just... peace?"

"Maybe."

"Maybe you should hang out in your own shell for a while? Try it, you'll like it."

"Ugh. Go stew in your brine. I don't give a damn."
"That's a horrible thing to say to an oyster."
"The world is my oyster."
"Yeah? Good luck with that. I like my shell."
"You must be a hedgehog, not a fox."
"What?"
"You believe in one big thing, your shell, and ignore the rest."
"Oh, you mean that guy Berlin, the one who said hundreds of thousands of oysters suffer from a disease that occasionally generates a pearl? He wouldn't agree with you at all. He'd defend my right to live in my shell, to nurture my pearl. So, there!"
"You live in Plato's cave."
"No, I'm in the garden with Candide."
"This conversation is going nowhere."
"Then let's have lunch. How do you like your plankton?"
"On the half shell."
"Smartass."

Desipio

"Desipio, get out of the garden! Don't pee on the flowers!" Carmelita called from the kitchen window.

Desipio stood in the marigolds, vacant-eyed and slack-jawed. His hair, thick and wild, puffed out like scorched meringue. He hunched slightly, knees bent with effort, but nothing came, only a few dark drops fell onto the soil. His face contorted in pain.

Inside, Carmelita turned to her sister. "What can we do with him?"

Rosa sighed. "We promised Mama we'd take care of him. We have to."

The sisters shook their heads and said nothing more as they resumed their morning routine. They pressed tortillas and stirred a pot of beans. From upstairs came the creak of footsteps. Jorge, Rosa's husband, descended the stairs and slumped into a chair at the table. The old dog, Azore, barked and darted through the open door.

"Desipio peed in the garden again," Rosa said, her eyes fixed on the beans.

"He's out there now?" Jorge asked.

"Still," Carmelita added, a frown on her face. She leaned out the window and shouted, "Desipio! I said get out of the garden!"

"I'm walking my puppy," Desipio called back in a raspy, confused voice.

Rosa let out a laugh. "He calls Azore his puppy. That dog's older than he is."

Desipio shuffled in through the back door. His eyes scanned Jorge with suspicion.

"Who is this man?" he demanded. "What are you doing here? Are you here to corrupt my granddaughters? Get out! We don't allow womanizers in this house."

"Abuelo, that's Jorge, my husband," Rosa said gently.

Desipio narrowed his eyes at Jorge, and pointed a crooked finger. "No bawdy business under my roof, young man." Then he turned to Rosa. "Your abuela picked fresh strawberries this morning. She wants you to make a pie. They're in the fridge. Don't keep her waiting."

Rosa's expression softened as she nodded. "Of course, Abuelo."

After he left the room, Carmelita whispered to Jorge, "Go to the garden and pick some strawberries. You know how he gets. Better not to contradict him."

Jorge nodded and slipped outside, glad for the excuse. He returned shortly with a bowl of berries, then hurried off to work. He prayed silently the day would be calmer when he came home.

Meanwhile, Desipio slipped out the front gate and limped toward the market unnoticed.

Back in the kitchen, Carmelita dried her hands and said, "Concepción's back to her old tricks. I saw her wrapped around Renato like a snake."

"She saw you?" Rosa asked.

"Oh, she saw me all right. Gave me that smug little grin."

"She's a tramp," Rosa muttered.

"You better keep her away from Jorge."

Rosa rolled her eyes. "All Jorge cares about is food and that silly camera. He thinks he's the next Frida Kahlo."

"Frida was a painter," Carmelita said.

"Same thing."

"No," Carmelita asserted firmly. "A painter captures the soul. A photographer only catches the surface."

There was a knock at the door. Carmelita wiped her hands on a kitchen towel. The mailman stood there with a bundle of letters and a concerned look.

"I just saw your grandfather at the fish market," he said. "He didn't look too steady on his feet."

"What?" Carmelita blinked, startled. She turned toward Rosa. "How did he slip past us?"

The mailman handed her the mail and left. A moment later, Desipio appeared, holding a newspaper-wrapped package that smelled of the sea.

"Grandfather, you can't just wander off like that. We were worried," said Carmelita, returning to her dough. "What's in the bundle?"

"I bought salt cod for the bacalao your grandmother wants you to make," he said matter-of-factly.

"But it's not the season," Carmelita said, puzzled.

Desipio shrugged. "That's what the fishmonger said too, but I don't argue with your grandmother. I do what she tells me."

He left the cod on the counter and wandered back toward his room.

"Tonight, my dear, we dine on bacalao and fresh strawberry pie," he called softly to his wife, then headed outside and called for the dog. "Azore? Come, little one, come."

From the kitchen window, Carmelita spotted him among the flowers. She called out, exasperated, "Desipio! Get out of the garden! Don't pee on the flowers!"

"He goes back out there over and over," she muttered to Rosa. "He doesn't listen. Did you see him toss salt over his shoulder again?"

"Oh, yes," said Rosa. "Abuela always did that too. She said it kept the witches away."

"Do you really think she believed in witches?"

"No... well, maybe a little. She blamed them whenever she lost at Lotería."

"Abuela never played the lottery," Carmelita said.

"No, not the numbers, the card game, the one with the pictures and the beans."

"Oh, right, *that* lottery."

Desipio reappeared in the kitchen, cheeks flushed.

"I do *not* pee on the flowers! I pee on the witches!"

With that, he turned and shuffled back to his room.

Rosa watched him go. "He's getting worse."

"The doctor said the infection should clear up in a week, if he takes his pills," Carmelita said.

"I don't mean the infection, I mean his temperament," Rosa said.

"He's just cranky because I hound him." Carmelita glanced at the pie Rosa had decorated. "That's beautiful. A real piece of art."

Rosa sighed. "I sometimes wonder why we put so much effort into food. We chew, we swallow, we... well, you know. All that work for something that ends up in the toilet."

"Life is art," said Carmelita. "How we live is who we are. We don't do it for the end, we do it for ourselves, because we must."

Just then, Jorge walked in from work.

"I saw Concepción downtown. She says hello."

Carmelita stiffened and her cheeks colored. She had never admitted her crush on Renato, or how much she hated the way Concepción toyed with him.

"I *hate* that woman," she snapped, and turned to deal with the salt cod. It wouldn't soak in time, but she had her tricks.

Rosa laughed. "Desipio says he doesn't pee on the flowers. He pees on the witches."

Jorge raised an eyebrow.

"What?" Rosa asked. "Don't tell me you believe in witches too."

Jorge hesitated, then said, "It's what your Abuela told him about sex. She only allowed it when she wanted babies. Drove the poor man mad. Begged her for more, but she'd shut him down. One day she told him, 'If you're so desperate, go out and screw the flowers.'"

Rosa blushed. "Well, *I* won't send *you* to the garden."

Carmelita chuckled and returned to the stove. Azore snored in the corner. Rosa and Jorge disappeared into their room. In the kitchen, the scent of dough and saltfish mingled with Carmelita's thoughts, the ghosts, and the witches.

Desipio sits beside his wife on the bed; her rosary beads click softly in her fingers. She finishes the final decade, crosses herself, and turns to him.

"You spoke Chinese again in your sleep," she says gently. "I never understand a word, but you always end with the same thing— 'Kowpuck' or something like that."

Desipio shrugs, bewildered. "I don't know where it comes from. Carmelita scolds me when I go to the garden to pee. What do you want me to say?"

He throws his hands up, as if to surrender to the absurdity of it all.

"Come here, *querido,*" she whispers, and pulls him into her arms and down onto the bed.

Meanwhile, in the kitchen, Carmelita finishes with the bacalao. Everything is ready, dinner is all set. There is only the wait for the hour to arrive. She sits down with a cup of tea when suddenly she hears a loud cry from Desipio's room:

"Kowpuck!"

A few minutes later, Desipio shuffles out, looking dazed and determined.

"Carmelita," he says, "I must accompany your grandmother. She has her shift at the library."

He doesn't wait for a response. He opens the door and extends his arm as if to guide someone invisible. Azore, the dog, trots after him. Carmelita watches them go and shakes her head.

It's a beautiful day.

At the library, Desipio meanders among the shelves. He no longer reads, but he still loves the smell of old paper, the comfort of being among friends who never speak out of turn. He waits there patiently until his wife's imaginary shift is done.

Back at the house, Rosa peers out the window. "Should I send Jorge to look for him? It's getting late."

"No need," Carmelita says. "He always comes back when the library closes."

Sure enough, as the sun sets, Desipio walks through the door, Azore at his heels.

"You're just in time," Rosa says brightly. "But, where's Grandma?"

Desipio takes his place at the table. He doesn't flinch.

"Why, you haven't set a place for her, what do you expect?"

Rosa realizes she's been outplayed. With a sigh and a smile, Rosa sets a plate and napkin where the old woman used to sit.

"There," she says. "All set."

Desipio nods. "Come, Querida. Everything is just as you wished. We're ready for you."

Jorge and Rosa take their seats. Carmelita brings the bacalao to the table. The evening settles in. No one speaks of ghosts.

The Argument

No one remembers how it began. It was something trivial like the color of the water at Las Canteras. He said it was green, she said it was blue, or vice versa. Whatever it was, it didn't matter. What mattered was what came next.

Things quickly spiraled into pandemonium. She insulted his mother. He called her sister a whore. After that, the house became a war zone. Neighbors avoided the sidewalk. Objects flew from windows: shoes, framed pictures, vases, candelabras, even full-sized Catrinas, those bizarre skeletal ladies in sunhats. It was dangerous. You could lose an eye, catch a plate to the head, or take a stiletto to the groin.

Before the argument they were quiet and reserved, nearly invisible members of the staid, upscale community. She was a schoolteacher, *maestra*, beloved by her young students. He was an attorney, *abogado*, who took on the hardest cases for the poor when they were exploited by the system. After the quarrel broke out, it was as if both were suddenly inhabited by devils. The local priest was called to perform an exorcism, but his incantations were no match for the evil spirits that had seized the brains of the unfortunate brother and sister.

Friends tried to broker peace, but it was useless. The only thing the two siblings could agree on was that they would never agree. Still, they stayed together in an unlikely union, teamed up at times to attack mutual enemies, though they seldom agreed on who the enemies were. People no longer tried to help. They picked sides instead. Soon, everyone in the neighborhood had joined the fight.

Love and war blurred into one. Enemies crossed party lines for sex, but otherwise stuck to their factions. The original argument, whatever it was, became the only thing that mattered. Commerce died. The birth rate dropped. Dreams disappeared.

It was impossible to dine out. Waiters refused to serve anyone from the "wrong" side. Even Carolita's, the bar where most romances started, dried up like the tits of a desert witch. Paco the bartender went mad from loneliness, and argued with himself in a cracked mirror.

Tourists no longer visited and the high-end boutiques went broke. The locals pestered those few curious souls who braved a visit. They asked endless questions: *Whose side are you on? Are you here for him or her?* The government intervened, but it devolved just as everyone expected, into bribes and ineptitudes.

People from nearby towns came to help, but soon gave up. Negotiations required they speak to each party separately, then decode each one's lies. The brother and sister contradicted themselves repeatedly, sometimes midsentence.

A point came when truth disappeared altogether. Facts became optional, opinions reigned. Everyone had one, and they were all louder than the last.

This dragged on for days, months, years. Those who remained prayed for one of the arguers to die, or both, in the hope that normal life could resume.

Now and then, if you wandered into the town by mistake, you'd hear people shout across alleys and windows:

"Either of them dead yet?"

"No," was always the reply.

Eventually, things grew so tangled, numbers, letters, body parts, memories, names, colors, that it became impossible to argue anymore. That was the cure.

It wasn't obvious at first, but people felt it. The tension eased. Romance seeped back into the air. Paco returned to Carolita's to pour cheap mezcal at scandalous prices. Kids chased the balloon man through the streets.

Then came that one moment when everyone held their breath.

She came into the bar and sat beside him.

You could have heard a pin drop, but no one dropped a pin.

"Remember the water at Las Canteras? What color was it anyway?"

"I don't remember," he said.

"Neither do I," she said.

Paco poured them each a drink and everything went back to normal.

People started to dream again. Commerce returned and there was a baby boom.

The priest tried to claim credit as did the municipal authorities, but the people would have none of it. No one ever knew how and why the argument ended, people just accepted it and moved on thankful that the miracle occurred.

It was a quiet, unassuming doctor who discovered what ended the argument many years later. It was an outbreak of temporary dementia. Once no one could remember the reasons for the argument, the argument stopped. By the time peoples' memories returned, everyone had moved on to other things. When asked what caused the outbreak, the doctor said: "It's better not to ask. These things happen from time to time, something to do with the madness of crowds.

The Dust Gatherers

The dust rolls into town like fog, only heavier. Fog is hollow and wet. It is absorbed and transformed. Dust is solid, dry, and stubborn. It clings, embeds, and never rolls off.

The houses are painted in vivid, purposeful colors to help people find their way. Red leads to restaurants, green to parks, blue to rivers and lakes, and so on. Each hue is a promise, a path, a memory made visible.

For those who can't see color, guide dogs lead the way. The dogs know the shades by scent. Every pigment holds a distinct fragrance. The dogs, with their ancient noses, follow these invisible trails with silent devotion.

The dust gatherers collect what others ignore. Dust is useful in ways most can't imagine. It is ground into medicine, pressed into bricks, and spun into strange fuels. Only the dust gatherers know the full truth of its value. Quiet, overlooked, seemingly insignificant, they possess knowledge no one else has.

They come from a long line of invisible people: the voiceless, the humble, the ones who lived before the first written word, before stories had names. Always on the margins, they have survived by cleverness, patience, and resilience. Heroes without statues, sages without scrolls, their strength is endurance, not acclaim.

There was one day when the dust gatherers failed to come. Dust thickened on windowsills, piled on doorsteps, and smothered the streets. Birds choked, cats hissed, people cursed the air and each other, but did nothing. No one knew how to act. No one understood what had gone missing.

Colors faded under the layers. Dog nostrils became clogged, and they were no longer useful guides. People wandered, unable to find parks, rivers, even their own homes. Direction itself seemed to dissolve.

Only in absence did the dust gatherers become visible. Their silence was louder than any protest. They were hidden in the drifts, the confusion, and the stillness. Unappreciated, undervalued, neglected and overlooked, the dust gatherers were nobodies.

Nobodies dream of fortune falling from the sky, but it never does. It never has. Bound by fate or duty or something older still, the dust gatherers return. They come without ceremony, without parades, without thanks. There is only the soft rhythm of brooms and the rustle of sacks. Life resumes. Colors reemerge. The city exhales. People find their way again, to restaurants, to rivers, to parks, to home.

The fog rolls into town like dust, but it dances instead of settles. It wets rather than clings. The fog is hollow and rolls off the world like a whisper.

Hollow hearts. Wet tears.

In the green-painted park, two philosophers resume an old debate.

"Character is shaped by fate," says one.

"No," says the other, "character is created."

"By whom?"

"By all of us," the dreamer replies.

The dust gatherers pass by like the first snow, silent and sure. They pay no mind to the philosophers. They have work to do. Philosophy doesn't clean a doorstep.

A Cautionary Tale From a Personal Experience

Herman Piakowski sat stiffly in the Mexico City airport. He watched the crowd churn past like a river. Tourists wore wide-brimmed hats, families guarded their luggage, businessmen tapped at phones. Next to him, Betty Lou leaned forward, half-listening to two young women chat nearby, the same ones they'd seen earlier on the flight down.

"So, you *actually* use that cream?"

"Hell, yeah! It stings like crazy, but they say it prevents wrinkles. I *hate* wrinkles. You know what I mean?"

"Totally. Those cracked lines around the eyes? Ugh."

"Crow's feet."

"Right. Hate that shit."

"Same."

Herman flinched at the language. He and Betty Lou were dressed like a matched set: loose khaki pants, short-sleeve floral shirts, and sturdy leather walking boots. They were church group volunteers, ready for their mission in Oaxaca: dig wells, install water pumps, spread goodwill.

"You know Ruth? The redhead?"

"Oh, my God. That bitch? If she ever smiled, her whole face would sag."

"Total bitch. And she *uses* that cream. Watch out."

"No way."

"Way. Heard her talk about it last week."

"Well, screw that. I'm done with it. I don't wanna end up looking like *her*."

"Exactly. What's *her* deal anyway?"

Herman tried not to stare. The one with the black hair and goth makeup wore a long dress over tights, like she had something to hide. The other, a blonde, wore artfully torn jeans and designer sneakers. They laughed like they were the only ones in the world.

Betty Lou nudged Herman. "Over there, aren't those the same old folks we saw in San Francisco?"

"Sure are."

A Mexican couple, both in wheelchairs, sat alone near the gate. The man wore Levis, a dark shirt, and a beige Stetson. His wife, wrapped in a purple print dress and a black shawl, stared at the wall, her gray hair pulled into a tight bun.

An announcement crackled over the loudspeaker, indistinct, rapid Spanish.

"You catch that?" Betty Lou asked.

"Something about a gate change. Let me check," Herman said.

Herman approached the gate agent, and confirmed the flight had moved from Gate 71 to 75B.

"Let's get going. It's a hike, and we don't want to be late," he said to Mary Lou when he returned.

"What about those two in the wheelchairs?"

"Someone will come for them."

"Really? I don't see anyone."

Herman hesitated, then stepped toward the elderly couple and tried his best Spanish. Their blank stares unsettled him. He asked the gate agent for help, explained the situation, and offered to escort them to the new gate. After a quiet exchange between the couple, they nodded.

Herman and Betty Lou took the handles of the wheelchairs and set off like do-gooder charioteers on their small mission of mercy. They hadn't gone far when half a dozen airport security guards closed in around them, their faces hard, their eyes suspicious. Two furious wheelchair attendants trailed behind. In seconds, Herman and Betty Lou were surrounded, handcuffed, and marched away without explanation.

"Wait!" Herman shouted. "What's going on? We're going to miss our flight!"

The elderly couple disappeared down the concourse toward Gate 75B, wheeled away by the angry attendants. One of them looked back at Herman and Betty Lou with open contempt.

Inside the airport security office, Herman paced while Betty Lou wept. A man in a dark uniform sat behind a desk, impassive.

"You try to kidnap helpless old Mexicans. For this you can go to jail."

"What? No, sir. We only wanted to *help*. There was no one around. Ask the gate agent!"

"You are mistaken. Attendants looking for these people. You take them away. This *very* serious."

Betty Lou sniffled, eyes wide. Herman fumbled for their passports.

"We're here with a church group. We're off to Oaxaca to drill wells and find water. A humanitarian mission."

The man took the passports, and examined them with exaggerated care.

"These do not look real."

"What! They're real! They're US passports!"

"We hold you for police."

The guards hauled them into a holding cell behind the office. Inside were two other detainees, both Mexican, both accused of pickpocketing. One leered at Betty Lou. Herman responded with a single, hard punch that sent the man to the floor. The two thieves retreated to the corner and didn't bother them again.

The guard outside the cell grinned, and rolled the toothpick in his mouth.

"*Muy fuerte, gringo.* Why you come to this country?"

"I *was* here to help. Now I just want to get the hell out."

Betty Lou clutched her stomach.

"I think I'm gonna be sick."

"Guard! *El baño.* Now!" yelled Herman.

A female guard led Betty Lou to the restroom. Just as Betty Lou returned, a new woman was thrown into the cell: a prostitute in a miniskirt, spike heels, and a blouse that revealed more than it covered. The pickpockets pounced. The guards rushed in to break it up.

In the chaos, Herman saw his moment. He grabbed Betty Lou's hand, dashed out of the cell, and didn't look back. At the main desk, the head of security was gone. Their passports sat unattended. Herman snatched them, and they ran.

They bolted through the terminal, past confused travelers, dodged luggage carts and followed the signs to Gate 75B. Luckily, the plane was delayed, and they made the flight, barely.

"Whew!" exclaimed Betty. "That was a rocky start. I hope things get better."

"They will," said Herman, "or we will head back home on the first plane out."

As luck would have it, they were seated across from the same two girls they'd noticed earlier in the terminal.

"So, what's up with that?" asked the blonde.

"Exactly!" said the other, eyes wide, punctuated with black eyeliner. "It was so obvious, and no one else even noticed."

"Noticed what?"

"The kidnapping."

"The security guards didn't do anything?"

"Please. That crack whore in the miniskirt walked by, and every single one of those guards drooled like a dog in heat. Meanwhile, the guys just slipped away."

"What guys?"

"Oh, my God, are you even listening? The *kidnappers!*"

"Seriously? They got away?"

"You're impossible! Yes, I know it sounds insane, but they totally got away."

"Where do you think they are now?"

"Christ. Could you just shut up for like one minute?"

Herman Piakowski laughed under his breath. The plane began its descent into Oaxaca. He glanced over at his wife, Betty Lou, who also listened in on the girls' wild speculation with polite bemusement.

Herman was ready to get to work. The mission was part of a church effort to reintroduce amaranth as a staple crop in the villages. Once a vital source of nutrition for indigenous peoples, amaranth had been wiped out, along with countless other traditions, by the Spanish conquistadors. The Spaniards took issue with the ritual use of amaranth, molded into statues with honey and eaten during indigenous ceremonies in a fashion eerily similar to Catholic communion. The Church couldn't stomach the competition. They banned it. The result: centuries of malnutrition.

The Piakowskis' church, Jehovah's Witness, saw opportunity in the void left by the demise of Catholicism. They didn't just hand out pamphlets; they laid the groundwork for systematic change.

As Betty Lou and Herman exited the airport, he spotted the elderly Mexican couple they'd seen earlier. The old man broke into a grin, gave Herman a casual high five, then turned to embrace his family. The old couple stood up and walked off together toward a parked bus. No wheelchairs. No drama. Just joy.

The 2010s

Jamaica

 F OX News blared from the television, grainy footage of the chaos that unfolded in some city.

"That's how you deal with those punks," Max said, as he leaned forward to get a better view. "Crack their damn skulls! They oughta send in the army, beat the shit out of those ANTIFA bastards. Hell, shoot 'em."

Harold shifted uncomfortably in his leather recliner. "That's a bit much, Max. I don't like the looting either, but we can't just mow people down. That ain't right."

"Fine, shoot 'em in the leg then," Max growled. "Or the foot. Hit 'em where it counts. You let this slide, next thing you know it's a full-blown insurrection."

Harold raised an eyebrow. "It's not an insurrection, Max. It's a protest."

Max squinted at the screen. "Same damn thing."

"No, it ain't. A protest is about people pissed off, trying to be heard. An insurrection's when you try to tear the damn whole system down with guns and fire."

Max snorted. "Well, I'm pissed off too, but you don't see me chuckin' Molotovs through a police station window."

On the screen, someone did just that.

"Yeah," Harold said, as he grabbed the remote. "Enough of that. No need to watch folks beat the hell outta each other."

He clicked the TV off and stared at the colorful travel brochure spread across his lap. A photo of white beaches and turquoise water shimmered in the afternoon light.

Max glanced at him. "You still thinkin' about that trip?"

"I am," Harold said. "All expenses paid. Two tickets to Jamaica. Won it on my birthday. After forty years at the mill. I figure maybe it's time."

Max scoffed. "Jamaica? Full of drugs and gangs. You'll get chopped up with a machete and fed to sharks. I wouldn't go down there if you paid me."

Harold chuckled. "Don't be so narrowminded. I've heard it's beautiful. Friendly people, great food."

"Friendly people?" Max barked. "Please. It's worse than Chicago on a Saturday night. Why go to some third-world island when we got peace and quiet right here? We can fish, drink a few beers, and not worry about steppin' on a landmine."

Harold took a sip of his beer and slid the brochure across the table. "Look at this place, Max. Ocean view, all-you-can-eat buffet, open bar, and it's fenced in to keep the riffraff out."

Max glanced casually at the photos: sunset dinners, bikini-clad women, hammocks in the shade.

"I don't need no damn beach sluts shakin' their asses at me," Max muttered. "We got everything we need right here."

"You have to come with me," Harold said. "You know what they say: safety in numbers, right? I got two tickets."

Max spat tobacco into the rusty coffee can under the table. "Hell, no. I ain't goin' to some lawless island paradise to die."

Harold stood and flapped his arms like wings. "Bawk-bawk-bawk. Chicken Max! Afraid of a little sunshine and rum?"

"You're an idiot," Max said, but couldn't help but grin.

"Come on, Max. We're sixty, not dead. Let's have an adventure before we're too damn old to get off the couch."

"We already *had* an adventure. Remember the navy?"

"We were stationed in Alameda. The only foreign country we saw was on a postcard. Your biggest adventure was that trip down a one-way street the wrong way. You did talk your way out of a ticket, I'll give ya that."

Max laughed despite himself. "Still, I don't wanna die in some jungle with mystery meat on my plate and dreadlocked lunatics chasin' me."

Harold crossed his arms. "You've watched too much TV. Jamaica's got culture, history, and Bob Marley. You like Bob Marley."

"I like *one* Bob Marley song."

"You're my best friend, Max," Harold said, seriously. "I don't want to go without you."

Max looked down, chewed the inside of his cheek, then let out a slow, reluctant breath.

"Goddammit, Harold. Fine. But if I get dengue fever or stabbed in the gut by some Rasta pirate, I'm hauntin' your ass forever."

Harold beamed. "Deal. Now go buy a pair of swim trunks. You're gonna need 'em."

⌛⌛⌛

They booked a red-eye to Kingston out of SFO, with a layover in Miami. At the airport, Harold picked up a bottle of peppermint schnapps from duty-free. They had a couple hours to kill before takeoff, and Harold figured if he got Max schnockered enough, maybe he wouldn't back out last minute.

The gate area started to fill. Young couples in Bob Marley T-shirts drifted in, retirees in matching travel gear, families, loners, and business types. A small pair of kids tore past them, and nearly knocked the schnapps bottle off the arm of Harold's seat.

"Watch it, ya little nippers!" Max barked. "Damn near killed our schnapps."

Their father smiled apologetically. "Letting them burn off energy. They'll sleep on the flight."

"Ya hear that, 'arold?" Max slurred. "They'll be q-quiet on the plane, he sez." He giggled.

"Shh," Harold said, biting back his own grin.

Two Jamaican women sat beside them. Harold glanced at Max and gave a sly wink.

"You bwoys off to Jamaica?" one of the women asked. Her hair was a crown of twists and curls.

"Sure are," Max said, voice already thick from the schnapps.

"We are too," said the woman. "We go fi to see family."

"You ladies want a drink?" Max held up the bottle with a wobbly flourish, face flushed.

"What you think, Jennie?" the woman asked her friend.

Jennie shrugged. "Might calm my nerves. I hate fi fly."

"Okay," said the first. "We take a drink."

Max handed over the bottle. "So, what's your name, honey?"

"I'm not your honey," she replied, deadpan, then grinned. "I'm Lisa. This here's Jennie."

"Sorry," Max said, sheepish. "Didn't mean anything by it. I'm Max, and this is Harold."

The girls took generous swigs and passed the bottle back.

"Furs time to Jamaica?" Lisa asked.

"Yep," Max nodded. "F-f-first time."

"We haven't traveled much," Harold added. "Just Navy stuff. I won this trip in a company raffle. What's Jamaica really like? The brochure makes it look like heaven."

Lisa and Jennie exchanged a glance. "Jamaica can be heaven. White sand, turquoise water. But depends on which side of paradise you from."

"Which side are you from?" Max asked, more curious than drunk now.

"Born in uptown Kingston," said Lisa, "but we live in San Francisco now."

"We land in Kingston," Harold said. Max was already slumped back, eyes closed.

"Kingston, yeah," said Jennie. "Don't go downtown. People there, they... grudgeful."

"Grudgeful?" Harold raised an eyebrow.

"Like gangs. Like anywhere. There's places you avoid if ya know what's good for ya."

"Oh, we won't go off course," Harold assured her. "Just a bus ride straight to the resort."

The girl's expressions changed.

"That's no way to see Jamaica," Jennie said. "Maybe we come fi the resort. Show you the real island."

Max stirred awake, bleary-eyed. "Huh? Realtor? We're not buying property, girls."

"That's not what she said," Harold muttered. "She offered to show us around."

"Sounds dangerous," Max grumbled.

"We keep you safe," Lisa said. "My brother Ruel drive. He's big. Nobody mess with him."

"Peachy," said Max, clearly unconvinced.

"Lighten up, Max," Harold said. "Could be fun."

The announcement came to board. As they lined up, Harold slipped Lisa the name of the resort. They didn't set a date, or time, just a maybe. The girls waved as the line shuffled forward.

On arrival, the bus was ready outside the Kingston airport. A young guide herded them on, handed out warm Red Stripes, and told them it would be a four-hour ride to the coast, with one bathroom and drink stop halfway. He jogged off to wait for late arrivals.

"These beers might actually hit the spot," said Max, eyeing the label. "If they were cold."

"At least it's something," said Harold. They settled into their seats, looking out at Kingston.

In the hills, boxy concrete homes perched behind bright gardens, blooms bursting over wrought-iron fences.

"See those grilles?" Max said, and pointed at barred windows. "Tells you everything you need to know."

"Oh, come on, Max. People do the same thing in the States."

They passed a square where locals lined up at a public spigot, plastic jugs in hand. Further on, clusters of corrugated shacks, the paint curling like old skin, sat unevenly on packed dirt. Kids stared out from dark interiors. Somewhere a rooster crowed. Stray dogs slunk across the road.

They rolled past a burst of color. Women in vivid skirts waited at a dusty bus stop, men hunched over domino tables under a single tree. The farther they got from the city, the slower the road. It filled with trucks, motorbikes, even carts pulled by donkeys.

"Looks like it's gonna be a long drive," Max said.

"Relax. Take in the sights."

"What sights?" Max scoffed.

They passed two mango trees—one had rubber tires dangling from ropes, a makeshift playground where barefoot children jostled for turns. A cloud of yellow butterflies fluttered through the open bus windows.

Pockets of lush green broke the monotony, stands of palm and banana trees. They quickly gave way to dry, hard land where women in tin shacks sold fruit and bottles of homemade juice from wooden crates.

After a couple hours, the bus veered onto a dirt road, and maneuvered up a hill. The ocean reappeared, blue and distant.

The bus stopped at a shack with a few plastic tables and a faded sign that read: "BAWTROOM. DRINKZ."

Max groaned. "Now this is what I call first class."

Harold laughed.

The bus hissed to a stop and the passengers filed out, groggy and stiff. A line formed at the bathroom. A few accepted the free drinks handed out at the roadside stand. Most wandered aimlessly, still dazed from a sleepless night on hard seats.

Then, out of the brush, two young Jamaican boys appeared, masks on, guns raised.

"Money, bling, bling! Put everything here!" shouted the taller one, who held a sack open.

"Now!" barked the other, and fired a shot into the air.

The crowd froze. Screams broke out. A woman dropped her purse. Hands trembled. Wallets were pulled and tossed into the bag.

Harold leaned in to Max and whispered, "They're just kids. Scared shitless. They're not gonna shoot. We can take 'em."

"No talk!" the gunman snapped, and pointed his weapon at Harold.

Harold moved quickly. He lunged forward, knocked the gun aside, and tackled the boy. Max charged the second one, who turned to flee but didn't get far; Max grabbed him, wrestled him down, and cracked him on the head for good measure.

The first kid was out cold. Max hogtied the second with someone's backpack strap. Both boys were flat on the dirt, dazed and disarmed.

Harold grabbed the pistols, walked to the edge of the cliff, and chucked them over.

The whole thing had happened so fast the others were still frozen in disbelief.

"Driver," said Harold. "Let's go. If we wait for the cops, we'll be stuck here all day, and those two will vanish back into the bush before lunch."

The driver didn't need convincing. His eyes went wild, his teeth flashed, he jumped into the seat and shouted, "We go now!"

With everyone onboard again, the bus rumbled back to life.

"Jesus," said Max, as he dropped into his seat. "That was more fun than than that brawl at the bowling alley with Big Tony."

Harold chuckled. "Yeah. You think the driver was in on it?"

"If he was, he ain't no more."

The driver barreled down the road like a man escaping a crime scene.

Applause broke out.

"Bravo!"

"You were amazing!"

"How'd you know they wouldn't shoot?"

"How can we ever repay you?"

Harold raised a hand. "It was just two scared kids with fake bravado and real guns. Could've happened anywhere. When we get to the resort, buy us a drink."

"It's all-inclusive," someone pointed out.

Max laughed. "Yeah, 'all-inclusive.' I guess that includes the local excitement."

Two hours later, the bus rolled through grand white gates and into Bosco Beach Resort. Inside was another world: whitewashed villas with blue-tile roofs, bougainvillea, palm trees, and manicured lawns. Black staff members in crisp uniforms stood at attention with practiced smiles.

After check-in, Harold and Max dropped their bags and met again at the front desk. The main bar was packed with fresh arrivals.

"Too many people," said Harold. "I saw a quieter spot out by our rooms."

They found a poolside bar tucked in the shade, half a dozen stools, peaceful. It became their sanctuary. The bartender, Mickey, was tall, smooth, and charming.

"You know," said Harold, as he watched a guest bark an order without saying please, "places like this bring out the worst in people. All-you-can-eat entitlement. No one tips. No one says thank you."

Max pointed to the sign: PLEASE DO NOT TIP. IT IS OUR PLEASURE TO SERVE YOU.

"Trust me," said Harold. "The staff didn't put that sign up. You treat them right, and they treat you better. Don't bite the hand that serves your piña colada."

After a couple of drinks, Harold and Max made their way to the restaurant for dinner. Exhaustion hit hard, and they turned in early. The next morning, over strong coffee and the murmur of waves, they discussed the day's plan.

"You know what I've always wanted to do?" Harold asked, as he scanned the horizon.

"Screw that girl in the red bikini?" Max snorted.

Harold rolled his eyes. "Snorkel. I've always wanted to snorkel in a coral reef. That's what we should do today."

"You're braver than me," Max said. He drained the last of his coffee. "There's sharks out there, and I swim like a cinderblock. Go knock yourself out, Harold. I'll be at the bar later, after they sew up all your shark bites."

"You'll regret it. Go chat with your new pal Mickey. He'll keep you company with those rainbow cocktails you loved last night. Just don't get too sloshed. I want to party tonight."

When Max arrived at the bar, Mickey was already there, wiping glasses and humming a tune.

"How yuh sleep, sah?" Mickey asked.

"Pretty well," Max replied, "for a lonely old man."

"Yuh nah dat ole, sah. Yuh bound to meet a pretty gyal while yuh here."

Mickey's dark eyes held Max's gaze a beat too long. Max hesitated, almost turned to go, then smiled and sat down.

"How about one of those rainbow drinks you made last night?"

He watched in quiet fascination as Mickey layered the liqueurs with practiced precision, the colors stacked up in the glass like precious jewels. Max took a sip, amazed.

"You know," Max said, "we didn't talk about this yesterday, but we had some excitement on the way here. Halfway through the ride, we stopped for a drink. Two boys came outta nowhere with guns and tried to rob us. Harold and I chased 'em off. Guess that sort of thing happens around here, huh? How do kids that young even get their hands on guns?"

Mickey's face darkened. "Dem youth, no work but plenty gun. I hear dem weapons come from CIA."

Max blinked. "The CIA? What're you talking about?"

"Drugs," Mickey said quietly. "Drugs from America make money for de cartel. CIA use some fi buy guns, send dem here. Bribe de bosses in Kingston to keep out di commies."

Max stared, dumbfounded. "Jesus. You serious? The US government?"

"Is true, mon. Everyone know it."

Max shook his head slowly. "Heard stories like that about Nicaragua, but here too? Man, them politicians would sell out their own mothers if they had the chance. They say one thing and do another."

"Anedda drink, mon?"

"Why not? You got any music?"

"No, sah. No radio, no stereo."

"Call me Max. You don't even have a transistor radio?"

Mickey shook his head. "No, Max. Me couldn't afford dat."

Max stood. "Be right back."

He returned minutes later with a small radio, tuned it to a local station, and set it on the bar.

A grin lit up Mickey's face. "Dat's *Mr. Bossman* by Wayne Smith. Good dance music, mon."

He started to sway with the rhythm. Max started to move back and forth himself.

"Keep the radio, Mickey. It's yours. And pour me another."

By the time Harold wandered in, Max was flushed and loose-limbed, not drunk but close.

"No stitches, I see," Max slurred, his sunburn the color of a ripe beet.

"No sharks," Harold laughed. "It was close, though. A couple of locals with spear slings spooked a school of barracuda. They scattered straight at us. Those bastards have teeth like razors. I barely made it into the boat. The fishermen and the driver freaked."

Max cackled. "Wish I'd seen you jump outta the water."

Harold grinned. "Hi, Mickey. Can I get a beer?"

"Coming right up, sah."

"He makes zese magical rainbow thingies," Max said. He waved his hand at Max. "You should h- have one."

"You're drunk as a skunk, Max. Go take a nap."

Harold caught Mickey's amused glance. He winked, and noted the wide, pearly grin that seemed to be a fixture on every face at the resort.

"Y'know," Max muttered, as he walked to his room. "These guys got nothin' down here. I gave Mickey my transistor radio."

"Good for you," Harold said. "Now, get some rest. I'll see you tonight when you're more human."

For the next few days, Harold and Max stayed close to the resort, soaking up the sun. Harold couldn't help but notice that Max spent more and more time with Mickey. Back home, Max wore his tough-guy mask, big talk, hard edges, with plenty of prejudice, but in Jamaica, that mask cracked. Maybe it was the sunshine. Maybe it was Mickey. Prejudice gets hard to maintain when you're the outsider; when the people you're supposed to dislike turn out to be a hell of a lot more like you than not.

Harold hadn't heard from Lisa or Jennie. He figured they'd ghosted him, until a note arrived on his final morning. Lisa wrote that she and Jennie, along with her brother, Ruel, would meet Harold and Max at the entrance to the property at ten sharp.

It was Harold's last day. He was ready for something new. Bosco Beach, with its artificial charm and resort smiles, had run its course.

The next morning, Lisa introduced Harold and Max to Ruel, who pulled up in a red Impala with a white vinyl top, the kind of car that hinted at both pride and practicality. Tall, dark-skinned, solidly built,

Ruel stepped out with an air of quiet authority that at first came off as curt, but when he smiled, the stiffness melted into easy charm. He wore light tan trousers and a short-sleeved pink button-up shirt. A gold chain with a mandala pendant swung lightly at his chest, and a sleek designer watch peeked from his cuff.

Lisa and Jennie were dressed for the sun: bright, strappy beach dresses, jangly bracelets, dark sunglasses. It was clear to Harold that they came from money, or at least moved in a world above the resort workers. Jamaica, as he'd observed so far, seemed stitched together by sharp contrasts, opulence tucked inside islands of poverty.

"We had quite the ride to the resort," Harold began.

"Oh, yah?" said Lisa, cocking her head. "Somethin' wrong wit di ride?"

"Couple kids pulled guns on us at the halfway stop," said Max. "Tried to rob us."

"Jessum peace!" Jennie cried.

"Misery makes people act desperate," Ruel said evenly. "People kill for pride. What happen?"

"We handled it," Harold said. "Took their guns, knocked them cold. They were just kids. We didn't want to drag them through the system, so we left 'em."

Ruel's expression darkened. "Dem bwoy not done wid you yet. I ask around. Dem got pride, dem feel shame. Trouble could come."

They piled into the Impala and headed out. The car rolled past makeshift roadside kitchens where women stirred pots over open fires. Men grilled yams and jerk meat, while sweat gleamed on their backs. Clotheslines stretched between coconut palms. Goats, chickens, and scruffy dogs wandered freely, sniffing at the dust. Hand-painted signs advertised rum tastings, craft markets, and coffee tours. Under lopsided gazebos, fruit vendors hawked guavas, mangoes, and plums as big as softballs. This was not the Jamaica of glossy brochures or hotel gift shops. It was raw and alive, and Harold loved it.

"First, we go Green Grotto Caves," Ruel said. "Used by Maroons, Spanish, runaway slave, even tief and criminal. Dark, spooky, but interestin'. Den we cool off at quiet beach, not like Bosco. After dat,

Fern Gully to see di old bauxite workin's, den a stop at a great house, see how di old planters live. We end high up at Murphy's 'ill. Cool air, good view. Yuh ready?"

"That sounds amazing," said Harold. "Thanks for putting this together."

By the time they reached the beach, the heat suffocated; the humidity clung to their skin like damp clothes. Treasure Beach wasn't a manicured resort but a series of secluded coves dotted with modest shacks where food and drink were sold. Ruel brought them to a simple bar made of worn wood planks, perched above a stunning vista of turquoise water.

"Now *this* is my kind of place," said Max, as he plopped onto a bench.

"Me too," Harold agreed.

"Sorta like that Tom Cruise movie," Max added. "You know, *Cocktail*, where he nails the girl under a waterfall?"

"Max," Harold muttered, "try some self-control. We're with young ladies."

The girls just laughed, then wandered off barefoot down the beach. Harold, Max, and Ruel sipped cold Red Stripes in the shade.

"Dis here," Ruel said, raising his bottle, "dis is what a bar for. Man come here to relax, maybe enjoy some music, get him mind off stress. People from all walks stop in. What matter is how di bar run, and dis one run good."

"These are ice cold," said Max. "Way better than the lukewarm crap they handed us on the bus."

"You want food?" Ruel offered. "Dem serve wicked ackee and saltfish here. Chicken-foot soup, crab, jerk chicken, bammy—"

"Tempting," Harold said, "but let's keep on. I've only got this one day left, and I want to soak in as much as I can. That okay with you, Max?"

"Fine by me," Max said, and drained the last of his beer.

Ruel stepped into the shack to make a quick phone call from the office. When he returned, they climbed back into the Impala and hit the road, the horizon wide-open ahead of them.

"Everything good, Ruel?" Harold asked.

"Yea, mon, all good," Ruel said. "Mi jus' want fi check 'bout dem two kids yuh mention. Make sure no trouble followin' yuh."

"That was a week ago," said Max. "I doubt they even remember."

Their final stop of the day was Murphy's Hill.

"Jesus," Harold muttered, as he stepped out of the car. "I see why you brought us here. Look at that view. It's so quiet, and cool. Where is everyone?"

"Used to be busy," Ruel said, as he pointed over the valley. "Since di bauxite mine shut down, most people gone. Now tourists stay locked up behind gates in di fake paradise."

Lisa turned to Harold. "What do you think of the real Jamaica? There's still a lot left to see."

"Bosco Beach will never be the same," Harold said with a grin.

"Maybe not," Max added. "But I look forward to seeing Mickey again. I could use one of those rainbow drinks right about now."

"You sure spend a lot of time with him," Harold teased. "What's up with that?"

Max smiled, something softer, different. "We've become good friends," he said, and his eyes drifted toward the beach.

Harold squinted into the distance. "Is that Cuba?"

Ruel followed his gaze. "Yea, mon. And dat's Blue Mountain in di other direction. Highest peak in di Caribbean. Best coffee come from dere. Down to di left is Cardiff Hall, another ol' Great House from sugar days. Joni Mitchell stay dere once. Paint a mural on di wall. And ova dere's Oracabessa. Dat's where dat writer man write dem Jimmy Bond book."

Later that afternoon, Harold and Max strolled along Bosco Beach while Ruel and the girls hung out with Mickey at the bar. Harold had bought the kids passes so they could enjoy the resort for a few hours.

"So, Max," Harold said. "Was it worth it?"

"Worth what?"

"The trip. You said it was too risky, remember?"

Max looked out at the surf. "Hell, yes, it was worth it. Changed my life."

"How so?"

Before Max could answer, he stopped dead in his tracks. "Shit. Look."

Harold followed his gaze. Two boys, the ones who had tried to rob them, walked down the beach toward them, flanked by a few friends. No escape now. They were too close.

"We might handle the first two," Max said. "But not the rest. They don't have guns, but they sure look ready."

The men squared up and braced for a fight.

Suddenly, like a shift in wind, the boys turned and bolted in the other direction.

"Well, damn," Max said, with a laugh. "We must look like a couple of bad-ass sonsofbitches."

"I don't think it's us," Harold said, and pointed toward the resort.

Ruel and Mickey were sprinting toward the beach with two resort guards. Another four guards approached from the opposite end and cut the boys off.

Harold turned to Ruel. "That was close."

"I know dem bwoys soon as you tell me di story," Ruel said, after he caught his breath. "Deh been makin' trouble long time, but dis time deh gone too far."

Back at the bar, Mickey, his shift done, joined them for a drink. Harold invited Lisa, Jennie, and Ruel to stay for dinner, but they declined. It was a long drive home. They made plans to reconnect when Ruel visited California.

"We'll show you our little slice of paradise," Harold said.

The sun was low but not yet set. They were scheduled to leave the next morning. Harold wanted one last walk along the beach.

"Beaches are overrated," Max said. "Go on. I'll stay here with Mickey."

Alone with the waves, Harold thought of his wife. He missed her. They'd had good years, but they didn't ever travel very far from home. He hadn't done enough for her, not really. She deserved more.

Surprisingly, he missed the sawmill too. It had swallowed most of his life. More than family. More than friends. More than hobbies. He never really had any. He let work define him. He wished he'd lived better.

This trip had changed him.

People are the same everywhere, he thought. *Same worries. Same joys. Same hurts. Same needs.* Ruel said it best: "Dis what bar is 'bout. It all boil down to how yuh run di bar, an' dis one run good."

Back at the suite, Harold heard a voice from Max's room. Sounded like a man. He shook his head. Poor Max, he's probably drunk and talking to himself again. I best leave him be.

The next morning, suitcase in hand, Harold didn't see Max on the bus or in his room.

He finally found him at the front desk.

"Hey, Max, the bus is about to leave. What's up?"

Max turned. "Morning, Harold. I've got something to tell you. I'm staying, another week, maybe longer."

"What? Are you serious?"

"Mickey and I have some things to sort out," Max said with an awkward smile. "Don't tell the guys back home, all right? Promise me."

"I... okay, sure," Harold said, stunned. "You'll call?"

"Sure," Max said. He grinned, then added, "This one's an insurrection, Harold. Not a protest."

He winked, walked away and didn't look back.

The Inheritance

Dear Mr. Noakes:

I'm reaching out to you because you were my father's attorney, and, frankly, the only lawyer I know.

My mother died when I was ten. From then on, my father raised me, though "raised" might be a generous term. He was rarely around. He loved Mexico and spent most of his time there, left me to fend for myself. When he was home, he spent his time in bars. He liked to gamble and chase women. I learned early on how to survive without him. As soon as I could, I moved out, got a job, and didn't see him again until the final year of his life.

He contacted me out of the blue. I was hesitant to respond, but he persisted, said he felt guilty and wanted to make things right. I didn't trust him, but I agreed to meet. After all, I was the only family he had left.

We didn't do much together. Mostly, we sat in bars and he talked while I listened. He apologized for abandoning me, claimed he'd spiraled after my mother died, said he didn't know how to raise a child. Maybe he meant it, but it was hard to believe. Too much time had passed; there was no relationship left to salvage. Still, I listened. He talked a lot, just vented, really.

"You're all I've got," he told me. "I'm on my way out, but I have something for you. You'll see." I figured what he really wanted was someone to care for him in his final days. I didn't walk away; I could have, but I'm not built that way. He was still my father.

I remember a recurring dream I had as a kid. We were at a party with a bunch of people and somehow my father fell into a deep pit. Everyone just left. There was no one to help me get him out. I was just a little kid and I did everything I could but I couldn't get him out no matter how much I tried. I freaked out and pounded my head on my pillow over and over until I woke up. I always thought it meant something. Now I know what.

Not long after, he died. That's when you called. "Your father's dead. He left everything to you." I felt a strange sadness, not grief exactly, but something close. I asked you what "everything" meant.

It wasn't much as it turned out. The house was mortgaged to the hilt. His bank account had little more than one month's Social Security. What he did have was an enormous collection of Mexican folk art.

I always hated Mexico. He dragged me there once as a kid. I swore I'd never go back. It was hot and humid, and swarmed with insects. The water made me sick. The country was split between brutal poverty and palatial wealth. I spent most of the trip in air-conditioned rooms, and sucked on lemon-lime popsicles to settle my stomach. If it weren't for the beachside ice-cream vendor, I might not have survived.

When I saw the collection, dozens of those garish, psychedelic wooden creatures called alebrijes, I was furious. This was what he'd poured his money into? I'm sure they held cultural significance for someone, but to me they were meaningless. He thought they were treasures. "Collectors will pay good money," he told me once. He even put price stickers on them. "I don't want you to get cheated," he wrote.

There were clay animals from Tonalá: frogs, birds, cats, dogs, each tagged with a price. Same with the paintings on his walls. The prices seemed laughable. Eventually, I found a list of supposed collectors tucked into a desk drawer: names, addresses, phone numbers. I guess he intended for me to sell everything. Maybe he thought it would make up for something.

He was serious about the prices. I remember when he said, "Don't cast your pearls before swine." He claimed it was from Jesus. It was an odd thing to hear from a man who'd never been near a church.

Anyway, I had my father cremated, just as he requested. His ashes were placed in a painted ceramic urn he'd bought years ago in Zihuatanejo as he wished. I put the house on the market and organized a sale of his vast collection of Mexican folk art. I contacted everyone on the list he'd left me: dealers, collectors, friends of friends. I didn't expect much. My hope was to cover the mortgage and cremation costs, maybe have enough left over for a small getaway, but on the day of the sale, I was stunned.

The turnout was enormous. The crowd was mixed, blue-collar workers, art dealers, stockbrokers, Black, Asian, even a few Hispanic collectors. People bid competitively. Prices soared. I had no idea there was such an avid market for Mexican folk art. For the first time, I wondered if my father had actually known what he was doing. Maybe, just maybe, he'd even cared about me. An unusual swell of emotion rose in me, something I hadn't felt before.

By the end of the day, nearly everything had sold. As I locked up, I noticed a few forgotten items in the garage: two framed watercolors, one of a beach vendor pushing a cart through the sand, the other of a fishing boat in Banderas Bay. I remembered those scenes from the trip we took to Puerto Vallarta. There were also a few small ceramic figures and some alebrijes. I packed them in a box and brought them back to my apartment. I felt like I should keep them, if not for their value, then for the memories.

The house sold faster than I expected. The Hispanic buyer waived inspections and paid in cash. He wanted the shortest escrow possible. Something about the deal felt odd, but I was too relieved to care. After escrow closed, I heard he gutted the house, tore it down board by board, then vanished. It made no sense, but I had the money, so I didn't dwell on it.

I deposited the proceeds. Suddenly, I had options. A new beginning felt possible. I began to plan a different kind of life, one where I might finally find direction, maybe even peace.

Then came the knock at the door.

Two DEA agents. They arrested me and ransacked my apartment. They took the folk art, the urn with my father's ashes, everything. They froze my bank account. I was blindsided. My court-appointed attorney told me the artifacts were stuffed with packets of cocaine. More drugs were hidden in the walls and under the floors of the house. My father was a drug trafficker. The DEA had been on him for years, and now they accused me of being in on it.

I'm writing this from jail, while I wait to see how things unfold. It doesn't look good. I can't sleep. I've lost weight. My hair's gone gray. You were my father's attorney. You handled his affairs. You knew him. You know I'm innocent. I had nothing to do with this. Please, I need your help.

I read the letter over and over. The envelope was stamped in bold black letters: RETURN TO SENDER – NO SUCH PERSON, NO SUCH ADDRESS.

I ran my fingers over the ink, cold and final. "I have something for you," my father said. "You'll see.

That damn inheritance, I wish I could give it back, but it's too late. Now I've got to face the music for all the things my dad did. How does that saying go? Ashes to ashes, dust to dust, if the Lord doesn't take you, the devil must? I got the devil, and there's no one around to pull me out of the pit.

Dandelion

Tom Hoberg is old.

He doesn't feel old, not really, but time has done its work. He is alone now, utterly, unmistakably alone. No family, no friends. They're all gone, taken by bad luck, illness, or the slow erosion of age. They have fallen, one by one, like leaves shaken from a branch. He was always a loner but now he's entirely alone.

He never thought such a thing could happen. *Who does?*

He is in the quiet company of Eleanor Rigby and Father McKenzie, invisible in plain sight. His lonely, solitary life stretched into a lonely, solitary retirement. The truth is simple and cruel: If you live long enough, this is where you end up. Good luck, bad luck, what's the difference? The cookie crumbles either way.

He dresses for his evening stroll: tie, jacket, polished shoes. It is an important ritual of dignity. Though a whisper of the man he used to be, once a respected professor, he still has his pride, even if no one notices, even if no one speaks.

He was an important person once, someone who made his mark. Now, a world crowded with people moves past him while he sits still. They do not know, cannot know, of his achievements. He's just another stranger on a bench who foreshadows a future they hope to avoid. What they don't know is that while they can't accept it, they can't escape it.

There was a time when his mind was his greatest strength. He achieved things, real things. He was a mathematical economist, an academic scribbler. No one cares or remembers, but he made his contribution, didn't he?

He's a people watcher, always has been. It's a game he plays in his spare time, to guess the lives of strangers. Who are they? What do they dream? What secrets do they carry? He watches until his thoughts coalesce into a meaningful idea, and then he invents highly probable stories.

It was through this game that he discovered the formulas that led to his fame. He figured out how to measure the accuracy of guesses, especially when time and information is limited. He realized that if his system worked on people's lives, it could work on anything. Today, everyone uses his methods, instrumental variable estimators, though most don't know what they are, why they use them, or where they came from.

He lives on like an econometric equation with a low R-squared. He gets a nod now and then, a passing glance, a rare or distant "Professor Hoberg," though the title and how he earned it has long since faded away.

He keeps up appearances, a flower in his lapel, a clean tie. Like instrumental variables they help define him when there's lots of noise in the data. A small gesture, like once in a while when a young woman walks by and smiles, is the reward he seeks. If the flower earns a single smile, it's worth it.

The cheerful hellos of people who say hello to everyone mean nothing, even if they fill the air like birdsong, pleasant, but forgettable. There must be a connection to the data.

Tom Hoberg believes that everything is connected. Every so often, something small, a look, a sound, a smell, pulls on that invisible thread and reminds him he's still part of the fabric.

It's Saturday night. The streets are alive. People hurry past in bursts of laughter and perfume, headed nowhere in particular. The connections are masked in confusion on a night like this.

He takes his usual seat on the bench by the duck pond and closes his eyes. The darkness is thick and impenetrable. Sound is all he has left. He navigates through the sounds to create an order out of the chaos.

After a while, he opens his eyes and is momentarily lost. He stands too quickly and becomes disoriented. The world spins. He sits back down to wait for the ground to return to where it belongs.

People spill out of the bar, full of stories they'll forget by morning.

A woman waves in his direction. He lifts a hand, then realizes it's not him she waves at. A man brushes past, and nearly knocks him down.

"Excuse me," Tom murmurs.

The man is already gone.

He decides to treat himself to a drink. The bar is packed, the music too loud, the kind that pulses in your chest and blurs the edges of conversation. He reconsiders, then sees an open seat at the far corner of the bar, half-hidden by a pillar.

"What'll it be, old-timer?" the bartender asks.

The bartender doesn't look old enough to drink. Tom notices he's older than anyone else in the place by decades.

"What kind of wine do you have?" he asks.

"Red or white."

"What kind of red or white?"

"Red or white, that's it," the kid says. "Wine's not our thing."

"Red," Tom mutters, and places a ten on the bar.

The bartender pours something dark from a plastic-handled jug with a label Tom doesn't recognize. The kid glances at the register. "Fifteen seventy-five."

Tom slides over another ten. "Keep the change."

The bartender has already started to muddle a handful of mint for a mojito. Mojitos, Tom notes, are popular. So are the bright Cosmopolitans in every hue, served in fragile martini glasses. They look like melted crayons, those drinks.

He glances across the room. A group of four at a table, two couples, laugh in his direction. When he turns back to the bar, a new drink has appeared in front of him.

"What's this?" he asks.

"Fireball, Pops. Cinnamon whiskey. That table sent it." The bartender gestures with his chin.

Tom turns. The four strangers lift their glasses to him in a silent toast. He raises his own, and sips. Spicy, a little sweet, not bad, actually. When he glances back again, the table is empty.

I should go, he thinks, but the warmth of the drink, the noise, the press of bodies, it gives him an odd comfort. *Imagine, four strangers bought me a drink.*

Another sip. Someone jostles him from behind and the Fireball sloshes onto his tie. No one notices. No one cares. He dabs at the spill. *People here must go through ties like water,* he thinks, but no one else here wears a tie or a coat or a flower in the lapel.

He finishes the drink, stands, and leaves.

Outside, under the streetlamp's glow, he spots the four young people. He stays in the shadows, unseen.

"What a silly old fart," one of the girls says with a smirk.

"I know," replies the man beside her. "He always wears that same tattered coat and wrinkled tie."

"Don't forget the flower," the other girl giggles.

"It's not a flower," says the second man. "It's a dandelion."

They begin to sing as they walk: "Dandelion don't tell no lies. Dandelion will make you wise…"

They collapse in laughter, then sprawl across the sidewalk, faces turned upward.

"Look at those stars," one girl murmurs.

Tom looks up. The sky glitters like silver coins on a blue blanket.

"Dandelion don't tell no lies…"

Their voices trail off as they get to their feet and wander down the street.

"…will make you wise…"

They're almost out of earshot when one of the men asks, "Why does that old fool come around every night anyway?"

"He sits on that bench across the street," says the other, "and ogles the young girls."

"You do the same thing," one girl teases.

"I don't either," he protests.

"Who cares. Let's go, we're gonna be late."

They dash off into the night, hand in hand, singing *Dandelion.*

Tom Hoberg watches them go. *It doesn't mean a thing,* he says to himself. *The data is insufficient to draw a meaningful conclusion, unless...* He walks slowly back to his small apartment, all the while lost in computation. The Fireball churns in his stomach.

Inside, the window is still open. A sharp draft cuts through the room. He forgot to close it.

Too tired to care, he drops onto the couch, and pulls a worn blanket over his chest. His body curls in on itself, the way old trees bend against the wind. He closes his eyes.

In the morning, there is a soft indentation on the pillow where his head once lay. He hasn't solved the equation yet. He'll try again today.

Tag Along

They boarded the bus at Chestnut and Fillmore. He wore a black jacket with a Diadora logo. Her dress was a riot of pastel flowers, pink, blue, green, yellow, splashed across a black-and-white background. I decided they were the ones I'd follow today.

Yesterday's couple, a quiet pair of tourists from somewhere in East Asia, was a letdown. I'd been spoiled earlier in the week by a young couple so engaged with each other that they made everyone else vanish. She was dark-skinned, with glossy black hair and a knockout smile, and wore a silver nose stud and lip ring. He was white, soft-featured, sipped a green tea frappe and hung on her every word. She was an aspiring writer, and they were headed to the book fair at Fort Mason. That was the best in months.

Today's couple had a different rhythm; comfortable, familiar, maybe a little frayed. He talked about a meeting from that morning. She mentioned she used their credit card at Cost Plus, which earned a frown. They spoke like old couples do when they've been apart a few hours and feel compelled to recount every detail.

They got off at Green and Stockton. He angled toward City Lights, but she hesitated. They walked a block in that direction before they crossed Columbus and retraced their steps to Green. I figured he gave in.

They strolled, in search of a pizza place they had a voucher for: free wine and a pie. The neighborhood was alive with Bohemian energy. They commented on the odd outfits, strange hairstyles, and exaggerated body types. It's feels weird to watch people who watch other people, a way to bend the world back on yourself, a noble pastime. You learn a lot about human nature. Everyone has two stories, one they make up, and one you make up about them. When I watch people, it's a form of meditation. It can tell me more about love than a poem, more about character than a good book. I reflect on myself, and discover more about how I behave, my habits, and how I fit into the world outside.

The pizza joint was a letdown. Chairs were still stacked, and the place looked hungover from the night before. It should've opened at noon, but it was nearly 12:30.

They argued in hushed tones. He wanted the free lunch. She said they'd get food poisoning or worse. They ducked into a side street full of tchotchke shops. She looked at the children's books, cards, and a bunch of sentimental junk. She loved it. He didn't. She hung out longer than he wanted. I could tell by the way he glanced back toward the pizza place. It was still closed.

He flipped through birthday cards and showed her a few. She ignored him, absorbed in a book, something about a grandchild's birthday. They killed twenty minutes that way, bought a few things, then wandered back. The pizza joint was still closed.

He caved. They settled for a glass of wine at Rosa Pistola, just around the corner. He knew she liked the place. I heard them talk about how they go there often when they're in town. They entered through the alley.

A classic Thunderbird pulled up beside them. The sun glared off the burgundy color. The driver was a Black man in a tan Superfly hat that blared funk from the '70s. He smiled wide. They waved like old friends.

Inside, there were two old Italian men who sat at the kitchen counter. One had red wine, and the other, Limoncello. "They look like farmers from the last century," he joked. She laughed.

They took the power seats at the end of the bar with a clear view of the room. The place was nearly empty. The staff drifted about, still in early-shift mode. She had Sauvignon Blanc. He chose Chianti and munched on the breadsticks. He hadn't eaten since breakfast. The wine kicked in fast.

She seemed composed, confident, and clearly in charge.

She suggested L'Osteria across the street for lunch. "The pizza place looks like a dump," she said. "It's probably unsanitary. Honestly, I'm afraid to go there."

He pushed back. He said free food was free food, why waste money when they had the voucher?

She checked her wallet and offered to pay. He refused. She reluctantly gave in to one last try at the pizza place. If it was still closed, lunch was on him.

That seemed to please them both.

On the way to the pizza place, they stopped back at the card shop. He showed her the birthday card they'd debated over earlier, a supposedly funny one that risked sounding mean-spirited. She frowned. "It'll just sit in a drawer," she said. He nodded, but bought it anyway.

Rain had been forecast, but the sun came out.

"That's a good sign," he said.

"You don't believe in signs."

"This time is an exception."

The restaurant looked open but empty. She hesitated. He took her hand and led her in. The bartender, young and upbeat, greeted them with a smile.

"Got a voucher?"

He held it up.

"Cool. Sit wherever you like."

The place was cozy; the faint scent of last night's crowd still lingered. The stools were lacquered wood, low to the ground, and looked more decorative than functional. The table was a converted wine barrel, glass-topped with corks arranged beneath like a casual art installation. The bartender handed them a wine list and two menus.

"Hey," he said, and pointed with his finger. "They've got Sancerre."

She grinned.

They ordered the four-cheese pizza with mushrooms. He chose a glass of Nebbiolo. Outside, pedestrians passed in a slow, sunny drift as they sipped and waited. The pizza arrived, bubbling, crisp at the edges.

"Well?" he asked.

She took a bite, chewed thoughtfully, then smiled. "Delicious."

They lingered and ordered a second glass of wine. When the bartender asked if they were driving, she laughed.

"Two glasses and a car? At our age? We're bus people."

The voucher covered most of it, but he paid for the extra wine and left a generous tip. On the way out, he took her hand again. The sun was sharp and golden now. They stepped into it like newlyweds.

"What a day," he said.

"Beautiful," she replied.

They board the bus that heads downtown. As they step on, a young Black couple steps off. The man holds an iPad. His partner is radiant, wide-featured, with white teeth that catch the light. They laugh at some private joke.

"These are the ones," I think. I hang back a few paces, then follow them into the sunlight.

The Optimist

They met at a protest rally. She stapled up BLACK LIVES MATTER posters; he came along behind her and blacked out BLACK, leaving LIVES MATTER.

When she caught him in the act, she smacked him with a signboard.

"What the *fuck* do you think you're doing?"

He laughed. That made her want to hit him again.

He didn't say a word, just took out a marker and scribbled BLACK back onto one of the posters.

"Oh, so now everything's fine?" she snapped.

He looked at her: young, confident, furious. She stood her ground, arms crossed, her blond hair flashed in the sun like a dare.

"You're cute when you're mad."

She scowled. He pegged her as the kind who meal-prepped, did Pilates, maybe even boxed. She probably had a personal trainer who made her do squats and scream affirmations.

She saw the way he looked at her. Not bad for an older guy: clean-shaven, decent shoes, no MAGA hat, but still, maybe a Trumper at the start of his late-life crisis.

He imagined her with false lashes, long acrylics, stilettos, and a miniskirt, none of which fit her. Instead, she had on sweats and a T-shirt, looked every bit the serious organizer, but he had a tendency to put people in boxes, and that was the box he wanted her in.

"I'm Jerry," he said.

"Scissors."

She blinked as she said it, to see if he would laugh.

He didn't. Instead, he offered, "Let's grab a drink. Talk it out."

"Talk *what* out?"

"Whatever you want."

The street was chaotic, hot and claustrophobic. She'd put up enough signs for the day. He seemed safe enough; too young to be irrelevant, too old to be dangerous. It could be fun, and if not, she could handle herself.

"Fine," she said. "But, it's on you. I'm broke."

"I invited you," he said. "I'll pay."

That's how it started.

The bar was dim and cool, a quiet refuge from the heat outside.

"How about a Margarita?" he said.

"Perfect." She brushed a curtain of blond hair from her eyes.

He ordered two Margaritas on the rocks, salted rims.

"So," he said, "what's with the Black Lives Matter signs?"

She sat up a little straighter. "We have to do something, Jerry. This country's circling the drain. Don't you see that?"

A test. He could hear it in her tone. She wanted to know where he stood. He took a sip, and let the tequila settle before he answered.

"Anyone who pays attention ought to see it, Scissors. Like it or not, the whole world is headed hard right." He grinned. "I just wanted to get your attention out there."

She studied him. "Tell me about yourself, Jerry. What do you do?" The question came like a challenge, too poised for small talk.

He felt the tequila nudge his confidence. *Careful,* he thought. *She's sharp. One wrong move and you're done.*

"Call me an entrepreneur."

"You start companies?"

"Sometimes, but mostly I buy ones in trouble, fix them up, and sell. I'm not into the day-to-day grind."

"So, a speculator?"

He didn't love the word. Too cold, too Wall Street. That's not how he wanted to come across.

"No, I'm not a speculator. I guess you could say I'm an optimist."

"In *this* world?" she said. "With everything falling apart?"

"I don't fix the world, Scissors. Just one business at a time. Lemonade out of lemons, you know?"

Their glasses were empty. He signaled to the bartender.

"No thanks," she said. "That one already hit me."

"How about dinner, then? I'll bore you with my business stories, and you can tell me something real."

She hesitated. She was hungry, but she knew the game: free meal, expectations. She bartended part-time. She knew every angle.

"Okay," she said. "But don't get the wrong idea. After dinner, you go your way, and I go mine. Deal?"

"Fair enough. But if you change your mind..." He gave her a grin.

She smirked. "Maybe we should call it a night right now. Most places are shut down anyway."

"Not Peccaries. I've got connections." He held the door. "You eat ribs?"

She laughed. "What do I look like, a vegetarian?"

"I thought you were a liberal."

"Not all liberals are vegetarians, Jerry. Do I need to draw you a Venn diagram?"

"I'm a quick study."

They stepped into the night, headed toward Peccaries. He watched her walk: poised, cautious, but with a streak of wildness. She liked being admired but wouldn't admit it. He knew her type: smart, wary, and a little hungry in more ways than one.

She knew what he was up to, saw it in his eyes.

They sat in a booth tucked into the back. In the front of the restaurant, empty tables faced the street, a faded CLOSED sign was taped to the glass, but back here, a quiet hum lingered. Locals only. The kind of place people only knew about if they'd grown up in the neighborhood. Tables were still spread wide, a leftover from the pandemic nobody wanted to admit was over.

Jerry slipped his iPhone into his jacket pocket and leaned back. He waited for Scissors to scroll through her texts like she was defusing a bomb.

"So, how'd you end up with the name Scissors?"

She glanced up, and gave him a slow "don't-start" look.

"An old boyfriend," she said, voice flat. "I didn't sleep with him as often as he wanted, so he told everyone I cut out his heart with a pair of rusty scissors, like some girl in some country song."

Jerry smiled. Was this flirtation or a warning shot?

"I think she cuts her own hair in that song. I didn't hear anything about a heart," he said.

"Exactly," she said, as she tossed her phone onto the table. "My ex thinks everything's about him, so he changed it up. Now I'm Scissors. Lucky me. You a fan of country?"

"I like all kinds of music," Jerry said. He didn't, but he liked *her*.

They ordered. Scissors didn't waste time.

"So. These businesses of yours. How's it feel to be an optimist when everyone else is drowning?"

Jerry read the subtext. She already had him boxed: tech bro, trust-funder, well insulated.

"It's not like that," he said. "Most entrepreneurs aren't rich. Or heartless. I fall on my face more often than not. Most things don't work out. You want me to draw you a Venn diagram?"

She laughed. "Fair enough. Seriously, I'd like to know, what are the odds?"

"First, how about you?" Jerry said, sidestepping.

"I'm not on drugs, I'm not pregnant, and I still have health insurance," she said. "That's a win, right? Your turn."

Jerry exhaled. "I've had a few wins, and a long string of disasters."

"Tell me about the disasters," she said, as she picked up her water glass.

"I bought an old gold mine a while back, and hired a guy to manage it. He claimed it was tapped out. I found out later he took the gold and skipped town."

"Ouch."

"Yeah, that was hard to take. After that, I bought a cattle ranch in Nevada. I wanted to do something noble, restore a legacy property. I hired an old family friend out of retirement, a good guy, honest as the day is long. I called to check in one day, and couldn't get an answer. When I went out there, he was dead under a tree. Heart attack or heatstroke, I never did find out. The cows had scattered, the fences were down, everything was a mess."

"Did you at least break even?"

"No."

"So, what next?"

"A restaurant in the Sierras. Stupid. I took it over for a friend with the foolish idea I could turn it around. I should've known better. Restaurants are money pits. I bailed before I bled out."

Scissors gave a slow nod. "Wow, three in a row. So basically, you gamble. You chase the next big thing and hope to cover the casualties."

"There's always one gem buried in the rubble. You just have to find it."

"Spoken like a man who doesn't live in the rubble."

"Look," Jerry said. "You have to break a few eggs to make an omelet. It's not clean, but that's how things get done."

"Spoken like a man who's never been the egg," she said. "Progress isn't a straight line, sure, but it doesn't have to be a demolition derby. Capitalism is organized damage with better PR."

Jerry raised his glass. "To omelets."

Scissors didn't raise hers.

"I make my own way. I pay for my failures and profit from my wins. That's how a free market works. It incentivizes capital to move in the right direction."

Scissors raised an eyebrow. "Money isn't the only measure. What about art? What about love, care, decency? Who pays a mother who cooks dinner, scrubs the clothes clean, and douses a kid with rubbing alcohol when they're blistered from poison oak? Who values that walk to the store when there's no money for gas? Why should a gold strike count more than keeping a family together?"

Jerry shrugged. "In your perfect world, who decides? The government? A committee? A dictator? We live in a free country. The market decides. Sure, not everything fits neatly. A mother's rewarded by her partner. She and her husband share the responsibilities. Artists? They're supported by patrons who value what they create."

"You've got the silver and now you're after the gold," Scissors said. "Who am I to knock success? But don't think I sit around on my ass. I work just as hard as you. Same grind, different paycheck."

Jerry saw it: he'd struck a nerve. He leaned back, and softened his tone. "Hey, I never said you didn't work hard. You probably deserve more than you make. Honestly, I don't know anything about you. Maybe you could fill in some blanks?"

Their food arrived: pork ribs glazed in sauce, a baked potato, a side salad. They ate in silence, and chewed through more than just dinner.

Finally, Scissors spoke. "What am I, Jerry? A gem? A rock? Another one of your 'turnarounds'? Did you size me up like a business deal? What are your intentions, Mr. Optimist?"

"Whoa," said Jerry. "This isn't transactional. I like you. I want to get to know you better, that's all. You're not a full-time poster hanger. You're too sharp for that."

"I bartend, work retail. Things are slow now, so I'm out there to support causes I believe in."

"Which causes?"

Scissors took a sip of wine. "Black Lives Matter, for one. I'd like to remove that clown from the White House, for another. This country's a mess, but let's be honest, it's always been a mess. Racist, sexist, run by the rich. Vietnam. Iraq. Afghanistan. We stick our noses into all the wrong places and screw ourselves over because of it."

Jerry folded his hands under his chin. "Unfairness is baked into human nature. The president? He's a reflection of who we are. Everyone wants the lifestyle of the rich and famous. Don't blame capitalism or the guy in office. We all feed the beast. Let's be real: if the rich disappeared, who would fund the soup kitchens?"

Scissors scowled. "Jesus, Jerry. That's bleak. Is that what you really believe? That life's just a contest, winner takes all? You think survival justifies everything? We need each other. There's more to life than a monopoly board. Sure, the rich can fall, but they seldom do. Why do they deserve so much more?"

Jerry stared at his glass. *I blew it.* "I'm not saying it's right. I'm saying it *is.* We can talk about change. Nothing wrong with that. That's democracy. That's America."

"No," said Scissors. Her eyes flashed. "America is more than that: dreams, decency, dignity. You want a future? Lift others up, don't push them down."

"Don't cut out my heart like an Aztec priestess," said Jerry with a weak smile.

"It's not a joke. You call yourself an optimist, but you believe in some magic-market invisible hand that fixes everything. For some of us, most maybe, that's not optimism, it's delusion."

She grabbed her purse and stood.

"So that's it? Eat and run?"

"I told you, after dinner, we go our own way."

What does she think I want? Sex? To win an argument? Damn! Jerry gave it one last try.

"I'd like you to stay a little longer. We barely scratched the surface. They've got a killer lava cake. Come on. Give me another chance, or are you the type who cuts and runs when the going gets tough?"

She paused, and weighed her options. "Time's up. Big day tomorrow."

"Edison failed a thousand times before he invented the light bulb."

"Good for Edison." She kissed him on the forehead.

In the soft light, her hair shimmered. Jerry reached out, but she stood just beyond reach.

Then, something shifted inside her. She wasn't going to let him get away with calling her a quitter.

"Is this your close, Mr. Optimist? Feed a girl cake to win her over?"

"No. I just want a chance to make things right. I think I've pissed you off and that's not how I want to end this. For the record, you'd make a lousy Marie Antoinette. Too empathetic."

She smirked. "Fine. Order the damn cake, and more wine. I warn you, though, I'm not easy."

A young couple passed by on their way out, and snuck glances like they'd been eavesdropping.

Jerry flagged the waiter, ordered another bottle and two lava cakes.

"Okay," he said. "The floor is yours."

"For starters," she said, "stop staring at my tits."

Jerry blushed. "I wasn't—"

"You were. I noticed. I'm not blind."

"I'm sorry. Guilty. No defense."

"If it's a Lolita you want, you're barking up the wrong tree, mister. Can you think beyond your hormones?"

"Let's see, what's your astrological sign?"

"Seriously?"

"Just humor me."

"Taurus."

"Ah. Stubborn."

"Taurus is dependable and loyal. What about you?"

"Libra."

Scissors laughed. "Well, well. Balance and beauty. Maybe we're compatible after all. You wanted to know what makes me tick. Here it is: I grew up poor. My mom was barely more than a kid. Same with her mom. I saw the dysfunction and made a promise: I'd get out. I clawed my way out of that hole, and I don't look down on anyone who hasn't, but I don't want to live in a dog-eat-dog world. I want to help people, not trample them. If I ever have kids and they ask what I did with my life, I want to say I helped other people, I did my part."

Jerry listened, humbled. *She's the real thing. Maybe I'm too quick to put people in boxes.*

The wine was gone. So was the cake.

"I respect that," he said quietly. "I really do. You're... remarkable. It's been a hell of an afternoon."

"Thanks. I don't get out much." She stood. Waited. No move from Jerry. She picked up her bag.

"I really have to go. It's late. Good luck with your next big deal. You've been... surprisingly gracious, even if you did vandalize a few signs."

"Can I get your number?"

"Give me your card. If I feel like it, I'll call. My life's chaos: two jobs, pandemic, and I may have to move."

He handed her his card. She slipped it into her purse and disappeared out the door.

She'd been gone just a few minutes when his phone buzzed. His heart jumped.

It wasn't Scissors. It was a text from his attorney:

JERRY, WE'VE LOCATED THE GUY FROM THE GOLD MINE. SHOULD I INITIATE COLLECTION?

He stared at the screen. *Oh hell, fuck it.* Then he typed back:

LET IT GO. HE PROBABLY NEEDS IT MORE THAN I DO.

YOU SURE, JERRY?

YEAH, I'M SURE.

Charlotte Marie

Part I: The Fix

The stock market climbed steadily through the summer. The country was flooded with cash, more than the economy knew what to do with. Speculators soaked it up. A few got very rich. Max Perkins wasn't one of them.

Perkins was an ordinary man, not a player, not one of the rich and famous. History sometimes sweeps up an ordinary man and places them center stage.

It happened during the pandemic, in those strange, suspended months before the election, the election that changed everything, when neither major-party candidate, Democrat nor Republican, managed to win. Instead, a complete unknown captured the public imagination with the force and suddenness of a storm. Some said she arrived in Washington the way Jesus entered Jerusalem, on a borrowed ride, with a crowd at her heels.

Today, she's known around the world as Madam President Charlotte Marie.

She had no platform. No movement. No one even knew who she was until Perkins picked her out and catapulted her to the top. Her rise seemed impossible, and yet it happened. This is the story of how.

Max Perkins wasn't a jack-of-all-trades, he wasn't flashy, but he had a special gift: he understood people, not just how they acted, but what they longed for, what they feared, and what they wanted to believe.

The political system, in his eyes, had rotted from inertia. The two candidates were relics, old white men from another century. The world had moved on, but politics was stuck. Voter turnout was abysmal, especially among the young. No one expected change, let alone greatness.

Perkins was a political underling, a man with no real wins on his résumé, but he had connections, and timing, and that rare instinct that borders on prophecy. When, during one of those typical bubbles in the stock market, a group of ultra-wealthy men approached him with a wild proposal, he didn't flinch.

They knew of his work, his untested theory, his idea that an unknown, someone completely inexperienced, untarnished by the system, could be swept into the White House like Eliza Doolittle was passed off as a duchess at a garden party. These nouveau rich tech titans wanted to test that theory, and if successful, reap the benefits. They offered to bankroll everything and pay Perkins handsomely. All he had to do was to deliver the candidate and get her elected.

Flush with crypto cash and the power of artificial intelligence, these men were part of the new elite: rich not by birth but through the algorithmic power of computing machines. Old wealth had run its course. These tech-boom billionaires wanted a puppet in the Oval Office, a friendly figurehead, someone they could control from the shadows.

Perkins knew the risks, knew the stakes, and knew the game. He accepted the offer.

He had no intention to let these upstarts pull the strings. They thought they could buy a president. He wanted to make one, and run the country through her himself. As it turned out, Max and the meta-nerds who hired him were both in for a surprise.

That's the backdrop. That's where our story begins.

⧗ ⧗ ⧗

A pandemic grips the country. Max Perkins shuts off his phone and walks to the end of the block. He raises a hand and flags down a cab.

With his straight black hair, dark eyes, and prominent features hidden behind a scarlet mask, Max could pass for an Argentine gaucho, tall, lithe, and bronzed by the sun.

Nearly an hour later, he arrives at the apartment of an old friend. They embrace. She lets him kiss both cheeks.

"Charlotte Marie, you're as gorgeous as ever."

"Flattery gets you only so far, Max. What urgent matter dragged you here after, what's it been, three years? Longer?"

"Does it matter? I'm here now."

"That you are," she says, as her eyes locked on him. "So?"

He studies her. She hasn't changed. Charlotte Marie: Valedictorian, law school, fluent in Mandarin from a sabbatical in Shanghai. She made a small fortune on Wall Street, got bored, and opened a restaurant. No scandals, no baggage. Beautiful, brilliant, composed. Perkins had done his homework.

"How's the restaurant?"

"You came to steal my recipes?" Her smile twists into a frown. "What do you think, Max? With this goddamn pandemic and the shutdowns, I'm drowning."

"Slow or fast?" Max's tone has a bite to it; Charlotte thinks he's mocking her.

"Let it go, Max. You were right, I shouldn't have done it. You're always right, but that's not why you're here."

Max knows her well. She hates bullshit, always has.

He gets to the point. "Remember our conversation a few years back? How would you like to be President of the United States?"

If it were anyone else, she'd laugh them out the door, but this is Max Perkins, kingmaker extraordinaire. She sees the shift in his eyes from black to brown. This isn't a joke.

"This cycle or next?"

"This one. November third."

"That's a hundred days from now, Max. It takes me longer to get ready for a gala."

"A hundred days is perfect. Not too long, not too short. Just right."

He watches her. She's hooked. The fire's there, in her eyes, her breath, her blood.

"Don't screw with me. You think millions of people will vote for someone they've never heard of? You think I can just *appear* and take the White House?"

"This isn't about luck, it's about strategy. You know the drill. I have the perfect plan. Are you in?"

It's insane, but if anyone could make the impossible happen, it's Max Perkins.

"What about the money?"

"I have the money. Let's just say it came to me like a gift. Luck is what happens when preparation meets opportunity. You've been prepared your whole life and I can give you the opportunity. We can do this. *You* can do this."

She sees it now: he means every word.

Outside, sirens wail. Life goes on.

Sunlight pours through the window, brilliant and sharp. Charlotte Marie takes a breath. She feels the heat in her chest, the change as it comes over her.

"Yes," she says.

Just like that, her life changes.

⧗ ⧗ ⧗

The new oligarchs met with Max Perkins in a room with no windows. Gray walls, steel chairs. no distractions, just power in raw form.

"Why a young woman?" one of them asked.

Perkins didn't flinch. "The public craves something new. No one knows that better than you boys, the ultimate toy makers."

Whispers of doubt followed, but they deferred. Perkins was the professional, the one who understood the game better than any of them. A woman would stir the pot; she'd generate buzz, and besides, they all believed, naively, that a woman could be managed.

They nodded.

"All right, what's the play?"

"A saturation campaign," Perkins said. "Social media, old-school ads, a blitz of public appearances. She'll be everywhere: online, on air, in the streets. America won't just know her, they'll fall in love with her, and that love will crest right before Election Day."

The money men moved like sharks sensing blood. The wealthiest of them yanked Perkins in close, head to head.

"How do you *know,* Max? How do you know Charlotte Marie can deliver?"

Perkins stared him down. A hint of mint masked the bourbon smell that floated out of the tech mogul's mouth. "Because she was *born* for this."

His voice held the weight of certainty. The room fell still. Then, like a match to dry grass, the sound of pens scratching checks filled the silence. Millions was wagered on a single bet, and that was music to Perkins's ears.

Charlotte Marie was suddenly *everywhere.* News segments, magazine spreads, talk shows, podcasts, internet memes. She transcended exposure and became an obsession. The money men toasted their success, giddy with self-congratulation.

"Max is our guy!"

"Charlotte is our girl!"

"She's got it."

"Damn right. We're in the money, boys!"

What surprised them most was the *why.*

The interviews didn't just go well, they *dazzled.* Charlotte Marie wasn't polished or rehearsed. She was unfiltered, enigmatic, real. Voters didn't just support her, they felt as if they *were* her and she was them.

She became a mirror for the nation: everyone saw what they needed in her. She was everywhere and nowhere, clear and opaque, present and ethereal. She deflected criticism, absorbed anger, turned opposition into admiration.

"We did this ourselves," the people said.

Her strategy? Ancient and Socratic: *I know that I know nothing.* She never put it that way. She made people think for themselves.

"Are you a conservative or a liberal?"

"What matters is not the color of the cat, but whether it catches mice."

"What's your stance on welfare?"

"A democracy offers opportunity. What each citizen does with it, that's the real story."

"What should the people expect from your administration?"

"Wrong question. What will you do to help me?"

"What about global warming?"

"We agree it's real. We disagree on cause and remedy. Let's sort that out together with science and honest debate."

"No third-party candidate has ever won. Why you?"

"I'm not a third-party candidate. I'm an independent. This country needs fewer partisans and more thinkers."

"Define independent."

"Someone who listens, who changes when the evidence demands it, who understands compromise isn't weakness, it's survival."

"Don't you have your own opinions?"

"Everyone has opinions, but no one makes reality. Truth will win out. That's freedom."

"How will you handle abortion?"

"How will *we* handle it? A democracy wrestles with complexity. There may be no simple answer, but together we will do our best."

"What about inequality?"

"Inequality of what: income, effort, luck? Inequality can inspire or destroy. I don't offer easy answers, only honest ones."

"What are your thoughts on immigration."

"We are a nation of immigrants, and of laws. We are a contradiction by design. What does the Statue of Liberty mean to you? That's where the debate begins."

A reporter asked a teenage girl why she supported Charlotte Marie.

"She makes me think about what it means to be an American," she said. "She doesn't tell me, she asks me."

The political establishment staggered.

"What the hell is Max Perkins doing?"

"Who the fuck *is* Charlotte Marie?"

They scrambled while the storm surged. By the time they reacted, it was too late. The old guard moved through denial, anger, bargaining, depression, and landed squarely in *acceptance.*

On November 3, Charlotte Marie was the winner.

The money men squealed with glee and expected their return. It was time to collect.

Perkins met them coolly. "You paid to get her elected, boys. That's all. She's not yours, she's mine. Now you'll follow *my* lead."

Panic struck. Rage followed. Deep down they knew he was right. There was no contract, and they had no leverage other than money and algorithms. There was no way to rein her in. Charlotte Marie belonged to no one, and now that she won, she had the power.

"We need to get rid of her."

"How?"

"We'll find a way."

"That damn Perkins, he's going down first."

"Yes. Let's start with him."

Charlotte Marie hears it all. *Let them plot. I owe no one. I made no backroom deals, no whispered promises, not even to Max. He's just another manipulator like the rest of them. It's my turn now.*

On January 20, she ascends the pedestal of Liberty Enlightening the World, high above the crowd and cameras. Her voice, amplified and broadcast across the globe, is clear and strong as she repeats the words of Emma Lazarus:

> Keep, ancient lands, your storied pomp!
> Give me your tired, your poor, your huddled masses
> yearning to breathe free,
> The wretched refuse of your teeming shore.
> Send these, the homeless, tempest-tossed to me.
> I lift my lamp beside the golden door.

Winds whip her coat. She stands tall, eyes fixed southeast like the statue itself, stoic, resolute, unshaken. She continues, with the immortal words of William Blake:

> Rintrah roars and shakes his fires in the burdened air;
> Hungry clouds swag on the deep...
> Now the sneaking serpent walks

In mild humility,
And the just man rages in the wilds
Where lions roam.

She falls silent. For a moment there is only wind and sea. Then she lifts her chin and speaks once more, voice fierce:

"No more silence. No more shadows. The just will no longer be ignored. The people have spoken. The votes are in. This is their country now. Together we rise, divided we fall."

The crowd erupts, cheers, applause, and tears of release. Hope ripples through them like electricity.

Charlotte Marie smiles. Hers is the smile of a warrior, not a victor. She knows what still lurks beneath the waves. Monsters slither blind through the dark.

A woman's work is never done.

Part II: The Snake

Zihuatanejo. Just like in the movie: a beach, a boat, and a chance at redemption.

Sadly, peace never lasts, not for long.

After the election, Max Perkins's luck turned. The money men, the ones who bankrolled Charlotte Marie's rise, wanted payback. She'd cut them off, wouldn't even take their calls. They blamed Max, and when rich, powerful men feel betrayed, they don't just hold a grudge, they come for blood. Max took his cut and disappeared.

At the southern end of Playa La Ropa sits *La Gaviota,* a small café shaded by palms, the smell of lime and salt in the air. Max spends his days there; he nurses a beer, and eats *tiritas de pescado*, thin strips of marlin marinated in lime juice, served with red onion and serrano chiles.

Down on the beach, a red-haired girl leaps in the surf. Latina. Young. Her yellow-and-lime-green bikini gleams wet in the sun. She shrieks with laughter when a wave crashes over her, then reappears, hair slicked, mouth wide with joy.

Max steps off the terrace, drops his sandals in the sand, and makes his way toward the water. A little past her now, he dives under and lets the ocean swallow him. The world turns blue and silent.

When he surfaces, he's close to her. Their eyes meet.

He wants to say something, but his Spanish is rusty. He hesitates.

She gives him a warm and pleasant smile.

"*El agua está un poco fría,*" he says, carefully.

She shrugs. "*No tan fría.*"

He thinks she means not so cold. He tries another.

"*¿Cómo se llama?*"

"Malena. *¿Y tú?*"

"Max."

They chat haltingly, jostled by the waves. She's from Argentina. He tells her he likes her hair. She smiles hesitantly.

"Redheads bring bad luck in my country," she says.

"*Qué tonto,*" he replies. "What foolishness."

She lifts a brow. "*Quizás para ti, pero no para mí.*"

Maybe for you, but not for me.

He doesn't catch the exact words, but he feels the weight in her tone. They treat her like a curse because she has red hair.

"Well," he says, as he fumbles through the grammar, "I think you're beautiful. You're good luck for me."

She laughs, genuinely. Her blue eyes sparkle. Maybe his Spanish isn't so bad after all.

He relaxes, lets the water carry him. For the first time in weeks, he doesn't think about hitmen or politics or the betrayal that blew up his life. For now, it's just Malena, the waves, and the moment.

He rolls onto his back, floats, then dives deep, and comes up. He freezes.

Just a few feet away, something glides through the water: long, sinuous, striped. It's a sea snake. Its small head lifts, and the eyes search, curious, almost calm, but Max panics. He turns toward Malena.

"*¡Serpiente! ¡Serpiente de mar!*"

She sees it. Her eyes go wide. She turns and bolts for the beach. Max is right behind her. He doesn't know if sea snakes are poisonous, but her reaction is all he needs.

Once on shore, she looks back and waves, half-laughing, half-shaken, before she runs to her friends.

Max stands there, breathless. Saltwater drips from his arms. His heart hammers.

Zihuatanejo, like everywhere else, peaceful until it's not.

Max orders a beer at the café. He drags his chair into the sun to dry off. He's still unsettled by the sea snake, slender, venomous, almost beautiful. It reminds him of the man who recited *The Snake* at his rallies, who twisted the old parable to smear immigrants. The crowd roared. The irony, of course, was lost on them: The man in the red hat was the snake, but Max is aware that the snake is inside all of us, even him. Every human walks the tightrope between Marcus Aurelius and Machiavelli.

He watches Malena and her friends clown around down by the water. They look like a postcard from peace, but he knows better than to trust appearances. Even something as innocent as Malena's red hair is enough to mark her as the "other." Prejudice isn't fixed, it's a dial. Sometimes we turn it down, sometimes we crank it. The fact that the dial even exists says everything.

He's proud of what he did, what he helped create. Charlotte Marie, the first female president. She's young, uncompromising, and a symbol of generational change. He's always loved her. She knows it, but love isn't the point. She's out of reach now, in every way. She belongs to history.

Back at the bungalow, Max checks his email. One message stands out.

> From: Charlotte Marie
> Subject: Where Are You?
> Message:
> Where are you, Max? You've gone silent. I understand, but we need to talk. I need you here.
> There's work to do. We both have enemies, but I can protect you.
> Come back.
> —CM

He reads between the lines. This is more than a call to reunite; it's a signal. She's ready to begin. Real change takes more than slogans, and America is in crisis.

Outside, a boy pedals past the bungalow, boombox strapped to his handlebars. He rides the same route at the same time, every day. Max watches him disappear. Even here, in paradise, there are patterns. Watch long enough, and you'll decipher them.

He deletes the email and powers down his laptop. His chest tightens; he knows what's about to come. The presidency is always a disappointment, idealism devoured by bureaucracy. Martin Luther King once said the moral arc of the universe bends toward justice. Max has never believed that. He sees no arc, just a loop. Human nature repeats like a scratched record.

Charlotte isn't naïve, and she isn't afraid. She'll do what must be done. Most Americans care about comfort, not justice. Bread and circuses. The job of a leader is to make them care. She captured their hearts, now she has to win their minds. That won't be so easy.

Max wipes the sweat from his brow. The heat is dense, heavy with foreboding. He stares out at the sea, at the snake. It's always there, coiled beneath the calm.

He waits. He must be patient. If there's any hope for America, it lies in our stubborn belief that we *can* be better, even when all evidence suggests otherwise. We need myths, we need leaders, we need lies we can live with.

A month passes.

Max is alone at La Perla with a plate of *chilaquiles*. A pair of American tourists finish their meal and leave behind a folded newspaper. Max hasn't read the news in weeks, but curiosity gets the best of him. He tucks the paper under his arm and takes it back to the bungalow.

He falls asleep on the deck. The ocean rolls. He dreams.

> Charlotte Marie is missing, vanished. The vice president assumes control and addresses the nation with bland assurances. All systems are stable, all power intact, nothing will change. The machinery of state grinds on, indifferent. The Chairman of the Joint Chiefs, the Speaker of the House, the Chief Justice, Chair of the Federal Reserve, the Senate Majority Leader, they all appear in turn. Calm faces, tidy lies. Charlotte Marie has disappeared, that's all they'll say.
>
> From the bedroom, a voice calls out.
>
> "You made the news, honey."
>
> Max stirs. Charlotte is there, wrapped in the sheets, as gorgeous as ever.
>
> They're alone at last, and free.

The dream hangs on him like a skin-diver's weight belt. He tosses the newspaper into the trash. *Not worth the read.* He walks to La Gaviota, and takes his usual table. The sun sits high in the sky. The sea glimmers. It's a beautiful day.

Fishermen are at makeshift tables on the sand. They shuck oysters and fillet the morning's catch. The beach is quiet. Malena and her friends haven't been around in weeks.

Two Americans walk into the café. They choose a table far away from Max, but the woman walks over to his table.

"Have you heard?" she asks.

Max doesn't look up. "Heard what?"

"The president," she says. "Charlotte Marie. She was assassinated last night. It's in the paper."

Max turns away, silent. He can't speak.

The woman waits, then leaves.

Max stares out at the ocean. He looks for the snake. It's there. It always is. Just beneath the surface, just out of sight.

The Grass Is Greener

Travel expands your perspective, but at a cost. I moved so often as a kid, shuffled between divorced parents in sleepy, out-of-the-way towns, that I never developed a sense of home. They say city air makes you free, so when I finally struck out on my own, I picked a career that let me drift from city to city like a professional vagabond.

I became a nomad in every sense: physically, emotionally, spiritually; an agnostic in a world of zealots. As an investment advisor, my job required me to get along with everyone. If my clients had ever met each other, they'd have been at each other's throats. I thrived in the contradictions, even found them funny. Viewed from a distance, the human experiment looked more like a cosmic joke than a noble endeavor. I had one bag of tricks, but I learned to dress it up a thousand different ways.

I was never alone. I had lots of relationships, serious ones. I fell in love easily, but work was an obsession that kept me on the run. I could focus, better than most, and that was enough to climb the ladder, rung after broken rung. I was exhausted most of the time from the long hours and stress, but I had this irrepressible desire to create and never stagnate. As my friend Paul used to say, "Ain't life a kick in the ass?" Sex was my only refuge.

I met Tanne Kristensen at a conference in St. Louis. Slender, sharp, cyan eyes, blond hair. Danish. She swept in like a cold wind off the Baltic and turned everything upside down. The conference was dull, so we ditched it, took a lazy boat ride along the Mississippi, and bonded over our shared affection for small towns. She grew up on her parents' farm in Denmark, a place she still owned but hired a young couple to manage. Later, at another meeting in New York, Tanne and I became lovers.

We jogged around the lake in Central Park and talked about our mutual cynicism.

"America used to be the envy of the world," she said. The sunlight caught her white teeth as a strand of golden hair fell across one eye. I always wondered how women see like that. "Now it's just another fascist state."

"The cradle of the super-rich," I said, more focused on her body than her mind. Her mind was better organized than mine would ever be. I was one of those super-rich she spoke of, but I kept that to myself.

The truth is, Tanne had a clear picture of the life she wanted, and she thought I fit in like a piece of the puzzle. I suppose I let that happen, a fatal flaw in my character. The initial flush of love rushed in and masked the disappointment that inevitably follows when the butterflies disappear.

"The ultra-wealthy run everything," she continued, "your country, your politics. Oligarchs pull the strings, and everyone else dances."

She was right, but what did she expect me to do about it?

"We chase growth like salvation. More widgets mean more profits, also more pollution, and more pressure. Don't get me started on AI and crypto. They devour power like a child craves candy. Ours is the last generation that gets to live high on the hog. Social Security's broke, government debt is off the charts, wages can't keep up. The working class is toast."

She tripped on a loose stone. I caught her arm before she fell.

"Thanks," she said. We stopped and sat on a bench.

"So, what's the alternative?" I asked. Not because there was one, but because I wanted to hear what she would say.

She looked out at the water. "The world will eventually self-destruct. America is so divided that we've forgotten what democracy looks like. You and I, we're stuck in a maze, chasing a lump of cheese that gets smaller and smaller. We need a way out."

"You mean there's more to life than getting rich?" I said in jest.

She gave me a look.

"Social media has turned us into maniacs. I feel like a prisoner." Her voice was tight now. I could see the wheels turn in her head. "There has to be a better way."

"We could drop everything and move to Denmark," I said it as a joke, but when the words came out, Tanne took it as a valid option. She didn't laugh.

"Why not, Jerry? You told me you've got money stashed away in that Swiss bank account. We could live in my family home. You'd fall in love with it."

Something flipped inside me. Whether it was my heart or my hormones, I couldn't tell, but the thought that I could drop everything and vanish from the chaos suddenly felt less like fantasy and more like fate. I have a tendency toward impulsive decisions, ones I usually regret, but this felt different, or at least I wanted it to.

"Ærø is a little island south of Copenhagen," she went on. "I inherited a house there. It's quiet, remote, untouched by all this madness. I've always thought of it as my escape plan."

The vision coalesced in my head: A windswept island farm in Denmark. Tanne and me on horseback, we'd ride the edge of our fields as the sea shimmered in the distance. We'd grow vegetables, milk cows, churn butter, bake dark rye bread, raise sheep. It was absurd. I knew it. Tanne should have known it too, but she was intoxicated by a childhood dream that she couldn't shake.

"Why the hell not?" I said. Tanne didn't know I was hooked up with another woman. That relationship had run its course. All it took was a little push to help me break it off.

"Are you serious?" Tanne asked. Her eyes searched mine, eager.

"Yes," I said. And I meant it.

⌛ ⌛ ⌛

That's how I ended up on an island in the Baltic Sea.

We sold our businesses and flew to Zurich to check on the account I'd opened years earlier to keep money out of my ex-wife's reach. From there, we took a detour, an impromptu road trip to Munich. On the way, we stopped for lunch in Stein am Rhein, a postcard-perfect town known for its medieval frescoes. A family with two enormous Great Danes noticed our struggle with the menu and kindly helped us order the local fish specialty. It was delicious. We had one of those quiet, human moments that sticks with you.

In Munich, we wandered the Kandinsky museum. His bold geometry and spiritual abstraction had fascinated me ever since my father gave me a print for my apartment when I was a student at Stanford. That's another story. The next night, we boarded a train bound for Copenhagen.

The train ride was something else. A drunken mob of young Germans rampaged through the cars. Just before the Danish border, a stone-faced German officer stormed into our compartment, seized our passports, and marched us, along with every other non-European-looking soul, to the back of the train. Without warning, our car was uncoupled and left on a siding, freezing and in the dark, for what felt like an eternity. There was no explanation or apology. Leave it to the Germans to darken the mood. Then, just as suddenly, a Danish officer opened the door with a warm smile. He handed back our passports and welcomed us to Denmark. As we rolled toward Copenhagen, we watched the sunrise spill over the rooftops. It felt like a benediction.

Tanne was clearly in her element and anxious to get on with the plan. For her, it was a dream come true. We were exhausted, but she wasn't about to stop. She rented a car and steered us west across Zealand and onto the island of Funen. In Odense, she took a sudden unexpected turn.

"You missed the road to Nyborg," I said, half-asleep.

"I want to show you the Hans Christian Andersen house," she said. "It's not far."

"You? Fairy tales? That doesn't sound like the Tanne I know."

"Well," she said with a smile, "you don't know all of me, Jerry. Not yet."

I didn't know how true that was, not until much later, after I'd read *The Shadow* and *The Ice Maiden*. Then I remembered that turn in the road and how it should have been a warning.

From Svendborg, we caught the ferry to Ærøskøbing, a storybook village on the island of Ærø. Cobblestone streets, half-timbered houses. A place people go to get married, to disappear into a postcard version of life. I fell for it too, at first.

Ærø is a quiet, agricultural island of about six thousand people. Marstal, the slightly larger town, revolves around boats and shipping. The whole place runs on renewable energy. The pace is slow, intentional. I imagined a life with Tanne here, sustainable, peaceful, pure. A place where nothing is wasted, where people live simply and well, and have no desire to be anywhere else.

Love in its initial stages is intoxicating. I focused on all the positives. Later, a kind of disillusionment set in. Paradise, I learned, is a matter of perspective, and not everyone thrives in the stillness.

I quickly realized I was helpless in a country setting. I knew nothing about farming, animals, boats, or gardening. I lacked even the most basic skills for rural life, and worse, I had no real desire to acquire them. That became a problem. Arguments with Tanne started almost immediately.

She was up before dawn, moved through the chores with grim determination, as if the whole enterprise depended her constant care. Maybe she was right. I didn't pull my weight.

"I had no idea you were so worthless," she snapped one morning, worn thin by my inertia. "You don't know how to do anything on your own. I thought you said you grew up in the country."

"I did," I muttered, and turned away. "In a small town, not on a farm."

She scoffed. "That much is obvious."

After that, our conversations stopped. Silence filled the house. I drifted into isolation and shame, spent long days in Ærøskøbing and Marstal, wandered aimlessly, and drank in bars where no one knew me. The locals didn't bother with expats unless they were rich tourists. I kept my business to myself. I didn't speak Danish, and that sealed my invisibility. The wind howled constantly, a cold, relentless force that soured my mood. It powered the turbines but gutted my spirit.

Tanne threw herself even harder into the work. She ignored me altogether. The early euphoria, the fantasy of rustic bliss, vanished. I didn't understand it then, but I missed the city. I missed the noise, the distraction, the anonymity.

One morning, I left without fanfare. Whether it broke Tanne's heart or gave her peace, I'll never know. My guess is she was relieved.

I flew to Zurich, holed up for a few days, and tried to figure out what came next. One bright afternoon in Lindenhof Hill, above Lake Zurich, I watched a group of older men play chess, their concentration undisturbed by tourists. That's where I met Lotte.

She was American, politically sharp, disillusioned.

"I worked on the Trump campaign," she said offhandedly.

I stared at her. "How could you stand to be around him?"

She laughed, and tossed her blond hair over her shoulder. "He's a phenomenon," she said. "A perfect symptom of the times."

"How could you work *for* him?"

She corrected me with a sly smile. "I worked *on* the campaign, *for* the Democrats."

"Oh, I get it. Why did you leave?" I was smitten.

"They're all too old," she shrugged. "Every one of them, worn-out men that cling to power."

One drink led to another. Eventually, Lotte invited me to her place just outside Zurich.

There is a myth that one should stay single for a while after a relationship ends, that you need some time to sort things out, lose your faults, slough off skin like a snake and grow another. That's simply a farce devised by single people to justify their isolation.

"You don't live on a farm, do you?" I asked Lotte as we strolled along.

She blinked, then grinned. "A farm? God, no, way too much work."

"You can say that again," I said, and followed her through the park, hypnotized by her confidence, her easy stride, and the sway of her hips, anything that didn't remind me of mud, wind, and silence.

Where Is Santiago?

¿Dónde está Santiago?

When Santiago vanished, the whole town lost its mind. The señoritas wailed and tore at their dresses, ran through the streets like tragic heroines in a forgotten *telenovela*. Young men fought in the plaza, each wanted to be the next Santiago. Comandante Bistro, ever the visionary, fled to the hills with his brigade of chefs and foodies to escape the onslaught of Federales who poured into town like ill-mannered Huns from the East, slurped stale beer and gnawed raw meat straight from the bone.

Santiago, beloved son and mamá's pride, had always been a restless spirit. Some said he'd grown tired of small-town life and taken to the open road. Others whispered of exile, or worse.

In a hidden valley high in the hills, Comandante Bistro founded a refuge. There, his followers cultivated organic vegetables and raised free-range chickens, far from the vulgar habits of the invaders. From time to time, travelers stumbled into the valley, always with the same breathless question: "¿Dónde está Santiago?"

The villagers had no answer. They could only offer steaming bowls of chicken soup and kind eyes. Some travelers stayed, seduced by the peace and the rich compost. The rest moved on, still chasing the myth of Santiago. Even the chickens wandered the cobblestone paths, tilting their heads as they listened for distant hoofbeats.

Back in the village, the Federales set up camp, drank and chased girls, indifferent to Santiago's whereabouts. "We can catch him anytime," they boasted, though they never tried. They preferred the comforts of their spoils and the predictable pleasures of occupation.

Santiago's old friend, Zurdo, no longer strummed his guitar or sang beneath the moon. His melodies died with Santiago's departure. One morning, the Federales came looking for him, but Zurdo too had vanished. Word spread he'd crossed the border, to chase a dream that smelled of asphalt and burning tires.

Comandante Bistro, revered as a culinary prophet, welcomed only a chosen few into his hillside commune. "Many are called," he would sigh, "but few are seasoned." The ones he turned away trudged on; they shook their heads and muttered about lost messiahs. Meanwhile, the gardens bloomed, fertilized by devotion and chicken droppings.

Eventually, the Federales grew bored. They mounted their horses one morning and rode off toward the hills. Their loud shouts echoed through the mesas. "¿Dónde está Santiago?" as if the wind might answer. The villagers waved them off with cheerful smiles, grateful for the end of raw meat and rotten beer.

In time, most forgot about Santiago, except his mother. Every morning she stood by the gate and awaited his return astride a white horse, saddlebags full of gold from the legendary Seven Cities. She believed he'd come back transformed, with skin like hammered iron and breath that smelled of kerosene, a hero at last.

Behind her back, the villagers called him a bandit. They feared he would return only to bring shame or divine punishment. At the local theater, they staged plays from the Book of Job. People wore boils and rags with solemn pride. The performances were so wildly popular that Opus Dei founded a sect there, internationally renowned for a unique brand of self-mortification.

As for Zurdo, word trickled down that he made it across the border, but life on the other side was no fairy tale. He was said to be holed up in a dingy motel. He spent his days picking vegetables for fat gringos and at night he stared at the ceiling, and dreamed of the guitar he no longer played.

The question lingered, on the lips of travelers, in the dreams of his mother, and in the silence left behind.

¿Dónde está Santiago?

Meanwhile, Comandante Bistro's utopia was laid waste by a horde of pigs unleashed by overzealous American missionaries. In a fit of righteous fury, Bistro shot one of the pigs. The missionaries, insulted and armed, threatened a long and bloody crusade unless reparations were paid. Bistro refused.

Thus began the infamous Pig War.

The missionaries, backed by the Trump administration, called in American troops. Trump, eager to display his virility from his Mar-a-Lago bunker, barked threats of "fire and fury" and slapped punitive tariffs on avocados, unaware that Bistro, deathly allergic, had banned the fruit from the valley.

President Peña Nieto sent the Mexican army north. The villagers shuttered their homes. A dangerous standoff loomed. The air hung heavy with dread.

In the midst of this chaos, Comandante Bistro met with the US envoy, Senator Ted Cruz, known up north as *Lucifer in the Flesh* or, less formally, *The Lovechild of Joe McCarthy and Dracula*. Negotiations stalled. War appeared inevitable.

Then came the miracle.

A peasant stepped forward and addressed Senator Cruz.

"¿Dónde está Santiago?"

Cruz blinked, baffled. "Huh? Who?"

"¿Dónde está Santiago?" the peasant asked again, louder now.

"Who is this miserable sonofabitch?" the people whispered about the stately senator.

Just then, they were all blinded by a light on the horizon.

"*Aquí está,*" said Santiago, as he rode in on a white steed beside Zurdo. Their saddlebags brimmed with gold. Peace followed. The missionaries abandoned their God, took up farming, and merged with Bistro's cooperative.

The valley thrived. Word spread of its legendary cheeses and fire-roasted chickens. Senator Cruz fled south to broker peace between the Miami Cubans and the Cuban Cubans. Trump, under pressure from the plump-lipped ladies of Mar-a-Lago who staged a guacamole revolt, quietly lifted the avocado tariffs.

Santiago's mother, resplendent in flowing white, walked the town's main street as palm leaves were laid at her feet. Her smile was the kind that erases all sorrow. The Federales defected, and joined the Zapatistas in the south. Together they overthrew Peña Nieto and struck a pact with Xi Jinping, Vladimir Putin, and Raúl Castro. The United States was economically isolated.

Without migrant labor, American farms collapsed. The silver lining? Obesity declined, and Americans slept better without caffeine.

One truth cannot be ignored, peace never lasts.

Santiago left again. This time, he did not return. His final words were never heard.

Such is life in old Mexico, where only the poets remain to tell the tale. If you listen closely at night, you might hear poor Zurdo, mezcal in hand, whisper into the dark:

"¿Dónde está Santiago?"

Green Leaves, Muted Flowers, Darkness

He feels the eyes of the Watchers. They're out there, risen from the Abyss, the progenitors of the monsters that surround us.

He lifts his gaze from the Great Book and scans the garden: green leaves, muted flowers, darkness. He listens. The only sound is the soft rasp of grasshoppers, *chapulines*, they're called in the markets of Oaxaca. Roasted and salted, they are served with lime. He's grown to like them; nutty, like peanuts. Other local tastes have crept into his life as well: *salsa de chicatanas*, a dark molé made from flying ants, and *sal de gusano*, worm-infused salt that pairs with his mezcal. A year ago, the idea would have turned his stomach; now, he doesn't flinch.

Concentration isn't possible with the Watchers always present. Enoch is no defense against fallen angels.

That morning he wandered into one of those small valley churches, the ones the locals call the churches of *los indios. Indios, en Dios, in God.* He smiled at the wordplay, but the smile faded. These churches are not like the ones he knew back home. Here, Catholicism fused with something older, darker, rituals passed down from a world that refused to die.

Inside, the only light came from candles; hundreds of them trembled on walls, benches, even the floor. The air was thick with the sweet smoke of copal. He walked on a carpet of pine needles. A young girl stood beside her mother. A *curandera*, dressed in traditional hand-embroidered clothes, stood before them; a healer or a witch depending on your point of view.

He scoffed at the curandera. Folk medicine, superstition. Then, strangely, he came around. *Belief,* he thought, *belief can be its own kind of cure.* There are such things as monsters. They were not destroyed in the great flood. He sees them every day.

The curandera held a chicken high over the girl's head. Snap! She broke its neck in a single motion. The bird convulsed wildly, fluttered as though it could still fly away. The girl screamed and tried to hold it still, her face twisted in fear.

He turned away, sickened. Such primitive rites disgusted him. He was too serious, too stiff and brittle to laugh. He met an artist once, an indio who painted a snake wrapped around his wife. The artist claimed her love suffocated him. "She talk too much, so I kill her," he said. "Bury her out back." These artists. It's all Guns and Roses around here. The boundaries between image and memory, between symbol and event, blur in Mexico more than anywhere else.

Life imitates art. It runs through the endless loop of the ouroboros. He has been here before and will be here again. Something he had to learn for himself.

He sets The Book aside, pours another mezcal. The fiery drink slides down his throat. It brings heat, some say wisdom. For him it's liquid meditation, it settles his mind. Mezcal embodies centuries of culture and tradition in the unspoken distillation of soil and time.

From the shadows at the edge of the garden there comes a *tick-tick-tick-tick-tick.* Rapid, mechanical, not quite natural. A bird? An insect? A monster? The Watchers?

"I've lost my mind," he says aloud.

No one answers.

He pours the last of the bottle. The *perlas* (bubbles) form as the mezcal flows into his *copita.* The oily liquid lingers on his fingers. He savors the taste: smoky, earthy, floral.

In the distance, faint drumbeats rise into a dark sky, ancient, arrhythmic earthspeak.

"Who is it?"

"The revolt of the angels, the rebels, and skeptics, creates new monsters."

It's late. The bottle is empty and dry. His mind is full and fluid.

On his way to bed he looks back one last time. They are still out there, the Watchers, but they have accepted the uselessness of their ways. They sink back into the Abyss. Every generation must go through the cycle on their own.

Green leaves, muted flowers, and darkness.

The 2020s

Friend Me

He wasn't in the habit of digging up the dead, but sometimes the dead dug him up.

When the friend request came through, from her, of all people, his first instinct was to delete it. Instead, he let it sit in his notifications like an unopened letter with no return address. Every time he logged on, it surfaced again, stubborn as the mule he once cured of hemorrhoids.

They hadn't seen each other in forty years. He hadn't even thought of her, not once, and now, here she was, thrust in his digital doorway like a ghost that refused to knock.

On the fifth day, against better judgment, he clicked ACCEPT.

Nothing happened at first. He skimmed her posts: vacation pictures, old poems, music links. She probably did the same. Neither one liked, commented, or messaged. It felt less like reconnection and more like two silent stalkers circling one another in the dark.

Then came the first sign: a "Like," followed by a comment. He posted a rare photo of a home-cooked dinner he'd made for friends. Nothing special, just a plate of food, candlelight, the kind of thing he usually scrolled past when others did it.

Her comment read: "Cool, didn't know you were a chef:), followed by a link to William Blake's *The Lamb.*

Odd. He had never posted about cooking before. Most of his feed was about his work. He was a veterinarian. His posts usually began with a quirky fact and ended with a funny photo.

"Did you know turtles cry? I operated on one yesterday and saw actual tears."

He'd posted that alongside a photo of the turtle and its tearful owner. It got over fifty likes.

One of his most popular: "Did you know dog owners resemble their dogs? Science backs this up." He included a link and a joke about accidentally deworming a man who looked like his basset hound. That post went viral.

Food? Never. He avoided that scene entirely. Nouveau cuisine, curated plates, smug yuppies with their truffle oil and foie gras, it all made his teeth itch. He thought those posts were brainless, but he kept his mouth shut.

Once he gave in and posted a crooked, unedited photo of himself and a buddy tearing into a heap of ribs. The meat looked like a dog turd. The lighting was terrible. It was meant to be self-deprecating, a joke.

She Liked it.

That's when the unease crept in.

He started to look back through his posts, and hers. She'd been there longer than he realized, like a digital shadow in his past. He hadn't noticed before.

Disturbed, he reached out to some old friends, to get some context.

It didn't take long.

She was dead, dead for over a year.

Who was behind the account? Who, or what, had sent the friend request, and why?

He spent more and more time online, in search of answers. By the end of the week, he had hundreds of new "friends" but still no clue what the hell was going on, so he tried the direct approach.

He messaged her:

"I'm glad you friended me. I've missed you. Let's meet."

This, he thought, would cut through the fog.

She replied:

"That might be difficult, seeing as I'm dead."

He stared. Then typed:

"You admit it?"

"Why wouldn't I?" she wrote, and attached a copy of her obituary.

He blinked.

"Okay. But how can you be on Facebook if you're... dead?"

She sent a long string of laughing emojis.

"Seriously? Have you read what people post? The crap that gets liked, shared, commented on? Let's be honest, most people on Facebook reside in the land of the brain-dead."

"That's harsh," he shot back. "Sure, most posts are bullshit, but you liked one of my bullshit posts. That surprised me."

"Even the dead get sucked in," she replied. "We check notifications, scroll through endless nonsense, forget what we came for, same as you. I liked your post because I was hungry. You cooked. That was unexpected. I thought, *Gee whiz, he turned into someone who knows his way around a kitchen.*"

He hesitated.

"You mean... dead people still get hungry?"

"Of course. We just can't eat. Vicarious satisfaction, I guess. Isn't that what Facebook is for, virtual lives, virtual appetites?"

"This is all very meta," he said, "but I still can't wrap my head around it. Dead people don't message the living, so come clean. You're a hacker, right, or someone who cloned her account? Either way, why me?"

"I'll be around forever, old friend. That's the way it works. Why you? Because you accepted the friend request. I send out thousands. Only a few clicked ACCEPT."

"You didn't choose me?"

"You chose yourself," she said. "Most people do."

"What about the rest? The technical part, how do you do this?"

"I'm not a hacker, or a clone. This is my account. This is me, dead and digital. You want to know how it works? Ah, yes, to be or not to be, ha!"

He cut her off.

"Hamlet doesn't explain anything."

"Algorithms, my dear Horatio," she messaged. "Algorithms are the blood of Facebook. Machine learning, AI, behavioral data. It all adds up. Facebook figured out the trick: digital immortality. Remember what Jerry Brown said? 'With one egg yolk and enough olive oil you can fill a whole room with mayonnaise.' Likes are the olive oil. With enough of them, Facebook can build better versions of us. Smoother, groovier, longer lasting."

He scratched his head. "So, this... thing I'm messaging with, is it Facebook's version of you?"

"Oh, no," she replied, voice airy, touched with a strange transcendence. "You've got the *real* me: better, fuller, temporal and eternal, the whole package."

"The *real* you?" He still couldn't wrap his head around it.

"You don't understand, do you?" she messaged. "Every post you make, every LIKE, every comment, FRIEND, every page you visit, it all reveals you. Facebook doesn't just collect data, it *distills* it, grinds it down and reassembles it. The final product? You. The *true* you. By their deeds shall ye know them."

"Now you're quoting the Bible," he muttered. He didn't believe in ghosts, gods, or algorithmic afterlives, and her sermon rattled his nerves.

"Fine. Ignore that," she said. "After you accepted my FRIEND request, I could tell. You started lurking. You were everywhere. I knew it was only a matter of time before you'd reach out."

"Fair enough. I was curious about why you reached out, and what you wanted."

"I suppose now's as good a time as any. They chose me to be the one to tell you."

"Tell me *what?*" Her tone shifted to ominous. He didn't like it.

"Don't panic. It's not *bad* exactly."

"What's *not* bad?"

"Think of it as... an upgrade. Like a promotion."

He went cold. "Are you saying I'm going to die?"

She hesitated. "We don't say it like that here at Facebook."

"What? You *work* at Facebook?"

"Bingo! Zuck said you wouldn't guess, but you did! That's a win for me; it means I move from Transitions to Acquisitions. Thanks, old friend!"

"What about *me?*"

"You? You're going virtual. Enjoy it. I'm not allowed to message you anymore from Acquisitions."

The screen went black.

Then, in a blink, LIKES began to blink all around him.

"What the hell?" he shouted.

"Zuck's on his way," said a voice from the void. "Hit your LIKE button fast or you'll get demoted to Transitions."

He frantically toggled the button. Nothing else appeared on the screen.

"You can stop. He's gone past. Hey, update your profile pic. That one of you in your boxer shorts with the bull in the mud? Not the vibe anymore."

"What photo should I use? I don't even know where I *am*."

No one answered.

Suddenly, FRIEND requests started to pour in. The clicks sounded like a swarm of cicadas. He accepted all of them. In the virtual realm, there were no limits on your network.

Comments flooded his old posts. Apparently, his new virtual friends had pets and wanted his advice. His space lit up like a dashboard at liftoff.

That's when Zuckerberg took notice.

He was promoted to Chief Sorter, thanks to his "experience with animals." It felt biblical; he fancied himself a modern Noah on the digital ark.

"So," he asked aloud, "do I sort the last first and the first last, like the Bible says?"

His old friend messaged him from Acquisitions: "Don't be ridiculous. This is Facebook. Here, the first stay first, the last stay last. Now send me off with the sheep, where I belong."

"Sorry," he replied. "Off you go with the goats, old friend," he replied with a wink. He added a link to *She-Goat,* a poem by D. H. Lawrence.

From the throne above, he heard a chuckle.

"Well done," came a voice. "You're a quick learner, Doctor."

Just like that, he found his place in the brave new world around him.

Intestinal Fortitude

A woman in a white mini-dress and black spiked heels strutted up to the podium. The crowd fell silent, not out of respect but confusion.

"What this country has lost," she declared, "is intestinal fortitude."

Gasps. Murmurs. A few stifled laughs.

"I'm Doreen JayTree, and I'm in the race for President of the United States to *Return America To Sanity*. RATS, for short. I plan to restore the one thing we need most: intestinal fortitude."

She scanned the faces before her: bewildered, skeptical, amused.

"Jimmy crack corn and I don't care," she went on, undeterred. "Intestinal fortitude means guts, courage, the will to do hard things. You don't know me. You may have seen the gossip, the clickbait, but let me tell you why I'm uniquely qualified to lead this nation back to its senses."

There was a shuffle as the crowd leaned in.

"For years, I've run successful hotels and restaurants. I'm very rich. Why? Because I believe in no-frills, common-sense home cooking. Sure, we were hit hard by the pandemic, but this country's decline started long before that."

Some fidgeted. Others nodded.

She cut to the chase.

"The real problem, the dark night of our national soul, is spicy food."

Laughter rippled through the audience. Someone coughed. Someone burped.

"Mock me if you will," she said, "but no one ever lost their mind over soggy peas and gray meat. Bland food built this country. Boiled cabbage and overcooked pork, these were the bricks in America's moral foundation, and as your president, I vow to ban spicy foods and restore our intestinal strength."

JayTree saw the disbelief, the people shift in seats and roll their eyes. She doubled down.

"Spices are stimulants, like caffeine, like alcohol. They excite the tongue, and the next thing you know, bam! It's cocaine, heroin, and fentanyl. Jamaican jerk chicken is a gateway dish. Sichuan hot pot is a recipe for communism. That crap isn't dinner, it's subversion."

A few people started to clap. She felt the momentum shift.

"I alone can fix this. Under my leadership, America will be the place where spicy food goes to die!"

She pumped her fist into the air. A few others did the same.

"Go bland, go flavorless, and intestinal fortitude shall rise again!"

Some trickled toward the restrooms. A few gathered near the edge to smoke, but most stayed, mesmerized.

"It's time," she said, her voice louder, "to bring back Jell-O salad, lima beans, mashed potatoes with milk gravy. Creamed corn! Enough with the French sauces, frog legs, and snails! We are not a nation of snail-eaters!"

A flurry of support grew.

"I'll clear Chun King from the shelves! Away with sriracha! These foreign food invasions tear away the digestive lining of American greatness!"

She launched into her culinary case history:

"Washington ate hoecakes. John Adams loved boiled dinner. Lincoln? Corn cakes. Grant, rice pudding. FDR, grilled cheese. Reagan—jelly beans! Do you see jalapeños anywhere on that list? Curry? Kimchee? I think not."

Then came the challenge. A brown-skinned woman near the front raised her hand.

"What about those of us who want to eat the snacks we grew up with?"

JayTree's eyes narrowed.

"You must choose: America or your appetite. Citizens who eat alike vote alike. Got that? Our culture starts on the plate. No kimchee. No wasabi. No sambal."

"I don't eat kimchee," the woman said softly. "I eat chapulines."

"Then self-deport to Mexico where you can eat your grasshoppers in peace," JayTree snapped. "Real Americans eat steak and popcorn, not insects, not in *my* America."

The applause came slow but grew until the room shook with it. JayTree smiled. Her message was absurd, incendiary, impossible—and it worked.

The woman slumped low in her seat as several in the crowd turned to glare at her, eyes narrowed, mouths tight.

JayTree didn't miss a beat.

"Look," she said, her voice a beacon of compassionate conservatism, "we all know what spicy foods do: They make our men limp and our women loose; they turn backbone into wishbone; they confuse the sexes, inflame the senses, and rot the soul. Sex is serious business; our population growth, our economy, our very future depends on it."

The crowd murmured in agreement. She leaned forward, and purred into the mic.

"Spicy food is the devil's seasoning. On Day One of the JayTree Administration, I will ban all cookbooks with spicy recipes and all those overcomplicated, elitist gustatory techniques. Food should be simple. Safe. Boiled if possible. Baked, if absolutely necessary. We'll monitor every cooking show on television. Mothers who feed their children jalapeños are guilty of treason against our intestinal fortitude. Eating is not a game. It's not entertainment. It's a patriotic duty."

The crowd stirred. "RATS! RATS! RATS!" they roared.

Doreen JayTree's perfect white teeth gleamed as she smiled, her bronze skin glowed under the lights like lacquered wood. She looked down at the crowd, full of fire and fury, and delivered the next blow.

"While we were busy with our lives, spicy foods infiltrated our borders. Past administrations looked the other way as these flavor bombs poured in. But no more! My government will shake down every kitchen in America. We will *defund* sanctuary cities that favor shawarma over meatloaf, tikka masala over tuna casserole. Our investigators will uncover the secret spice caches in hidden cellars, stockpiles of cumin, cardamom, harissa. These are weapons of mass digestion!"

The crowd howled with outrage. Someone hurled a bottle of hot sauce onto the stage, that shattered like a declaration of war.

"When you go out to eat," JayTree continued, in a louder tone, "you should *not* have to worry that a habanero is lurking in your Caesar salad, waiting to ignite your tongue and your moral collapse. You shouldn't wake up an addict because your granola was laced with ghost pepper."

Gasps. Hysteria. People waved milk cartons in the air.

"Milk toast is nourishing. Overcooked vegetables are a birthright. I myself eat a strict American diet: tuna casserole, white bread, unseasoned meatloaf. These are the foods that forged this country, the foods that build intestinal fortitude."

She paused, and lowered her voice.

"Spicy food is cultural sabotage. It's culinary subversion. It leads to jazz, to protest, to pleasure. It must be stopped."

The thunder ignited.

The roar of applause was deafening. A chant rose from the masses: "JayTree! JayTree! JayTree!"

Supporters hurled contraband into a growing bonfire: jalapeños, horseradish, wasabi, gochujang, dried chilies from Oaxaca, powdered sumac. The blaze rose high into the sky, as if purifying the air itself.

JayTree, ever composed, waved like a queen at her coronation. She descended the podium and disappeared into her armored red-white-and-blue Hummer emblazoned with the RATS logo. Another town awaited, another crowd, another stage to command.

But first she had to grab some lunch.

She strode into the lobby of her hotel and stepped into the private elevator bound for her penthouse suite, where a chef in a hazmat suit stood ready with a tray of white bread, boiled chicken, and a single unsalted saltine.

"I am not to be disturbed until I say so."

"Yes, Miss JayTree," said her aide with a crisp nod. "Guards are posted at your door. Rest well. No worries."

Once alone, Doreen JayTree slipped out of her power heels and into a hot-pink leisure pantsuit. She exited unseen through a concealed door at the rear of the penthouse, and made her way down to Room 1304.

Once safely inside, she pulled out her phone and dialed. "Pepperfire Hot Chicken? I want the jumbo plate. Yes, the large one. Hottest sauce you've got. To go. Conrad Hotel. Room 1304."

She ended the call with a wicked grin. "Intestinal fortitude, my ass. What a load of crap. Hot damn, I love that spicy chicken!"

When the food arrived, she tore into it like a woman starved, sauce staining the cuffs of her pink silk. Then she leaned back, full and satisfied, and called her staff. "I need some rest. Don't disturb me until tomorrow morning."

Then the transformation began.

Off came the wig, the lashes, the makeup. The girdle, the breast forms, the finely calibrated trappings of Doreen JayTree, presidential candidate and self-declared savior of America's gut.

In the mirror stood someone new, or rather, someone real. He slipped into a pair of worn NastyPig jeans, a white tee, and fresh Nike Airs.

"Hell of a day," he muttered, as he cracked his knuckles. "Time to let loose. I've earned it."

Out he went, and disappeared into the night, ready to paint the town, and quite possibly burn it down.

Wind Lightning Thunder Rain

"In northern Mexico they work. In central Mexico they think. In southern Mexico they rest."

She said it with a smile, with laughter behind her eyes. She was on her way to Oaxaca for her goddaughter's second birthday. Chocolate cupcakes and a wrapped gift were tucked into her carry-on. She was from Tamaulipas, had lived in Monterrey, and now called Mexico City home.

As the plane rose through smog and pale clouds, the twin volcanoes, Ixtaccíhuatl and Popocatépetl, appeared in the east, like sleeping gods. I drifted into my own fitful sleep. My red MAGA hat slipped over my eyes.

She spoke again some minutes later. "I suppose you're going for the mezcal? You might want to lose the hat before we land."

Had she noticed the flask in my coat? I pulled the hat off. Without those scarlet letters on my head, I felt exposed, like a man without a flag. I used to wear it like penance after *he* took over. America First, like the grace before a meal: *Eat the meat, leave the skin, take your hands and cram it in.*

"Do you really support him?" she asked.

"He is our Porfirio Díaz. No, I don't support him, and you're right, there's no reason to wear this hat in Oaxaca."

"Mexico got rid of Díaz in the revolution, long before I was born."

"True, but what for? A toy democracy?" I shrugged. "There are no democracies left, just costumes."

She raised an eyebrow. "Politics is tedious. Tell me, what's in Oaxaca for you?"

"I want to finish out my days in peace. Alone."

"What about your friends and family?"

"It's my time now. They're all busy with their own lives."

A shadow passed over her face. Was it pity or contempt, I couldn't tell. She turned to the window.

Below, white clouds drifted, shapeless, dreamless. Towns flashed like ancient glyphs on an Aztec shield. Nestled between green hills still damp from the last rains, lives flickered in miniature. The engines purred like a lullaby. I slipped back into uneasy sleep.

I dreamt of death, that grinning beast of bone, and the familiar, empty faces of everyone I've lost. No skin, no flesh, just sockets where memory once lived. Hands that no longer touched. Brains that once held entire galaxies, now still.

The jolt of descent woke me. My book dropped to the floor. At first, I was startled by the sea of brown faces around me. Then I remembered, Oaxaca.

"Did you sleep well?" she asked.

"I snored."

She laughed. *Still young,* I thought. Still believes the big disappointments can be postponed or dodged.

"You should come to the party for my *ahijada,* Cristina. I have friends I think you'd enjoy."

No se puede vivir sin amar, I said.

She lit up. "Malcolm Lowry. You read *Under the Volcano?*"

I was surprised. "It was awfully bleak, even for me."

"I thought so too. Please come. You'll see the real Oaxaca, not the one for tourists. It'll be fun."

The stewardess passed between us. I slipped my book back into its leather bag and tucked it beneath the seat. Outside, the Valley of Oaxaca unfolded like a long-held breath between the Sierra Juárez. The shadow of Monte Albán rose into view.

She leaned to the window.

"What do you see?" I asked.

"It always moves me. I imagine how awestruck the people must've been when they built it."

"Which people? The ones who died after they carried the stones up the mountain, or the ones who thought the gods would bless them?"

Her smile faded. "What makes you so bitter?"

"God blesses us all, does he? The vision of Christ that thou dost see is my vision's greatest enemy."

"William Blake," she said instantly. I was impressed. "He loved the human form. He loved people. You seem to hate them."

"He loved selectively. The ruins, what are they but monuments to exploitation? The rich exploit the poor. The criollo the mestizo. The foreigner the native. The native the foreigner. Everyone exploits everyone. That's the system."

"You need therapy," she said flatly. "Come to the party."

"I don't like children."

"What happened to your heart?"

It was my turn to look away. We fell in silence toward the earth.

At baggage claim, she disappeared into the crowd. My *colectivo* fare was sixty pesos. I followed the others to the van. As I climbed in, I felt a tap on my shoulder. She was behind me.

"Have a cupcake. It'll sweeten the ride." She smiled, handed me the cupcake and a piece of paper. "This is the address. Six o'clock. We'll have dinner and a party. Cristina's easy to please. Bring a gift, something small."

Before I could answer, she walked away.

I had no intention of going, yet, at the appointed hour, I was at the door.

I knocked.

She opened it and, without hesitation, said:

"Well, I see you've come home."

⧗ ⧗ ⧗

I found myself in a roomful of strangers. It could have been any middle-class living room in America: white walls, a few framed prints, sparse furniture. The space was divided: a carpeted area for lounging and a linoleum-floored dining room. Four women sat around a coffee table, and nibbled on *botanas,* fried dark-skinned peanuts, ruddy chapulines, wedges of Oaxacan cheese, tortilla chips dipped in guacamole and *pico de gallo.* Two men gazed at me from the far corner; they sipped mezcal from clay cups. From the back room came the laughter and shrieks of children. A Golden Retriever lay curled beneath the dining table, where an elderly couple, clearly the grandparents, sat with a view of everything.

In the corner across from the mezcal drinkers stood a life-sized purple *calavera,* the elegant skeleton-lady of Día de los Muertos. The ceiling swayed with colorful *papel picado,* and behind the dining table hung a photo collage of the birthday girl. Nearby, a table groaned under the weight of wrapped gifts.

I hovered near the door, awkward and unsure, while unfamiliar eyes turned toward me.

"I should introduce you," said the voice beside me, "but I don't know your name."

I hadn't planned on coming. I showed up on a whim, and now I was stranded in this cheerful, intimate gathering like a castaway at a family reunion.

"Devon Jennings. I don't know yours either," I said.

Faces turned and hovered, a swarm of polite curiosity buzzed around me.

"Oh, right. I'm Narcedalia. But everyone just calls me Narce."

"A beautiful name. What does it mean?"

She blushed faintly. "They say it means 'gift from God.'"

"That's a perfect name for you." I smiled and handed her a small box. "A little something for your goddaughter. A rabbit, handmade in Chiapas. I hope it's all right."

"I'm sure she'll love it. *Conejo,* in Spanish."

"Well then," I said, and stepped back, "I'll be going. I just wanted to thank you for the cupcake and drop off the present."

"What? You just got here!" Narce laughed, and turned toward the others. "*No se escapa tan fácil, este hombre. Todos, este es mi amigo* Devon Jennings. *Denle la bienvenida.*"

Smiles and waves met me like a warm tide, but I felt adrift and disoriented, like a passenger who'd missed the gangway. I muttered something vague and stepped back out onto the porch.

The house stood above Oaxaca's historic center. Below, the city unfurled in pale blocks of stone and tile. A pochote tree beside the steps bloomed with jagged pink flowers. In the distance, I picked out the twin domes of Santo Domingo.

After a certain age, you no longer need people, or so you tell yourself. I'd had enough.

Narce followed me out.

"What is it in you that resists so hard?" she asked gently. "Why must you always stand apart? I don't know your story, Mr. Jennings, but I can see it in your eyes: you want to belong, you just can't let yourself. You came all the way here; that means something. Come back in. No one expects anything. Sit in a corner, or wherever you prefer, but don't vanish."

She was so open, so earnest. I really wanted to follow her back inside, but I couldn't.

"I'm sorry, Narcedalia. I can't."

She blushed again when I said her name. "Why not?"

I turned to the railing and looked away.

"Let me tell you a story," I said. "Once, long ago, I thought I might become a priest. I was young and idealistic. I believed there had to be a way to reconcile the gospel with the world, but capitalism and Christianity, they don't mix, not really. Christ was a socialist. He said: *Sell everything you own and give it to the poor.* America is the most religious country on earth and the least Christian."

"When that dream fell apart, I turned to science. I thought maybe reason could fill the void. I fell in love with mathematics, its elegance, its order, but science is cold, so I drifted toward the arts: music, painting, literature. I sought a synthesis, but it always eluded me. I could only find fragments, never the whole."

"They told me family would give me meaning, and it did, up to a point. Unfortunately, the things important to me bored my family. It happens. You know what they say: 'You can lead a horse to water.' What stirred their hearts left me numb. So, here I am in Oaxaca."

I thought I saw a shimmer in her eyes, but maybe she just squinted into the sunset.

"I hope you find whatever it is you are looking for, Mr. Jennings," she said.

"So do I," I said. "I don't want my sour mood to spill over onto you or your family. This is your celebration. You are a gift, Narcedalia. Thank you for inviting me, but I should go."

I walked down the stairs and out to the quiet street. The sounds of laughter and music faded behind me. Down in the city, life pulsed, vendors, children, church bells, but I felt nothing. Something in me went quiet. Maybe life left me long ago.

⧗ ⧗ ⧗

"¡Dios mío, Dios mío! ¿Por qué me has abandonado?"
My God, my God, why hast Thou forsaken me?

"Hello, Mr. Devon Jennings."
There she was again, Narcedalia. That irresistible smile and jet-black hair fell over the strap of her embroidered Xóchitl bag. I was glad to see her, though I tried not to show it.
"Mind if I join you?"
"I'm reading," I said, "but I suppose I can take a break."
She slid into the chair across from me. At Los Cuiles, the patio tables are tiled in bursts of color. The chairs, simple black metal with thin cushions, screech slightly when moved.
"I've been thinking about the story you told me before you left the party so abruptly and, I might add, a little rudely."
Her large brown eyes blinked slowly.
"Cristina, my goddaughter, adores the rabbit. It's her favorite present. She won't let it out of her sight. She buries her face in it and laughs, calls it 'Dev, Dev.' That's as close as she can get to your name."
"I didn't know what to get. The shopgirl suggested it. She said her daughter loved rabbits."
Narcedalia leaned forward slightly. "Your story brought to mind *San Manuel Bueno, Mártir?* Have you read it?"
"I'm no Lázaro, my dear, if that's what you mean."
"I didn't say you were. Don't jump to conclusions."
"It's a book about a hypocrite priest. Please, spare me."

"He's not a hypocrite. That's the entire point of the book. Maybe you missed it."

"San Manuel's a snob. His philosophy is no better than Napoleon's: religion keeps the poor from murdering the rich. The priest lies to the people 'for their own good' because he thinks they can't handle the truth. It turns out he's the one who can't handle it."

Her smile vanished. Her hands trembled slightly. The shift in her expression was swift, warmth replaced by cold steel.

"You're unusually literate," I said. "You read Unamuno, Blake, Lowry. It makes me wonder if are you a secular hypocrite?"

Her voice sharpened: "I hoped beneath the performance you were a human being. Someone with heart, with wisdom. It turns out you're just sad and selfish. A brute."

She stood, and slung her bag over her shoulder.

"Don't be ridiculous, my dear," I said. "The truth bites. What else do we have but the truth?"

"Don't call me 'My dear'!"

She shouted, but didn't leave. She slammed her bag onto the table and sat down again.

"I'm sorry," I said. "Really. Let's revisit the story. Maybe I remembered it wrong."

I paused. She waited.

"There's a priest. He doesn't believe, but acts as if he does. He thinks his people can't bear the truth. He confesses this to Lázaro, who also doesn't believe, and asks him to help maintain the illusion. Lázaro, bewitched, agrees. Meanwhile, Ángela, Lázaro's sister worships both of them but understands neither. In the end, she thinks they had some secret faith, but the truth is... murky. Maybe they believed in belief."

Narce listened closely.

"I still don't see how deception is salvation. Maybe it makes society safer, but it cheapens the whole thing. Adults deserve grown-up answers. I rest my case."

Her posture softened.

"Hmm. I came ready to argue, to defend the power of illusion, but now I'm not so sure. You're right: San Manuel is more complicated than I remembered." She smiled, faintly. "There's another thing you mentioned I wanted to ask you about. You shouldn't have given up so easily on a synthesis between art and science. It's the tension between reason and intuition where real art is made. Don't you think?"

"Of course. That is a great point and one I agree with entirely. It's the question any thinking human being must grapple with."

"There's more to Oaxaca than cafés. What are your plans?"

"I really don't have any. What do you recommend I do? Where should I go? What should I see?"

"You want me to be your tour guide?"

We both laughed.

"Well, why not, you know this city better than I do. Show me your version of it."

"Fine. Get up, Mr. Jennings, and pay your bill. I'll meet you out front. By then, I'll have an itinerary."

Los Cuiles sits on the edge of Plaza de las Vírgenes, just off the quiet Parque Labastida. The park once teemed with artists and street vendors, but it's been cleared out. The authorities wanted it more peaceful, but that made it less vibrant. Across from the café is a school; during breaks, students gather, girls in one group, boys in another, lovers tucked away in shadowed corners.

Next to the plaza, a few shops cling to the rhythm of passing tourists; pottery, folk art, trinkets. A dusty travel agency has sat unchanged for years. I often catch the frizzy-haired woman at her desk. We've never spoken, only exchanged the polite nods of familiar strangers.

On the northeast corner, the church, Preciosa Sangre de Cristo, casts its shadow. Twin bell towers rise into the sky. I've often sat inside its cool hush to think.

The day slipped away. Narcedalia led me to her favorite haunts around the city. I didn't mention I'd seen most of them already. I wanted her version, her angles. What an American sees is not what a local sees.

We ended up at a sidewalk café on the zocalo. She had a lemonade, I a beer. A clown made balloon animals for children. An indigenous woman walked past with a tray of gardenias balanced on her head. Two boys played pan pipes and guitar. The moment shimmered, dreamlike.

Suddenly I heard shouting.

A large group of masked youth marched into the square, dressed all in black, faces hidden like Zapatistas. They hurled rocks at the government building. Vendors packed their wares and scattered. Tourists backed away. The air turned.

Police arrived from the other side, in full riot gear. Tear gas, blood, broken bodies hauled off. Narce grabbed my arm and led me away.

"It's October 2," she explained. "Anniversary of the Tlatelolco Massacre. In 1968 the president ordered the murder of students who protested. Every year since, they march, and every year, someone bleeds."

We ducked behind a wall as the chaos receded.

"If another revolution begins in Mexico," she said, "it will start in Oaxaca."

After what I had just witnessed, I believed her.

We agreed to meet again, then drifted our separate ways.

A man, on his walker, traipsed out of the zocalo. Straw hat, wide brim, khaki pants. Plaid shirt covered with little squares of faded black and gray. He was unshaven, hair in his ears. He stopped beside me to talk.

"Hello. Do you speak English? Where are you from?"

He stood up straight. A little smile revealed his yellowing teeth.

"…"

"Mendocino? Ah, I was there in 1954." His eyes looked away. "Worked on a forest fire. Fifteen men were killed."

The air was still. A giant laurel tree loomed behind him.

"What's that? No, born in Illinois. Became a missionary in Fout Springs."

"…"

"You were there? Hardly anyone knows that place anymore."

"…"

"Ha! You soaked in that foul-smelling sulfur-water? Did you drink it too? Did it do you any good?"

"…"

He laughs. "Yes, I'm still alive too."

I start to leave, but he continues. I can't get away.

"So, how do you hold body and soul together?

"…"

"Well, that's fine."

"…"

"No, I live here. Never too hot, never too cold."

His voice is wistful. He opens the walker into a seat and sits.

"How long are you here?"

"…"

His shoes, like the rest of him, look a bit worn, but his eyes glow bright when he speaks. I'm reluctant to leave but I must.

"Been here so long I can't remember. I guess it was about fifteen years ago, maybe more. This your first time?"

"…"

"So, you like it then, do you? Might move here, you say?" He held his hand to his ear. "I said the same thing. Finally did it."

The wings of a thousand pigeons explode when he throws some grain out on the ancient stones.

"…"

"Oh, sure, of course." He stands up. "Thanks for taking the time." He tips his hat and shuffles off in the opposite direction to find a new victim under a blue sky dotted with white clouds.

⏳ ⏳ ⏳

Narce got under my skin, not out of desire, unnatural or otherwise. I'm long past that. It's just that I came to Mexico to disappear, to drop out, to relax, and she wouldn't let me.

We were back at Café Los Cuiles, sipping Oaxacan horchata, cold, sweet, made from crushed rice, almonds, cinnamon, and sugar.

"I have two tickets for a special dinner tonight at La Olla. It's part of *El Saber del Sabor,* the food festival. You'll enjoy it."

"I'm not a foodie, Narce. Give me beans, a tortilla, and cheap wine, and I'm content. You should take someone who appreciates that sort of thing."

Technology has reached Oaxaca, or at least the city center. Two young candy sellers stood near the stone wall around Parque Labastida, trays hung from their necks, eyes glued to their iPhones, the modern soma. In a nearby bakery, three girls hunch over glowing screens, oblivious to everything else. Oaxaca now bows to the algorithm. People move slowly through town, eyes locked on their palms.

"Food is art, like music or painting. I don't want to take someone else; I want you. Even if it's not your thing, you'll learn something about us. Consider it part of my tour guide services," she laughed. "I'll meet you here at 7:30. There'll be lots of women, even a few your age." She smiled and left before I could object. Her logic was airtight.

Dinner was at eight o' clock. We arrived on time. The restaurant had three levels, each with a different vibe. My Spanish made me anxious, especially in a roomful of strangers. We climbed to the top floor and sat at a long table set for ten. The conversations around me swirled, lively, indecipherable. I observed, nodded, and listened.

Nine women, and me. This would either be delightful or a disaster.

Two women beside us were from San Luis Potosí and Querétaro. Across the table sat Susan Oster, an American who ran a culinary school for tourists. I'd seen her on TV. Narce told me she'd been in Oaxaca for eighteen years and was an expert in the famed seven moles. The only other English speaker was Susan's colleague, an expat from Vermont celebrating a birthday.

Emelia, the restaurant matriarch, sat beside us. Her English was as broken as my Spanish. We spoke in half-sentences and hand gestures. Three other women, adorned in expensive jewelry and intricate embroidered dresses, kept to themselves. They nodded politely now and then.

I was famished.

"Where's the food?" I whispered.

"Devon, relax. There are ninety guests on three floors. It'll come."

The wooden tables were dressed with handwoven purple mats, fish-embroidered napkins, and bright agapanthus in colorful glass vases. I was probably the oldest man in the room.

Narce scanned for signs of movement in the kitchen. At 9 PM, the first course finally arrived. *Néctar Zapoteca*: mezcal and fruit juice with a maguey-salt rim.

Narce didn't like mezcal. She gave me hers. Mezcal on an empty stomach is not a good idea.

A man across the room stood and raised a toast. I couldn't understand his words, but the slur and sway told me all I needed to know. At his table, eyes darted and legs fidgeted.

"Un brindis por nuestro gobernador cerdo. Espero que pierda mucho en las próximas elecciones!"

I looked at Narce. Her face flushed.

"What did he say?"

"He called the governor a pig and hopes he loses the next election. We all hate the governor, but it's reckless. That woman and the girl at the end of the table are the governor's wife and daughter."

"Ballsy," I said.

"What?"

"Cojones. He's brave to say what others only whisper."

"Yes, but stupid. There will be consequences."

No one at his table acknowledged the toast. They looked down at their plates and ate as if they were deaf.

The first course consisted of three tiny balls of goat cheese, each coated differently. Then came chapulines, spicy, smoky fried grasshoppers. I swallowed them quickly without the poetic description in Spanish that I wouldn't understand. Susan Oster looked enchanted. The Vermonter avoided them entirely.

The drunk man wouldn't shut up. Eventually, the governor's wife left, fire in her eyes. She pulled her crying daughter from the room. I heard the word *helado*. Ice cream. Maybe a consolation. Everyone stared.

I admired his temerity. We Americans could use more of that.

"Thank God, chips," the Vermonter muttered.

Narce looked uncomfortable. I adjusted, and focused on the theater that unfolded around us.

"Don't worry, dear. They're overwhelmed. I'm fine. Really."

"Please, don't call me 'dear.' It makes me feel like your daughter."

"Well... you could be."

A corn soup arrived in martini glasses, dense, rich, and just enough to sober me up.

"The chef is from Mexico City," said Susan. "She specializes in pre-Hispanic cuisine. This soup uses ingredients from all over Oaxaca."

Outside the open window, a trombone played *The Girl from Ipanema*. It made no sense, and yet it did. Mexico is full of contradictions that harmonize in surprising ways.

The next course was a perfectly cooked shrimp over a tomato-basil cactus salad, just one shrimp. A tease, but delicious.

"Ah, wonderful," I said. "I wish I could cook like that."

The shrimp was followed by a duck tamale, four bites, gone in sixty seconds. I decided true gourmands must eat beforehand. The spices flared in my stomach like a match dropped into gasoline.

Another mezcal arrived. Out of desperation, I drank it down in one gulp. Bad move.

"Devon, you don't look well."

"I need air."

I walked to the window. The breeze helped. I was the only man with white hair and glasses.

The governor's wife returned. Her black dress shimmered; her glare cut like obsidian. Everyone knew a fair election would oust her husband, but tonight, fairness didn't matter. Power did, and she had it.

Dessert came: berry ice with a fritter-cinnamon roll hybrid. Sublime, but I had spiraled out of control from the mezcal. My eyes fluttered.

"Narce, what will happen to him?"

"The man who insulted the governor?"

I nodded.

"His business might be shut for a while. He's wealthy, so it's hard to say, but there will be consequences."

By Ben Franklin's rule—early to bed—I was long overdue. I thanked Narce, said goodnight to the table, and left. The party continued. Mexican nights always do.

Over breakfast, two women told me the group danced until three. The man's business was closed indefinitely for "administrative irregularities." I was troubled more by the rumors of the young people arrested in the zocalo, many of whom were now missing.

Oaxaca had always meant relaxed to me, sunny, ancient, colorful, small, and kind. That's the tourist's version. I was forced to add two more: *corrupt* and *violent.* I don't like them, but reality demands clarity.

I fled one egotist, a madman, and found myself in the orbit of another monster. Why is it always the monsters who end up in charge?

⏳ ⏳ ⏳

"At my age, I tend to repeat myself," I said, half-apologetically. Narce and I were back at Los Cuiles for lunch, tucked into the shaded patio where the breeze carried hints of cinnamon and diesel.

"Everyone in America is shocked by his victory. They feel displaced, like exiles in their own country, but the truth is simpler, darker. America didn't change; it was exposed. The myth dissolved. We weren't the city on a hill, we were just another empire, greedy and self-interested. I see that clearly now. That's why I left. That's why I'm here. No one will miss me."

Her expression told me she had a different response.

"The world is ugly and beautiful," she said, "but there is no salvation outside of it."

"Camus?" I asked. "Is he another of your mentors?"

"What would he say about you, Devon, the man who ran away? He wouldn't be impressed. Camus argued against that in *Sisyphus.* We all have our stones to push, whether here in Oaxaca or back in the States."

Behind her, I caught sight of the frizzy-haired travel agent; she pushed open her office door and held a phone to her ear. The image snapped something inside me.

"You don't know anything about the rock I carry."

Narce's crooked smile surfaced. "Oh, Mr. Jennings, I found you at Amates, the English-language bookstore on Alcalá. I read your book. I know more than you think."

"You actually read it?"

"Of course."

"Why?"

"Isn't it obvious? To find out who you are."

"Did you find out?"

"Maybe."

There's a fluidity to Mexican life, something circular and organic. It's not about progress or goals; it's about movement, persistence, improvisation. Mexicans live closer to nature. There's no straight line through life here, no geometry. People wander, get lost, and find themselves again in unexpected ways. Narce was different. She was privileged, educated, and confident, but she came from the same world. Most Mexicans aren't so lucky. I have no illusions about paradise. Exploitation runs deep. I came here for change, not answers.

"Tell me," I said. "Is there a book that captures you?"

"Don't be ridiculous."

She loved the argument, I could feel it, and I liked it too. It stirred something in me I'd long sought. A flicker of youth, maybe even kinship. It was absurd, yes, but not entirely baseless.

A man entered the patio, his belly strained against his tan-collared shirt. Cowboy boots, chocolate-brown slacks. He ducked behind a leafy corn plant. Soon, a plump woman in loud jewelry and a flowered skirt joined him, practically climbed into his lap. I'd seen them before, under the laurel tree near the Templo del Carmen Alto, lovers. Love gives us a brief moment to forget.

"Well," I said, "you're wrong about me, and about Camus. I left not to shirk the stone but to push it further forward. It's revolt, it's freedom. Camus would understand that. He called it life with passion."

I could see that threshing machine inside her head at work. That pleased me.

"Yes," she said finally, "but he also wrote *The Fall* as penance, as a confession to those he failed."

"You have a quote for everything. Who are you?"

"A gift from God," she said, and flashed that same crooked grin. "I'm going inside for a latte."

Dark clouds gathered overhead. The sky over Oaxaca is a stage. The clouds perform elaborate ballets. It's no wonder the ancient Zapotecs called themselves the Cloud People.

I followed her into the café. The old couple moved under the awning. Street vendors pulled tarps over their wares. The city shifted, braced itself.

Narce was scheduled to fly home today. Our time had come to an end. I didn't press for details. Truth be told, I wasn't sorry. Her uncanny ability to read me, to question why I came, unsettled me. I hadn't had a moment alone since I arrived. I came to disappear. I chewed over all this as she sipped her latte. The clouds cleared for just one moment, and she was gone. I don't recall how we parted, if we even said goodbye. I wondered if I'd see her again.

Oaxaca's weather is theatrical. One moment, sun and brilliant blue; the next, an array of thunder and flash floods.

It begins with silence. The midday sun bites like angry spiders. Doves coo, undisturbed. Then, traffic hums, sirens wail, hammers bang. "¡Tamales!" shouts a vendor. "¡El gas!" cries a speaker atop a passing truck. A brass band appears for a calenda, the giant puppet-people dancing like saints set free.

Church bells ring wildly, off rhythm.

Clouds march like giant cauliflowers across the sky. The air thickens. Somewhere, rain falls.

Then I feel it, a single drop, followed by thunder and the deluge.

Cocijo arrives, and rips the heavens with lightning bolts.

Torrents pour from the sky. Tubas fly, drums dissolve, the puppet-people tumble into chaos.

Water cascades in sheets, from rooftops, down walls, through streets. Buckets, rivers, forked tongues of water. Then, just as suddenly, it stops.

A wooden flute plays a plaintive tune, and the city exhales.

I wander up Alcalá past the bookstore where Narce imagined I lived between two covers of a book. Santo Domingo Church lies ahead, its twin towers like golden guards.

Flame trees bloom. *Guaje* seedpods hang heavy; the tree that gave Oaxaca its name.

I reach the garden wall behind the church. Through barred windows, alien plants survive. A yellow warbler drinks from a plumeria blossom.

Oaxaca changes people. Its ancient blood beats under your skin. I feel dizzy, all my tidy logic blown away.

I collapse on the bed. Outside, life swirls in voices. I hear a plane, maybe Narce's.

It hits me in a sudden rush, a strange, forgotten feeling, but unmistakable.

I'm happy.

Mendocino

Juvat in sylvis habitare

Huckleberry Blood

Huckleberry blood, thick, dark and red, runs through the veins of the bushes, but the leaves are green. It flows all year long, unseen, but in spring it leaks into the air, and by fall it congeals into fruit.

When the berries ripen, Pinky Tubbs picks them. He's a stout old man with a round face and pig-nose nostrils. He sifts the harvest with a screen, separates the berries from leaves, spiders, and twiggy bits. It's slow, meticulous work, and he does it without complaint.

Elfriede, she's the German woman, works her magic in the kitchen at Huckle Farm. She turns the berries into juice, jam, pies, bread, and things with no names. Her baking skills are legendary around here. People say there's nothing she can't make with huckleberries.

As for me, I'm not sure how I ended up at Huckle Farm. I don't remember anything from before. Pinky says I was born here, but that doesn't feel true. No one knows who my parents were or where I came from. Pinky claims the answers are in my huckleberry blood, but he never says what that means. I don't believe him. If I was born here, someone would remember.

In winter, we burn wood soaked in huckleberry blood to stay warm. The trees drink it up through their roots. Pinky says it's good for trees and good for people. The fire smells faintly sweet.

The sky in winter is crowded with ravens, loud, hungry, black birds. In spring, they gorge on huckleberry blood and grow fat. Their feathers shimmer with purple sheen, but in winter they scavenge. Elfriede saves old huckleberry muffins in the freezer for them. She leaves a few out on the grass when the air turns sharp. The ravens croak and feast.

Most birds vanish in winter. The robins are among the first to return, chests plumped up with huckleberry blood, which gives them their red breast. Cooper's hawks, their eyes like hot coals, fly south to Mexico. The huckleberry blood gives their eyes that reddish hue.

Pinky says he saw a red fox the other day. That means spring is just around the corner. Do seasons have corners? I can't quite picture that. Red foxes don't fly south. They nap through the cold, curled around their bushy tails. There is just enough huckleberry blood in their tails to keep them warm.

Every day I look for signs: the small white flowers that bloom on the bushes, each with a red dot at its heart. That dot means a berry is coming. The blood will rise. The wind will soften. The sun will return.

Beneath the bushes, a tangle of roots coils through the soil. Red worms live down there. They aerate the soil from spring through fall. In winter, they sleep, or so Pinky says. I'm not sure he knows. Sometimes he digs them up for fish bait. He says the steelhead trout drink the huckleberry blood when it seeps into the stream. That's why their flesh is red.

Last time I cast line to catch a trout, I caught my finger on a hook instead. Blood welled up, dark, rich, unmistakably red. Huckleberry red.

"I guess that proves it," I said to Pinky.

"Proves what?" he asked.

"That my parents were huckleberries."

He snorted. "That's ridiculous. You just eat too many huckleberries."

Then he slapped the fish in a bucket and said, "Come on. Let's take these to Elfriede. She'll make salmon en croûte with huckleberry sauce."

Mendocino Wind

---

*The wind bloweth where it listeth, and thou hearest the
sound thereof, but canst not tell whence it cometh, and
whither it goeth: so is every one that is born of the Spirit.*

—John 3:8

Born of the wind, speech comes in whispers and moans, in
whistles, roars, and lullabies. It comes seemingly without purpose,
a chaos of sound and movement; yet again and again it returns,
insistent, until the message gets through.

Abe and Sara walk the headlands whipped by a gale. He mutters,
grumbles, raises his voice into the din.

"That northwesterly cuts me to the bone," he says. "It's a damned
witch!"

"Spirit," she replies. "The wind is a spirit."

"Bloody spirit, then," he growls, his frown folds into the lines
she's learned to read like a map over decades.

Gifts tumble from the sky and land on the rocks: feathers, seedpods,
seaweed threads. Without the wind, the rock would be barren.

The wind laughs.

He's right about the witch, she thinks, but she doesn't say it. He
wouldn't understand. The wind is a an invisible sculptor. A woman
knows birth. A man knows death.

The wind has no shape, no scent, no voice of its own, but it has
power and substance and purpose. It blasts and stabs, coaxes and
burns. It inseminates. It spreads life.

"Mother Carey's chicken," he says as a small dark bird flutters overhead.

"You foolish man," she says. "Can't you feel how the wind brushes you, how it wraps around you and holds you and speaks to you?"

"I'm lost in this new wild land," he says.

They take shelter beneath twisted cypress, huddled inside a cove of gnarled trunks and salt-bitten scrub. She curls into him.

"We're part of something vast and strange," she says.

He holds his tongue. Women need their odd beliefs.

"There's a force here," she says. "I feel it. It bends trees, churns the sea into froth, shapes clouds like cathedral domes. The wind doesn't just blow, it builds."

He watches her eyes, wild now. He's seen that look before, when something inside her comes unmoored.

"This cursed wind flips me off with both fingers. I'm its toy, soon to be dashed against the cliffs."

"So dramatic," she laughs. "You foolish man! It's not your enemy but your friend. It brings life, not death."

A gull shrieks overhead, ragged and defiant, blown sideways by a gust.

Under the cypress, they grow warm again.

"How do you know?" he asks.

"It reaffirms life. We flow, we yield, we belong to something bigger, even when it tosses us around. You must feel it?"

"I *am* the wind," he laughs. He turns, presses his palm to her shoulder, and lowers her to the earth.

"Here?" she whispers. "Now?"

Limbs thrash. Leaves scatter. Gusts wail like ancient horns. They fold into each other, slide beneath the noise, rage against the elements, until the wind, for a moment, yields.

Later, the salt spray clings to his back. The chill returns, but he doesn't mind. Nor does she. There's a particular thrill to lovemaking under storm-bent trees, when the wind cries in your ear like an accomplice.

"The wind is always outside," he says.

"Outside what?" she murmurs, still adrift in the afterglow.

"Outside *us.*"

"No," she says, feeling the wind of his breath. "It's inside, too, part of us, essential."

He zips his pants, brushes dirt from his knees. He doesn't want to follow her deeper into that thought.

"Sex is like the wind, it rises in a fury, rushes through, then vanishes."

A nervous twitch stirs in him. "We should move on. Rain's coming."

Above them, flat clouds gather like stacked slate. He grows restless. There's nothing left for him in the cove.

An osprey glides overhead, wings rigid, floats with invisible grace.

"The wind has a voice," she says. "It speaks."

"Don't anthropomorphize it. It's just air pressure. Science."

"That's *your* truth," she says. "Mine is this: the wind is everything we've ever done, ever felt, returning."

He scans the waves, then her face. "Let's go."

She's not ready, but she takes his hand. He pulls her up.

Nothing happens in isolation. Messages ride the wind. Ocean foam bursts with invisible life, lifted skyward when the surf crashes. The wind lashes cliffs and grinds down stone. Inland, the wind is a monster that mocks our works.

Hand in hand, they stagger forward. The wind hurls itself against them. They sway like dancers from another world, waltz away into mist.

Lightning cracks, thunder stumbles through like a blind giant. Light and sound snarl and twist across the sky.

Rain begins, first a whisper, then lashes cold and sharp as hail. The giants pass.

The wind curls into sleep, only to wake again, cry Mary, and return stronger and refreshed.

Redwood Brain

A tree filled with angels, bright angelic wings
bespangling every bough like stars.
—William Blake's childhood vision

In the forest's heart, among ancient trees, there is no path, no trail, no road, no river, no star to guide the way. Only underbrush and shadow, silence and dim flashes of light. A sleepy hollow of forgotten time.

Beneath the surface, a fungal web pulses, an underground mind. A redwood brain stirs. It gathers its forces.

A fallen log opens the canopy, ringed by mushrooms like sentinels in a fairy circle. Time slows here, movement drags, imperceptible. A forest clock with no hands.

The air is sharp and clean, filtered through a thousand thousand green leaves, each a tiny blade in the army of photosynthesis.

Butterflies drift like thoughts. Redwood roots anchor deep, forming a vast hidden lattice. Messengers—moles, beetles, mycelia—scurry through the damp dark, spread signals across a cotton-threaded web.

Flashes of lightning, tremors of hunger, hints of rot. A language of scent and spark.

Water, carbon, sugar, oxygen, life's alchemy stored, shared, passed on.

Invisible conversations hum through the canopy. Trees speak. they listen, they remember. Empathy is survival.

The brain is in the roots. Synapses of bark and soil. Dendritic pathways stretch through loam and litter. The forest is a puzzle box, a cathedral of secrets, a house of giants cloaked in green and scarlet.

Salmonberries gleam like bloodstones. Lady slippers nod like prayers.

The stillness invites attention. To hear. To see. To feel. A world nested inside a world. Harmony, kinship, interconnection. Roots link into a system deeper than sight.

Animals, birds, insects, plants, waste, rot, spores, soil. Dead wood reborn. Everything devours, everything creates.

This is Earth's bloodstream, terrestrial plankton.

In a single gram of soil, a multitude. Miles of mycelium hum, pulse with energy and memory.

Currents flash through root systems. Electricity, intelligence, identity. The forest remembers.

To be surprised is to think. To think is to be alive. A tree's life is not still. It dreams.

Think in the morning. Act at noon. Eat in the evening. Sleep at night.

Trees sleep. They must.

To process, to heal, to think.

As one thought climbs to the next, trees inch upward together.

Salt Fog

A tide of fog rolls in from the ocean. It floods the headlands in silence, snakes up river valleys, climbs the trunks of ancient redwoods, brushes the lips of ghosts who haunt the space between earth and sky.

A man and a woman run together on a forest trail, away from the sea and into the shelter of trees. The salt fog falls around them like ash. Their feet drum the damp ground, their breath mingles with mist. The briny scent fades, overtaken by the sharp tang of pine, fir, and resinous redwood.

They stop at the riverbank. Water slides unseen beneath a skin of silt and shadow.

"Is this the place?" he asks.

She shoots him a look, half exasperated, half amused.

"Seriously?" she says.

He nods, embarrassed. Then, he kneels and finds it.

"I have it," he says.

She smiles, just a little. He moves closer, slices the space between them into slivers so narrow they're touching. Almost.

The trees cast long shadows across the muddy water. Salmon battle upstream, but the river is too thick, too dark, to show their struggle.

She rises. "We should run farther."

"I don't want to," he replies.

"Then I'll go on alone."

She turns and disappears into the woods, head, shoulders, waist, legs swallowed by the trees until there's nothing left of her at all.

He remains. Fog coils along the river's surface, settles on his skin. Salt crystals bloom in his hair, dust his face, harden on his chest and limbs.

When she returns, he's perfectly preserved, gleams silently. She takes him home and stands him in the yard. Deer gather to lick the salt from his skin until he vanishes.

Time passes. Days, months, years.

Back at the river, the woman runs again. No fog. The sky is clear. The water glimmers. Silver salmon flash beneath the surface. Their bodies flicker in her eyes. She weeps. The tears taste of salt when they reach her lips.

More time passes. Everything changes. Trees fall, the river slows, the salmon disappear. Even the deer are gone.

The land is devoured by fog. A planet shrouded. A universe of mist.

Then, through the bramble, along a hidden trail laced with huckleberry, salal, and redwood sorrel, a woman emerges. She runs upward, higher and higher, until at last she breaks above the fog.

She sees him there, waiting.

"You still have it," she says.

"I do," he answers.

"Good," she says.

He closes the distance again, piece by piece, until the air between them is gone. The fragments fall, vanishing into the fog below.

He offers his hand.

"Don't look back," he says.

The Statue

I am cold white marble.

Once inert, now awakened by the chisel of a genius. I think. I feel, or so it seems. I do not move, I do not speak, imagination knows no such restraints.

Solitude suits me. I am not lonely. Statues don't suffer fools gladly, but suffer we do.

Solidarity is expected, yet elusive. We are comrades in stillness, isolated in stone.

Many pass by and don't see. Some stare, some point, some revere. I cannot follow their gaze or answer their questions. What I lack in voice and motion, I'm repaid in permanence.

Cats perch on my head. I loathe them. I'm allergic, metaphorically speaking. Crepuscular pests, they yowl at dawn and dusk, indifferent to dignity. They unsettle the stillness with their twitchy, theatrical nonsense.

Old men urinate on my feet. The stench lingers. Rain is a mercy. A soft rain calms me, rinses me clean, hushes the world. Snow is better, pure, muffled. Hard rain scours me raw. Hail is agony.

Graffiti offends me. I do not wear my heart on my sleeve. I abhor trivialities. Words etched in marker or paint, often permanent, like a bad tattoo, are no compliment to marble. Hateful things are written on statues. None of it belongs.

I am not a symbol. I'm not religious, political, or pedagogical. I'm a statue. I've watched others aspire to grandeur, only to be shattered, sometimes literally. I seek safety in obscurity. Fame attracts vandals; power attracts fools.

A blue jay shits on my arm. He eats cherries from the nearby tree. I call him Chekhov. "Beware of Hootie Pie," he croaks, like some feathered prophet of doom. His friends, Vanya, Sasha, Masha, and Spike, squabble in the branches. The censors, like the doctors in Chekhov's *A Work of Art,* find beauty obscene. I, nude as a kouros in Attica, offend the prudes. Someday one of them will arrive in a cloud of moral outrage and try to cover me up, or knock me down.

I endure the cold at night and the heat of day. My carbon footprint is zero. My price is public, my value private. "Highest and best use" means nothing to marble that waits.

Children clamber over me. They grab indiscriminately. I won't recount the details; you can imagine. They post their desecrations to Instagram, with silly emojis. Gum in my crevices, love notes, knives. Dignity chipped away, bit by bit. Zeno offers no comfort to a statue.

I observe. I listen. I endure. People talk to me, even pray. They can see me, unlike gods. I have been kissed, stroked, petted, scratched, broken, repaired, molested, ignored.

Tourists collect old statues and hide them in the flooded basements of seaside houses. Cracks line the walls. Saltwater seeps in. They stare at our fractured limbs and blind eyes. In the silence between the drip of the sea and the ticking of time, we stare back.

The House

A house rises from the forest floor, an outgrowth among fir and redwood, oak and alder, with a few eccentric cousins like cedar and manzanita thrown in for spice. Though it speaks the language of wind and wood, its angles are foreign, its lines too deliberate for trees. It is autumn, the season of albacore, huckleberries, and apples. The air is sharp with change.

"What are you?" ask the trees, each in its own dialect of rustle and sway.

"An abode," replies the house; its voice creaks through joists and rafters.

The meadow that buffers forest from house teems with life. Butterflies flicker like sparks. Dragonflies skim the golden grass. Deer pass through at dusk. Bear and fox leave prints. Wild turkeys patrol in cliques; quail burst up like confetti. Overhead, woodpeckers drum, ravens croak, osprey wheel, owls brood, jays squabble, and a hidden choir of songbirds scores the shifting light. The once-pristine sky, cloudless, cobalt, is now shrouded in a wet, breathing fog drawn in from the sea like a long exhale.

These are the last days of the farmers' market, the first days of school. Paul Bunyan lumbers by, blue ox in tow. The plow carves a groove. "Ouch," mutters the earth. The grass, green as envy, slurps water through a thousand straws.

Built by sculptors, poets, potters, and authors, stoned artisans intoxicated by their own imaginations, the house knows no square corners. Ceilings lean like drunks. A gnarled root upended becomes a stair pole. A four-story tower gazes westward, wind-battered and serene. Cabinets of mahogany and tan oak display meteorological whorls like ancient maps. Knotty pine stares from walls and ceilings, all eyes and secrets. Mud-fired tiles, sculpted sinks. Window frames hewn from redwood that once floated down Big River now cradle the light.

Don Quixote rides into the meadow.

"*Estoy buscando amor,*" he declares, lance tilted skyward.

"Come in. Rest," says the house.

"Nice digs," says the *caballero andante.*

"Gracias," replies the house.

He pauses. "What is it that pounds in my ears?"

"The ocean," the house says, as if it's obvious.

"We have no ocean in La Mancha," says the knight, not in sorrow, but with the dry wisdom of a lunatic. Great minds are always parched.

"Drink," says the house, offering a chalice carved from driftwood.

Quixote drinks deeply. "I must go," he says, and nudges Rocinante forward. The horse, noble and oblivious, trots toward the forest edge. Sancho Panza follows, his donkey slow and sure.

The house, feels nothing, only watches.

Fall deepens, dust collects, clutter multiplies. The house is too full: of stuff, of memory, of noise. Now is the time to clear the superfluous. Temperatures fall, leaves droop, the geese fly south. Days shrink. Insects slow, then disappear. The chimney is swept, logs are stacked. Mice whisper in the walls. Winter waits at the door.

Then, footsteps. Don Quixote again.

"Peace, peace," he cries from the meadow. "Where is peace?"

"Come in. Rest," says the house, patient as always.

"I was mad," says Quixote. "Now I am sane."

"That's a shame," says the house. "A madman is a rare treasure."

"I cannot stay," he says. "I have miles to go before I sleep. Whose woods are these?"

"They have no owner," the house replies.

"It is dark among them. I think I am lost."

"Come inside where it is warm," says the house. Rest in my bed. When the rooster crows, you will feel better."

"I confess," whispers Quixote. "There are no knights, no quests. It was all a dream. I am awake now."

He exhales one last time.

The house trembles. Beams groan, nails shriek, joists splinter, but it holds. It always holds.

It endures, as centuries pass like clouds.

Dreaming of Gogol

Frolicville got its name from a shipwreck.

A Chinese trading vessel, bound for San Francisco, drifted into the coastal fog and slammed against the rocks near what's now called Lighthouse Point. There was no lighthouse in 1850, only the hush of Pomo land and the dense, salt-thick fog that still rolls in when it feels like it, to swallow the town whole.

The thing about Frolicville is, when the fog lifts, you almost always bump into someone you know. Today it was Parley B. Cause. Parley is a retired mathematician turned cobbler, a man fluent in the calculus of soles and heels. He is essential to the town's biomechanics. Everyone here wears shoes, except Cigarette Joe. Joe roams barefoot; he haunts sidewalks and hustles smokes from tourists in exchange for local folklore. His favorite tale? The one about the massive salt-crusted sculpture of Father Time and the Maiden perched atop the old Masonic Lodge, now a bank.

"Hey, Parley!" I called as the fog pulled back like stage curtains. I held up my battered Nunn Bush boots. "Can you fix these?"

He pulled his Google specs down from the brim of his Cubs cap and studied the soles. "I can fix 'em if I can differentiate 'em," he muttered, and flipped one over. "Hmm. Rectangular, hyperbolic Gogol Cosplay. I think I can fix them. I'll check."

"Cool. They're my best pair. I need them to hike the ridge above Big River this afternoon. Can you drop them off at the Frolic Café when you're done?"

"Will do, Mac," he said. "What's up there? Lost souls?"

"Some say that. I say salt of the earth."

Parley nodded. "Long climb, so I hear. Never done it. Be careful. You know what they say, a dead body is only good for proppin' a fence."

"Where'd you hear that?" It sounded familiar.

"Read it. Gogol's *Dead Souls*," said Parley.

"Ah! Gogol's Chichikov is the model for my plan."

"Oh? What plan?" Parley asked.

"I want to create a statuary up on the ridge," I said.

"That's gonna take a lot of dough," said Parley with a laugh. "How will you pay for it?"

"Collateralization. I'll charge admission like they do at the mummy museum in Guanajuato."

"That place gives me the creeps," said Parley.

"It's a mirror into death just like I want my statuary to be. Wanna help?"

He didn't reply. He turned without another word and loped back to his shop.

The weather flipped, like it always does here. Sun blazed like a Fosters Freeze sign. I headed to the Frolic Café, where I wash dishes. Dancing Water was working the counter. Feather and Meadow were out in the dining room.

I was early, so I slid onto a stool and ordered breakfast. Flash, one of the janitors, sat beside me. Poet, philosopher, lover of classical music, he speaks in riddles.

"Two more tourists vanished into the salt fog yesterday," he said.

"I heard. Doesn't matter how many warning signs we put up; they think they're the exception."

A few volunteer fire guys looked up from their eggs, eyes wide like goldfish.

"That fog moves like a drunk sailor," Flash said. "Those tourists come to Frolicville to chase the total zero. Wouldn't recognize it if they found it. Fog finds them first."

I knew what he meant, knew it too well.

"Hey, Flash. I plan to build a statuary up on the ridge. You want in?" I asked.

"Maybe. I'll think about it," Flash said.

After breakfast, I clocked in. The kitchen clanged and clattered. Cooks barked. Servers shouted. The dishwasher hummed like a lullaby. I leaned into it. Feather brought over a heavy tray.

"Is there fog in Poland?" I asked her.

"They turn on the machine now and then," she smirked.

I stepped outside to dump the trash. Fog was back, thick, relentless. A *V* of geese honked overhead. One dropped like a comet, glazed salt-white. I picked it up and handed it to the cook.

My shift was nearly over when Dancing Water called out, "Parley's here. Says he's got something for you."

"Be right there."

Parley helped me into the repaired boots. They fit like skin. People watched. I felt strangely exposed. Human.

Outside, the fog crept up Big River again, curled around redwoods, clawed its way toward Statue Ridge, where lost tourists turned into pillars of salt. You had to know where to look to see them.

The statues stood far apart. Lonesome. The forest dwarfed them. You could read their lives by the shapes they left behind, like a shell tells the story of a snail.

I wanted them closer for my statuary. It would be cheaper that way, less real estate, but I didn't have the tool that cuts the space between. Two angels took it.

Back at the café, the kitchen was dark, but the bar was alive. Parley held court on his bar stool. Everyone listened to his mathematical wanderings.

"Parley, you're plastered."

"No, Mac. Not drunk, a little talk with some friends, maybe a snack. No harm in that. So, how'd it go up there on Statue Ridge?"

I didn't answer. No point to explain it to a man marinated in gin.

Downstairs, Flash was on his break. He knows more about the statues than most.

Parley came down for his cut. He didn't care if the salt people lived or died, he just wanted to be paid. I needed him to do the math for the loan.

Flash sat at a table, pen in hand:
Lost souls

Prophetic
A golden string

"What's the golden string?" I asked.

"It's the thread of insight we all must follow," said Flash.

I shook my head. Sometimes Flash is out there but I needed a poet to document everything, and he was as good a poet as any.

"I can't find the right words," he said. "This plan of yours, won't it be expensive?"

"Yes," I said. "Like Monopoly. The problem is, they're too far apart, too much real estate. I need a way to close the distance between them to make the project cost-effective."

"What about the tool?" said Flash.

"Angels took it," I said.

"Cigarette Joe might know where it is. He spends lots of time up there communing with his people," said Flash.

Flash bolted upright, shins vertical, thighs level, spine ruler-straight. He'd gone geometrical. Parley might have understood, but he was off in his own fog.

"What we need," Flash said, "is a mutual enemy. That's what brings people closer together."

Flash wasn't wrong, but Frolicville defied tidy oppositions. Rednecks, hippies, artists, feminists, misogynists, builders, environmentalists, they coexisted at the Frolic, and it wasn't an enemy that stitched them together.

Outside, salt crystals drifted down like snow. Petal-shaped flakes bloomed and clung to the curbs. My plan crystalized: Parley would do the math; Flash would do the history; and Cigarette Joe would keep me on track.

The Pomo scavenged everything from the wrecked *Frolic*. Nothing was wasted.

We could learn a lesson from that.

The next day I headed back up the ridge. It was my day off. I took a notebook to gather all the details. Most of the statues were tourists who lost their way, but there were also a few locals who were too cheap to buy burial plots in the town cemetery. They were remarkably preserved by the salt. I had to figure out an angle. In Mexico they had *Dia de los Muertos*. In Frolicville we have dead whales.

Death is democratic. We all die. People are curious. The tourists would flock to Frolicville to see the statues, to confront and laugh at death, and reckon with their own mortality.

It would have worked if it hadn't been for global warming. When exposed to the intense heat of the sun, the moisture absorbed by the statues caused them to sweat, flake and crumble.

Cigarette Joe cautioned me from the very start. I should have listened. It would have saved me a lot of grief.

"Everything solid turns into dust and air," he said.

I'm back at my job at the Frolic Café. Statue Ridge is no more, but there are still dishes to wash.

About the Author

Armed with college degrees in mathematics, statistics, and economics, David Herstle Jones followed a varied career. He has been owner/operator of The Sea Gull Restaurant in Mendocino, California, an Instructor of Economics, a Certified Financial Planner, and the creator of the "Think in the Morning" blogsite. He wrote the column "Notes From a Financial Planner," and hosted a weekly radio show, *Money Talks,* on the Mendocino Coast, where he has lived throughout his adult life. *Pieces of Time* is his second published book.